AN ENEMY AT THE HIGHLAND COURT

THE HIGHLAND LADIES BOOK FIVE

CELESTE BARCLAY

 Created with Vellum

To those who have found love with the most unlikely of partners.

Happy reading, y'all,
Celeste

SUBSCRIBE TO CELESTE'S NEWSLETTER

Subscribe to Celeste's bimonthly newsletter to receive exclusive insider perks.

Have you read *Their Highland Beginning, The Clan Sinclair Prequel?* Learn how the saga begins! This FREE novella is available to all new subscribers to Celeste's monthly newsletter. Subscribe on her website.

Subscribe Now

THE HIGHLAND LADIES

CHAPTER ONE

A crack of thunder followed only moments later by a blaze of lightning made several ladies-in-waiting jump within the queen's solar. The early autumn storm seemed to rattle one's bones as much as it did the window embrasures. Cairren Kennedy glanced around Queen Elizabeth's private salon and stifled her chuckle as the newest ladies-in-waiting trembled. Mostly Lowlanders, these young ladies were not yet accustomed to the raging storms the Highlands flung upon Stirling from the north. Cairren arrived at Robert the Bruce's court three years earlier as a wide-eyed and quiet girl. But in the time she'd spent there, she'd developed a thick skin and a significant cynicism. As she watched the newer arrivals, she wished she could return to her days before becoming a lady-in-waiting to Elizabeth de Burgh. It had been just over a year since her best friend, Allyson Elliot, married Ewan Gordon and moved to the Highlands. During that year, Cairren awaited the announcement of her own betrothal, and with each passing month, she found her mood increasingly matched the weather outside.

Cairren received a hint from her father around

the time of Allyson's wedding that he was in the midst of arranging a betrothal to a Highlander, but he'd volunteered no specifics. Cairren suspected that news came several prospective suitors ago. Growing up near the border, with constant strife between the Scots and the English, made life among the contentious Highlanders seem peaceful. While her clan's land sat along the coast, their allies were the Dunbars and Armstrongs, which meant the two border clans often called upon the Kennedys to lend warriors to the cause. She understood her father wanted her away from the ever-shifting political dynamics that were a daily part of life in the south. However, moving to the Highlands sight unseen terrified her. She was blessed with a doting father who always had her best interests at heart, but she couldn't help but wonder how he thought the Highlands were a better option. She'd rather move to her mother's people in southern France. At least there, she would blend in.

"Lady Cairren," Queen Elizabeth's voice drew Cairren out of her pensiveness, forcing her to abandon her thoughts. "Please pick up where you left off yesterday."

Cairren retrieved the vellum copy of *Summa contra Gentiles* from the table upon which she'd laid it the day before. With a slight French lilt to her voice, Cairren was among the queen's favorites to read aloud. She was also one of the few women who read fluently. She accepted that the queen had committed her to an hour of droning prose on providence and the soul. While she was as devout as the next person, Cairren swallowed her sigh as she prepared to read the divine insights of Thomas Aquinas. As she settled onto a stool, a page entered the solar and whispered to the Mistress of the Bedchamber who, in turn, cast an eye at Cairren.

"Your Majesty, I beg your pardon, but Lady Cairren has been summoned to see her father and mother, who are newly arrived," the Mistress of the Bedchamber announced, all eyes swinging to Cairren.

Cairren froze. It was rare for her parents to visit court, so it was with trepidation that she laid aside the manuscript and rose. Awaiting the queen's permission to leave, her stomach twisted into a knot that would have made a sailor proud. She could think of only two reasons for Innes and Collette Kennedy to travel during a week's worth of torrential downpours: news of death or her betrothal. If asked, Cairren would have said they were one and the same. At the queen's nod, Cairren did her best to maintain her poise and glide from the salon. Once in the passageway, she gathered her skirts and darted to her parents' chamber. Fear that something had happened to her sister, Caitlyn, prompted her to hurry, but anxiousness that it might be news of a betrothal caused her to slow her pace two doors down from the Kennedys' suite.

Cairren knocked but didn't wait for an invitation to enter, pushing the door open and stepping inside. Her parents turned as one, opening their arms to her, and she was certain she flew across the chamber rather than walked. The relief she felt each time she reunited with her family stole her breath away. She'd learned to manage her homesickness by reminding herself that she couldn't change the duty she served to her queen and her clan, but in moments like this, her loneliness flooded every nerve. Her mother's familiar scent of myrtle, from her hometown in the south of France, soothed the ache in Cairren's chest. Her father's pine and fresh air scent reminded her of the countless hours of her childhood spent touring villages on the back of his horse.

"*Maman*, Papa," Cairren breathed.

"*Ma petite-fille.*" My little girl. The three words Collette said no longer applied to a woman of three-and-twenty, but Cairren's mother had called her that since the day of her birth. "*Common ça va?*"

"Everything is going well, *Maman*. I'm so happy to see you." Cairren turned her cheek one way, then the other, to receive her mother's customary kisses before Innes engulfed her in an embrace that lifted her toes from the floor.

"My wee lassie, it does my heart good to see you," Innes's deep voice rumbled against Cairren's chest before he settled her back on her feet.

"You both seem in good spirits, so I assume all is well at home." Cairren looked between her parents, praying she hadn't presumed the wrong meaning to their warm welcome.

"All is as well as to be expected, with the bluidy English breathing down our necks every two minutes. They seem to have forgotten that there is a truce," Innes grumbled. "Your sister sends her regards and is quite put out with me since I refused to allow her to accompany us."

Cairren hadn't realized she'd been holding her breath until her chest suddenly deflated. However, this meant there could only be one other reason for her parents to travel from the southwestern corner of Scotland to Stirling, which formed the boundary between the Lowlands and the Highlands. She held her breath once more as she waited for the axe to drop.

"There's no reason to look as though the headsman is after you," Collette's gentle smile only made Cairren more nervous.

"*Oui, Maman.*" Cairren forced her own smile, but she could tell it was more of a grimace when her father straightened and his stern "Laird of Clan Kennedy" expression settled upon his face.

"I ken you've deduced why we've come, but there's naught to frown aboot," Innes's voice sounded far from reassuring. Instead, it sounded like an order.

"Papa, I don't mean to frown, but the unknown is frightening," Cairren confessed, and her father's paternal smile returned.

"I ken that, lass. But we must all grow up, and we must all move from one duty to another. You've loyally served the queen for nigh on three years. It is time for you to move on."

"Who is he, Papa, and how far north does he live?" Cairren asked, but dreaded the answer.

"His name is Padraig Munro. He's the second son of the Munro laird and he's the same age as you," Innes explained.

"Munro? They are in the heart of the Highlands. That's so far from you and *Maman* and Caitlyn. I'll never see any of you or the clan again." Cairren fought the tears that burned the back of her eyelids, but gave in when a sob rose from deep within her soul.

"*Ma chérie, pas de panique.*"

"'My dear, don't panic' doesn't make me feel better, *Maman*. How can I not panic? Not only is it far from everyone and everything I know, they're Highlanders. They'll never accept me." Cairren closed her eyes as she tried to do as her mother instructed, but the nausea proved she was failing. "I don't look aught like them. I can't even pass for a Lowlander. How will I manage in the Highlands when I'm still learning Gaelic and I look like a foreigner?"

Cairren stuck out her arm, showing her parents what they already knew was there. Her olive complexion was in constant contrast to the lily-white skin that was the norm in Scotland. Her maternal grandfather's Arab traits still showed strongly in Collette and her oldest daughter. Cairren had always thought it was a blessing that Caitlyn's skin was lighter and didn't tan as easily as Cairren's. Her sister fared a better chance of making a match with a man who would want her.

"You've made a place here for yourself because you are good and kind," Innes reassured her.

"Barely. It took nearly a year before most of the ladies didn't whisper in front of me. Now they only do it behind my back. They allow me in their circle because the queen demands it, but if they had their choice, they would exclude me. Now that Allyson's married, there are only a few who bother to remain pleasant. Only Blair Sutherland and Arabella Johnstone are willing to be my friends." Cairren forced herself to stop. She hadn't meant to divulge the truth about her loneliness at court, but she needed her parents to understand why marrying her to a Highlander would be a disaster.

"Lass, it's done. Laird Munro and I have already signed the documents."

"So, I am already betrothed. I am as good as married," Cairren's despondency must have shown because her parents pulled her back into their embrace. "Why him?"

"The king chose, Cairren. He knows I want to get you away from the border."

"And the Munros are the only ones who would take me." Cairren pulled away from her parents. "How desperate are they for my dowry?" Cairren suspected her father had been in contact with a dozen clans, but the Munros must have been the only ones who showed an interest. More likely, forced their hand.

"A bride's dowry always comes in handy," Innes offered. The noncommittal nature of his answer said more than his words.

"Do they know that their new wealth comes with a brown bride?" Cairren crossed her arms but refrained from tapping her toe.

"Of course they are aware of your ancestry, *ma petite-fille*," Collette reassured.

"But that doesn't mean they know what I look like."

"Are you ashamed of your family?" Innes cocked an eyebrow.

"Never." Cairren's answer was emphatic, but she followed it by whispering, "That doesn't mean I can't be scared of what they think."

Cairren's tears started once again. Collette led Cairren to a chair before the fire as Innes stoked it. Both women were slight in build and could share the wide chair. Cairren leaned her head against her mother's shoulder as Collette stroked her hair.

"I fell hopelessly in love with your mother," Innes reminded Cairren. "Your mother's skin color is only one part of her; it's the whole, inside and out, that is so beautiful."

"But you chose one another. I'll be delivered to a mon who has no choice but to take me," Cairren buried her face in her mother's shoulder.

"Cairren," Collette's French accent softened the middle consonants and once more soothed Cairren's fraught nerves. "It wasn't easy for me in the beginning either. It took time for our people to accept me, to accept their laird's son's choice of bride. Your *grand-père* disapproved of me on sight. But with hard work and an open heart, I won our clan over. Now I can't imagine living anywhere but on Kennedy land."

Cairren nodded, but she didn't voice her thoughts. *Why couldn't you just send me to France where I could marry? I speak French as well as anyone born there. I wouldn't stick out there. Caitlyn belongs in this world more than I do. Her marriage could solidify an alliance. My move to France and her marriage would remove us both from the border area. The difference between you and me, Maman, is you married the laird's heir. I'm marrying a second son. He won't hold the same power to demand they accept me.*

"We will accompany you north and remain for the wedding. We depart in two days for Foulis. It'll take us a sennight to travel. We will hold the wedding within a sennight of our arrival," Innes explained. Cairren recognized the hard edge to her father's voice signaling her time to air her grievances had ended, and he wouldn't entertain any more of her complaints.

"We will speak later, *ma petite-fille*," Collette reassured, and there was little else Cairren could do but nod.

CHAPTER TWO

Cairren eased into her seat at the ladies' table as the evening meal began. She'd remained with her parents throughout the afternoon, hearing stories and the latest news from their clan. Her mood lightened as she listened to her mother regaling tales of Caitlyn's continued attempts make perfume. Collette Aubert hailed from the Grasse region, the area of France best known for its perfumes and soaps. Her father had been an Arab trader shipwrecked along the southern French coast when his Moroccan ship bound for Italy was blown off course during a storm. Collette's mother, Marie-Claude, was already a widow and was willing to take the foreigner in while he recovered.

As Collette had recounted countless times, her parents' love story was much like Innes and Collette's —love at first sight. Ebrahim Boukhriss traded myrrh and frankincense from the Lovat region to cities along the Mediterranean, so settling in Grasse was ideal. Collette described him as a quiet man who would have barely come to Innes's shoulders. He was shrewd and bookish, which made it easy to expand Marie-Claude's soap and perfume trade. While Cairren had inherited her maternal grandfather's olive skin, almond-shaped eyes, and deep chestnut hair, she'd inherited her paternal grandmother's translucent grey eyes. There was a tinge of green that made them appear silver at times. She and her sister shared this feature, and it was the indisputable proof that Innes was their father.

Innes met Collette when the French hired him as a mercenary. When he sailed away from Kennedy territory, he was a second son, and there seemed little chance that he would inherit the lairdship. The money he earned while in France lined the Kennedys' coffers and helped them finance the on-going skirmishes against the English. It was while Innes was away that an English neighbor killed his older brother, during a standoff over land that had changed hands many times. It thrust him into the role of the laird's heir and forced Innes to return, but he refused to do so without his French bride. He'd married Collette without telling his family, having planned to remain in France permanently. When Innes and Collette had no choice but to go to Scotland, Collette adopted her mother's surname, Aubert, hoping to make her transition easier, but a single glance at Collette spoke of her Arab lineage.

There were few who could contest that Cairren was a stunning woman, but she was not the epitome of Scottish beauty. While her features were striking and created an exotic appearance compared to the fair-haired and fair-skinned Scots, her appearance was an albatross around her neck. As a young woman taught to read, she discovered ancient practices rumored to lighten skin tones for women whispered to have foreign heritage. She'd even gone so far as to try various tonics and herbs to lighten her skin when she learned she was to serve among the queen's retinue, but nothing she used made a difference. She'd often worn peasant straw hats at home to protect her face and neck from the sun, but somehow her skin tone always deepened in summer. The veils many women wore at court did nothing to deflect the sunshine when she rode or strolled in the garden. She'd spent her first summer at court inside as much as possible, but the queen enjoyed a long morning constitutional through her gardens and insisted her ladies-in-waiting join her. Now she stayed in the shade whenever she could, claiming too much sun gave her headaches and strained her eyes.

"Why did your parents come?" Laurel Ross asked as a servant placed a trencher before Cairren.

"I will be leaving court to marry. My father informed me of my betrothal," Cairren shrugged, hoping to play off her sense of impending doom that returned with the mention of her upcoming nuptials.

"Do you know who it is?" Blair Sutherland asked.

"Aye. Padraig Munro." Cairren's gaze shifted to Laurel as her friend began to cough. The look of shock made the hair on Cairren's arms stand up.

"Just went down the wrong way," Laurel gasped as she lifted her mug of ale to her mouth.

"The Munros aren't far from Sutherland!" Blair bubbled. "Perhaps I could visit the next time I travel home."

"I would like that very much," Cairren smiled, but she was still watching Laurel, who seemed to have recovered but had grown withdrawn. Cairren wasn't about to inquire while the worst gossips in the kingdom surrounded her, but she intended to ask Laurel about her reaction when they could speak in private. Fortunately, they were roommates.

"When do you leave?" Arabella Johnstone asked

softly. Her best friend, Blair's sister Maude, left court just before Cairren's friend Allyson. Maude married Kieran MacLeod after a whirlwind romance that set every tongue on fire at court. Cairren grew closer to Blair and Arabella after Maude's departure, but they hadn't become genuine friends until Allyson left to marry Ewan.

"In two days," Cairren plastered a smile on her face that hid her regret. She'd worked hard to make the few friends she had, and now she would have to start over again. "I'll be wed within the fortnight."

"So soon?" Laurel blurted.

Cairren narrowed her eyes at her roommate, but she was resolved to keep her questions until later.

"Aye. It'll take a sennight to travel, and then my father says I'll be married within a sennight of our arrival. My parents will have another fortnight's journey ahead of them to return to Dunure. With the weather as it is, I suspect we'll have an early winter. I wouldn't want them trapped somewhere along their route. They'll be gone more than a moon as it is. My father doesn't care to be away from home that long with how things stand. There have been English ships spotted off our coast several times since Beltane." As Cairren spoke about the upcoming journey, she groaned internally as she pictured the days spent on horseback and camping outside. There was no sign that the weather would improve, and as they moved further into the Highlands, the likelihood of experiencing all four seasons in a day increased. If she and her parents were departing from home, she might have convinced her father to sail along the western coast and come inland near Assynt. Then it would only have been a couple days' ride to Foulis.

"Which gown will you wear?" Blair prodded.

Cairren recognized Blair's attempt to cheer her up, but any thoughts of the wedding soured her mood as much as it did her stomach.

"I suppose my mother brought the gown I made before I left for court. It's pale blue with embroidery at the neckline, the waist, and the hem." What Cairren didn't mention was the higher than fashionable neckline and the billowing sleeves that covered as much skin as possible, no matter how she moved.

"That sounds lovely," Laurel offered, but Cairren caught the uncertainty in her voice.

The women eventually turned to other topics of conversation before the dancing began. Cairren was never short of dance partners, but their intent was rarely innocent. When she was newly arrived at court, it had shocked her to hear the propositions courtiers made to women, but the ones she received were often among the lewdest she heard. Men who had no intention of an honorable outcome suggested acts that Cairren initially believed were depraved. As she grew more accustomed to her new way of life, she learned that the acts were normal parts of bed play, but they were inappropriate to suggest to a maiden. The men assumed that she was desperate for a guardian to offer his protection and often reminded her that she wouldn't do better than to become a man's mistress. She'd hidden in her chamber more than once during her first year, and she'd learned to never walk alone in the passageways and to steer her way into the crowd if an unsavory courtier or guest approached for a dance, but it was inevitable she could not avoid some of the brasher ones. She never considered relenting. She had always trusted her father would find her a match, and if not, she would happily retire to Dunure when her tenure as a lady-in-waiting ended.

"Lady Cairren, it's always a pleasure to partner with you," an Armstrong delegate whose name she couldn't recall spoke from behind her shoulder. Cairren turned to see the attractive man sweep his gaze over her, lingering overly long just below her waist and at her bust.

"I thank you for the compliment. Please excuse me. I must join my parents," Cairren sidestepped the callow man's implied request.

"I am certain they won't begrudge you a turn around the floor with a neighbor."

They may not, but I will. The man didn't give Cairren an opportunity to refuse before he grasped her hand in a hold that was far too tight and virtually dragged her into the mass of dancers. The set was one where each dance was with the same partner. Unlike a reel, she would be stuck with the Armstrong warrior who held her too close.

"You're even lovelier than the last time we danced," he whispered beside her ear. The shiver that raced along Cairren's spine was from fear. She understood where the conversation would go before long. "You are enticing and could lead a mon to sin."

"Then perhaps you should make your way to the kirk, and I can make my way to my parents," Cairren's tone was like syrup, but the put down was clear.

"Where would the fun be in that?" The man steered them toward a door that led to a darkened passageway Cairren knew couples often used for trysts. She dug her slippered heels into the floorboards, but the man took little notice, or rather he ignored her opposition.

"Cuthbert, who is this fine piece?" Another Armstrong asked as they came closer to the door than made Cairren comfortable. She recalled now that the delegate had an English name because his mother had English parents.

"Don't you recognize the Kennedy's daughter, Nevil? I intend to discover if she's as smooth as French women are reported to be. She'll be good for a tupping. I've heard her people own women just to pleasure men."

Cairren gasped, understanding Cuthbert's meaning. She recalled Cuthbert and Nevil were brothers. She had no intention of allowing any man besides her husband discover what her grooming habits were. She twisted away, but the man's hold on her hand made it impossible to break free. She grabbed his little finger and pulled it back as hard as she could. His hand dropped from hers only for his brother to wrap what felt like an iron manacle around her arm.

"Let go of my daughter," Innes's quiet hiss made Cairren and both Armstrongs halt. Suddenly, Cairren was free and stumbling toward her father. He pulled her against his side, dropped a kiss on her crown, then pushed her behind him as he cracked his knuckles. "I heard what you said to my daughter. I saw my daughter trying to get away. To me, it looked like you intended to accost her."

Innes took a menacing step forward, but the men were foolish enough to stand their ground. Innes's grin made the men finally realize the grave error they made. It was an expression that made warriors cower on the battlefield. He grasped a handful of hair on each head and slammed their foreheads together.

"Perhaps if you put your heads together, you'll come up with some sense." Innes pulled them apart only to ram them together again. "You can tell your laird that I expect a proper apology or our alliance is through."

"We offer that apology now, my laird. We beg your pardon and Lady Cairren's for the slight."

"Nay," Innes growled. "Not good enough. You're here to represent the Armstrongs and your laird. Since you act on his behalf, your behavior is a reflection of him. He will offer an apology or he can fight the English without the Kennedys."

Cairren listened to the exchange and was prudent enough not to interfere, but she wished her father would let sleeping dogs lie. She didn't want this to become public fodder for her last two days at court. While she appreciated her father's intervention, his overprotectiveness was creating a scene. As if sensing his daughter's growing anxiety, he released the men and spun on his heel. He wrapped his arm around Cairren and led her back to where Collette sat with the senior guardsmen who traveled with them.

"*Qu'est-ce qui s'est passe?*" What happened, Collette asked as she noticed their approach.

"*Rien, Maman.*" She knew her father would say it was more than nothing.

"Two Armstrong swine tried to pull our lass out of the Great Hall and made inappropriate comments. I handled it," Innes stated as he took his seat on the bench beside Collette. A speaking glance at his men had them hurrying away from the table.

"You don't seem very surprised, Cairren," Collette observed. "What did they say?"

Cairren's face flushed as she glanced at Innes, whose temper seemed ready to flair again. She looked back at her mother and shook her head. "They were interested in learning aboot French grooming customs. They intended to see for themselves."

Collette's French temper was shorter than Innes's Scottish one, which meant her mother was ready to commit bloody murder to defend her daughter. The older woman's eyes swept the crowd, narrowing when she recognized the Armstrong contingent.

"*Maman*, please. Just let it go. I'm used to it." Cairren wanted to swallow her tongue. She hadn't intended to admit that she was accustomed to such insults.

"*Pour quoi?*"

"Because that wasn't the first time I've heard that. Court is not a place known for morality. The ladies-in-waiting receive uncouth offers, but most refuse them."

"But most aren't likened to a harem slave," Innes growled.

"Harem?" Collette's eyes narrowed as she left her seat.

"*Maman, s'il vous plaît. Non,*" Cairren begged, but Collette was already winding her way through the crowd until she reached the Armstrongs. Silence fell among the men as they recognized Lady Collette Kennedy.

"*Qui?* Who?" Collette demanded. She kept her voice low, but the steel edge cut through the awkwardness.

"Who, what, madame?" Cuthbert spoke up. His smarminess dripped from his words. But Collette refused to play his game. She reached out, grabbed his groin, and squeezed mercilessly.

"*C'est vrai.* It is true. They say the English have tiny cocks. Perhaps your mother shouldn't have lain with one and kept herself to a good Scotsman." Collette squeezed once more for good measure. "Give my regards to your mother, Lady Anne. And I'm certain your uncle will offer the apology I imagine my husband demanded."

Those surrounding them chuckled at Collette's put-down. She stepped away as the crowd of onlookers parted to allow the angry Frenchwoman through. But she turned back to face the Armstrongs once more. "By the by, if I learn a single one of you insults another young lady, you'd better guard your cods because I will cut them off." She made a slicing motion through the air, and more than one man winced.

Cairren wanted to melt into the floor. Her humiliation was complete, even if she recognized her parents' good intentions. It was just as well she was leaving because she wouldn't be able to show her face again. She prayed she could spend the next two days hidden away.

CHAPTER THREE

Cairren finished scrubbing her face and neck before turning to Laurel. She eyed her roommate before putting the drying linen aside and pulled on the chemise she preferred to sleep in. Steeling herself for whatever she would learn, she cleared her throat. Laurel looked over at her as she combed her hair.

"Why won't I be welcome at the Munros? Is it because of how I look?" Cairren saw no point in mincing words.

"There's that," Laurel glanced back at her before settling in to braid her hair. By silent agreement, both women had dismissed their maids.

"Then what else?"

Laurel lowered her arms and studied Cairren for a long moment before sighing. "You've been a good roommate to me. You tolerated my rudeness to you and your friends yet never had a harsh word to me. You're not a gossip, and you don't spread untruths. Perhaps I should have appreciated that more. Cairren, you won't be welcome because Padraig wants to marry my sister, Myrna." Laurel lowered her eyes and shook her head. "They're in love."

Cairren sucked in a breath as the room spun. As

though her ethnicity wouldn't be enough of a challenge, she faced a life with a man who would resent her for taking him away from the woman he loved. She was doomed to fail before she arrived.

"Thank you for telling me," Cairren murmured.

"Be careful, Cairren. My sister isn't known for her kindness. How she's fooled Padraig for this long, I can only imagine."

Cairren closed her eyes as she imagined her faceless groom in bed with a woman who resembled Laurel. She wanted to cry, but she also wanted to heave. "At least I know and won't walk in blind."

"I suppose you could look at it that way. Cairren, Laird and Lady Munro have wanted to secure an alliance through marriage with my clan since I was a child. They've practically turned down the covers to Padraig's bed for my sister. If she had a greater dowry, they would already be married. But they must need your dowry even more than I thought. Padraig's not a cruel mon, but he's devoted to Myrna. He won't welcome you either." Laurel stood up and tentatively moved toward Cairren. "I'm sorry to tell you this. But I feel you deserve the warning. It will be hard enough without adding the humiliation of discovering the truth in front of your new clan. Hopefully, you can prepare yourself. I suspect Myrna will be there when you arrive. Padraig won't have kept this from her, and she'll want to eye her competition." Laurel drew Cairren into an embrace. The women had never shared physical affection before, but Cairren found surprising comfort in Laurel.

"I don't think I'll be much competition if Padraig is that in love with your sister. I suspect he'll do his duty once and then forget aboot me."

Laurel nodded, but Cairren couldn't read the

emotion in her roommate's eyes. If she'd had to describe it, Cairren would have said speculative, even hopeful. What Laurel hoped for, Cairren didn't know.

The morning of Cairren's departure couldn't come soon enough. She'd faced the other ladies-in-waiting the morning after her parents arrived when she joined them for Mass. She continued to read Thomas Aquinas's manuscript as the queen requested, but she slipped away from the solar and took her meals in her chamber. Neither Laurel nor Cairren broached the subject of Padraig and Myrna, but it hung as a leaden weight between them. Laurel helped Cairren pack and offered her a set of earbobs that Myrna would recognize. Laurel insisted her sister would know they were a token of friendship and believed it would ease some of the inevitable hostility. Cairren thanked her, but she suspected Myrna would more likely accuse her of stealing than believe they were a gift. Cairren said her goodbyes to Queen Elizabeth, who offered her a blessing and a kind word.

Then it was time to leave, and Cairren found herself mounted on her horse with a dozen Kennedy warriors guarding her and her parents as the sun raised its sleepy head over the horizon. She wished they headed south instead of north, but as the Kennedys passed through the Stirling city gates, Cairren resolved not to think about how much she dreaded their destination or how her homesickness grew with each clop of her horse's hooves. A light drizzle seemed like nature's way of commiserating with Cairren's feelings, but by midmorning the sun shone, and she found her spirits lifted.

When they made camp the first night, Innes and several of his men went hunting. One of the men felled a doe, so Cairren worked alongside her mother as they butchered the animal, careful to salt and store the meat so it would last the fifteen-person party for a couple of days. Cairren relished each moment she had with her parents, even during the less-savory tasks. She'd never been an avid hunter even though she knew how, but she'd enjoyed spending time with her mother in the kitchens. Not a noblewoman by birth, Collette grew up in a small cottage where she helped her own mother with cooking and housekeeping. Collette insisted that Cairren and Caitlyn learn each task needed to run a keep so the sisters would appreciate the labors of servants and to remind them of their great fortune as the laird's daughters. Innes often praised his daughters for their humility and willingness to always assist in any task inside or outside of Dunure Castle.

"Be sure you clean all the entrails out and put twice as much salt as you think you need, *comprends?*"

"*Oui, Maman.* I understand. I haven't been away so long that I've forgotten," Cairren grinned. She looked forward to the roasted venison that would feed them for the first half of their journey. It made the arduous cross-country trek less intimidating, knowing she would have a full belly rather than the hollowness bannocks and dried beef never really filled. As she and one of the guardsmen lifted the skewered flank onto the spit, Cairren looked around at the men who traveled with her. They were men she'd known her entire life; some were childhood friends close to her age, while others were closer to her parents' ages. As some of the men sang, Cairren relaxed for the first time since her parents arrived. Laurel's warning was ever present, but Cairren was able to push it to the back of her mind. When the men opted to sip their whisky, Collette dulcet tones eased many into slumber.

> *"L'autier jost'un sebissa*
> *Trobei pastora mestissa,*
> *de joi e den sen massissa,*
> *Si cum filla de vilana,*
> *Cap' e gonel'e pelissa,*
> *Vest e camiza treslissa,*
> *Sotlars e caussas de lana."*

Cairren followed along, softly translating each line.

> "The other day beside a hedge,
> I found a humble shepherdess
> Full of joy and good sense
> Like the daughter of a peasant girl;
> A cape, a coat and fur
> She wore, and a shirt of rough cloth, shoes and woolen
> stockings."

As more men settled on their bedrolls, Cairren abandoned the English version and sang along with her mother. By the end of the thirteenth verse, mother and daughter sat with their arms wrapped around one another. Cairren's alto was the perfect complement to her mother's soprano. They'd sung together since Cairren could speak, with Caitlyn's voice eventually offering harmony with its mid-range octave.

"I shall miss this, *ma petite-fille*," Collette whispered. "But remember when you miss home, Caitlyn and I are singing along with you, even if only in spirit."

Cairren nodded as she gazed at the twinkling stars and wondered if her sister was doing the same. She wondered whether Padraig ever stargazed, but the image of a woman who resembled Laurel pushed to the forefront of her mind. Her thoughts became locked on the notion that Padraig didn't bother to look at the stars because he preferred to stare at Myrna.

"What is it? Where have you gone?" Collette's whisper broke through the quagmire that threatened to pull Cairren's mind under.

"*Maman*, I learned something from Laurel Ross the night you and Papa arrived."

"*Quoi?*"

Cairren looked around the camp at the sleeping men, but even as snores drifted to them, Cairren opted to continue their conversation in French. "Laurel told me that Padraig has been in love with Laurel's sister, Myrna, for years and wants to marry her. Laurel said that if Myrna had a larger dowry, they would already be wed. She warned me that Myrna would likely be there when we arrived. *Maman*, how am I supposed to marry a mon when the woman he loves is watching? How can I go to a mon's bed when he wishes I was someone else? What if he mistakes me in the dark and calls out the wrong name? I don't know that I could survive that humiliation."

"You can and you would. It breaks my heart to learn you are entering this marriage at such a disadvantage, but you are a woman with much to offer your husband and new clan. And before you say that what you have to offer is a fat dowry, you know that isn't what I meant. You will never be able to make everyone like you. Some may never respect you, but as long as you show everyone kindness and dignity, then most will come around. I wish I could have promised you a love match like your father and I have, but we know how rare that is. Try to build an accord with your husband. Don't attempt to replace this Myrna but carve out a place where you and Padraig can get along. Perhaps in time, his feelings will change."

"I will try, *Maman*. Is it wrong that I pray he gets me with child quickly? Then I will have someone to love and who will love me, and I won't have to share a bed with a mon who doesn't want to be there."

"It isn't wrong, but don't set all your hopes on that. It might not happen so easily. Cairren," Collette paused as she bit her lip. "I explained to you when your courses came how a man and woman join to make babes. I suspect you've learned even more since arriving at court. Padraig may not love you outside your bedchamber, but if he desires you within your chamber, you may find pleasures of two types. The obvious is the pleasure your body enjoys. But the other pleasure is finding a common ground where you can nurture trust. I won't give you false hope and say satisfying your husband will make him faithful, but it can keep you in his good graces."

"I know, *Maman*. But he may already be bedding Myrna. If he is, then why would he bother to bed me once we've made the marriage binding?"

"Then ensure he wants more than one night."

"How can I do that without coming across as a wanton? How would I know to do those things if not from experience?"

Collette chuckled. "I'm not saying you should perform the acts of a courtesan, but welcome him to your bed. Don't lie there like a dead fish. Pay attention to what seems to spur him on, and whether or not he arouses you, for God's sake, make it seem like he is."

"How do you know this if you and Papa were in love when you married?"

"My mother didn't love her first husband and could barely tolerate him at first. She had to learn these lessons with no one's advice. She made peace with her marriage and made the most of it until he died. She explained these things to me before I met your father, and they have stuck with me. It saddens me that I must impart them to you, but I pray they serve you well."

"*Merci, Maman*," Cairren whispered as she yawned. She slid down her bedroll, and Collette kissed her temple as she drew the plaid over Cairren's shoulder for what would be one of the last times in either of their lives.

"*Fais des beaux rêves*." Make good dreams. It was the phrase Collette had said every night as she tucked her daughters in. And Cairren offered the same response she always did.

"*Toi aussi*." You too.

CHAPTER FOUR

Foulis Castle came into view on the seventh morning of their journey. They'd been delayed when a horse threw a shoe, then went lame. They'd had to make a detour to a village where the horse could rest and a blacksmith refitted the horseshoe. It was a blessing in disguise as Cairren enjoyed a night in a bed, even if the frame creaked when she so much as breathed. It was still warmer and softer than the ground.

Cairren gathered her reins in one hand and shielded her eyes as she took in the imposing keep that was to become her new home. The Munro banner flapped in the wind, signaling the laird was in residence. Cairren was certain that at least one patrol had seen them as they crossed into Munro territory, and likely a scout raced ahead to inform the laird of their imminent arrival. While Cairren couldn't make out any figures on the battlements, she knew that the superior height meant the guardsmen had already spotted their entourage. She rode in the center beside her mother with her father in the lead. Kennedy guardsmen surrounded the women, and with her short stature, Cairren suspected no one would notice her until she dismounted. She intended to use that to her advantage as she cast surreptitious glances around the bailey as they passed beneath the portcullis. The walls were well maintained, sentries were posted along the battlements, and the people looked healthy and well fed.

Just how badly could they need my dowry? Cairren turned her attention toward the steps as a couple about her parents' age led the way down the keep's steps. Two more couples followed. Cairren's eyes riveted on the blond, willowy woman, and she knew in an instant that Myrna was walking beside Padraig, her betrothed, to come and greet her. Her stomach sank, and she struggled to keep a scowl from clouding her expression. She adopted the look of serenity and grace that she'd cultivated during her earliest days at court. Allyson had helped her, and it hadn't taken Cairren long to appreciate its value. She suspected she would wear it every day for the rest of her life.

"Laird and Lady Kennedy, it is a pleasure to welcome you and your daughter to Foulis Castle and Clan Munro," the giant who approached them boomed. The man was not much taller than Innes, but his chest seemed twice as wide. Innes had always been one of the largest and brawest men Cairren knew, but Laird Micheil Munro fit every whispered rumor she'd ever heard about Highlanders. Lady Mary Munro sniffed, her nose curling as though a foul odor wafted toward her as she passed an assessing eye over Cairren and Collette. It was clear the Kennedy women did not pass muster, at least not by Lady Munro's standards.

The man who stood directly behind Laird Munro

smirked as his eyes raked Cairren. She recognized the action, and she prayed the man wasn't Padraig. There was something about him that made Cairren uneasy. When the man scowled at the sallow-looking woman at his side, Cairren realized that the couple must have been the older son and his wife. Cairren finally turned her attention to the man who stood silently with Myrna's arm now wrapped around his. Cairren's heart lurched as the most handsome man she'd even seen stood before her. He still hadn't spotted her, even if Myrna had. His black hair was cut shorter than most Highlanders, sitting above his collar. He had piercing brown eyes that appeared nearly black from a distance. Cairren wondered briefly if they were truly windows into his soul. She hoped not. His jaw was finely chiseled, but his nose had a slight bump where she supposed someone once broke it. It appeared to be the only flaw in his otherwise perfect visage. He was as large as his father, which made him a few inches taller than his older brother. It was clear both sons were trained warriors, but where there was an air of arrogance about the older son, Padraig appeared confident.

"*Tha iad le chèile cho donn,*" Myrna murmured. Cairren understood enough Gaelic to know the woman had said "they're both so brown." It wasn't an observation but an accusation.

"*Et tu es si grossier,*" Cairren muttered. And you're so rude. At her quiet comment, Collette shot her a look of warning. While they might not expect Lowlanders to speak Gaelic, which Collette didn't, there was always the likelihood that a noble family spoke French.

As Cairren looked away from her mother, her

eyes locked with Padraig's, and she recognized the surprise when he finally caught sight of her. She cocked an eyebrow in challenge before her eyes darted to Myrna. Padraig didn't hurry, but he removed Myrna's arm from his. When Cairren's eyebrow nearly reached her hairline, Padraig stepped forward.

Padraig Munro feared he would swoon for the first time in his life. He hadn't expected the stunning beauty who stood among giants. Nor had he expected her pluck to cast such a withering gaze within moments of their eyes meeting. He'd been curious as the Kennedys rode into the bailey, so he hadn't noticed when Myrna wrapped her arm around his. It was something they had done so many times over the years that it felt natural. When Cairren's expression hardened and both her chin and eyebrow lifted, Padraig noticed Myrna once again. And how inappropriate their behavior was. He'd been struck dumb was his only explanation. He'd always believed Myrna was the loveliest woman he'd ever seen with sky-blue eyes, long flaxen hair, and a lithesome figure, but Cairren took his breath away. He stared into the astute silver-gray eyes that seemed to see far too much in too short a time. While she'd pulled her hair into a braid, the plait sat over her shoulder, grazing her waist. The rich brunette color shone red where the sun caught it. Her diminutive body was lush and softer than Myrna's, and he found his fingers itched to trail over her breasts and hips. He'd never felt such a spark of lust for any woman. He and Myrna had an understanding, or at least there had been one until he learned of his betrothal, that until they wed, Padraig was free to find his pleasure with other women, but he swore he would be faithful once they married.

He'd heard Myrna's comment, but it was several long moments before it registered with him, and Padraig gathered his wits enough to notice Cairren's skin tone. His heart dropped, and the lust fizzled. He wanted to squirm, embarrassment that his new bride was so dark-skinned already setting in. She would be a constant source of mockery among his clan and their neighbors. He swallowed the bile that rose in the back of his throat as he wondered how his father could have agreed to the match. They weren't in that desperate need, were they? As though his mother divined his thoughts, she glanced at Myrna and frowned.

"*Coigrich ghràineil. Chan eil feum againn air an òr cho mòr. Is e masladh a tha seo,*" Disgusting foreigners. We don't need their gold that much. This is an insult, Lady Mary Munro griped as she returned her glower to Cairren, who reared back as her eyes widened.

Cairren stepped forward and offered the angry woman a curtsy befitting a queen. When she rose, she locked her eyes on her soon-to-be mother-by-marriage and spoke in a clear voice. "*Maitheanas dhomh, chan eil mo Ghàidhlig glè mhath fhathast. Ach tha e na thoileachas coinneachadh riut. Màthair.*" Forgive me, my Gaelic isn't very good yet. But it's a pleasure to meet you. Mother.

It was Mary's turn to gasp. Cairren wasn't sure if it was the use of Gaelic or the fact that she called the woman Mother—perhaps it was both—but she derived smug satisfaction from startling the woman. With an angelic smile she didn't mean, Cairren turned back toward Padraig and offered him a curtsy, one that conveniently accentuated the low neckline of her gown. She and Collette had chosen it for that reason, and

Cairren had donned it just before Foulis Castle came into sight. While it was a risk showing so much of her olive-toned skin, they banked on her betrothed noticing her bosom. She wore a fresh gown, had braided her hair again, and dabbed on perfume, so she was as well presented as she could be after a week on the road. When Myrna hissed, Cairren tilted her head and offered her a soft smile before looking back at Padraig.

Padraig didn't know where to look. His mother and beloved were practically hissing and snarling while Cairren the kitten proved that she had claws. He never imagined she would understand Gaelic. It made him wonder how she'd learned. While his mind railed against taking a wife who couldn't have been more different from the women he was used to, his body had a different idea entirely and was already eagerly considering their wedding night. He remembered to bow and extend his hand. When Cairren looked at it as if to tell whether it was dirty, he almost pulled it back, but she brought her fingertips to just above his. When he bent over it, a floral perfume wafted toward him, a scent he didn't recognize.

"Myrtle," Cairren whispered. Padraig's eyes jumped to Cairren's, and he spotted a moment where she lowered her armor and sincerity shone through, but Myrna huffed, and the shield went back up. Cairren pulled her hand away and turned to Myrna. "Lady Myrna, your sister Laurel sends her regards. I have a missive from her in my chest. I will be certain to deliver it as soon as possible."

"Laurel? You know my sister?"

"Aye. We've been roommates for nearly three years. Did she never mention it?" Cairren infused innocence into her voice when all she wanted to do was swipe the smug look from Myrna's face. Her introduction to the laird's family and their guest wasn't going well.

"Nay. We—we—aren't close," Myrna explained.

Cairren looked as if to contemplate something before nodding. "I suppose she spoke of Katherine or Elizabeth or Margaret when she told me she wrote to her sisters." Cairren waved a dismissive hand as she turned toward the couple that had remained silent as the unpleasant exchange played out in the middle of the bailey.

"Lady Cairren, I am Duncan, tánaiste to my laird father. This is my wife, Lady Wynda." Duncan didn't glance at his wife, instead fastening his attention to Cairren's bust. Cairren nodded but kept her attention on the rather mousy-looking woman. Wynda returned the shallow curtsy and smiled timidly. As she lowered her chin, her collar shifted, and Cairstine was certain she saw a bruise. Her eyes darted to Duncan, but he was still shamelessly staring at her bosom.

Padraig's gaze was riveted on Cairren, no longer noticing anyone around him. His body refused to calm, and as she stepped forward when his mother ushered them toward the Great Hall, her gown pulled snug across her chest. Padraig's lengthening rod bumped against the back of his sporran, and he was grateful that it hid his rampant cockstand. He shifted his eyes to Myrna, who was glaring at him. She wrapped her arm back around his so tightly that he wouldn't be able to extricate it without causing a scene. He frowned at his beloved before turning back to Cairren, who walked with elegance and poise, studiously ignoring him and Myrna. His discomfort grew when Myrna settled into the seat she always occupied, but should have been offered to Cairren. His mother abetted Myrna's rudeness, and the two women showed no shame in insulting their guests or his bride-to-be.

"The wedding will be tomorrow," Micheil boomed. "I'm certain you are eager to be on your way home, Innes."

"I am certain I'm eager to see my daughter well settled before I go anywhere," Innes spoke softly, but the resolve in his voice made Padraig once again want to squirm. He didn't want a showdown between the two lairds in front of his clan. They were already abuzz about the two women who sat at the dais, their appearances an oddity in the Highlands.

"Tapadh leat." Padraig heard Cairren say thank you to the servant who brought her food and a mug of ale. While her pronunciation wasn't perfect, it was more than passable. Her effort impressed him, even if the serving woman sneered in return. Cairren kept her smile in place as though the servant hadn't been rude to her.

"Manipulative witch," Myrna muttered. Padraig glanced down at Myrna, who pouted at him. "She's just trying to suck up to everyone with her pathetic attempt at Gaelic. Does she think our people are too uncouth to know Scots? She's the heathen here."

Myrna's vehemence unsettled Padraig, even if he understood her anger. They'd been planning a Samhain wedding at the end of the following month when the news arrived that King Robert decreed that Padraig must marry Cairren. The announcement devastated Myrna and Padraig, and she begged him to run away with her. The idea tempted Padraig, but he couldn't overlook the ingrained sense of duty to his clan. He couldn't make the Munros face the king's wrath so he could get what he wanted. He'd accepted the inevitable more easily than Myrna.

Mayhap I should have listened to Wynda and sent Myrna home. I never imagined Cairren would know of Myrna, and I assumed she would turn a blind eye once she did. But then, Myrna hasnae offered a warm welcome to a woman who now calls Foulis home when Myrna never will. That's surely what has Myrna upset. Perhaps a walk will sooth Myrna's temper.

As though Myrna read his mind, she looked directly at Cairren and said, "Padraig, shall we leave for our walk?"

All three Kennedy faces turned toward them, and Padraig wanted to melt into the floor. Discretion didn't seem to be Myrna's aim. Cairren's mocking smile made him feel uncomfortable, but Collette's surprise and hurt made him feel ashamed. He barely dared to look at Innes, who looked ready to murder him.

Cairren lifted her chin and smiled serenely at Padraig. "You should take all the walks together you can while you can. It shall be rather difficult once Myrna returns to Balnagown."

"Myrna is Wynda's companion," Mary interrupted. "She lives here."

Padraig choked on the ale he'd just gulped. His mother spoke a lie, and when Cairren's smile didn't falter, he was certain she knew it too.

"Congratulations on your new position, Myrna. How convenient that it should be offered so recently."

"It wasn't recent at all," Myrna huffed.

"I'd call a sennight recent. Laurel mentioned you'd likely be here to greet me, but I would think your own sister would know if you'd taken up residence with another mon—I mean clan." Cairren spoke with a straight face, daring Myrna to argue, daring Myrna to correct her. For once that morning, Myrna wisely backed down. "I'd do it before the sun gets too high. You wouldn't want to freckle. Or worse, turn brown."

Innes cleared his throat. Cairren leaned back in her chair as she shifted her attention back to the people sitting below the dais, who strained to hear the conversation between Padraig's long-time love interest and his betrothed. Padraig was trapped, knowing the right thing to do would be to send Myrna home that very day, yet wanting to draw out every last minute they could spend together before he was bound to a woman he desired but didn't want. He glanced at Innes, whose eyes shot daggers at him as Myrna leaned against him to whisper. He didn't even hear what she said as Innes twirled his eating knife between his fingers, weaving it under and over.

"There will be no whiling away the day walking hand in hand," Micheil decreed. "The men will adjourn to my solar to discuss the dowry's delivery and the bride price's exchange."

Padraig felt his cheeks flush as his father put into words his very plans. Words his betrothed was forced to hear. He'd never been in a more uncomfortable position than he was now, but he suspected it would only go downhill as the wedding drew nearer. As Myrna sulked, the pout he'd once thought so provocative appeared mulish and petulant while Cairren continued to smile graciously despite the servants' ongoing rudeness and his family's hostile greeting. She'd given as good as she'd gotten, but she did so with a smile. It softened her edges while Myrna appeared ungracious. A moment of doubt flickered through his mind as he considered how Myrna might treat other guests she didn't favor if they were to marry. The woman he often claimed to be inordinately proud of embarrassed him. He couldn't make it to his father's solar quickly enough, but he dreaded being in an enclosed space with Innes, who looked ready to geld him.

CHAPTER FIVE

Padraig eased the door closed behind him once his father, Innes, and Duncan preceded him into the laird's solar. Innes rounded on him and leaned so far forward their noses nearly touched.

"Disgraceful," Innes hissed. "If she says one more word aboot my lass, the wedding is off."

"Hold on now, Kennedy," Micheil intervened. "The lad has had his eye on Myrna for years. It came as a surprise that the king ordered Padraig to marry your daughter. He needs a period of adjustment, a chance to get used to the idea."

"He's had two bluidy moons to get used to it!" Innes erupted.

"Two moons? Nay. I learned of the betrothal a fortnight ago," Padraig corrected.

"Then that is between you and your father, but this betrothal was set and signed two moons ago." Innes cracked his knuckles as he continued to block Padraig against the door. Padraig wasn't about to test who would win if it came to fisticuffs with his soon-to-be father-by-marriage. The man might have been smaller than him, but Innes was an irate father. The only thing scarier would have been Collette staring him down. He hadn't been able to meet the woman's eye after Myrna began taunting Cairren. The woman's disgust radiated from her, and Padraig had felt like the direct recipient of her disdain.

Rightly so. I doubt I could have mucked this up any more if I'd tried. I didna mean to hurt the lass's feelings or dishonor her, but I certainly managed that and more. I need to sort things out with Myrna and send her to Balnagown until I can see her again without upsetting the apple cart.

"Guilty is written across your face," Innes growled. "You're planning to set Myrna aside long enough to marry Cairren, then you'll figure out how to see her. Don't you think my daughter wanted something else for her life than a mon who rejected her before you even met? If King Robert hadn't insisted, I would have taken her just aboot anywhere but here."

"This is my home, and you will not insult my family," Micheil insisted, but he snapped his mouth shut when Innes rounded on him.

"And this is now my daughter's home, and she is part of your family. Yet neither of you have protected her." Innes turned away from Micheil and looked back at Padraig. He lowered his voice, so only Padraig could hear. "She doesn't deserve this. If you hurt her, I will tear your clan asunder. You may not ken, but I am Tristan Mackay's godfather. His father and I fought together in France. Our clans are allies. With the Mackays come the Sinclairs and Sutherlands, who now count the MacLeods as allies too. That seems to name most of your neighbors."

Padraig narrowed his eyes, not appreciating being threatened within his home, but he wisely remained silent. While he chafed at the warning, he understood the man's need to ensure his daughter's wellbeing.

"Lady Cairren will be well taken care of, I assure you."

Innes's look of revulsion made Padraig feel like a chastised wean. "How very pretty of you to say. You still haven't promised to set your other woman aside. I don't think you're yet mon enough to be a husband."

Innes pulled folded parchments from his doublet and moved to the table in the center of the chamber. He spread out the contracts, and the conversation shifted to the practical discussion of how Cairren's dowry would be delivered since they hadn't brought everything. There was also discussion over the bride price. Without saying it in so many words, Micheil tried to negotiate that Padraig was receiving less than the finest quality goods. Innes stood to his full height and stared at Micheil until the Highlander backed down and mumbled an apology for insinuating Innes's daughter was an unsatisfactory object.

Padraig remained silent throughout the meeting as he watched the difference between his father and Innes. Micheil was patronizing and condescending while Innes's temper settled, and the latter came across as the more reasonable man. Innes's insistence on the terms the two lairds had already brokered were in Cairren's best interest. He seemed unconcerned about their impact on his clan, and Padraig realized how much more financially stable the Kennedys must have been than the Munros. Ongoing animosity with the Mackenzies had cost the Munros greatly. Razed fields along with dead and stolen cattle depleted their funds and made Padraig's marriage to a woman with a substantial dowry a necessity. Without the income, it would be several years before his clan rallied again. It would keep them weak, and with the Mackenzies and Camerons breathing down their neck, they couldn't afford to lose.

Padraig had to admit that he respected Innes's forthrightness and savvy negotiating skills. He easily backed Padraig's hotheaded father into a corner more than once. But despite his growing appreciation for Innes, Padraig sensed the man's estimation of him continued to sink. Padraig couldn't name why that bothered him, but he found he disliked the sense of disappointing Innes. When they concluded their business, Innes left to find his family, and the Munro men remained in the laird's solar.

"Catch the bitch in heat and get her with child. Once you have your son, you can ignore her. Perhaps a croft in an outlying village would suit her," Micheil huffed. Padraig couldn't believe his ears. His father's words stunned him. He'd never heard his father speak of a lady in such a vulgar manner, and he couldn't believe he was advocating Padraig abandon her.

"You can't be serious," Padraig spluttered.

"As serious as a wart on a witch's lip," Micheil snarled. "The king never mentioned he'd be sending us some brown bitch to pollute our clan. She's a disgrace. How Innes Kennedy can show either of those women's faces in public is beyond me."

"You don't even know her," Padraig argued. "How can you be so certain she's that horrible?"

Micheil surveyed his son before sneering. "Let your cock have its fun. Swive her until you tire of her. But she's naught more than a disgusting heathen."

Duncan had remained silent throughout the meeting but chose that moment to voice his opinion. "I wonder if her mother taught her the tricks of French courtiers? It's obvious the woman is Saracen. Perhaps she's taught your wee bride how to service a mon like the women do in those harems the Crusaders tell stories of." The speculative gleam in Duncan's eyes made Padraig wary. His brother already had a wife, and Duncan was far too excited about Cairren for Padraig's taste. He glared at Duncan until his brother took the hint.

"I'm going for that walk with Myrna," Padraig announced.

Padraig breathed easy for the first time since the Kennedys arrived. He strolled along the loch with Myrna's hand safely tucked in his, just as they had done for the past two years. They'd met as children, and their parents made it clear that they expected a match between them, but Padraig had waited until Myrna was of an age to marry without him feeling like he would bed a child. Now at eight-and-ten, Myrna was a desirable woman ready to marry. Padraig glanced down at her and couldn't remember a time when he hadn't been in love with her.

Myrna stopped and turned toward Padraig, tears brimming in her eyes. "This is just wretched. It's so unfair, Padraig. Tomorrow's wedding is supposed to be ours. What will I do without you? How will I go on?"

"Wheest," Padraig cooed as he pulled her into his arms and kissed her temple. "This is just as hard for me, and I am just as heartbroken."

Myrna jerked away. "I doubt that. I saw how you looked at her. You want to bed her. You desire her," Myrna accused.

"I will have to bed her, Myrna. She'll be my wife.

But that doesn't mean I'll enjoy it, nor does it mean I want to."

"That's not what it looked like to me," Myrna argued. "It looked like you want her more than you do me."

"That's ridiculous," Padraig scoffed.

"Is it? I have never objected to you coupling with other women. Men have needs. I wasn't old enough to wed. But now I know whose bed you're going to. I'll have to watch you during the bedding ceremony. Another ceremony that should have been mine," Myrna wailed. "You'll have to touch—that."

Padraig attempted to console Myrna, but the more he tried to sooth her, the more distraught she became. It was an hour's ride to the Ross's keep, and Padraig considered taking Myrna home, but when he suggested it, she erupted.

"You're kicking me out? How dare you! You want to be able to tup your little bride without having to look me in the eye the next morning. You're abandoning me for—for—that!"

Myrna's repeated referral to Cairren as "that" chafed, and Padraig stood to his full height. "I was trying to spare you and protect you, just as I have sworn to always do. I would keep you from being hurt by everything that will happen tomorrow, Myrna."

"I don't trust her," Myrna seethed.

"Don't trust her? What is it you think she'll do?"

"She's already trying to seduce you."

"Seduce me?" Padraig was incredulous. Cairren appeared more likely to tear off his head and spit down his throat before inviting him into her bed. "Hardly."

"You haven't denied that you're eager to bed her," Myrna countered.

"I didn't realize I needed to, since that isn't the case." *Well, ma mind might nae be eager even if ma body is. Myrna needs to go. What will I do if ma cock points at Cairren tomorrow eve right there with Myrna watching? She'd never forgive me. But if today's been any sign, it'll be at full attention before the chamber door closes.*

Myrna sobbed, "Don't kick me out. Please, Padraig. Let me stay. I just want to be near you."

Padraig's heart ached for the desperation in Myrna's voice, and he couldn't bring himself to deny her anything. "Very well. But Mother's lie can't become the truth. You won't be able to stay here permanently. If for no other reason than it would destroy your reputation to remain after I marry. People will speculate that we're carrying on an affair."

"Would that really be so bad? I mean to have an affair. It's the closest—"

"No," Padraig interrupted. "Absolutely not. I will not take you as my mistress. You are a lady, gently bred, who must be a maiden when she weds."

"If I can't marry you, then who would want me? Obviously, I don't have the dowry needed to make a clan want me."

"That's not true. Oh Myrna, I don't want to imagine you in the arms of another mon. It tears at my soul, but one day you will be another mon's wife. I can't take what isn't mine. Your maidenhead will belong to another."

"It belongs to me!" Myrna hissed. "Why don't you want me anymore?"

"I do. I'll never stop wanting you," Padraig insisted. "But I won't ruin your future. I love you too much."

Myrna whimpered, and Padraig pulled her back

into his embrace, but she pulled away once more. Padraig's stomach clenched at the gleam in Myrna's eyes.

"If you must bed that whore because it's your duty, I can overlook you being with another woman. If I return to you no longer an innocent, then you won't have wronged me."

"What?" Padraig's arms dropped from Myrna's waist. "You would toss your skirts up for some other mon just so you could slip into my bed next?"

"If I'm no longer an innocent, then you won't have taken aught that doesn't belong to you. Someone else will have."

"No." Padraig shook his head.

"No?" Myrna mimicked. "Are you suggesting you'll be faithful to the heathen?"

"What? No. Yes. I don't know." Padraig shook his head, unable to keep up with Myrna's unexpected train of thought. He'd always intended to be faithful to his wife, but until a fortnight ago, he'd always thought he'd marry Myrna. He hadn't considered taking a leman, and he'd never imagined making Myrna his mistress. None of it sat right with him. He might not want to marry Cairren—in fact he dreaded it—but even he could see she didn't deserve an unfaithful husband. If he couldn't offer her his heart, at least he could offer her fidelity. "As much as I despise what I will have to do, I will make a pledge before God to keep myself only unto my wife. That will be Cairren. And I won't disgrace you, Myrna."

"So, you're choosing her over me," Myrna demanded.

"I'm choosing honor," Padraig countered.

Myrna squinted. "Honor won't pleasure you the way I hope to."

Padraig's eyes widened. They'd shared many kisses over the two years he'd courted her, some less chaste than others, but they had never gone beyond that.

"Don't look so horrified. I have two married sisters. They've explained things to me." Myrna's eyes narrowed once more. "I probably still know less than your slattern bride."

Padraig opened his mouth, but his thought died when movement in the distance caught his eye. He turned to see Cairren and Collette returning to the keep, each with a basket of wildflowers over their arm. Half a dozen Kennedy guardsmen surrounded them. They weren't close enough to hear Myrna and his conversation, but it was likely the mother and daughter spotted the couple before Padraig noticed them. He knew how incriminating it would appear. As the women drew nearer, he observed Cairren's chin notch up an inch, but she studiously ignored him. Collette didn't spare them a glance either.

"We should go," Padraig muttered once the women had their backs to Myrna and him.

"Chasing after her already like she's a bitch in heat," Myrna snapped. Padraig stared at Myrna for a long moment before he took her arm and steered her toward the keep in silence. Myrna and Micheil both described Cairren the same way, but the only one who seemed like a bitch was Myrna.

CHAPTER SIX

The bluidy bastard can't keep his hands off her. He must have bolted to find her the moment he left his father's solar. Then easy as you please, they're standing together where anyone can see them. As though his entire clan doesn't ken his betrothed arrived today, he's standing there clinging to her. I understand, plain and simple. I'm not simple. Cairren kept her smile in place as she sat beside Padraig at the evening meal. With the announcement of the wedding the next day, it forced Mary to seat Cairren beside her son, but the older woman kept casting withering glares at Cairren and heaving pitying sighs when she looked at Padraig.

Despite sharing a trencher, the betrothed couple appeared to barely notice one another. Cairren spoke softly to Collette through most of the meal, even speaking once or twice with Wynda, but she never looked at Padraig. He wanted to offer her an apology, but he wasn't certain what he would apologize for. Would it be the incredibly rude comments his mother and —he didn't even know how to think of Myrna— made when the Kennedys arrived? Would it be the way Myrna clung to him whenever she could? Would it be the disgusting things Cairren hadn't even heard

Myrna and Micheil say? Or would it be his cowardice for not being able to talk to her even though they sat shoulder-to-shoulder? He swallowed and made his first foray into a peace offering.

"Would you care for more duck, my lady?" Padraig whispered to Cairren. He watched her eyes drop to their trencher, where a pile of duck still sat on her side.

"Thank you, no." Cairren's tone was polite but cold.

"Perhaps more wine?" Padraig tried again. He watched Cairren bite her lip as if she was steeling herself for whatever would come next.

"I am well. I have more than enough to eat and drink, but I thank you all the same." Cairren's accent, a blend of Scots and French, intrigued Padraig. He caught himself wondering what he could mention that would draw her into conversation just so he could listen.

"I imagine the weather made the journey rather arduous."

"It did on the days it rained. On the days it didn't, it was pleasant."

Padraig wracked his brain for another topic, since something as banal as the weather didn't elicit much of an answer. *Perhaps I should ask her a question. A question other than if she wants more food. I havenae a clue what a safe topic is at this point.*

"Would you tell me aboot your time at court?" Padraig assumed this would be something she could speak at length about since she lived there for three years. But he watched Cairren's expression, and he could tell her instinct was to say no.

"It was interesting," Cairren paused, unsure of what to say next. "I hadn't met the king or queen before I arrived, and I knew no one there. I recognized the names of a few ladies-in-waiting. Most are Lowlanders, so some were neighbors, but Dunure is rather isolated, being on the coast. I had traveled little before joining the court. Now I have seen much of Scotland since I've accompanied the queen on summer progress."

"It is certainly different from being on one's clan territory. What did you find most different at court from being at home?" Padraig began to feel more confident since he elicited more than one sentence at a time from Cairren, but he caught his breath as she turned to stare at him. The hurt in her eyes was so penetrating that he didn't know where to look.

"How unwelcome I was," Cairren whispered.

"Lass—" Padraig was at a loss for words. Rather than smooth things over, he'd ripped open an unhealed wound. "I—That was thoughtless. I'm sorry." His words sounded lame to his own ears, but he didn't know what else to say.

"There is naught to be done aboot it, and you couldn't have known. Think no more on it," Cairren's voice was strong, but Padraig noticed her chin tremble as she forced out the words. He glanced at his family, and shame washed over him as he considered how their behavior must have mirrored what Cairren had already endured once.

"Would you take a walk with me after the meal?" Padraig prayed he'd have a nimbler wit once they were not surrounded by so many people.

"No. I don't think that's wise."

"Why not? We're betrothed and marrying tomorrow."

"Exactly."

"I don't understand."

Cairren turned an exasperated face to him, and he could tell she clenched her jaw. "I would prefer not to spell it out to you."

"I'm afraid you must because I'm not following."

"No one wants me here. They all wish you were marrying Myrna tomorrow rather than—what was it—someone so brown. If they discover you've taken me for a walk, they will despise me even more for what they'll assume is me seducing you, and they will resent you for turning away from Myrna. It's best that we don't."

"We should talk, Cairren," Padraig pressed. It was the first time he'd spoken her name aloud without the honorific, and he liked how it felt rolling off his tongue.

"No, we shouldn't. At least not tonight. We have a lifetime ahead of us to talk."

"Are you always so disagreeable?" Padraig muttered.

"Are you always so naïve?" Cairren returned. Padraig opened his mouth to respond, but Cairren lifted her palm off the table, signaling him to wait. "I'm not trying to be disagreeable, Padraig. You're the only person who's been..." Cairren didn't know how to describe Padraig's welcome. It hadn't been warm, but neither had it been hostile. "It would be unwise of me to create any more animosity. Eventually, it will spill over to you."

"You're protecting me?" Padraig was aghast.

"Call it experience hard learned. You would do well not to be caught in the storm's eye. I'm here to serve a purpose. Neither of us needs to pretend it's aught else. I brought a dowry, and I will bear your children." Cairren swept her eyes over the diners seated at long tables beneath the dais. She glanced down at her hands and flinched. "Perhaps we shall settle on I brought a dowry."

"What's that supposed to mean?"

Cairren's gray eyes met Padraig's, and once more he recognized hurt in her gaze. But this seemed soul deep. He watched her swallow several times before she felt composed enough to speak. "Perhaps it would be best if I didn't bear you any children. In a few years, you can claim I'm infertile and set me aside. Perhaps you'll be able to have the marriage you want." Cairren glanced at Myrna before returning her gaze to Padraig. "They might be brown like me."

Padraig sat back, the wind let out of his sails. He hadn't considered what their children might look like, not even when his father spoke of her polluting their bloodline. His eyes swept over Cairren's clear complexion, noticing a smattering of freckles on her nose. Her brows were finely etched as if each hair had been placed just so. Her lips were plump and glistened from when she licked them before speaking. While he understood the ramifications of having a wife who didn't resemble anyone in his clan, he couldn't deny that she was beautiful and would likely one day have beautiful children. He wondered if all of her would be the same bronze hue or if she were paler under her clothes. He realized that he was more curious about the contrast and being able to see her undressed than hoping that she would have lighter skin.

The longer he gazed at her, the less he cared about her skin color. But he doubted anyone else in his clan would have the same reaction. He'd seen how many of the men looked at her, and it set him on edge. He could only describe it as leering, but he'd watched Cairren pretend not to notice, and it saddened him to realize that she was accustomed to such lecherous behavior. The men appreciated her beauty and the desire it stirred, but Padraig knew none of them respected her. Once more he felt trapped in the middle. He realized he'd sat quiet too long when Cairren dipped her chin and returned her focus to the uneaten food on her side of the trencher.

"We will only say you're infertile if it proves to be true," Padraig said.

"You can't mean you're willing to risk..." Cairren couldn't say it again. It tore at her to acknowledge that if she had children, no one would see it as a blessing other than her.

"Did your father see having children with your mother as a risk?" Padraig prodded.

"He loves her," Cairren whispered. She couldn't continue this conversation. The musicians tuning their instruments as the servants pushed the last tables to the sides increased her need to escape. "Excuse me."

Cairren pushed back her chair, grateful she sat on the end and could step off the dais without drawing attention. She attempted to make her way to the stairs, but too many people were milling around for her to cut a direct path. As she wound through the crowd of Munros, she caught the snide comments and disdainful glares. She kept her chin up and back straight as she tried to navigate the least congested parts of the Great Hall.

"Hope his cock doesn't shrivel up after touching that quim," Cairren heard a man's voice.

"Nay. He's a lucky bastard. Perhaps she'll swive us once he's through with her. Her whoring type can never get enough." Another man's voice carried to her along with the laughter that followed. But suddenly, Cairren was surrounded by silence. She looked over her shoulder and caught sight of Padraig's murderous glare. For a moment she feared he directed it at her for causing a stir, but when he narrowed his eyes at a man standing beside Cairren, she realized he must have heard what she had.

"Rest assured, I don't share what is mine," Padraig growled. What he heard disgusted him, but it mortified him that Cairren heard it too. "You two have just earned yourselves a moon of mucking out the motte. Anyone who feels the need to voice similar opinions will find themselves knee deep in shite."

Padraig wrapped his arm around Cairren's shoulders and steered her toward the massive doors that led to the bailey. He hadn't trusted his clan not to harass, even harm, Cairren as she tried to leave the Great Hall. He had been right not to. He never imagined he would hear such filth directed at a lady, and he was certain the men were aware she could hear. He was sure that was exactly why they'd spoken. They'd painted the gentle lady at his side as little more than a tavern whore. *Call it experience hard learned.* Cairren's words rang in Padraig's ears, and he realized Cairren was far too familiar with the insults spewed around them.

As soon as the doors closed behind them, Cairren refused to budge. "You shouldn't be out here. You need to go back inside."

"Would you let me worry aboot myself for a while? I'm not a child. I can choose for myself where I go and with whom I go." Padraig found himself pulling Cairren's Kennedy plaid over her shoulders before he realized what he was doing. He had a flash of an image of Cairren wrapped in a Munro plaid; Padraig was unsettled by how right it seemed. "It's chilly."

Cairren watched as Padraig turned away and proceeded down the steps, assuming she would follow, but she refused. She would return to the Great Hall before anyone could claim they'd slipped away together. The cool northern night air eased much of the tension between Cairren's shoulders as she inhaled deeply. She turned her face toward the stars and searched for her favorite constellations. Her father often sailed and had taught her about how the stars were a navigation tool. She oriented herself to the south, looking off into the distance as though she might spy Dunure all the way from the Highlands. When Padraig returned to her side, she felt too depleted to reject the embrace he offered. She rested her cheek against his chest. She began to relax but the memory of seeing him in the same position with Myrna only hours earlier had her reeling back, shaking her head.

"I'm not who you wish to be out here with. I'm less than a poor substitute. I'll go back inside." Cairren turned away, but Padraig grasped her arm. Unlike the Armstrong representative who waylaid her at Stirling Castle, Padraig's grip wasn't punishing. Just the opposite. It was gentle, and Cairren knew she could pull away, but she found she didn't want to. The fight had gone out of her, and she was suddenly too exhausted from the months of anxiousness, the interminable journey, and the open hostility. She just wanted to climb into bed and close her eyes.

"How do you know who I want to be here with? Have you asked? Do I look like I want to be somewhere else?"

"You will when Myrna finds you."

"Let me worry aboot that." Padraig was firm.

Cairren's laughter held no mirth. "You haven't

spent the past three years surviving the social politics of a hoard of young women who are mercilessly competitive. She may be displeased with you, but I will pay for this."

"You don't know Myrna. She's not like that." But even as he defended his beloved, Padraig feared Cairren was right.

"You defend the woman you love to the woman you're marrying." Cairren crossed her arms.

"I do love Myrna. I may not be able to offer you my heart, but I can offer you the protection of my name and fidelity."

"That's laughable at best." Cairren's lip curled. "Fidelity? You mean coming to my bed at night while spending your days, cow-eyed and lovestruck, with the woman you want. How long will that last? Just don't seek me out when you smell of her."

"That's unfair," Padraig protested.

"Unfair? To you? Let me guess what she said to convince you she should stay and witness *our* wedding. She can't believe you'd abandon her. That it will devastate her to be away from you. That she can't live without you. That she just needs time to find a way for you to be together." Cairren waived a dismissive hand in front of her. "I've heard that drivel from desperate women more times than I have fingers and toes. But it still surprises me how many men believe it. Though I can't say you surprise me at all. You're wholly predictable."

Cairren turned away, but Padraig's arms drew her back against his broad chest. His heated palm rested on her belly, wide enough to cover most of her abdomen. He leaned in to whisper beside her ear. "That is a future you concocted. I will swear my oath before God, and I will keep it."

"You may claim you'll be faithful, but you don't deny Myrna made those pleas to you."

"So what if she did? You will be my wife by this time tomorrow."

Before Cairren could respond, he eased her around and cupped her jaw, bringing his mouth within a hair's breadth of hers. When she didn't pull away, his lips brushed hers before pressing more firmly. His tongue pressed against the seam of her lips twice, but she did little more than part them, making Padraig realize Cairren was more innocent than he realized and didn't understand what he wanted. He used his thumbs to press down on her jaw, coaxing her to open for him. When his tongue swept across the satiny depths, Cairren stilled. She didn't pull away, but Padraig suspected she didn't know what to do. Possessiveness unlike anything he had experienced before swept over him as he realized that no man before him had enjoyed the drugging effects of Cairren's kisses.

She tentatively twirled her tongue with his, a gasp of surprise confirming Padraig's suspicions. He could recall every moment of his first kiss with Myrna as though he were sharing it with her again rather than kissing Cairren. He never recalled Myrna being as hesitant. He'd assumed her eagerness came from curiosity and long-restrained want, but as he thought about it, Myrna seemed to have known exactly what to do, her mouth open and ready to receive his tongue even before the kiss began.

His hands were almost wider than Cairren's narrow frame, and he feared for a moment that she wouldn't be able to manage coupling with him, let alone bear children. But he groaned as his hand cupped her backside while the other slid along her ribs until it captured the swell of her breast. He marveled at how such a slender woman had such lush curves hidden beneath her gown. He noticed how easy it was to hold her against him even when he had to stoop to reach her. Cairren came to the middle of his chest, and as he held her, he had a surging sense of protectiveness blended with desire that surpassed any he'd felt with other women. He'd been attracted to the women he'd been with between the sheets, against walls, even in haystacks, but the need to bury himself within a woman had never consumed him as it did now. His aching cock throbbed behind his sporran. It tempted him to push the pouch out of the way and let his sword press against her sheath. He'd long believed that he would never desire a woman more than Myrna, but he found his body ached for Cairren with an insistence he doubted he could ever satiate.

Footsteps behind him in the bailey brought Padraig back to reality, and as he looked around, he realized the torches blazing near the doors would have illuminated everything he did to the men on the battlements. His broad shoulders might have hidden Cairren, but they didn't hide his obvious movements as his hands explored her body. Shame washed over him, knowing the men would believe his actions represented his view of Cairren: she was little more than the whore the men in the Great Hall had called her if the laird's son pawed at her in plain sight. As he watched Cairren bring her fingers to her lips, as though still shocked by the kiss they shared, he recalled once again that Myrna had never seemed so innocent and transfixed by any of their early kisses, and he had a moment of niggling doubt that Myrna had more experience than he'd believed. When Cairren gasped again, it wasn't the breathy sound of surprise. It was disgust. She covered her mouth with her hands and shook her head.

Cairren felt lightheaded and drugged as the world fell away around them while she shared her first kiss. Her head seemed to float above her body, all of her senses but touch dulled. But when she pulled away and noticed Padraig's distant stare, her world crashed to smithereens around her.

"Even now you're thinking of her. Picturing being with her rather than stuck here with me." Cairren's expression was so filled with loathing that Padraig wanted to turn away rather than accept the shame that flooded him. "Consummate this marriage, then leave me the hell alone."

When Cairren dashed inside, Padraig remained outside. He'd ruined Cairren's first kiss and what was undoubtedly the most earth-shattering one he'd ever shared. His rod throbbed with unspent need, so he opted for a dip in the loch rather than return to the Great Hall. He stood in the same spot he had countless times before, prepared to conjure an image of Myrna as he took himself in hand, but only Cairren materialized in his imagination. Remembering her swollen lips and glazed eyes as he pulled away from their kiss made his cock pulse and leak. He continued to work his length as he recalled how she'd felt in his hands, and it was her name on his lips when jets of seed sprayed into the water. He longed for the feel of her in his arms once again as the euphoria waned. He was certain taking himself in hand while thinking of Myrna was never as satisfying as picturing Cairren. As he trudged back to the keep, he'd never been more miserable in his life.

CHAPTER SEVEN

Collette brushed Cairren's hair as they sat before the fire in Cairren's chamber. They'd spent the day with Innes away from the keep and away from the Munros. Innes and Collette had lain awake late into the night, both fretting about the future they'd unwittingly forced Cairren into. They'd finally agreed they would insist on a handfasting instead of a regular marriage. They would gladly forfeit all of Cairren's dowry if it meant she could return home in a year and a day if she were miserable. After they broke their fast, Innes pulled Micheil aside to discuss the desired change in plans. Cairren hadn't understood why the conversation appeared heated in the beginning, but Micheil's expression turned from enraged to smug as the two lairds returned to the dais. He cast her a priggish smile that made Cairren go cold and desperate to learn the newest development.

Her parents' news stunned her, but she confessed it was a great relief to know that there was a possibility that she wouldn't be sentenced to a lifetime with the Munros. After three years as a lady-in-waiting, she was confident she could endure a year in the Highlands. She wondered how much more relieved

Padraig would be than her when he learned the news. If it was only for a year, she found she didn't care what Padraig did or with whom he did it. She would gladly turn a blind eye and let Myrna have him. With a lighter heart, Cairren enjoyed her family's trip to the loch. They picnicked and even swam together. She'd grown up swimming in the frigid waters and rough currents of the Irish Sea and the Firth of Clyde. As she dove and turned in the warm summer water, Innes teased her.

"You're still more seal than woman," Innes chuckled, then spluttered as Cairren splashed water in his face.

"Catch me if you can," she called before diving below the surface. He easily caught his daughter's ankle and reeled her back in before lifting her overhead and tossing her just as he had when she was a child. She hooted as she sailed through the air and emerged giggling, as though she hadn't a care in the world. And for the brief time the trio spent together that afternoon, Cairren could pretend that she had none.

But now she sat with Collette, freshly bathed as her mother wove the flowers into her hair that they'd picked the day before. She was scrubbed clean, and as her chemise brushed against her skin, her body felt sleek from the waxing they'd performed the night before. At four-and-ten, Collette taught Cairren how to use honey to remove the hair from her mons. At the time, the anticipated pain terrified her, and it shocked her that her mother would propose something so indecent, but she soon preferred the feel. She hadn't enjoyed the luxury frequently at court, but she waxed often enough to keep from being miserable each time she did.

"*Maman*, are you certain being smooth won't repulse Padraig? Won't he think he's bedding a child? This isn't something any Scottish mon expects, or at least none that aren't courtiers. What if he rejects me?" *Even more.*

"*Ma petite-fille*, I can almost certainly agree that he will never have seen the like, but I can also promise that it will intrigue him more than you suspect. You will feel different from any of the women in his past, and it will surely increase his pleasure. As long as you remember what I said about not lying there like a dead fish and at the least pretend to enjoy his attention, he will return to your bed."

"But what if I only want this one night? I can't risk getting with child if I intend to repudiate the handfast."

"*Mon cher ceour.*" My dear heart, Collette sighed. "Don't go into this assuming it will end. You will make yourself even more miserable if you do naught but count down the days. Approach this with the open mind and open heart you bring to all things. If you close yourself off to the mere chance you might find happiness here, no one will accept you. People will be able to tell. They'll sense that sentiment, even if you never speak aloud your intentions."

"But, *Maman*, now that Padraig and Myrna must know it's only a handfast, they'll be even more resolute to marry. What's keeping them from speaking of their marriage or their wedding plans in front of me? I really will be just a chest of gold to them. How can I not look forward to the end?"

"*Chaque chose en son temps*," Collette reminded Cairren. While Cairren knew the words meant each thing in its own time, she understood her mother meant not to worry until there was reason to. But Collette hadn't been standing outside while Cairren and Padraig kissed. She hadn't experienced the light-headed feeling that engulfed Cairren as Padraig kissed her and his hands roamed over her. She'd been able to forget who they were and why their match was a disaster. Or at least she had until she realized that he was thinking about Myrna rather than her. Then the bliss crumbled, and the hurt returned. She replayed the kiss over and over, convinced Padraig must have been imagining he was kissing Myrna to offer her such passion. The rejection stung, even if she reminded herself that she never should have expected more. She once again dreaded climbing into bed beside Padraig, fearful that he would always be fooling himself into thinking it was Myrna rather than Cairren he coupled with.

"*Oui, Maman. Je sais.*" Cairren might know what Collette meant and even agreed, but it didn't make it any easier. Collette patted Cairren's hair into place one last time, and Cairren had to admit that her coiffure exceeded even the most beautiful she'd seen at court. "*C'est tres joli. Merci, Maman.*"

It was very pretty, and she was thankful, but she knew they would judge her appearance not by her hair, but what people had already decided was the truth about Cairren. She sighed but twisted to view the entire hairstyle in the looking glass. Her mother had fashioned a circlet from a braid before nestling a gold circlet within the circle of the plait. Collette banded the hair that remained hanging down Cairren's back every few inches with brightly colored ribbons that complimented her pale blue gown.

The gown was more conservative than the ones Cairren wore at court. It was even conservative compared to most of the ones she wore at home, but it created a stunning effect. Cairren had designed it to cover as much of her as possible, but the fabric draped around her like a second skin. The high neckline accentuated her breasts without hinting at the skin that lay beneath. Collette understood the intrigue it would create in men, but she'd said nothing to Cairren, knowing her daughter's intent was to decrease attention to her body. Collette's gentle smile played at the corners of her mouth as she watched Cairren don the kirtle. The embroidery around the collar drew the eye to Cairren's swan-like neck and defined jawline. Her face was rounded and soft, each feature dainty. The embroidery at the waist resembled a girdle, but a vee rested at the center, pointing to the place Collette was certain Padraig would enjoy discovering. The full skirts shimmered each time Cairren moved, and the overly long sleeves were looser than what was *à la mode*, but they made each of her arms' movements elegant.

A knock at the door sounded as Cairren took a deep breath, steeling herself for what came next. She knew it was Innes coming to escort mother and daughter to the kirk. Collette opened the door, and Innes's face immediately shone with pride. He stepped inside Cairren's chamber and held out his hands, which Cairren eagerly took. His massive hands dwarfed hers, but their difference in size had always made Cairren feel safe. She'd had a brief sense of that when Padraig held her the night before—before it all came crashing down.

"My wee lassie, you are the bonniest sight this side of the Cairngorms. You're radiant, and I have never been prouder to be your papa." Innes blinked several times, and Cairren saw the wetness in his eyes. "You're hardly a wean anymore, but you will always be my wee lassie. Remember that always." Innes pulled Cairren into his embrace and tucked her against his chest, careful not to muss her hair.

"Thank you, Papa. I will happily remain your little lass forever." Cairren strained to kiss the bristles that ran along Innes's jaw, his beard having tickled her since she was a child. Innes shifted his attention to Collette, and she stepped forward as Innes wrapped one arm around each of them.

"I am the luckiest mon alive. God has blessed me with a wife and daughters I love with all my heart." Innes's words sparked regret in Cairren that Caitlyn wasn't there beside her. They'd been the best of friends their entire lives, and it had felt like Cairren lost a limb when she went to court. The phantom pains she'd felt returned as her arms tingled to hug her sister.

"We are just as lucky to have you, *mon cher amour*." Just as Collette had always called Cairren her little girl, she'd always called Innes her dear love. To Cairren's ear, it sounded even better than its equal translation of beloved, somehow more sentimental. Cairren forced away the disappointment that she would never hear such an endearment from the man she was handfasting. While she dressed, she'd resigned herself to what was to come and chided herself for self-pity. Duty came before the individual, a mantra she'd adopted when she left home. She would accept come what may with an open heart and an open mind, just as her mother advised.

"Are you ready, wee one?" Innes whispered. Even though she wasn't, she nodded. She would discover soon enough what was coming.

Padraig slipped away from his nagging mother and Myrna's constant sighs. His head ached, and he needed peace to collect himself before he would be forced to stand on the kirk steps handfasting with a woman who couldn't be more opposite in appearance from the woman he loved, the woman he longed to marry, the one he was supposed to marry. He'd accepted his fate and resigned himself to accept his immediate future. Micheil pulled Padraig aside and explained the wedding would be a handfasting instead. While it was an inordinate relief to know an end was in sight, he dreaded listening to Mary and Myrna counting down the days until Cairren left. Until the number was in the single digits, Padraig feared it would demoralize him more. And he admitted to himself that Myrna's attitude was becoming tiresome. Her aggrieved huffs and wistful sighs were wearing his nerves thin, a first between them.

Their courtship had been idyllic, both cherishing every moment they spent together, planning their life together and the family they would build. They'd been so like-minded in all things that Padraig assumed he would never find fault in Myrna. But now her petulance and insolence made him wonder what she would be like if they did ever disagree. For the first time, she seemed less attractive to him.

Cairren had made her dislike of their situation clear, but each point she raised had been valid. Padraig had thought about their conversation both inside and outside the keep for most of the night. Cairren's accusations had been truthful, and her concerns about Myrna were honest without being spiteful. He'd tried to imagine how Myrna would feel if she were put in Cairren's place. His heart ached at the thought, and some sympathy that welled in his chest from his fictitious scenario spilled over to Cairren. If he'd intended to keep himself only unto Myrna when they thought they would marry, he'd accepted that he should do the same for Cairren. Now that he knew that it was only for a year, the sacrifice seemed less significant.

Laughter carried to him on a breeze as he wandered toward the loch. He caught snippets of French and knew the Kennedys were nearby. He assumed they were there for a walk like he was, so the loud cry and splash startled him. He feared one of the ladies had fallen into the lake if they'd been standing on an outcropping. The rocks were slick even in dry weather, and it was easy to fall. Padraig sprinted toward the shore, but came to a halt when he spotted Cairren giggling as she soared through the air before tucking into a tight ball just before landing in the water. Innes's chuckle turned Padraig's attention toward his soon-to-be father-by-marriage. The amusement and fondness on his face spoke of his affection for his daughter. He noticed Collette sat on a rock dangling her feet in the water, wearing only her chemise. But his attention reverted to Cairren as she swam close to Innes, then flipped onto her back, kicking water in her father's face. In the blink of an eye, she was on her belly and disappearing beneath the surface. Padraig watched as Innes took off after his daughter underwater, and it was only a moment later that Cairren's head emerged as Innes dragged her back to him.

"What am I to do with such a naughty lass who splashes her father?" Innes teased.

"Toss me out, Papa!" Cairren replied. Innes hoisted Cairren over his head, her petite body weighing little more than a feather to the braw warrior. He bounced her thrice before hurling her forward. This time, instead of tucking into a ball, Cairren stretched into a graceful arrow, entering the water headfirst. The Kennedys' playfulness mesmerized Padraig. He'd seen no family, noble or otherwise, so relaxed and happy in one another's company. He supposed the Sinclair siblings were the closest he could think of. The four brothers and their little sister were famous for their bond. The four mountainous men were no match for their sister, who didn't even come to their shoulders. Padraig had never shared even a remote closeness to Duncan. They'd been rivals and adversaries their entire lives. When Padraig surpassed Duncan's height, the rift between them became irreparable, as though Duncan blamed his younger brother for growing taller and broader than him. While neither had control over their height, Padraig spent far more hours training than Duncan, who took for granted his position as tánaiste. His inheritance was secure, and he believed himself a better fighter than he was, so he often skipped the hours in the lists that Padraig spent, preferring to bed women other than his wife.

Padraig's musings ended when he realized Collette had caught sight of him gawking. He nodded and moved further down the path, but Cairren's voice drew closer as he passed by a bush and tree that provided camouflage despite the red brick color of his plaid. Padraig ducked and spied through the leaves as Cairren hoisted herself onto the rock beside her mother. Her wet chemise clung to her, and it granted Padraig a spectacular view of full breasts and dark nipples. As she rang out her hair and lifted it off her neck, the transparent garment pulled tighter, and Padraig's cock roared to life.

"*Ma petite-fille*, we must return to the keep, so

you can prepare for the ceremony. Slip into those trees and change back into your kirtle." Collette nodded toward trees near where Padraig hid. He wondered if Collette suspected he lingered or if she meant privacy for Cairren. Before he could consider whether he should walk away, Cairren yanked her sodden chemise over her head. She stood there in the buff with a body more glorious than anything his imagination could divine. He'd bedded enough women to know they weren't all created the same, but Cairren's body surpassed even the ripest tavern wench. His feet seemed to have taken root as he remained frozen in place, fearing that any movement would alert Cairren to his presence. A sense of urgency to conduct the ceremony and begin the feast so he could take her to his chamber soon pulsed along with his straining rod.

Shame and disloyalty soon pushed desire out of the way. He was ashamed to spy on Cairren when she believed she had the benefit of privacy, and he felt disloyal to Myrna and ashamed for wanting Cairren with a physical hunger that surpassed any he'd experienced for Myrna. He closed his eyes as he tried to calm his racing heart and thoughts. He knew there would be an unavoidable bedding ceremony. As he'd lain in bed the night before, he'd considered Cairren's suggestion that he just stay away once they consummated the handfast. It would make the repudiation easier, especially since he wouldn't risk siring any children. It eased his guilt for hurting Myrna by bedding another woman. But all of his good intentions evaporated as he watched Cairren. She was a siren, and he was a sailor willingly lured. Cairren didn't even know the effect she had on him, but he feared she might grow manipulative when she realized she had the power to bring him to his knees. However, that thought didn't sit right with him. Something about Cairren made him doubt she was the manipulative type.

Mayhap we can form a truce if we at least get along in the bedchamber. If Myrna isnae here to see, then mayhap bedding Cairren every night will make it easier for us to get along. If she's satisfied, well...What the hell am I saying? I want to send Myrna off, so she doesnae ken how much I enjoy bedding another woman! How fickle and disloyal can I be?

But I will be sworn to Cairren for at least a year. She deserves some of ma loyalty. Having the woman I want, the one I intend to spend the rest of my life with after this debacle ends, living under the same roof as ma wife is a slight. Even I ken better. But the thought of nae seeing Myrna, nae talking to her even if I canna hold her, is excruciating. I may enjoy bedding Cairren, but entering the chamber every night that I've believed meant for Myrna with a woman who isnae Myrna dulls the appeal of even the most enticing woman I've ever seen. Padraig rubbed his forehead as the ache continued. He remained out of sight until the Kennedys passed through the postern gate. Then he returned to his chamber to prepare for the handfasting.

CHAPTER EIGHT

Padraig pinched the inside of his wrist to see if he was dreaming. A vision of angelic beauty floated toward him as he waited on the steps of the keep's kirk. Cairren walked with grace and dignity through a crowd that looked more prepared to lob rotting vegetables at her than cheer her on. The blatant rudeness galled Padraig. Even if they didn't agree with his marriage, their duty to their laird was to accept and respect his decision. Micheil accepted the king's offer, and so it was as much by Laird Munro's decree as King Robert's that Padraig marry Cairren.

Padraig noticed Cairren looked straight ahead, as if she didn't notice the surrounding people, but her eyes weren't locked on him. Instead, they appeared vacant, as though she saw nothing, as though she wasn't present in the moment. It was disconcerting as she drew closer. When she stopped before the steps, she curtseyed to his bow, but she seemed far away. When she placed her hand in his, Padraig squeezed it gently, and her trance disappeared. Her eyes swept the crowd, and Padraig felt ill as once more fear haunted Cairren's eyes. He regretted drawing her back to reality.

"Look at me, lass," Padraig whispered as he squeezed her hand again. Cairren lifted her gaze to Padraig's as she swallowed. It was as though she registered his presence for the first time. Her eyes swept over him, taking in the crisp leine and ceremonial plaid. He'd polished his boots, and the dirks he sheathed at his waist. Even though the sheaths hid the blades, their handles shone. For a reason he dared not entertain, he'd wanted to look his best for Cairren. Her eyes met his, and her gaze softened as she noticed the strands that were darker from still being damp. He'd shaven, and she seemed to appreciate the smooth skin. If nothing else, Padraig realized, she approved of his appearance.

He more than approved of hers. She appeared exquisite in a gown that clung to her like someone poured her into it, drawing the eye to the most enticing parts of her body. While he could only see her front, he suspected the gown would hang close enough to her bottom to hint at what lay beneath, just as the gown did over her breasts. His mind flashed to the sight of Cairren in the soaked chemise and his first glimpse at the dark nipples unlike any he'd yet seen. His arousal stirred yet again as he recalled the vision of loveliness that she was when naked. He sported what seemed like a permanent cockstand since Cairren arrived at Foulis. No woman had such a visceral effect on Padraig. He forced his eyes away from devouring his bride, letting them sweep his clan members before landing on Myrna. Her blond hair shone like spun gold as she stood beside Mary. Defiance radiated from the glare she fixed on Cairren. The hard set of her mouth and chin detracted from her beauty. Once more, Padraig considered how he'd been convinced that no woman existed who was lovelier than Myrna, but now he held hands with one.

Cairren's shift away from him brought his attention back to her, and he realized she'd caught him staring at Myrna. It was obvious he'd amplified the hurt Cairren already suffered, and he wished he could pull Cairren aside and share his thoughts, make her understand how constantly conflicted he felt. How he desired her and appreciated her appearance even as he pined for Myrna. But he suspected Cairren wouldn't find those words consoling, that it would only dig him deeper into the pile of manure his life had taken residence in. As the priest wrapped the cord around their wrist, Padraig stroked the back of Cairren's hand, trying to sooth some of the pain from her eyes. Her hand jerked back, but she caught herself before it was noticeable to anyone beside Padraig and the priest who glowered at her. Father Mitchell had christened Padraig and had supported Padraig's pursuit of Myrna's hand. While Padraig understood the priest's disappointment, even disdain, for the bride who stood before them, the open hostility seemed overmuch now that they were to handfast.

Father Mitchell cleared his throat before casting Cairren one more sneer. He turned his attention to the crowd.

"Dearly beloved, we are gathered together here in the sight of God, and in the face of this clan, to join together this mon and this woman in holy matrimony; which is an honorable estate, instituted of God in the time of mon's innocence, signifying unto us the mystical union that is betwixt Christ and his Church; which holy estate Christ adorned and beautified with his presence, and first miracle that he wrought, in Cana of Galilee; and is commended of Saint Paul to be honorable among all men: and therefore is not by any to be enterprised, nor taken in hand, unadvisedly, lightly, or wantonly, to satisfy men's carnal lusts and appetites, like brute beasts that have no understanding; but reverently, discreetly, advisedly, soberly, and in the fear of God; duly considering the causes for which matrimony was ordained."

Cairren's nails bit into Padraig's hands as the priest intoned the first verse of the traditional Church marriage vows. They were not the words of a handfast. Cairren turned horror-filled eyes toward the priest, who pretended to ignore her. As he drew breath at the end of the verse, it tempted Padraig to shield Cairren from the man's hateful glare. It was as though he blamed Cairren for their marriage. Padraig looked at his parents, and he knew immediately who had done this. Micheil's self-satisfied expression said it all. He was forcing Padraig into this marriage to ensure they kept Cairren's dowry.

"Papa," Cairren whispered. The sense of betrayal in her voice nearly made Padraig come undone. When she spoke again, there was a plea to the single word, as if she begged her father to rescue her. "Papa?"

Innes Kennedy stood shocked beside Collette, who had tears streaming down her cheeks. He was prepared to bash Micheil Munro's brains in, but there was nothing he could do. It was a courtesy to agree to a handfast, and Micheil was well within his legal rights to insist that their children marry, making the union permanent. He looked at Micheil and mouthed, "You will pay for this. I will not forget." But Micheil had the audacity to grin even wider.

"He didn't know," Padraig whispered to Cairren. "Neither did I."

Cairren's face crumbled, but no tears came. She turned it, so his clan couldn't see her shock and despondency. She remained stoic, and Padraig drew courage from this pint-sized woman. If she could endure the shock of the situation, so too could he.

"First, it was ordained for the procreation of children," Father Mitchell continued. "To be brought up in the fear and nurture of the Lord, and to the praise of his holy Name. Secondly, it was ordained for a remedy against sin, and to avoid fornication; that such persons as have not the gift of contingency might marry, and keep themselves undefiled members of Christ's body. Thirdly, it was ordained for the mutual society, help, and comfort, that the one ought to have of the other, both in prosperity and adversity. Into which holy estate these two persons present come now to be joined. Therefore, if any many can show any just cause, why they may not lawfully be joined together, let him now speak, or else hereafter forever hold his peace."

Padraig tensed, waiting to hear Myrna's voice, or Innes's. The words forewarning against lust and fornication mocked Padraig, as though they knew they were the only reasons Padraig looked forward to the marriage.

"I require and charge you both, as ye will answer at the dreadful day of judgment when the secrets of all hearts shall be disclosed, that if either of you know any impediment, why ye may not be lawfully joined together in matrimony, ye do now confess it. For be ye well assured, that so many as are coupled together otherwise than God's Word doth allow are not joined together by God; neither is their matrimony lawful."

He feared Cairren would speak out, but when silence ensued, Father Mitchell picked up where he left off. Cairren's expression was once again distant, as though she weren't attending her own wedding and wasn't standing before him.

Father Mitchell looked at Padraig. "Wilt the have this woman to thy wedded wife, to live together after God's ordinance in the holy estate of matrimony? Wilt the love her, comfort her, honor, and keep her in sickness and in health; and, forsaking all other, keep thee only unto her, so long as ye both shall live?" This was the vow Padraig dreaded but swore to keep even though he didn't love Cairren. Unable to offer her love, he felt an obligation to hold true to the other promises.

"I will," Padraig's clear voice spread across the now silent clan. There was no doubt or hesitation in his tone, and it seemed to bring Cairren back to the present. And now it was Cairren's turn to agree to the vow that would bind her to Padraig until one of them met their Creator.

"Wilt the have this mon to thy wedded husband," Father Mitchell intoned. Padraig didn't miss the challenge in the priest's voice, as though he dared Cairren to fail. "To live together after God's ordinance in the holy estate of matrimony? Wilt the obey him, and serve him, love, honor, and keep him in sickness and in health; and, forsaking all other, keep thee only unto him, so long as ye both shall live?"

Cairren drew in a deep breath. Pain seemed to consume every inch of her. It was agony standing before Padraig when he promised to love, honor, and comfort her when she knew he didn't mean any of it. Now it was her turn to lie. While she might have been willing to love him, Padraig already made it clear that such tender feelings would be pointless. Her pledge to obey a man who took her hand in marriage after being paid to do so, made her chattel. But what choice did she have? None.

"I will." Cairren's voice gave no hint to her inner turmoil. She met Padraig's eyes, determined to pretend to be the devoted bride to Padraig's doting groom.

Innes stepped forward, prepared for what came next. Father Mitchell directed his derisive tone at Collette as he stared with equal disgust at Cairren's mother. "Who giveth this woman to be married to this mon?" He managed to make the word "woman" sound distasteful and condescending each time he spoke it.

"Her mother and I," Innes lifted his chin, not afraid to challenge the man of the cloth. Cairren's father was already beside himself that Micheil fooled them into the marriage. He wasn't willing to cower before a priest who mocked him.

"I, Padraig Angus Munro take thee." Padraig froze. He had no idea what Cairren's full name was. He hadn't paid attention to the contracts, and he hadn't thought to ask.

"Sabine," Cairren whispered.

"Cairren Sabine Kennedy, to my wedded wife, to have and to hold from this day forward, for better for worse, for richer or for poorer, in sickness and in health, to love and to cherish, till death us do part, according to God's holy ordinance; and thereto I plight thee my troth." As though agreeing to the terms hadn't been bad enough, the ceremony now forced them to voice each promise aloud.

"I, Cairren Sabine Kennedy, take thee, Padraig Angus Munro, to my wedded husband, to have and to hold from this day forward, for better for worse, for richer or for poorer, in sickness and in health, to love, cherish, and to obey, till death us do part, according to God's holy ordinance; and thereto I give thee my troth."

Padraig pulled a ring from his sporran that he rubbed between his thumb and forefinger. It was the ring he'd always intended to give Myrna, but now he was sliding it onto Cairren's finger. Once more, her hand jerked as if she would pull it away, as if the ring scorched her finger. Padraig glanced at Cairren and knew she'd realized the ring wasn't really meant for her. He pushed the ring over her knuckle where it settled at the base of her finger. With her fine bones, the ring looked as though it had been crafted just for her. The deep emerald reflected the sunlight as Padraig tried not to sigh with resignation. It wouldn't make Cairren or him feel better.

"With this ring I thee wed." As Padraig stood before his stalwart bride, a woman who would endure a lifetime of rejection from the clan she joined, he discovered a reverence for his pledge that he hadn't expected. He admitted to himself that he wasn't sure that he could have survived the past day with the dignity Cairren had. He admired her for it, and he felt pride that King Robert entrusted her to him. None of his clan might appreciate the gift he'd been given, but at least Padraig could respect her. "With my body I thee worship, and with all my worldly goods I thee endow: In the Name of the Father, and of the Son, and of the Holy Ghost. Amen." His body agreed with his vow to worship her, so Padraig felt as though not everything he'd said was a falsehood.

"Those whom God hath joined together let no mon put asunder." Father Mitchell seemed to choke on his words before he shifted his attention once more to the gathered clan members. "Forasmuch as Padraig and Cairren have consented together in holy wedlock, and have witnessed the same before God and this clan, and thereto have given and pledged their troth either to other, and have declared the same by giving and receiving of a ring, and by joining of hands; I pronounce that they be mon and wife together, In the Name of the Father, and of the Son, and of the Holy Spirit. Amen."

Padraig eased Cairren into his arms, cautious not to startle her. She looked up at him as though she were adrift, and the protectiveness and possessiveness he experienced while standing with her on the keep steps reemerged. He lowered his mouth to hers but whispered, "Open for me."

Cairren's eyes flared, but her lips parted on a soft mint-scented breath. Her eyes drifted close, and Padraig brought their mouths together. The heat and intensity from the night before sparked with the merest graze of their lips. He pressed his tongue into her mouth as she opened to him. His hold tightened as he felt her hands rest on his chest. He remembered they had an audience when an angry screech rent the air. He pulled back and saw Myrna's hands curled into claws as though she prepared to attack Cairren.

Where there would normally be cheers and applause, there was stunned silence. Padraig pulled Cairren against his side and tucked her against him, trying to shield her from the looks of revulsion and disgust. But she refused to remain hidden. She donned her courtly facade, an expression Padraig already recognized as her defense, and stepped away from him. She steered toward her parents, but just before she reached them, she tilted her head toward Myrna and tossed her bouquet toward her. Reflexively, Myrna caught it. When she realized the significance of catching Cairren's bouquet after watching Cairren marry the man she wanted, she dropped it and ground her heel into it.

Cairren laughed merrily, even though Padraig sensed it was an act. "Thank you. They've been making me want to sneeze the entire time."

Padraig blinked several times as Innes and Collette linked arms with Cairren, and the trio moved toward the keep. Cairren didn't bother to look back to see if Padraig followed. He'd been left at the altar—except they were already married.

CHAPTER NINE

Padraig pulled back one of the seats of honor for Cairren, then slipped into the one beside her. As servants circulated among the diners, Padraig watched the stares directed toward his bride and him. He hadn't intended to shock his clansmen and women or hurt Myrna, but lust swept him away as Cairren returned his kiss. Now Myrna sulked, his mother and father could barely hide their disgust, the people seated before him gossiped, and his bride was already in the midst of a conversation with her parents. It was as though he no longer existed to Cairren, as though she intended to set the example for how leaving one another alone would work. Seated next to her mother and two seats down from her father, Cairren spoke softly in French. Padraig had given little thought to whether Innes spoke French since he hadn't heard him, but Padraig realized the laird must have since he met his wife in France. It intrigued him to hear the burly Lowlander speak French with a Scottish brogue. It didn't resemble any French Padraig had heard, but Collette and Cairren understood him. Cairren's French sounded flawless, as though she'd spoken nothing else. She'd continued to use Gaelic for "please" and "thank you" despite how the servants turned up their nose. She'd understood what Myrna said when they met, and she'd even offered Mary a complicated greeting. He respected and appreciated her effort.

When a servant stepped between them to place a dish on the table, the woman intentionally tipped it toward Cairren's lap. Padraig watched in horror but snapped to attention in time to push the servant's hand away, making the food splatter the tablecloth rather than Cairren's gown.

"Return to the kitchens and don't let me see your face at this table again. Ever," Padraig hissed. Cairren turned wide eyes to him before she glanced at the tablecloth, then at her lap. Fortunately, none had spilled on her, but Padraig knew she understood the slip hadn't been an accident. He had her attention, and he intended to seize upon it. "You speak French and Scots. Do you speak any other languages?"

"I can read and write Latin; my Italian is passable. It's not even a day's ride to Italy from where my mother grew up. She learned enough to assist my *grand-père* with their soap and perfume trade. She taught me." Cairren offered him a shy smile. "I'm working on my Gaelic."

"You've impressed me with what you know. Do your parents, or at least your father, speak it?"

Cairren shook her head. "Nay. My father mentioned last year that he would look for a husband from the Highlands for me. I didn't know how long I would have, but I asked a lady-in-waiting from here, Blair Sutherland, to help me. She's been tutoring me for months."

"You wanted to impress your new clan?" Padraig

asked, but he wanted to retract his words when Cairren looked at him as though he were an imbecile.

"I want to understand what people are saying," she replied. Neither of them needed to say aloud that she wanted to understand what people were saying about her.

"You barely had a Scots accent when you spoke yesterday. You're bound to impress people with your knowledge."

"I doubt that, and that's not my intent."

Padraig couldn't blame Cairren for being on the defensive, but it was their wedding feast. He wished for a reprieve from everyone's animosity for just a while. He served Cairren the choicest cuts of food as the dishes and platters moved across the table. She was gracious, but he noticed she pushed food to his side of the trencher, keeping very little for herself.

"Do you always eat so little?" Padraig murmured. Once more he wished he'd kept his mouth shut.

"Did you expect a gluttonous bride? One used to gorging herself during feasts at the royal court?"

"I didn't expect aught. I hadn't had time to. I learned of our betrothal a fortnight ago."

Cairren's smile didn't reach her eyes. "And in that fortnight, I'm certain you were far too preoccupied to wonder who you might be marrying." Her gaze shifted to where Myrna sat glaring at her. Cairren sat back and looked away from their food. "And you wonder why I don't feel much like eating."

Cairren and Padraig reached for their shared chalice at the same moment, their fingers brushing together before Padraig's hand covered Cairren's. Padraig felt Cairren's sharp inhale before she released the stem, but her hand was still beneath Padraig's. He pulled them away and tucked them beneath the table, out of anyone's sight, particularly the glowering blonde at the end of the table.

"Let us get through this feast and tonight, then perhaps we can talk properly."

Cairren canted her head to glance at Padraig as his fingers entwined with hers beneath the tablecloth. His hand was warm, and she could feel his callouses rub against her knuckles. It was the hand of a man accustomed to work, and she found the feel arousing. "Aboot what?"

"Aboot how we will go forth. We are both healthy and young. We can expect to be married for many years. I would like us to start out with a truce."

Cairren yanked her hand away. "Then the first term of our agreement is that she leaves. I can't, so she must."

"Be reasonable, Cairren. She is our guest, and a lifelong friend to our clan."

"'Our?' She isn't our anything. She is yours. Yours to deal with. Take her home and stay there if you'd rather, or ride back and forth. Balnagown is less than a morning's ride. You can see her every day if you want, but I wouldn't have to share my new home with a woman who looks like she'd murder me in my sleep."

Padraig was prepared to disagree, even tell Cairren she was overreacting, but he spared a glance at Myrna, and the hatred that oozed from her turned her normally serene face ugly. When he returned his eyes to Cairren, she'd already turned back to her parents. He always ruined things by failing to keep his attention away from Myrna. He'd done it several times in the day he'd known Cairren, and he wondered how many more times she'd endure the unintended slight before something had to give.

The meal progressed with Padraig sitting in silence, avoiding Myrna's doleful expressions, while listening to Cairren cheerfully talking to her parents. He'd learned French and could speak it, but he hadn't used it often. He rarely visited court, and that was the only time he needed it. When he tuned out the sounds around him and focused on Cairren and her parents, he could follow along as they discussed the border and England. It surprised him how deeply Cairren understood the politics of her home region. He could tell she took an interest, and he realized she was more intelligent than he'd given her credit. When their talk turned to her time at court, she became more guarded. But she told her parents stories about Blair and Arabella, and Padraig found it relieved him to learn she had two friends at Stirling Castle. He wondered if he could arrange for Blair to visit Foulis the next time she traveled to Sutherland.

When the music began, Padraig held out his hand to Cairren, who looked at it as though it were mottled with warts. Her incredulous expression made him think twice about offering to dance. But they were the bride and groom, and even if this irregular marriage meant no one expected them to act like a married couple, he found he wanted to dance with her. His body ached to feel her pressed against him, and he was curious to learn if she danced as gracefully as she did everything else.

"I'd like to dance with you," Padraig confessed.

"Why? No one expects it. I don't expect it," Cairren responded.

"Because I want to."

Cairren narrowed her eyes, and Padraig could tell she gritted her teeth, but she relented with a condition. "I will not dance any that require me to partner with someone else. I haven't a death wish." There was no humor but deadly seriousness in her last sentence. Padraig nodded, wishing he didn't have to agree. He helped her from her seat, then led her to the floor. Other couples had already gathered for the first dance, but when they noticed the groom and particularly the bride, they gave them a wide berth, as though breathing near Cairren would endanger them. Cairren pretended not to notice. At court, no one paid attention when she took to the dance floor. It was always too crowded to spot her, and courtiers used dancing for seduction and politics. She'd learned early on that while refusing to dance shielded her from the innuendos and propositions, not dancing was only fodder for more gossip. She'd chosen the lesser of the two evils. As she moved among the Munros, it was clear the lesser evil would have been to remain seated.

Padraig drew Cairren into the circle of his arms as they picked up the rhythm of the dance, and Cairren discovered he was light on his feet and skilled. Inevitably, her mind wondered how many dances he'd shared with Myrna to have become so at ease. She closed her eyes for a long blink, trying to clear the picture of them together.

"Cairren? Don't think aboot her. I'm not," Padraig murmured.

"Stop lying. It doesn't make me feel better, and it does you no service."

"Must you always believe the worst in me? Have I treated you like the others?"

Cairren's eyes met his, and the earnestness she found made her question her assumption that he just hid his disgust better than the others. She whispered, "No."

"I meant what I said earlier. I'd like to call a truce."

Cairren studied him again before nodding. "I haven't the strength to fight you too. I meant what I said earlier. I don't want her here, but that's not my decision to make. I will find things to occupy my days, and I won't question how you occupy yours."

Padraig didn't like that at all. The resignation in her voice hurt him in a way he couldn't describe. It wasn't quite guilt, shame, or pity. Perhaps it was a combination of them all. While he wanted to spend his days with Myrna and even intended to when he wasn't training, her acceptance reflected how down-trodden she'd already become. She'd given up, and they'd only married a few hours ago. *But why would she put up a fight? What is there to fight for? I dinna want to be married to her any more than she wants to be married to me. She kens I love another woman. I've told her I can never love her. We spent more than half of today believing we would be free of one another in a year. And I willna commit to sending Myrna away. I dinna want to send her away, yet I want to be bedding Cairren as we dance. I'm a hypocrite, and what's worse is that I suspect I willna hide it from anyone for long. Ma clan and Myrna already witnessed how I kissed her, ma lust was on display for everyone. I desire her too much to pretend tonight in ma bed that I dinna. I want to enjoy coupling with her. I want her to enjoy it as much as I do. Bluidy bleeding hell.*

The music changed to a country reel, and Cairren pulled away as though she'd been burned. She turned to the dais before Padraig could lead her. He was only two steps behind her when an elbow flew toward her face. There was nothing about the current dance that warranted such a move. Cairren ducked in time that it struck Padraig mid-chest. He knew that meant it would have struck Cairren in the face. Padraig grabbed the offending man by his leine and ripped him away from his partner.

"I would be within ma rights to kill ye for that. Ye tried to strike ma bride, a noblewoman, daughter-by-marriage to yer laird," Padraig seethed as he looked at those within earshot. He was so furious he didn't realize he'd lapsed into his burr. "I will make this clear to ye, and ye may tell everyone else. Any harm done to Lady Cairren is harm done to me. It willna be punishment I'm after. It'll be vengeance, clansman or nae. It wasnae her idea to be here. She never asked for this marriage. But she is, and ye will treat her with the respect due ma wife. If she can follow the king's decree with honor, ye bluidy well can too."

Cairren watched in horror as Padraig appeared ready to murder the man in the Munros' Great Hall. A small—miniscule, really—part of her appreciated Padraig coming to her defense. But fear of retribution consumed her. Padraig was naïve to think his warning carried weight. He was an imposing figure when he was calm, and positively terrifying when he was angry, but his people vastly outnumbered him. Even if no one attempted such an obvious attack again, she would pay for him lashing out. When she stepped toward Padraig, people lurched out of her way as though she were a leper. She put her hands on the arm that held the man, and she looked up at him. She wouldn't speak aloud her plea, but she knew he understood because he released the offender immediately. She turned back toward the dais, and just as she always did, she walked with her head held high and her shoulders back.

Padraig stepped beside her and wrapped her arm

through his as he walked with her back to the dais. He took in the scene at the laird's table, and his stomach sank knowing Cairren saw the same thing. Innes was on his feet, Collette and Wynda looked aghast, tears even streamed down his sister-by-marriage's cheeks. Duncan and Micheil were laughing, and Mary and Myrna had smug satisfaction written across their faces. Padraig was struck by a thought that chilled him to his core. *Did Myrna arrange for that to happen? Nay. She may nae feel sorry for Cairren that it happened, but she would never be so unkind as to do such a thing. The idea couldnae have crossed her mind.* Padraig was about to take the first step up to the dais when his mother rose.

"Let's get this over with," Mary called out. "There is a celebration to enjoy once it's done."

Padraig glanced down at Cairren, both understanding what Mary meant. It was time for the bedding ceremony. His mother's comment once again embarrassed him. There was no misconstruing that she meant the feast wouldn't start in earnest until they'd enjoyed Cairren's inevitable humiliation. Without a sound, Cairren released his arm and turned around. Those on the dais followed the couple toward the stairs, but before they ascended, Padraig turned back to the crowd that jockeyed for positions that would grant them access to his chamber.

"My wife and I will only entertain our family. No one else is permitted in my chamber."

"Son," Mary protested.

"My bride should be for my eyes only. There will already be too many of you there, and this will already take too long for my taste." Padraig's penetrating gaze swept over everyone gathered, even settling on Myrna for a moment. He couldn't prevent the bedding ceremony, but he could be sure everyone understood he didn't dread coupling with his wife. *Mayhap if I show that I accept her, then others will begin to, too. Mayhap I can convince maself of that while I'm at it.*

Padraig led Cairren to his bedchamber and opened the door. Before she could step forward, he scooped her into his arms and carried her over the threshold. When he placed her on her feet, he kissed her cheek.

CHAPTER TEN

Cairren tried not to tremble as her mother lifted the gold circlet from her hair and unwound her braid. Once her hair hung loose, Collette arranged it over her shoulders and unlaced her gown. Cairren nodded to her mother and peeled the kirtle off her shoulders and down to her breasts. Padraig realized the chemise was sheer, even more transparent than the one she'd worn when she swam. His eyes darted to the other men in the chamber. Innes appeared uncomfortable in the presence of his daughter as she undressed, and Padraig sympathized. But it was Micheil and Duncan's lecherous gaze—followed by Duncan's elbowing Micheil—that pushed Padraig too far.

"The men will turn away," Padraig commanded.

"That's not the custom," Micheil disagreed as he shook his head.

"If you won't turn around, then you will leave. No mon sees my wife but me." Padraig rested his hand on the handle of one of his dirks. He cocked an eyebrow in challenge as he looked at Duncan.

"*Chan fhiach a 'ghalla an trioblaid. Ma tha thu air fear fhaicinn, tha thu air am faicinn uile,*" Duncan spoke clearly, and Mary and Myrna snickered.

Padraig was certain his family was aware Cairren knew enough Gaelic to understand "the bitch isn't worth the trouble. If you've seen one, you've seen them all." He looked at Cairren, who in turn looked at Duncan and Micheil, but rather than appear shocked or even hurt, her expression was defiant. It was as though she knew something they didn't.

"*Qu'ont ils dit?*" Collette murmured.

"*La garce n'en vaut pas la peine. Si vous en avez vue un, vous les avez toutes vus,*" Cairren responded, and Padraig knew she'd translated for her parents before Innes growled.

"Out!" Innes bellowed. "Both of you out before I kill you."

"You can't kick me out of a chamber in my own home," Micheil sneered.

Innes brandished a dirk in both hands, pulled from hidden folds of his plaid. He lunged at Duncan, pressing the tip just below the man's throat. "Leave or I will kill him," Innes spoke to Micheil, but he never took his eyes off Duncan. When Micheil didn't respond immediately, Innes pricked Duncan's skin. "I'll die before I allow you to talk aboot my daughter like that."

"Father, Duncan, out. Now. This is my chamber and my wife. Leave." Padraig opened the door and glared at the men of his family. Micheil muttered, "not worth it," before he and Duncan exited the chamber.

Innes walked to Cairren and kissed her cheek. "I don't trust them. Get yourself to the Sutherlands if ever you feel in danger. I will come for you," Innes whispered in French. He walked through the door, and Padraig closed it behind his father-by-marriage.

Padraig stepped back to where he'd stood at the

foot of the bed, watching Cairren. They stood no more than three feet apart, and Cairren was certain she could feel the heat coming from Padraig. His nod encouraged her to push her gown down her arms and over her hips until it pooled at her feet. Padraig's body reacted immediately when he caught sight of her dark nipples beneath the sheer fabric. He'd already been partially aroused as they entered the chamber, his mind and body knowing he would finally feel Cairren beneath him. Once the gown slipped to her shoulders and a hint of her cleavage showed through the chemise, his cock had grown hard and uncomfortable with the weight of his sporran pressing against it. When Cairren stepped out of her gown, Wynda gathered it for her with a sympathetic smile before hanging it over the screen that kept the chamber pot out of sight.

Cairren reached under her chemise to roll down her stockings after she slipped out of her slippers. As she removed them, she watched Padraig unpin the brooch from his shoulder and drop it into his sporran, then he unfastened his belt, letting it fall to the floor. Once he pushed the extra length of wool from his shoulder, his plaid unraveled. The hem of his leine rested at his knees, but with no plaid wrapped around his waist, there was no disguising the length that rested against his belly. As Cairren watched Padraig undress, she understood what she saw. Lowlanders preferred leggings, which made an aroused shaft harder to disguise. She'd seen the outline many times at court, but none drew her attention like Padraig's did. Her eyes met his and locked until they were blocked for a moment as he lifted his leine over his head.

It was Myrna who gasped, but Padraig didn't look

away from Cairren. It wasn't even his conscience that warned him not to. Cairren solely captivated his attention. As his eyes traveled over her body, he noticed that there was no shadow at the apex of her thighs. His gaze met hers again, and the defiant look had returned. She eased her chemise up her legs, watching him as she teased him. When the hem hung just below her mons, she gathered the material, inch by tantalizingly slow inch. In one sweep, Cairren pulled the chemise over her head and let it drop. Padraig's heart raced as he took in the unblemished skin that ran the entire length of her. He'd never seen a woman with a smooth mons, and his cock jerked for one and all to see.

"*Slut teas-meadhain*," Myrna hissed. Cairren glanced at Myrna and smirked; Padraig was shocked to realize that Cairren knew Myrna called her a heathenous slut. He never imagined those words would be part of her vocabulary.

"*Salope païenne*," Cairren translated for her mother.

Collette glared at Myrna. She muttered, "*une vache*," but neither Highland woman seemed to know Collette called Myrna a cow—a bitch, really, but Padraig did. It took him a moment to realize that he didn't intend to rush to Myrna's defense. He even believed she warranted the comment.

"Let us move this along," Padraig commanded. The venomous glare Myrna shot him made him remember this couldn't be easy for her, and his sympathy returned as he considered how she must have been suffering to see another woman had aroused him and to know he would bed Cairren, and not her, on his wedding night.

Mary tutted as she stepped forward to walk

around Cairren, inspecting her for any defect, even lifting her breasts and jiggling them. Then she pointed to Cairren's hairless mound. *"Cha dèanadh ach brathaidh, feòladair Frangach, seo."*

"Seule une pute, une pute française, ferait ça." Once again Cairren translated, telling her mother that Mary believed only a whore, a French whore, would do this.

"Tu es fini. You are done," Collette stepped between Cairren and Myrna, who blocked Collette from reaching Mary. "You can see that not only is there naught wrong, she's flawless."

"Flawless?" Mary narrowed her eyes, and Padraig feared what she would do next. He couldn't believe his eyes when Mary's hand shot out and pressed between Cairren's legs, her fingers curled. Before she touched Cairren' sheath, Padraig lifted his mother away from his wife.

"Mother!"

"No woman who comes to her wedding bed clean as a newborn bairn is a virgin," Mary insisted.

"I told you she would try to seduce you! I told you!" Myrna wailed. "She's a whore!"

"Get out!" Padraig roared.

Myrna froze as she looked at Padraig with disbelief before she pointed to herself. "Me? You're telling me to leave? What, so you can hurry up and swive your slut?"

"Get out because I'm ashamed of you. I never imagined for a moment, Myrna, that you could be so disgustingly hateful. I have never been so disappointed in someone as I am in you, right now. Get out." Padraig shocked himself as he spewed forth the truth, uncaring whether it hurt Myrna's feelings. His duty was to protect his wife, not Myrna, no matter how much he loved her. He lowered his voice, but there was no way that Cairren didn't hear. "I love you, Myrna, but you can't do this. It's not right."

"Right? What is right aboot this—this—" Myrna pointed toward Cairren. "That getting into the bed that should have been mine with the mon who should have mine?"

"We can't change any of this, so go."

"You want her more than you do me," Myrna accused.

"This has naught to do with you or me. This is my duty to my clan." Padraig growled. Cairren moved out of the corner of his eye, and he recalled that she was hearing everything he said. He'd once more become so focused on Myrna that he forgot how his actions hurt Cairren. He looked at her as she fought back tears. Padraig looked around the room; he and Cairren stood naked, the lack of clothing obviously humiliating Cairren, with his mother and would-have-been-betrothed spewing vulgarities at her while his mother-by-marriage could do nothing to stop them. Wynda unabashedly cried, her hands covering her mouth, her eyes filled with horror. "We are done here. You will all leave. What happens now is between me and my wife."

"No." Mary pointed at Cairren. "She's not a virgin, and we shall all witness you coupling that way she can't spill chicken's or sheep's blood on the sheet to fool us."

Cairren stepped forward. "Where the devil would I get that? I've never been in this chamber before. I have no clothes on, and I brought nothing with me. I am a virgin, and I will prove it." Cairren turned to Wynda. "Would you stand outside the door until Padraig and I are—are done? He will bring you the sheet immediately. They can hang it from the railing before the night is through."

"That's not good enough," Mary argued.

"Then you are saying you think your son is such a fool that I could trick him. You are saying that he is dishonorable and wouldn't send out the sheet, or that he'd trick his own parents. You are saying that you don't trust your other, Highlander, daughter-by-marriage. It's one thing to insult me, but you needn't drag the rest of your family into it." Cairren crossed her arms beneath her breasts. The sight of them pushed up and together made Padraig's cock jump. Myrna burst into tears and ran toward him. Just like her instinct had been to catch Cairren's bouquet, his was to embrace her. He raised his arms, but at the last minute he realized what he was doing. He saw the betrayal and rejection on Cairren's face before it turned to loathing. He'd expected the bedding ceremony to be awful, but he'd never imagined it could be so horrendous. He grasped Myrna's upper arms and kept her away from his body.

"Don't do this, Myrna. Leave," Padraig said as gently as he could. He released one arm and led her to the door. He opened it and ushered her through. Collette and Wynda hurried to leave, but Mary remained. "Get out, Mother, or I will pick you up and carry you out."

Mary huffed and stormed out, leaving Padraig finally alone with Cairren. He didn't know what to do, what to say. He didn't know if he should look at her or look away. He walked to the foot of the bed and rested his head in his hands. But he couldn't sit still. He ran his hands through his hair as he stood and looked at Cairren. The atrocious scene had caused his arousal to wane, but the moment he looked at Cairren again, his rod lengthened and hardened. He'd never felt more of a cad than he did in that moment. His body continued to react at the most inopportune times. He closed his eyes and turned his head away. With no one else to look at, Cairren's last words came back to him.

"Why did you defend me? Why do you keep trying to protect me? Wynda I can understand, but why me? Why after what you heard me say?" Padraig's voice was hoarse as he gazed at Cairren, who now wrapped her arms over her chest and waist.

"Did I lie? What I said is what your mother's words implied. Wynda has done naught wrong in any of this. She's been the only kind face that I've seen. She seems—timid," Cairren tried to pick the right word to say aloud, but she would have better described Wynda as skittish. "I've watched the stronger pick on the weak before and not spoken against it. I'm ashamed of that, and I won't stay quiet after I watched it nearly destroy Maude Sutherland's chance at happiness and love. If I don't speak up, then I'm complicit and just as foul a soul as the person being cruel."

Padraig took a step closer but wasn't sure if Cairren would allow him any nearer. "But why me? Why protect me?"

"As you said. This is aboot duty. Yours and mine to our clans. Despite this mess, you strike me as honorable. To insinuate you're aught other than that is wrong. You're doing your—doing what you can with this." Cairren waved her hand toward the bed, then between them. "Padraig, I'm not a child. I can take care of myself, and that means I can manage to speak out against a wrong."

"But you worried earlier that upsetting Myrna would cause you more problems."

"Oh, it will. I won't come out of this unscathed, but that doesn't change that I should do what's right. Honor is important to people other than just the men in the Highlands. If I stand by and do naught when a wrong is committed, then where is my honor?" Cairren shook her head and shrugged. Padraig was in awe of the tiny woman who stood before him with more integrity than any member of his clan, including him, had shown since the Kennedys arrived. He took the last two steps until he could tuck his finger under her chin and lift her head until their eyes met.

"I'm sorry. Those words may feel insignificant, but they are sincere. I thought earlier tonight that I wasn't sure that I could endure what you have without breaking down and crying. Now you've suffered even more. Cairren, I can't undo any of this, but I can try to make up for it. I will keep them away from you as best I can. I will make it clear I won't tolerate any further insults to you. And—" Padraig shifted uncomfortably. "And I can at least make something aboot being here feel good."

Cairren's turned a pretty shade of pink as her lips twitched. Her eyes darted down to his rod that pointed toward her. She smiled and nodded. "There is little point in pretending you're not attracted to me, and I won't pretend I'm not attracted to you. Our two kisses proved that." Cairren glanced at the bed before looking back at Padraig.

"Are you scared?"

"A little," Cairren admitted.

"For all my faults and errs, what we share in this chamber will always be for your pleasure. When we are in here together, the rest of the world doesn't exist.

It's just the two of us and what we want." Padraig spoke without realizing that he admitted that he intended to bed Cairren more than just that night.

"Thank you," Cairren whispered. She lifted her chin as Padraig lowered his mouth to hers. She came onto her toes as she reached to wrap her arms around his neck. She opened to him without hesitation, welcoming the thrust and parry of their tongues in her mouth. Padraig brushed her hair away from her chest before cupping her breast. His thumb brushed back and forth over her nipple until it pebbled. His other hand skimmed down her back until he cupped her backside, pressing her hips to his. He bent to take her breast in his mouth, but their height difference made it awkward. Cairren giggled. "Apparently, I've found something else I'm too short for."

"Cheeky," Padraig grinned as he patted her backside. "Then I shall have to solve that."

CHAPTER ELEVEN

Padraig lifted Cairren into his arms and carried her to the bed. Someone had already turned down the sheets. He laid her down with such gentleness that Cairren's heart lurched. Padraig slid onto the bed beside her. He lay on his side as his fingers grazed over her breasts. It was the barest contact, but it made Cairren shiver as an ache began low in her belly. She rolled onto her side and tentatively raised her hand. When Padraig nodded, she ran her hand over the bronzed skin of his chest and shoulders. It was clear that he trained outside without his leine; his torso, arms, and calves were darker than his thighs. She hadn't anticipated how much tanner he would be without his shirt covering him. She marveled at how strong Padraig's muscles felt under her palm. He'd carried her twice, but the moments were so brief that she hadn't a chance to discover the power he possessed. She trailed her hand up his neck until she cupped his jaw.

"May I kiss you?" she whispered.

"You never need to ask, Cairren."

She scooted closer until she could press her lips to his. He let her control this kiss, opening to her but not thrusting forth his tongue. Hers flicked out, brushing the inside of his mouth. He groaned as the need to thrust into her sheath grew, but he kept himself still, encouraging her to explore, to gain more courage to discover what she liked. She pulled back, offering him three quick kisses before she rolled onto her back, her arms open to him.

"There is no rush," Padraig murmured, but Cairren's eyes flashed to the door. "Shh. Wynda will wait. She's on your side, Cairren. I hate saying there are sides, but we both know there are. She won't want you to miss out on what should be special for you. I know my sister-by-marriage. Her first time was not enjoyable. I know she'd want better for you."

Cairren darted another glance at the door before she nodded. Padraig rested on his forearm as he leaned in for another kiss. He'd tasted nothing so sweet at Cairren, her floral scent enticing, her lips soft and plump, her mouth warm and inviting. He kissed his way down her neck, shifting down the bed to take her breast in his mouth. As the heat from his tongue swirled around her, he flicked her nipple before drawing it into a peak. Cairren couldn't contain her moan or keep her back from arching, offering herself to him. He kneaded the supple flesh of her other breast as he continued to worship the one he suckled. He shifted again, capturing the other breast in his mouth. His hand slid along her belly until it brushed over the satiny skin of her mons. He'd felt nothing like it. As his fingers explored the bare skin, Cairren's legs fell open, the invitation clear.

Padraig used the hand of the arm he rested on to massage her breast as he continued to suckle the other. With no thatch of hair hiding the hood over her pearl, he found the source of her pleasure and slowly ran circles over it with the pad of his thumb. He dipped a finger into her entrance, dew coating it. She sighed at the feeling of him finally touching her where her body felt like it would go up in flames. The ache in her belly spread, making her writhe under his ministrations as her body searched for relief. As he dipped a second fingertip into her, she moaned again, and Padraig recognized the sound of frustration. He eased the fingers in until he brushed her barrier.

He'd known all along that she was an innocent, but the unprovoked possessiveness he'd already experienced twice swept over him. He couldn't recall every feeling this way about Myrna. He'd always assumed he would be her first and only, but the need to know, to claim what he believed was his, had never consumed him, never even entered his mind before Cairren. He pushed thoughts of Myrna away, refusing to think of another woman while he coupled with Cairren. She deserved more respect and loyalty, and he refused to risk her suspecting where his mind drifted to. He worked her sheath as her hips rocked against his hand. The women he'd bedded in the past were all experienced. The feel of his touch was nothing new to them, and he rarely paid as much attention to their responses. But watching Cairren discover the pleasure they could find with one another was captivating. Her changing expressions, the sound of her breathing, how she moved as she learned what she enjoyed. All of it mesmerized him, and his cock pulsed with unspent need. He glanced down and noticed he was leaking, but he wanted to draw out her introduction to passion before he inevitably caused her pain.

"Padraig," Cairren moaned. She didn't know what to do. Her body ached, and it was so strong that the places he touched burned with the need for something more. She knew her body was begging for him to join his with her, but she didn't know how to ask. Her heels dug into the mattress but slipped along the sheets as she tried to bring his fingers deeper.

"Wheest, Ren. I know. You're almost there." Padraig circled her bud again as he added more force to both his thumb and his fingers as he worked her sheath. Her chin tilted up as her eyes squeezed shut, and he felt the spasms grip his fingers. Cairren felt breathless as pleasure spread from within her core out through her belly as though she glided along a wave. "Open for me, little one."

Cairren heard Padraig's request through her haze, and she felt something thicker than his fingers pressing against her entrance. She looked down to find Padraig's length slowly disappearing within her. There was an ache and a burn of a different sort as he pressed further into her, but she fought to remain calm and breathe. She'd heard plenty of women speak of their first time and the pain. She'd also heard plenty tell how their partner had been rough and uncaring. Padraig seemed attuned to her and how her body reacted to his.

"Look at me, Cairren. I wish we could skip what comes next. I don't want to hurt you, but I believe it's inevitable. Give it a moment, and the pain will subside. But if it's too miserable, tell me, and we will stop."

"Won't that make you miserable?"

"Not as much as knowing I've hurt you. I've done that enough already," Padraig hung his head.

"Padraig?" Cairren waited for him to look at her, then she cupped his jaw. "I trust you." And she found that she did. In that moment as they lay together in bed, putting aside all that had happened and the undoubtable fallout they would face in the morning, she trusted him. "Will you kiss me while..."

Padraig pressed his mouth to her, his tongue sweeping inside then thrusting, mimicking what he intended to do with his sword in her sheath. He drove into her, breaking her barrier and barely withdrawing his tongue before her teeth snapped shut. She whimpered as her nails dug into his upper arms where she'd wrapped her hands to brace herself.

"Ren, look at me. Shh, it'll pass. Lie here with me, catch your breath." Padraig's voice soothed her as he brushed hair back from her temple. He kissed away the stray tear that fell from each eye.

"Will you kiss me again? I promise I didn't mean to bite."

Padraig's smile was boyish and soft. "I ken you didn't, little one." As their kiss deepened and Padraig felt Cairren's body soften, he rocked his hips against her. The moan that reached his ears was once again one of passion and need. As his hips thrust forward, she raised hers and tilted to meet him. Her hands ran over his back, leaving a trail of tingling skin until she reached his buttocks. The next moan was deep and purely carnal as her hands grasped his chiseled backside. She'd never imagined a part of any person's body could be so hard and taut. Her hands slipped into the grooves at the sides, and she found they were the perfect place to hold on.

Padraig couldn't slow down. He was racing toward his climax faster than he could control. His body demanded relief, but his mind demanded he ensure Cairren climaxed at least once while they were joined. He wouldn't cheat her out of the pleasure he was on the cusp of grasping. He feared he was too rough, and his conscience screamed that he should be gentle. He recognized she was far smaller than him and this was her first time, but as she met him thrust for thrust, and her moans filled his ears, he couldn't control himself. He panted as he tried to regain some restraint, but when he tried to slow, her fingers dug into his backside.

"No. Don't stop. Please," Cairren begged.

"Ren, I could only stop if you told me to, but I need you. Dear God, how could aught feel this good and not be a sin?"

"You'll keep going?" Cairren's eyes drifted closed as her concentration centered on how their bodies moved together.

"God, yes. Cairren, I want you more than I've ever wanted aught in my life. What're you doing to me?"

"I don't know." Cairren's innocent response made Padraig smile. His sweet bride with the luscious body was temptation incarnate. "I feel it again, Padraig. Like before. That feeling."

"Good, little one. You should. I want you to."

"Will you? I mean, will it be that way for you?"

"I suspect even better than ever before." Before he could say more, he felt Cairren's core clamp around him as her breath hitched. He let go of the restraint he'd mustered, and his climax consumed him. He'd never experienced such physical pleasure before, and as he watched Cairren with her eyes closed, he'd never felt so close to another person. Not even Myrna.

Padraig felt as much as saw Cairren's heaving chest, and he feared he was crushing her. When he made to roll off, her eyes sprang open and her arms and legs held him in place. He saw a flash of uncertainty in her eyes, almost fear, but she whispered. "Please, not yet."

He lowered himself back down to his forearms, brushing hair from her damp forehead. "I don't want to go anywhere." He kissed her with a tenderness he didn't know he possessed. When they pulled apart, Cairren pushed hair away from Padraig's eyes and caressed his cheek.

"Thank you for being gentle with me, for making sure this was—I don't even know how to describe it. I'm just thankful that you thought of me." Cairren froze as her own words sunk in. He felt her tense, and he knew what she feared.

"You fill every one of my senses, my need for you consumes me with such power that the keep could burn down around us, and I wouldn't be able to think of aught but you." The kiss he pressed against her mouth was passionate. The tender sentimentality was gone, replaced by hunger he thought he'd surely sated. But his need for his wife made him harden within her narrow frame. "I don't want to hurt you any more than I have. We should stop. I should let you rest."

Cairren shook her head. "I need this. Padraig, I don't understand how my body aches so much when you touch me or why it's so strong that it hurts, but please, I don't want to stop."

If Padraig feared he'd been too rough the first time, he'd underestimated how little control he had around Cairren. He thrust into her over and over, holding little back as she pushed her heels into the mattress, lifting her hips to meet his every time he drove into her. Her moans encouraged him as their kisses grew wild.

"I may never let you out of this bed," Padraig growled.

"Only if you stay in it with me," Cairren panted.

"I'd stay buried inside you like I am now."

"I wouldn't stop—" Cairren's release ripped through, and she screamed.

"Ren!" Padraig bellowed as he followed her over the edge. He rolled them over, so she lay sprawled across his chest. "There is no way my arms will hold me up. I can barely breathe," he panted.

Cairren could only nod. She'd only been this breathless once before. It was when she was ten summers, and she fell from her horse. The landing had knocked the wind out of her, and she'd panicked that she would never draw another breath. This time, with Padraig beneath her and his arms cradling her, she wasn't afraid. She closed her eyes, but she needed something else. She strained to kiss him, not sure why it felt so urgent when she still hadn't caught her breath. When they pulled apart, she rested her head over his heart, the steady thump calming.

"Where'd you go just now? Before we kissed. You seemed far away."

Cairren tilted her head back and smiled. "I was remembering when I was ten and fell from my horse. The impact left me breathless. It felt like I would never draw air into my chest again, and I remember the sense of panic. A moment ago, I felt just as breathless as I did then, but I didn't panic. I wasn't scared, and I felt..." Cairren trailed off, suddenly uncomfortable admitting her feelings.

"How did you feel, Ren? Tell me. Please don't shut me out. Not now," Padraig's voice was just as soothing as listening to his heart. His fingered caressed her back, and she relaxed again.

"I felt protected," she whispered. Padraig could see her face, and a lump rose in his throat as she flinched, then squeezed her eyes shut. It was as though she expected him to scoff at her or reject her. Padraig realized, for Cairren, that fear was reasonable. Nothing in the past day had made her feel protected except for when she was with her parents. She'd admitted something that made her vulnerable, and it scared her that he would use it against her. His heart ached to know that while she trusted him with her body, her mind—her heart—was nowhere near as sure.

"I will protect you. Not because I'm a Highlander and honor bound. Not because you're a lady and my wife. Because you're you, Cairren, and you deserve to be safe." Padraig felt her swallow and a slight nod. She took a deep breath before she lifted her head. Her smile was weak, but he saw relief in her eyes. She eased off of his body and moved across the bed.

CHAPTER TWELVE

Cairren looked at the streak of blood on the sheet, and a peculiar mixture of pride and humiliation warred within her. She was proud that it would vindicate her once Wynda hung the sheet. But it humiliated her that everyone would know that Padraig had just bedded her. They would congratulate Padraig for suffering through his duty while continuing to believe she was a whore, even though the proof existed to show she wasn't. She moved to the edge of the bed and pulled the sheet loose.

"That can wait a moment." Padraig didn't feel like moving, and he wasn't pleased that Cairren was no longer pressed against him.

"No, it can't. Wynda and whoever else out there who's waiting will know that we're done. If we don't take it out there sooner, they'll claim I needed the time to spill blood on the sheet. That I duped you. We've already lain here too long."

Padraig rolled off the bed, anger bubbling to the surface. "Is that all you've been thinking aboot? That you needed to hurry and get it over with?"

"What?" Cairren reeled back. "How can you ask that when I just told you—just told you how I feel," she finished on a whisper. Cairren pulled her lips in, and the tears she'd held at bay since she arrived finally broke the floodgates. "I'm scared."

Padraig raced around the bed and pulled Cairren into his arms. Seeing his wife, who'd endured much since her arrival, break down into sobs alarmed him. The fact she'd admitted her fear, and he'd heard the words, left him feeling inadequate and helpless. She wouldn't have admitted it if his clan hadn't worn her down and she wasn't truly fearful. She didn't have to explain what scared her. Even with her parents still in residence, if the clan thought she'd been unchaste before becoming his bride, they would demand retribution. It wouldn't just be her life at risk, but those of her parents and their guardsmen. Such a situation wouldn't be so dangerous if it weren't already so volatile.

Padraig released Cairren and grabbed the plaid from the foot of his bed. He wrapped it around her before snatching the sheet from the bed. He wrapped his own discarded plaid around his waist before walking to the door. He glanced back to make sure Cairren was covered before he flung the door open. As he'd expected, Wynda wasn't alone. Both sides of their family were present. He held up the sheet before bunching it in his hands and throwing it at his father. Myrna burst into tears and once more stepped toward him, but he turned to Wynda.

"I want a bath brought up here now. I don't care if you have to rouse every drunk servant in this keep." Myrna was almost to him when he slammed the door shut. He turned back to see Cairren had gone ghostly pale, and he feared she would collapse. When her legs wobbled, and she teetered toward the bed, he sprinted back to her side. He lifted her into his arms and carried her to the fireplace. Once he set her on a chair, he retrieved a flask of whisky and held it out to her. She didn't look away from the flames as she took a long draw before handing it back to him. She had the same vacant stare she'd worn as she approached the kirk that evening. It was as if she saw nothing in front of her. It was disconcerting. Padraig squatted before her and took her hands. "Where do you go when you seem so far away?"

Cairren turned her head toward his voice, but her eyes remained on the flames. "When I arrived at court, those first few months were dreadful. I wasn't shunned. I was the oddity, the curious stranger everyone wanted to learn aboot. My name was familiar to most, but few had ever met me. I told you, Dunure is remote. I've spent time sailing along the coast, but I didn't travel much before going to court. I like my home." Cairren shrugged.

Padraig was surprised to learn that her experience at court differed from at Foulis. He assumed she'd been rejected in the way his clan had done. It struck him that she still thought of Dunure as home, but he reminded himself that nothing about being at Foulis felt welcoming or familiar to her.

"People wanted to know why I looked so different. They wanted to know if my mother and sister looked like me. It was well known that *Maman* is French, but everyone assumed she would look like the Scots or the English. She and I don't resemble how people picture the French. My *grand-père* wasn't French. He wasn't even European. I told you before that at first people whispered aboot me in front of my face. I suppose it was hardly ever really a whisper, even if they held their hand in front of their mouth.

Eventually, they did it behind my back. I'm not sure which was worse."

When Cairren stopped talking, Padraig squeezed her hands again, encouraging her to continue. He found he was desperate to learn more about Cairren.

"But I learned how to pick a place to look at and let what was happening around me, what people were saying, fade away. Sometimes I pray, sometimes I recite a poem. Sometimes I don't really think aboot aught but concentrating on the spot I picked. It was the only way to make it bearable until people realized that I was raised no different from any other lady raised in the Lowlands. Plenty of them speak French, and it's spoken as often at court as Scots. The only reason people still gossiped is because they assumed I would be loose. They couldn't understand why I wasn't, since they believed I must be the slut your— like what they said earlier—because of my foreign heritage. Men gossiped and wagered to see who would offer the proposition I finally accepted. Women gossiped aboot when I would stop pretending to be better than I was. And most wondered what I believe you did: what do I really look like without my clothes on? Am I dark everywhere or just the bits that show?"

Padraig was about to speak, but the knock at the door signaled the servants' arrival with the bath. He opened it and found Collette standing with a bar of soap in her hand, but her eyes latched onto Cairren, who sat with her back to the door. Padraig nodded, and Collette rushed inside. He watched mother and daughter whisper together as the servants traipsed in with the tub and buckets of steaming water.

"Padraig," a woman's voice hissed from the passageway. He knew Myrna was waiting for him. He glanced over at Cairren and found she was looking back at him. The look of defeat when she nodded her head made him doubt whether he should step outside, but he felt bad for how he'd treated Myrna earlier. He'd let his temper take control, and he wanted to make amends before a rift developed between them. He stepped in the passageway and led her away from the door. "It's done! You never have to touch her again!"

Padraig's feelings didn't match Myrna's excitement. Only minutes ago, he'd been wondering when he could couple with Cairren again without fearing that he'd hurt her. Guilt for betraying Myrna swept over him. Her joyous expression reminded him of all the times he'd thought she was the loveliest creature he'd ever beheld. His mind flashed to earlier that night, but he justified her behavior to himself. In his mind, he excused her cruel and vulgar words as being overwrought with hurt and disappointment. He wrapped his arms around Myrna and kissed the top of her head, but she pulled away, curling her nose up.

"Don't touch me while you smell like that disgusting swine."

"Myrna," Padraig hissed. The door to his chamber was open, and he was certain everyone inside heard Myrna. He wasn't sure what was worse: Cairren hearing that he was touching Myrna or the insulting description.

"Why are you so worried aboot her feelings? You haven't cared aboot mine since she arrived."

"Myrna, I can care that someone is treated properly without it meaning I love you any less."

"She's trying to turn you away from me. We all heard you in there. It was like listening to a farmer hump a whore," Myrna spat.

"You have a filthy mouth, and it's making you

ugly. I've never had a moment where I haven't been proud to have you on my arm until yesterday. You're disgracing yourself and me." Padraig felt his temper boil and was ready to turn away from Myrna when she burst into tears. She sobbed as she wedged her way back into his embrace. He wrapped his arms around her, his heart aching for her.

"It just hurts so much, Padraig. Everyone kens what you were doing. That you liked what you were doing. It was so humiliating for me. She's taken my place," Myrna sobbed. Padraig drew in a deep breath, recognizing Myrna was suffering just as much as Cairren, just differently. He was sympathetic to Cairren, but he found himself wanting to make any promise that would ease Myrna's upset and end her tears.

"I know, Myrna. I'm sorry it has to be this way. I would protect you before all others if I could. The only way to make this easier is for you to return home."

"So you can keep coupling with her without me having to know. How could you, Padraig? How can you choose her over me?"

"I'm not. I'm trying to protect you. I'm married to her now, and that won't change. I don't want you to have to see me with her," Padraig explained.

Myrna pulled away once again, a hard glint in her eyes. "Why would you be with her if I'm here? You've done your duty. There is no reason for you ever to touch her again."

"I can't know if she's breeding yet. It can take once or it can many times before a woman gets with child."

"Gets with child? You don't need heirs. You're

only a second son," Myrna blurted. Padraig went stiff and pushed back his shoulders.

"*Only* a second son? That never seemed to bother you in the past. If that's the case, why should I marry at all?"

"Because you love me. Oh, Padraig. I'm so upset I don't even know what I'm saying. I'm sorry. I'm just so—" A sob cut off her last word. Padraig relented and once more embraced her, relieved she didn't reject him or point out Cairren's scent. Noise behind him made him turn around.

Cairren watched as her husband, the man who'd just taken her innocence and brought her pleasure she never dreamed existed, stood before her in the passage-way, holding the woman he really wanted. Humiliation, her constant companion these days, flooded through her. Myrna's blond hair shone in the torchlight, and it was the perfect contrast to Padraig's head of black hair. They were both strikingly good looking, and they made a stunning couple. With no way to get to the stairs without passing them, she took a deep breath then her first step forward. She was too tired to go into battle again, but she expected the blows to keep coming.

Padraig watched as Cairren approached, her mother and Wynda behind her. He hadn't seen Wynda enter, but he realized she must have brought Cairren the robe she now wore. Collette carried Cairren's wedding gown.

"Where are you going?" Padraig turned away from Myrna, but his arms remained around her.

Cairren sniffed. "We're done, so I'm going to bed." She looked directly at Myrna. "I'm exhausted now."

"You're leaving?" Padraig's brow furrowed.

"You didn't expect me to stay, did you?" Cairren scoffed. "We did what we had to, and now that I'd rather be in my own chamber, you can do as you please in there."

Cairren turned away and moved toward the stairs, but paused and looked back. "Just remember you'll need to change the sheets now that we finally finished coupling. You wouldn't want to smell like swine."

CHAPTER THIRTEEN

Padraig woke the morning after his wedding feeling like he was hung over. His head pounded, his body ached, and his stomach churned. He hadn't slept more than an hour at a stretch; the disaster replaying over and over in his mind. The hateful things his family said collided with Cairren's story of how people treated her when she arrived at court, making his ears ring. Every time he pictured Cairren as they coupled, the image was overrun by one of her sobbing and admitting her fear. Then there was Myrna in the passageway. He wanted to find her, to make sure that she would recover from her own ordeal, but he dreaded leaving his chamber and facing reality.

Nay. I dread facing Cairren. I dread seeing the hurt and betrayal from what she saw and heard between Myrna and me. I left ma bed where I'd just had the most exquisite experience with a woman I've ever had, and I went to another woman. I might have done naught with Myrna, but does that really matter? If I heard this tale, and it were aboot another mon, I'd want to thrash him. Instead, easy as ye please, I left Cairren behind. Yet, I still dinna feel as bad as I ken I should. It's Myrna I want to comfort. Padraig sat up and rubbed his forehead. *What the bluidy hell is wrong with me?*

He made his way belowstairs, finding his family and Myrna seated at the dais, but the Kennedys were nowhere in sight. He looked around the Great Hall but didn't see any of their guardsmen either. His heart tightened as he feared they'd left, but when he looked at his family again, he knew that wasn't the case. They didn't look smug enough for the Kennedys to have left. His eye caught the sheet hanging over the railing as it swung with the draught. There was no missing the bright red streak that marred the white sheet. Padraig swallowed as once more memories from the night before danced before his eyes. His bollocks ached as he remembered how it felt to be hilt-deep inside Cairren, and he wouldn't lie to himself and say he didn't want to do it again, didn't want to do it over and over.

Myrna wrapped her arm around his and beamed. "I'm sorry aboot last night, Padraig. I was awful, and I'm so ashamed." Padraig listened to her tone, which sounded contrite, but it didn't match the sunny expression on her face.

"I'm sorry too. I wish you hadn't had to go through that. I love you." He cupped Myrna's cheek and gazed into her blue eyes. He felt himself slipping into their depths, the familiarity calling to him. His thumb swept over her cheekbone until a clearing of a throat brought him back to reality. He was standing in the middle of the Great Hall, sharing an intimate moment with a woman other than his wife, the wife he'd married less than a day ago. He looked up to see Innes, Collette, and Cairren watching him.

· · ·

Cairren stumbled as she entered the Great Hall and caught sight of Myrna and Padraig standing together. They weren't just merely talking. They looked like lovers exchanging a private moment. Except it wasn't private at all with hundreds of eyes watching them. She despised him. She loathed him. But she despised and loathed herself more for letting her guard down. She never should have trusted him, and more fool was she for doing so when she knew better. Her time alone with Padraig had been the most incredible experience of her life, but what the Lord giveth, the Lord taketh away. She figured she'd spent two pleasant hours with Padraig while they explored one another, but that was a mere drop in the bucket compared to the time spent wanting to be anywhere but Foulis. She followed her parents to the dais, not sparing Padraig a glance.

Padraig wanted to groan. He'd believed himself to be a thoughtful and sensible man, but he couldn't seem to stop digging himself deeper and deeper into his own grave. He'd never thought himself fickle either, having wanted Myrna as his wife for so long. But he couldn't deny how much he wanted Cairren. *But the most disgraceful part is that I want to keep ma wife as though she were ma mistress. Nay acknowledgment of one another in the daylight while bedding her every night. Though from the look on her face, I may never touch her again.* Padraig watched as Cairren walked past him and Myrna, their arms still wrapped around each other for all of Clan Munro and the Kennedys to see. It didn't even dawn on Padraig that he should extricate himself until they'd already walked past and Innes growled. Padraig had grown too distracted by how beautiful Cairren looked in a burgundy gown with her hair pulled up as was appropriate for a married woman. Her cheeks were flushed, and the wisps of hair that had come loose appeared windblown. He noticed Collette looked much the same way, and Innes was running his hand over his hair to flatten it. They'd already been for a morning ride. Padraig wanted to groan as he thought about how the only morning ride he'd been planning that day had been Cairren.

"Let's eat, Padraig. I'm famished." Myrna's upbeat voice punctured his train of thought. He smiled at her and led her to the dais. Cairren sat at the far end of the table between her parents, nowhere near where she'd sat with Padraig during the feast. Mary scowled when she realized her son and Myrna couldn't sit together because there were no chairs left open next to each other. Padraig watched his mother rake a venomous glance over his wife and parents-by-marriage, as if they'd somehow created the situation. Padraig had little choice but to take a seat between Wynda and a senior guardsman while Myrna sat to Mary's left.

Wynda glanced at Duncan to be sure he was talking to Micheil before she leaned toward Padraig. It surprised him that his sister-by-marriage attempted to make conversation. She made it appear as though she were asking him to pass the jug of cream, but she whispered, "My heart has never hurt so much for someone before. I thought you were better than Duncan."

Wynda's comment stunned Padraig as he looked past her to where Duncan guffawed at something Micheil said. He'd never enjoyed being compared to his older brother, and this was the worst one yet. He looked into Wynda's eyes and saw pity, but he sensed it wasn't pity for him and his lost opportunity to marry the woman he loved. It was pity that he was a lesser man than she'd believed. As she leaned forward to reach for the honey, Wynda whispered again.

"There is more than meets the eye to both of them, but you will only like what you learn aboot one of them. It won't be the one you think you want."

Padraig opened his mouth to speak, but Wynda's eyes flared with fear before she turned toward Duncan. He watched his brother cast a disgusted look at Wynda.

"What're you babbling on aboot now? You haven't the sense God gave a gnat. Haven't I warned you aboot prattling?"

"Aye, Duncan. I was just—"

"Did I ask what you were doing?" Duncan interrupted.

"She was asking for the cream and honey," Padraig intervened.

"Did I ask you what she was doing? Stay out of the farce that is my marriage and I'll stay out of yours," Duncan retorted.

The sound of something being knocked over drew his attention away from Duncan and Wynda. He looked over to see Cairren blotting the front of her gown.

"I'm so sorry," Cairren mumbled. "I'm not usually so clumsy. Uh, Lady Wynda, would you show me where I might take this to be laundered?" Cairren was already moving around the table, then standing between Duncan and Wynda before anyone could remind Cairren that her maid was responsible for that. She held out her hand to Wynda, who looked at it before glancing at Cairren's encouraging smile. None of his family could see the exchange because Cairren's back blocked their view.

"Of course, Lady Cairren. Please come with me." Wynda rose and led Cairren to the end of the dais that wouldn't force them to walk past the Munros. Collette followed them as Innes rose. The man glared at Padraig before leaning forward to whisper none too quietly.

"You and me. The lists. Now." Innes didn't wait to see if Padraig accepted the challenge, instead turning and jumping down from the dais. He walked through the Great Hall with a sense of command that only a battle-hardened laird could. Padraig wanted to groan. Sparring with Innes was the last thing his body needed.

"But I thought you were spending the day with me." Myrna's voice seemed to fill every crevice of the Great Hall as members of the clan waited to see who Padraig chose. Myrna's innocent smile reassured him that she hadn't just tried to manipulate him.

"I'm afraid I can't. I need to train, and I can't refuse him. I will join you after the nooning." Padraig kept his voice low, but the grins from the people seated closest to the dais told him they'd heard him plan a rendezvous with Myrna.

▭

"Does he beat you?" Cairren demanded as soon as they were abovestairs. "I saw the bruise above your collarbone when I arrived."

"He loses his temper sometimes," Wynda demurred.

"Does the laird strike his wife?" Cairren wouldn't relent.

Wynda snorted. "You've met the woman. Would he live to tell the tale?"

"Then why does the laird allow his son to mistreat you?"

Wynda closed the door behind them once the three women were inside Cairren's chamber. She sighed and drew her lips in as she decided what to say. "Duncan and I married five summers ago, and I'm yet to give him an heir. I was an Urquhart before I wed. The alliance secured the Munros' access to the Moray Firth. I grew up along the coast, I suppose, much like you. The weather was milder there, and I was in good health. But since moving inland, I'm poorly much more often. Duncan becomes angry when I'm unwell, accusing me of being infirm and that's why I haven't carried any bairns to term."

Cairren watched Wynda as she spoke, and something didn't sit right with Cairren. Wynda appeared thin and sallow, but she didn't strike Cairren as being as being sickly so much as underfed. Though she supposed not eating enough and being beaten often would compromise anyone's health.

"Wynda, have you lost the bairns because he's beaten you too badly?" Cairren kept her voice low and tried to keep her tone soft. Her sister-by-marriage shook her head, but tears trailed down her cheeks. "Oh, Wynda, why haven't you told your father? Or have you, and he refuses to help you?"

"I can't ever reveal this to anyone. Duncan will kill me." Wynda grabbed Cairren's hands. "You can never let him know that I admitted this. Please, Cairren. Please."

Cairren pulled Wynda into her arms and stroked the woman's hair as she looked at Collette. When the women stepped apart, Collette took one of Wynda's hands and gave it a gentle squeeze.

"If your father knew, would he help you?" Collette asked.

"I don't know. I think so, but I can't be sure."

"Wynda," Collette's voice was laced with the authority she'd carried as the lady of Clan Kennedy for over twenty years. "If you want to go back to your parents, Innes and I will make certain you get there safely. You need only say you do, and you will."

Wynda stood quietly, considering the offer before her, but with great regret, she shook her head. "I can't. The Munros are far larger than the Urquharts. They could lay waste to my clan if I did that. I can't risk my family and my people just because things are hard for me here. It wouldn't be right."

Cairren and Collette exchanged a glance, knowing that Wynda was doing the honorable thing even if it was likely to get her killed one of these days. They had to respect her choice.

"Do you have to spend much time with him?" Cairren asked.

"Nay. I keep to myself during the day and help with the running of the keep. Duncan trains and meets with Micheil and the clan elders. He comes to my chambers some nights, but rarely these days. He only pays attention if he thinks I've done something wrong."

Cairren took hold of Wynda's hands, much like her mother had. "I will not endanger you by making it obvious that we are allies, but will you promise that if you're ever in fear for your life, you will come to me?"

"Yes," Wynda rasped as tears filled her eyes. The two women, neither wanted within Foulis Castle, formed a friendship more for survival than from things in common, but Cairren prayed she could protect Wynda just as she promised.

CHAPTER FOURTEEN

Breaking his fast and seeing Myrna had eased Padraig's headache and queasiness, but the five rounds of sparring against Innes that he'd just survived made him feel as though his head were inside a bell tower. The man had been relentless, proving that Lowlanders shouldn't be underestimated.

"Come now, lad. You can't be tired yet. Are your battles up here that short you get winded after ten minutes? You'd never survive along the border. The British would piss on you after severing your head from your shoulders." Innes taunted as Padraig wiped the sweat from near his eyes. They'd been circling one another, preparing for their sixth round.

"Perhaps he's tired from fucking your daughter all night." The wind caught the man's words, and even the warrior who uttered them realized his error. Innes swung around, dropped his sword and barreled into the crowd of onlookers before knocking the guilty man to the ground. He straddled the man, his knees pinning the warrior's arms to the ground, rendering them useless. His fist rained down one punch after another, while his other hand gripped the Munro warrior's throat. A couple of Munros attempted to pull Innes off of their comrade but they backed away, doubled over from Innes landing his fist in their groin. When the man's face was no longer recognizable, Innes lifted his head and slammed it down on the ground.

"Who's next?" Innes looked around the crowd. "I'm auld enough to be most your father. I've just gone five rounds with yon stripling," he pointed toward Padraig, "and I'm barely out of breath. Anyone else have comments to make aboot my wee lass?"

Innes stood and placed his hands on his hips, challenging any of them to step forward. When no one dared breathe in his direction, he bent and picked up his sword. He walked back to Padraig, and it appeared as though his temper had already settled, so Padraig was unprepared for the fist that plowed into his face, breaking his nose. Padraig stumbled backwards as Innes spat at his feet. "Where you lead, they follow."

Innes walked away from the lists while the men stared, unsure whether they should attack him and defend their laird's son's honor, or remain where they were, already terrified of him. Padraig pinched the end of his nose, tilting his head back to staunch the bleeding. He'd been unprepared for his father-by-marriage to lash out, but he couldn't deny he deserved it. He supposed he was lucky to be alive. Innes had outwitted him repeatedly as they practiced, overlooking multiple opportunities to injure Padraig when he let his guard down or misjudged Innes's strategy. Padraig had grown impatient, embarrassed to be bested in front of his men. But it was only after one of Padraig's warriors, one he'd trained alongside since they entered the lists as adolescents, insulted Cairren that Innes lashed out.

Padraig knew he was fortunate to walk away with only a broken nose, and he hadn't intervened on Denis's behalf because the man deserved the beating. But it was Innes's parting comment that made him feel the worst. Padraig had set the example that Cairren was of little consequence to him. He knew there'd been talk about them on the keep's steps the night she arrived. The guards had been gossiping about it for two days. Then the kiss outside the kirk, the scene during the feast, and Padraig's refusal to allow anyone outside of the lairds' families to enter the bedchamber angered many within the clan. His actions with Myrna that morning spoke louder than if Padraig stood on the battlements and screamed that Cairren was a whore. As Padraig continued to pinch his nose and walked back to the keep, he knew he was lucky to be alive.

"Padraig?"

Padraig looked up as his eyes adjusted from the bright sunlight to the dimmer light within the keep. Cairren stared aghast, and he knew he was a mess. He had blood splattered across his face and chest, and he could tell his eye was bruising. His nose hurt more than when a horse kicked him and broke it when he was five-and-ten.

"Padraig, what happened?" Cairren remained where she stood, but he could hear the concern in her voice. "Saints above! How'd you break your nose?"

Cairren rushed forward and yanked Padraig's leine from his hand. She swiped it across his chest and face as he raised his elbow to move his arm out of the way while his fingers still held his nose shut. Cairren gently pried his hand loose before finding a clean strip of cloth. She blotted his face and flinched when he hissed.

"I'm sorry," she whispered.

"It's not your fault, lass."

"I'll be more careful." But Padraig lowered her hands when she reached for him again.

"It's not you. I'm fine."

"You're not. You need to have your nose set and something cold put on your eye. Who's your healer? Can someone send for her?"

"We haven't one. She died last winter."

"She'd trained no one to take over from her? Do you at least have a midwife?"

"Nay. She was young and hadn't thought she would need a replacement. She was both the healer and the midwife."

"Who can set your nose? Your mother? Myrna?"

Padraig snorted, then groaned. "Neither. They can't stand the sight of blood or getting dirty from it."

"And they wanted to be warriors' wives?" Cairren shook her head in disbelief, but took Padraig's hand and tugged him toward the Great Hall. She guided them to the window that let in the only natural light in the gathering hall. People had already begun milling about in anticipation of the nooning. Heads turned to watch the couple as Cairren led Padraig to a bench. "Sit."

Cairren turned Padraig's face toward the light and tried not to grimace. Whoever broke his nose did so in a way that the bone cracked in at least two places. She was going to cause him terrible pain before it could feel better.

"Padraig, I'm sorry I'm going to have to hurt you. It's unavoidable. Do you want some whisky first?" Cairren glanced around, hoping to signal someone willing to come close enough for her to make the request.

"Nay. Just be done with it."

She positioned one hand to grasp the bridge of his nose while the other gripped his jaw. Her strong fingers pressed against his jaw and chin.

"Sit still. Are you re—" Cairren didn't finish her sentence before her booted foot kicked Padraig's shin. She used the distraction to realign his nose.

"Fucking shite, lass! Ye dinna need to kick so hard." It was the second time Cairren heard Padraig's brogue, and she rather liked it. She chuckled as she stepped back. "There's naught funny aboot kicking a wounded mon. As if ma nose dinna already hurt. I thought ye would fix ma nose, nae break ma shin."

"Your nose is fixed."

"What?" Padraig's brow furrowed, but he gingerly felt around his nose and realized she was right. It still hurt like the dickens, but it was straighter than it had been before. The bump from the last time someone set it was straightened, and he realized that the pain was less than it had been.

"I'm sorry that you're injured in a second place, but I needed to distract you. You would have pulled away the moment I put pressure on your nose, and I wouldn't have been able to get it straight."

"You evil witch!" Myrna squawked. "Get away from him. What are you doing to him?"

Cairren stepped back from Padraig, who blinked rapidly as he watched Myrna rush toward them. He attempted to stand, but Cairren's hand shot out and pressed his shoulder down, urging him to remain seated. She muttered, "Dizzy." And he was. She turned her attention to Myrna and tossed Padraig's filthy leine at her.

"You're just in time to clean up. You always manage to show up when I'm done with Padraig." Cairren canted her head and smiled. She brushed past Myrna as the woman fumed, but then Myrna remembered Padraig, or at least that Padraig was watching.

"Oh, my love. What did she do to you?" Myrna cooed as she reached for his face. Padraig swatted her hand away and stood.

"She set my nose since no one else here can."

"I would have!" Myrna exclaimed.

"Before or after you swooned from the blood? She's cleaned most of it up." Padraig looked for Cairren, but she'd disappeared. But his clan watched him. He was in no mood to deal with any woman or his clan gawking at him. "I'm going to bathe."

"I thought we would spend the afternoon together."

"Myrna, I just got my nose broken. It hurts like hell."

"But I can kiss you and make it all better," Myrna cooed.

"No, you cannot. I told you. I love you, but I'm not breaking my vow to Cairren."

"So you're picking her again," Myrna spat.

"No. I'm picking the vow I made before God. Myrna, my head aches, and my nose is throbbing. Please, just let me go and bathe. I'm sure I'll feel better after a dip in the loch."

"I'll come with you. I can scrub your back," Myrna grinned.

"What? No! You've never seen—I've never shown you my—I mean you saw last night, but that's different. You shouldn't have even been in there last night as an unwed woman." The truth of that statement dawned on Padraig for the first time.

"Well, I was. And now that it's not a secret, why shouldn't I see it again?"

"Because we're not married," Padraig hissed through his gritted teeth.

"But you did your duty. Now it's a marriage in name only."

"And you're still a maiden. It would be wrong even if I weren't wed."

"I told you I could solve that problem," Myrna raised an eyebrow and offered a knowing smile.

"Are you saying that just to get back at me?"

"No, I'm saying it so your stuffy honor will stay quiet, and we can move on with our lives."

"Move on to what? I told you, I'm not making you my mistress." Padraig rubbed his forehead and longed for a way to escape.

"What other choice is there if you still love me and want to be with me?" Myrna argued.

"There's the choice that we accept life didn't give us what we wanted. I will *not* dishonor you by making you my mistress."

"I don't think it has aught to do with honor. I think you care more aboot her than you do me. You tupped her once, and now she's bewitched you."

"Don't say that," Padraig hissed. He looked around to see who could overhear them. Many of his clan were very superstitious, and if they believed Cairren was a witch, or any sort of heretic, they wouldn't think twice before tying her to a stake.

"You're protecting her. Why? I demand to ken why you care what happens to her. Wouldn't that be for the best?" Padraig didn't have to guess what she meant. Myrna had already thought of the consequences if the clan turned against Cairren. Padraig leaned forward, so they were eye-to-eye.

"Are you saying you want her killed?"

"What?" Myrna's blue eyes widened, and she adamantly shook her head. "I'd never say that."

"Then is that what you're hinting at because that's how it sounds?" Padraig straightened. He was out of patience, and he was struggling not to lose his temper at Myrna. "I need to leave before one of us says something we regret. I will find you before the evening meal." Out of habit, he kissed her forehead before stepping around her.

Just as had happened that morning, all eyes watched the intimacy he shared with Myrna when he should have had more sense.

CHAPTER FIFTEEN

Cairren drew back the string on her bow as her eyes followed the buck they chased. She took a deep breath, holding it as she set her final sight, and exhaled as she released the arrow. It sailed through the air before landing through the deer's heart. It staggered several steps before falling to the ground.

"Well done, my wee lassie," Innes cheered as she rode pillion on his horse. He'd taught her to hunt from a moving horse when she was young, but it had been years since she'd tried it. She couldn't believe she bagged the buck on her first try. Collette rode up alongside them with their guards following. Innes had spurred his horse into a gallop when Cairren pointed out the animal. She'd clung to her father's waist until they drew near, then she nocked an arrow and squeezed her thighs to keep her from falling from the charging steed.

The Kennedys had decided to hunt, hoping that bringing back a catch would be a conciliatory action. Or at least they could say they tried. They dismounted and went to check Cairren's kill. The animal lay with its eye open but unmoving. Cairren said a prayer of thanks that the animal hadn't suffered. She enjoyed the challenge of hunting but always felt guilty afterwards. She preferred to shoot hay targets, but she'd relented when her father suggested that it might be a small act to smooth things over with her new clan. She doubted it, but she had a day left with her parents. She didn't want to ruin it.

"Lady Cairren, you've done better than any of us could have," a guardsman spoke up as six men walked past to retrieve the animal. It was a large buck that easily outweighed her, and its antlers were in perfect condition.

"That head should be a nice edition to their collection in the Great Hall. Perhaps you could present them to the laird and lady, *ma petite-fille*," Collette suggested. Cairren turned away but nodded. She walked back to her father's horse and stood on the far side, so she didn't have to see or hear the men preparing to move the animal. She knew they would dress the animal once they returned to the keep, so they needed only to get the buck's hooves tied to sturdy branches to carry it back. Cairren mounted on the back of Innes's horse once again, and the hunting party turned back toward the castle. They had to ride past the loch, and someone in the water caught Cairren's attention. As if she had a sixth sense, she knew it was Padraig before they were close enough for her to make out his features. He stood in waist-deep water and watched as they approached.

"Do I stop, lass?" Innes whispered.

"I suppose we have to unless we want to be rude."

"Would that be so bad?" Innes muttered. Cairren shrugged, but she knew her father couldn't see. Innes slowed his horse to a walk until they drew near enough to talk to Padraig.

. . .

Padraig had just surfaced from gingerly dipping his head beneath the surface when he watched eight horses gallop past the far side of the loch. He'd known in an instant it was Cairren seated behind her father. He wondered why she wasn't riding her own horse until he watched her pull something over her shoulder. From her movement, he knew she was preparing to shoot an arrow. It impressed him that she kept her seat without the use of her hands to hold on, but he didn't expect the party to stop. He watched as all the Kennedys dismounted, but they were too far for him to tell what they were doing. He scrubbed his hair and body as he watched them talking. Then the guardsmen moved away from Cairren and her parents. He'd finished washing by the time the warriors emerged from the thicket carrying a deer large enough for Padraig to see it from a distance. They'd remounted and were galloping back to the keep before he could leave the loch without flashing all of them. He opted to remain in the water, and he was glad he did when his cock stirred.

Cairren's hair had tumbled loose and tendrils danced in the wind as she held onto her father. Her cheeks were rosy, and she was smiling at they approached, but he knew the moment she recognized him. Her smile slipped as she sat straighter. Innes said something to her, and she shrugged. She didn't look as pleased to see him as he felt about seeing her.

"How's your nose, lad? I heard Cairren straightened it, and Myrna offered to kiss it better." Innes's penetrating eyes bored into Padraig. Padraig had no idea how Innes had heard about Myrna. Cairren had already left the Great Hall when Myrna made her salacious offer. Padraig's gaze swept over the Kennedys, and two guards in particular looked ready to murder him. He understood without words that they'd been in the Great Hall and had either heard Myrna or overheard people repeating what she'd said. He glanced back at Cairren to see how she responded to her father's words, but she was watching her father.

"I thank your daughter for tending to me. It feels much better already," Padraig smiled at Cairren, but she studiously ignored him.

"Then I didn't do a good enough job breaking it," Innes growled. He twisted in his saddle and murmured to Cairren, but Padraig couldn't make out what he said before the laird swung his leg over his horse's withers and slid to the ground. "Take the ladies back to the keep. Prepare the animal and be sure Lady Cairren gets her prize."

Innes walked to the edge of the loch and crossed his arms while he waited for his men to escort his wife and daughter back to the keep. Padraig walked out of the water and thanked Innes when he handed Padraig his plaid. The older man sized up the younger before taking a deep breath.

"You've made it clear in every way possible that not only do you love another woman, you will not give her up. So be it. There is naught I can do aboot it and neither can Cairren. My lass has accepted that you mean to make her your mistress rather than treat her as your wife. She's come to terms with that far faster than I have, and it's because she's a better person than I am."

Innes bent and picked up a rock. He rubbed his thumb along the flat side before skipping it along the surface of the water. He did it again before turning back to Padraig.

"I decided a year ago that since Cairren was an age to marry and would soon finish her expected service to the queen, I would find her a husband far from the strife and danger of the border. I considered taking her to France, but knowing she'd be so far from us broke her mother's and my hearts. I don't doubt you know you weren't the first candidate. And I'm certain you've guessed a reason why none of the other prospects turned out. But what I doubt you know, what even Cairren doesn't know—though I suppose I should have told her—is that I turned down the acceptances. Each clan was happy to take her dowry, but as I investigated more, I learned things aboot the men that might marry my daughter. I didn't feel she would be safe with any of those other men. Their clans might have accepted her, but the men themselves made me fear for her. You were the only mon I learned of who received praise from everyone I asked."

Padraig didn't know what to say. He'd made the assumption that Innes expected. He'd taken one look at Cairren once he got past the initial shock of her beauty and believed that every other clan rejected her because she looked too different.

"No one mentioned you were courting a Ross lass, perhaps it's not well known. I don't ken. But of those I asked, each and every one of them, swore you were honorable and would never hurt my daughter. They swore I could trust you with her, knowing I wouldn't be close enough to come to her with haste. And now I'm set to leave in the morn, and I don't ken if my daughter will survive her first night here without me." Innes looked at Padraig, and he didn't bother to hide the wetness in his eyes. "She's a good lass. She's bound to you now, and that can't be easily undone. But if you doubt for even a moment that you can protect her, tell me now, and I will defy the king and take her home. If you cannot or will not honor her, then tell me before I leave her in your care. If aught happens to her, I don't ken that my family could make it through. It would kill her mother and devastate her sister. I would lose all three of the most important people to ever enter my life. I don't know that I would survive it."

Innes's honesty stunned Padraig. The bear of a man who'd spent all morning knocking him on his arse, then broke his nose, was wiping the mist from his eyes. Padraig looked toward the keep for a long moment before looking back at Innes.

"I can't suddenly lie and promise that I will love your daughter. I believe I can grow fond of her, but my heart belongs to someone else. It has for years. I spent two years courting Myrna, and we planned to wed after Samhain. That's less than two moons from now. But I swore to protect Cairren and to be faithful to her. I will not take Myrna or any other woman to my bed, but neither can I suddenly stop loving Myrna. I don't ken what to do." Padraig sighed. "That's not true. I ken what I should do, but I'm discovering I'm more selfish than I imagined. I admit I've been trying to devise a way to keep both women here, to enjoy both of their company in their own way. But you pointed out what I realized myself this morning: I'm turning my wife into my mistress. I admit I desire Cairren in a way that I've never felt for a woman before. What passed between us last night was unlike aught I could imagine intimacy to be. But that doesn't mean I love her, and it doesn't mean that I'll stop loving Myrna." Padraig shook his head as he looked back at the keep. "I didn't intend to hurt Cairren. Truly. Not like the others have. I just keep mucking everything up with her."

Padraig looked at Innes, and he wished he hadn't. The man wasn't angry; he no longer appeared sad; he was nothing. It was almost like how Cairren drifted away when she felt trapped, but the look in Innes's eyes was pity for a man he'd given up on. Innes shook his head and sighed.

"It's time you stopped acting like a spoiled child and started being a mon. No one gets to have it all. You included." Innes walked away, leaving Padraig alone once again.

▭

Cairren climbed into her bed and stared at the ceiling in the dark. She'd presented the head and antlers to Micheil, and he'd stood speechless for a long moment before looking at Innes and laughing. He demanded to know who had really taken down the buck. The Kennedy guards were standing at her back as she made the presentation and explained that they gave the venison everyone ate that night in appreciation for the Munros hosting the wedding. Cairren sensed the disgust among the men as Micheil went along the line, asking each man in turn if he'd killed the deer. She'd stood with her back straight, as always, but she'd been most angry at Padraig for his cowardice. He knew she'd been the one to take the shot, the only one to take the shot. He could have spoken up on her behalf, but instead, he left her to stand in front of his clan to be ridiculed by his father. She hadn't spared him a glance the entire night.

Cairren rolled onto her side and hugged the spare pillow to her chest. She'd fallen asleep the same way the night before, remembering how it had felt to wrap herself around Padraig. For the few hours they had together, she'd felt accepted and wanted. She'd fooled herself into thinking Padraig would do the right thing. Even if he didn't give up Myrna entirely, that maybe he wouldn't contribute to Cairren's suffering. But it was less than a half hour after they left the bed where he'd introduced her to passion that she heard him with Myrna, then saw him holding her. She wasn't even angry with him at that point. She was furious with herself for letting her guard down, for making a fool of herself.

When someone knocked, she assumed it was her mother coming to say goodnight one last time even though Collette had tucked Cairren in just as she had when Cairren was a child. She opened the door, expecting to see Collette. "*Maman?*"

"Nay, lass. It's me." Padraig stood in the passageway with his leine and plaid on but no boots or stockings. Cairren pushed the door to slam it in his face, but he caught it before it closed.

"Leave me alone, Padraig, I will scream this keep down." Cairren turned away from him. "Close the door behind you."

"I'm not leaving, Cairren." At Padraig's refusal, she spun around and opened her mouth to scream. "Wait! I want to have that talk. We haven't come to a truce, and that's my fault. I would set things to rights."

"Set things to rights?" Cairren scoffed. "Get out."

"Not until we've talked."

"Talked? So you can make things all better between us so by morning you can—what did your man say—be tired from fucking me all night. Thank you. No. I decline."

"That wasn't why I came."

"You are a useless liar. It is. You came hoping to straighten things out enough to appease me and then convince me to let you bed me. Mayhap you'd have the decency not to ask for it tonight, but you plan to fool me into letting you into my bed or getting me to go to yours." Cairren crossed her arms but stepped toward Padraig. "Do you know what the most pathetic part of all of this is? Even knowing you want someone else, I'd bed you again. Every bluidy night because I enjoyed it, because I desire you and you desire me. But you're too weak. You can't balance everything, so you can't have it all. As long as I'm putting my life at risk to roll around with you, you're not worth it. You want to love Myrna, but you want to fuck me. I'm not the one trying to stop you from having what you want. I have no designs on trying to make you fall in love with me. I've never told you not to love Myrna. I only told you I wanted her to leave because I don't feel safe. I encouraged you to visit her every day. I even said I don't care if you bed her. I've been here three days, and there hasn't been a moment outside of lying on your bed or leaving the keep with my parents when I haven't feared for my safety. Myrna only fears not getting what she wants. You are naught more than a spoiled child in a mon's body. You tout doing your duty, but you haven't a clue what duty is. You want to play with your toys rather than lead by example. I wouldn't follow you into battle. I wouldn't even follow you to a chamber pot. Now get out." Cairren pointed toward the door.

Padraig stood dumbfounded. Cairren was ready to spit nails, but she looked magnificent. Her silver-gray eyes glowed in the firelight that drew out the red and gold in her hair. She spoke calmly and with conviction, and she spoke the truth. Even as his body reacted as it always did, he saw the sense in what she said. He wondered if she had spoken to Innes and learned what he'd said that afternoon. Her words were so close to her father's. He found himself nodding, but he didn't know what to say in response. He wasn't ready to leave. They had resolved nothing, and they needed to find a way to coexist. While he didn't want their intimacy to end after one night, he accepted that it might. But he still needed to get Cairren to learn to live alongside Myrna because the latter once again refused to consider leaving. She'd brought up the topic of staying in front of his mother and father, and even though he'd argued it would be best for her to return to Balnagown, his parents overruled him. A blind man could see what they were doing, but he was powerless to change their edict, and he needed Cairren to know that.

Padraig walked to one of the two chairs before the fireplace and sat. He looked back at Cairren to see if she would join him, but she shook her head. Instead, she went to stand by the door. He sighed but stretched his long legs out before him. He thought to wait her out, thinking she would eventually give up and join him, but the minutes drew out. He glanced back at Cairren, and she still stood with her arms crossed. He thought she might have given in to leaning against the wall, but she stood like a statue. He shook his head and sighed once more.

"I told Myrna she needed to leave when she brought up staying longer. She did it in front of my parents, and they disagreed with me. They said she is to stay. I would have taken her home, and I would have gone to visit her every day that my duties allowed."

"And then returned every night to tup me."

"Isn't that what you said you want? You want her gone, but you also want me."

"It's the best I could hope for. But that's all it is. Hope. And hope is often wasted."

"Then how do we move forward? The three of us shall live under this roof until who knows when."

"Why are you asking me? I'm not the problem in this little love triangle. I've accepted my role. It's Myrna who can't accept me. Bed me if you want, if you dare defy her. Don't bed me if you can't live with the consequences. One way or another, my parents leave at dawn, and I'm stuck here. Your clan loathes me, so whether we share a bed or not isn't my most pressing concern."

Padraig stood and walked toward Cairren. When she didn't shy away, he cupped her jaw, tilting her head back to look into her eyes. "You're being flippant and distant to cover how much you're hurting. And I'm the cause of that hurt, directly and indirectly. I wish there was more that I could do to fix this, but the more I try to please everyone, the more displeased everyone is."

"Am I supposed to feel sorry for you?" Cairren glared at him.

"No. That's not what I meant. I meant that while I've made a mess of everything, I am trying. I told you last night, that I know I'm making mistakes, but I can at least make you feel good when it's just the two of us."

Cairren closed her eyes and prayed for patience. "But it's never just the two of us. You don't think she'll know?" She blew out a breath in exasperation. "You do not understand women in the least. If she's not doing it this very minute, I guarantee you she will at some point tonight and every night coming. Myrna will check your chamber. She will look to see if I'm there or if you've left. You will not be able to hide this from her."

"She's not like that."

"Oh, and you're not a fool," Cairren mocked. "Court is filled with jealous lovers and mistresses who spy upon one another. This Greek tragedy is no different than what is played out every night in Stirling Castle. You may desire me, but you don't want me any more tonight than you did before we met. You'll bed me because now that you've pledged yourself before God, your honor demands you remain faithful. I'm the only option besides celibacy. Besides, you'd never besmirch Myrna's honor by treating her as your mistress. You wouldn't dare steal her maidenhead, even though I'm certain she's offered. Let me guess. She's even said she'll find someone else to do the dishonorable deed, so she'll no longer be a maiden, and you won't have to feel guilty." Cairren watched as surprise and recognition flared in Padraig's eyes. "I'm right, aren't I? Do you know why I guessed the truth? Because she isn't doing aught I haven't seen other women do to manipulate men. But she's too perfect in your eyes to sin, so leave. This is the last time I will say it before I scream. My father will butcher you."

"I'll go, but this isn't over yet, Cairren."

"You, me, and a bed is. Goodnight." Cairren opened the door, and Padraig passed through. She pushed it closed before he could say anything else, and he heard the bar drop into place. He sighed and trudged to his chamber, where another night of restlessness awaited.

CHAPTER SIXTEEN

Cairren waved one last time as her parents rode away from Foulis Castle. Her mother had kept her tears at bay, knowing that if she cried, Cairren would too. Cairren had sworn to Collette that she would never let the Munros see her cry. She would never show them her weakness. Innes whispered his reminder that if she should ever need to flee, she should head to the Sutherlands. They'd hugged and with great regret on all of their parts, Innes and Collette rode away with the Kennedy guardsmen surrounding them.

Cairren inhaled a deep breath before turning around. Some people in the bailey overtly stared at her while others were more covert, but she cared not. She was exhausted. She intended to return to her chamber, and if she never left it again, it would be too soon. She entered the keep as Padraig came down the stairs. His hair was disheveled, and he was bleary-eyed. He looked as though he'd barely slept, and Cairren felt a smug sense of satisfaction. When Padraig caught sight of Cairren walking toward him, his eyes darted to the doors leading to the bailey and back to her.

"Bluidy hell, did your parents leave already?"

"Aye." Cairren intended to keep walking, but Padraig stopped her.

"I'm sorry. I didn't mean to be rude. I overslept." Padraig ran a hand through his hair, making it stand on end even more. "I had a hard time falling asleep."

"That's a pity. I slept quite well. Good day." Cairren once again went to step around him, but he caught her elbow.

"Where are you going?"

"Where you are not, because where you are, Myrna is sure to follow." Cairren pulled her arm away, but in time for Myrna to see Padraig holding it when she entered the Great Hall from the kitchens. She cast him a pitying look before walking to the stairs. Padraig turned to greet Myrna, but she watched Cairren walking away.

"Good morning, my love," Padraig greeted her.

"They're gone, but they left her behind," Myrna mused.

"Aye." Padraig intended to change the subject. "What shall we do today?"

"Are you actually talking to me?" Myrna batted her eyelashes.

"Of course, my love. What would you like?"

"Let's start with a walk, and then we shall see from there," Myrna bubbled, and Padraig finally saw the woman he knew, the one he'd fallen in love with. Gone was the anger and spitefulness. He breathed a silent sigh of relief. He glanced back at the stairs once before he left the keep with Myrna. They spent the morning strolling around the loch and even sat together at the dais when they arrived late for the meal and Cairren wasn't in sight. He inquired later, but she'd requested no tray be taken to her.

He spent the afternoon playing chess with Myrna

and reading in his father's solar as she embroidered. It was just as it had been before Cairren arrived and turned his world upside down. But he grew concerned when the evening meal came and went, but she didn't make an appearance, and once again he learned she hadn't requested a tray. After everyone settled for the night, he went to check on her. He knocked three separate times, but she never answered, and when he tried the door, it was barred. He gave up and sought his own bed.

And so began their game of cat-and-mouse. They fell into a routine where Padraig caught glimpses of Cairren, but she never joined the meals, and she never lingered in the Great Hall. He had no idea how she spent most of her days because no one seemed to notice if she went anywhere. He only knew that she spent a few hours with Wynda in Cairren's chamber. He learned that Cairren read to Wynda, who was illiterate, while Wynda sewed. He kept to himself how similar that was to how he spent his time with Myrna in the laird's solar. Except Myrna seemed to listen only as a courtesy, while Wynda beamed when she told him about the stories Cairren shared and how she adopted unique voices for each character. He'd never seen his sister-by-marriage so vibrant as she was when she spoke about her time spent with Cairren. He was happy for Wynda, and it relieved him to learn that Wynda took food to Cairren, so she wasn't starving. He tried to be sly and inquire whether Cairren ever asked about him, but Wynda's smile always dropped as she shook her head. She'd give his arms a quick squeeze, then slip away with some excuse of a chore or duty calling her name.

By the end of the first sennight, he was driving himself crazy. Never seeing Cairren frustrated him, so he took it out on the men in the lists. He was certain they knew why he'd grown surly and easily riled, but after Denis's beating, they kept their comments far from Padraig's ears. None wanted to learn if he would react as Innes had. But at the same time, he felt like a joke before his men. It wasn't a secret that his wife refused to lay eyes on him while he lusted after her.

Padraig had heard someone moving about in the passageway each night, and he'd wondered the first couple of times if it were Cairren coming to see him, but when no one knocked, he crept to the passageway. He'd caught Myrna claiming to be going for a drink of water. He wouldn't admit it to anyone, but he realized Cairren had been right about Myrna checking to see where Padraig was and whether he was alone. She never opened the door and peered in, but he was certain she put her ear to the door. It amused him to picture her tiptoeing down the passageway, attempting to be stealthy, so he chuckled when he'd hear her moving around. She never found what she looked for, and Padraig had convinced himself that he could last without another midnight visit to Cairren.

But by the tenth night, he could no longer stand it. As he prepared to leave his chamber and traipse through the dark passageways, he wasn't certain if it was better that Myrna occupied a family chamber, or if it would have been better for her to be on the same floor as Cairren and in a guest chamber. Being on his floor meant it was easier for her to sneak to his chamber, but it also meant there was less likelihood that she would hear anything if he convinced Cairren to open her door.

His mother had given Myrna a chamber on the family floor when she first started spending extended visits at Foulis early in their courtship. He'd thought it odd that the chamber wasn't on the guest floor above, but it had made it convenient for him to steal kisses late at night. Now he realized that had been his mother's intention all along. He didn't believe Myrna had anything to do with the room assignment, but he resented knowing his mother tried to manipulate him.

He made his way to Cairren's chamber on silent feet, but he cringed when his knock echoed down the passageway. He waited, then knocked again. He pressed his ear to the door and heard movement on the other side, but no one approached the door. He knocked a third time and pressed his mouth near the door jamb. "Cairren, it's me. Please open the door."

A moment later, Cairren pulled open the door. Padraig's body had its usual reaction to Cairren, but after a week and a half of barely seeing her, his body ached to touch her again. His eyes swept over her as she stood before him in her thin chemise. He had only his plaid wrapped around his waist, and he watched her drink in the sight of his half naked body before her eyes jumped to meet his. She stepped back, and as Padraig passed through the doorway, he pulled her into his arms before kicking the door shut. Their mouths fused together as Padraig's hands roamed over her body.

When he couldn't stand the fabric keeping him from feeling her body pressed against his, Padraig yanked the offending garment off Cairren as she pulled his plaid loose. He lifted her, and her legs went around his waist. His fingers bit into the flesh of her bottom as her sheath rubbed against the tip of his sword. He could feel she was wet for him already, and he wondered if she'd been thinking of him as he thought of her every night. He carried her to the bed and followed her onto it as she settled against the pillows. He'd planned to go slowly, reintroducing her to the passion they shared, but their need was too urgent. She cupped his jaw, and their eyes met for a long moment before they returned to kissing, and Padraig eased his cock into her. She moaned as her kiss grew wilder. She moved against him as though they'd been lovers for years rather than one night. Their bodies found their rhythm with little effort, and they were both soon flying over the precipice and crashing into the waves of ecstasy.

Padraig rolled them, so he didn't have to fear suffocating Cairren. As they lay panting but sated, Padraig realized he'd spilled his seed into Cairren each time with no thought of pulling out. He'd always been overly cautious in the past, pulling out well before his release, using his hand to finish what he didn't dare to do within a woman. He also realized they hadn't spoken a word to one another since she opened the door. He caressed her back and shoulder, but when her breathing slowed and she hadn't moved in a while, he looked down and realized she'd fallen asleep. He shifted so he could see her face as she slumbered. It was relaxed, and she looked younger. Her flawless skin and features tempted him to run the pad of his finger over her eyebrows, cheekbones, nose, and chin, but he didn't dare lest he wake her. She was in a deep sleep quickly, and he realized she must have been exhausted. He wondered if this was the first time she'd slept deeply in nights.

Padraig dozed, but he woke as soon as Cairren

stirred. He watched as her eyes fluttered open and realization dawned on her. He held his breath, fearing she might scream or scramble out of the bed. Instead, she snuggled closer, her eyes drifting closed again, but her hand stroked his chest.

"I've missed you, Ren. Not just this," Padraig was quick to clarify as her eyes snapped open. "I've missed seeing you and talking to you. I've been worrying aboot you."

"I've missed you too," Cairren whispered. But a moment later, she pushed up onto her elbow. "Why do you call me Ren?"

"Because you're tiny and look fragile, but in reality, you're tenacious."

"But they're songbirds. You don't know if I can sing. I might sound like a magpie."

"Even if you did, it wouldn't change how I see you."

"And how is that?"

Padraig grazed his fingers over her shoulder, sending a shiver along her spine as she waited for him to answer. "As someone people often underestimate. Someone who will fiercely defend and protect those who matter to you. Someone far braver and more resilient than anyone gives you credit for." Cairren smiled at him, and his heart felt too large for his chest as the warmth radiated from her and took root deep within him. He brought her head down to kiss her, but before their lips met, she pressed her finger to his.

"I like it. That means a great deal to me, and I like that it's special between us. Thank you." Their mouth fused together as tenderness soon exploded into passion. Padraig lifted Cairren to straddle him. At her confused look, he helped her guide him past her entrance. He watched with fascination as she explored different ways to move with him buried deep within her. When she found what she wanted, her head fell back, her hair brushing his legs as her breasts bounced. He kneaded the globes until he couldn't resist suckling her. She looked down at him, and she'd never imagined a more erotic experience than watching Padraig tonguing her nipple before drawing it into the satin recesses of his mouth as her body rocked against his. His palmed wrapped around her nape as he kissed his way over her collarbone and up her neck until he nipped at her jaw before finally tugging her earlobe with his teeth.

When Padraig sat up and pressed their bodies together so that every part from their mouths to their hips melded into one, Cairren felt her release burst through her. She buried her head against his shoulder to muffle her cry. But it was only seconds later that their mouths were searching for one another. Padraig kept her tucked tightly against his body as he repositioned them, so he could watch himself sliding in and out of her slick heat. Cairren's hands roamed over his shoulders and chest, trailing over the ridges of his abdomen before wrapping around his back. Once more, their bodies pressed together, now slick with their sweat. Cairren tried to slow her body's response, fearing it would all be over too soon and not knowing if it would ever happen again, but the feel of every thrust and surge of Padraig's cock chipped away her resistance. Her body went taut, and Padraig couldn't control himself either. As her core squeezed his shaft, he gave in and release carried them away.

"I don't want to stay away from you any more, Ren," Padraig whispered.

She was slow to respond, as though she cautiously

considered her response. "I don't want you to either. But it must remain a secret."

"I hate that you're right." Neither said more after that. There was little they could say that didn't re-open fresh wounds. It was shortly before dawn that Padraig crept back to his chamber.

Another fortnight passed, but unlike before, Padraig sneaked into Cairren's chamber every night, where he remained until the first rays of sunlight threatened to peak over the horizon. While he never slept deeply between their bouts of coupling, he awoke more refreshed than he could ever remember after a full night's sleep. Nothing changed for them during the day, and Padraig continued to only catch glimpses of Cairren some days, but every night she asked how his day was, and every night she steered their conversation so he never had a chance to ask about hers. She never mentioned Myrna or the arrangement they had. They talked about their childhood and shared stories. They talked about their interests and where they would travel if they could go anywhere. Padraig helped Cairren learn more Gaelic while she corrected his French. They'd created a small haven for themselves, and they both cherished it.

CHAPTER SEVENTEEN

After a month, Cairren feared she would begin climbing the walls if she didn't escape her chamber for longer than an hour or two a day. When she'd initially adopted her plan to spend her life hiding away in her chamber, she didn't anticipate how soon boredom would monopolize her days. She spent a few hours with Wynda each day, and they were growing to be close friends. She found the woman bright and witty once she grew more confident around Cairren. The only bone of contention was she would never admit to when Duncan abused her. Cairren knew each time it happened, but when she asked, Wynda found excuses for being clumsy.

"I need more fresh air," Cairren said as she stood by the arrow slit. "Would you care for a walk?"

"Perhaps another day, but not today," Wynda smiled. "Mary asked, if you can call it that, for me to make another batch of candles for the upcoming Samhain feast."

Cairren nodded. It was yet another reminder that the day Padraig and Myrna had planned to marry was rapidly approaching. She'd noticed the past couple of nights, Padraig arrived tense and on edge. It didn't take long before he relaxed and was solely attentive to her, but she suspected that the impending feast was troubling him. She didn't know if it was Myrna or his mother or something else that was causing the problem, but he wasn't himself. She suspected that in part it was his own unhappiness that he wouldn't be marrying Myrna as they planned. It made it hard to welcome him when she was silently reminded that she was only worthy of Padraig's time and attention when they were in bed. Otherwise, nothing had changed. He didn't care about her beyond their mutual pleasure. He still pined for another woman. The woman he spent most of his day with.

"Then I shall go for one and describe all the flowers and animals to you tomorrow." Cairren grinned as she and Wynda left her chamber. They parted in the passageway, and Cairren slipped out to the bailey. She approached the guardroom near the gate and knocked on the door.

"What?" A guard barked at her. His aggressive response took her aback, but she plastered her courtly smile onto her face and proceeded.

"Good morn. I'd like to take a walk beyond the bailey wall. Please send two guards to escort me." Cairren infused authority she didn't feel into her voice while trying to be polite.

"Nay." She was unprepared for the man's curt response.

"I beg your pardon. Perhaps I was unclear. I'd like two guards to accompany me while I'm away from the keep."

"And perhaps ye're too daft to understand me. I said nay."

"You're not entitled to tell me no. I am not asking."

"If Padraig cared enough to have ye guarded, he would have assigned ye a detail already. Since he hasnae, ye're obviously of nay more worth to him than ye are anyone else. If ye want to leave, then leave. But no mon will escort ye." The guard slammed the door shut in Cairren's face, leaving her standing stunned outside the hut. She looked around when she heard laughter and realized there had been an audience to her humiliation. She turned toward the gate and walked out.

She considered walking until she couldn't see Foulis anymore and then continuing to walk beyond that. Instead, she walked around the bailey wall and out to the loch. It was a warm day even though it was already the middle of October. She didn't have a hat to shield her face from the sun, and she worried for a moment about her skin darkening, but she figured that ship had already sailed and sunk. She slipped her shoes off and rolled down her stockings before dipping her toes into the cool water. She found a rock to sit upon in the shade, and she spent the rest of the afternoon watching the clouds pass overhead fish splashing as they came up for air, and listening to the birds chatter. She heard a particularly persistent chatter and smiled when she recognized the sound of a wren. Alone together, Padraig rarely called her anything but Ren. She'd grown used to it, and she treasured how she felt when he used the name that they only shared between them.

When the sun shifted and began to set, Cairren sighed and accepted that she needed to return to the keep if she wanted to make it to her chamber before the Great Hall filled with people. She entered the bailey through the postern gate near the gardens. Two voices she would know anywhere drifted to her.

"I know, my love. It pains me that the day we were to marry draws closer, and it will be naught but disappointment and pain," Padraig cooed. "I love you, and I wish I could ease your pain." Cairren forced herself not to make a mocking face as she continued to walk past the garden.

"You could ease it, but you refuse," Myrna whined.

"Shh, my love."

"She's just so horrid. She may have finally found the decency to remain hidden, but I know she's here. I know she's keeping you from me. I wish she'd never come," Myrna moaned.

"I wish the same, Myrna." Padraig agreed. Cairren came even with where they stood and watched as Myrna drew Padraig in for a kiss, and he did little to resist. Cairren watched, knowing she wasn't the only one who saw or heard them.

"You're not the only two who wished that," she announced. Padraig jerked away from Myrna and spun around. Horror washed over him as he took in Cairren's expression. It was blank, and he knew what that meant. He hadn't even been thinking about what he was saying. He'd just been agreeing with Myrna because he didn't want her crying again like she had been earlier. It broke his heart to see Myrna so upset, and he did whatever he could to placate her, which included saying things without thought.

Cairren turned away and made to continue walking, but Padraig called out to her. Cairren pretended not to hear him, but the second time, his voice was closer. She turned to watch him approach.

"Ren—"

"Don't. You have no right to call me that. You don't want me here. You definitely don't need me here." Cairren looked away, but then glared at Padraig. "I held out a glimmer of hope that you were honorable. I know I said you could do as you please with her, but I thought maybe, just maybe, that the honor you claimed would keep you from being unfaithful would be real. Clearly it's not. Believe me, you are a far greater disappointment to me than I ever was to you. You just don't like the way I look. I don't like who you are."

Padraig stood speechless, watching Cairren walk away. He barely noticed when Myrna approached until she pulled his arm around her. "What did that hideous creature have to say?"

"Hmm?" Padraig continued to watch Cairren as she entered the keep. He remembered what Myrna asked, but rather than answer, he realized that Myrna hadn't been able to hear his exchange with Cairren. Unlike Myrna and him, who never considered who was listening or watching, Cairren hadn't broadcasted her disgust for all and sundry to hear.

That night, Padraig didn't consider going to Cairren's chamber. He knew she would never let him in, and he doubted she would even open the door to listen to an apology. He knew he was the spoiled child she and her father called him. He wanted both of his toys, and he would have apologized just to get what he wanted. He couldn't recall ever being so disgusted with himself as he had been since Cairren arrived. He wanted to blame her, but still had a thimbleful of honor and could accept the root of his problems lay at his feet.

Cairren was desperate to escape the keep again. She'd spent the morning with Wynda, but she decided she would go for a ride. She'd twice more, unsuccessfully, to request that guards escort her, but the responses grew cruder each time. She abandoned asking and left the bailey alone. She spoke to few people and avoided lingering anywhere overlong. She'd discovered an apple orchard, so she'd stored away several in her chamber since she was often hungry. She'd tried requesting trays several times since she retreated to her chamber, but none ever arrived. She scavenged or relied on Wynda to bring her food. She considered abandoning her self-imposed imprisonment, but she'd had a run in with Duncan one evening as she headed toward the Great Hall for the meal. He'd caught her on the landing as she made her way from the third floor to the second. He'd pinned her against the wall and tried to grope her, but she'd twisted away and ran down the stairs. His mocking laughter followed her as she hid in a passageway until she felt it was safe to return to her chamber.

As she slipped from her chamber with an apple in each hand, Cairren eased down the stairs but froze in the shadows when she heard Myrna on the floor below. Cairren peeked and recognized she was with her maid.

"I never knew a mon could do such things with his tongue until he did it. I enjoy it more each time. He swears I taste finer than the most extravagant wine. I'm certain I taste better than that bitch he married." Myrna's words weren't hushed. She wasn't trying to keep what she said a secret. Cairren wondered if Myrna was speaking for her benefit, but Cairren knew there was no way Myrna could know she was standing on the stairs above them. Tears pricked the back of her eyelids as she listened to Myrna continue to describe her tryst with Padraig. "The first time I learned how a mon enters a woman, I couldn't believe anyone would enjoy something so crude. But I swear, his cock is enough to make me steal the crown jewels." The two women giggled as they disappeared into Myrna's chamber. Cairren rested her head against the wall as tears streamed down her cheeks. She abandoned her plan for a ride and returned to her chamber.

Over the next month, Padraig saw Cairren five times, and it was always the back of her head. He discovered Wynda learned of the scene at the garden, not because Cairren told her, but because it was the juiciest piece of gossip for weeks. What Cairren hadn't known was it was the first and only time he'd kissed Myrna since he married Cairren. He'd battled with his desire to do so, but he'd mustered more restraint with Myrna than he ever did with Cairren. But the moment Myrna's lips touched his and familiarity flooded him, he gave into the temptation. The first moments had been divine, as though he was sipping water for the first time after wandering a desert for years. But it left a sour feeling in his heart as the kiss drew on. As he came to his senses and realized it wasn't Cairren but Myrna he kissed, the giddiness evaporated. Then there was Cairren's voice, echoing the wish that she'd never come to Foulis. He hadn't considered what he said until she said the *three* of them wished the same thing.

It worried him when one morning Wynda approached him and shared that Cairren hadn't left her chamber once in three days. He offered to check on her, but Wynda adamantly shook her head. She reassured him that Cairren was well, but Wynda still felt he should know. Padraig thanked her but went to Cairren's chamber, anyway. He knocked, but she never answered. When he pressed his ear to her door, he didn't hear any movement. He wondered if she'd changed her mind.

Cairren heard Padraig outside her door, but she refused to open it. She'd been hiding for days after separate near encounters with both Duncan and Myrna. Three days earlier, Cairren returned from a walk and cut through the garden to enter the keep through a side passageway. She'd spotted Duncan approaching, and the memory of being pinned against the wall flooded back. She knew he'd seen her because he leered and licked his lips. She'd passed him in a passageway one other time since he'd pinned against the wall, and he'd whispered lewd comments about what he could do with his hand and her quim. She darted through the door and into the dark passageway. She knew there were storage rooms along the corridor, so she ducked into one and left the door open a crack. Rather than spy Duncan following her, she recognized Myrna and her maid walking toward where she hid.

"What did he do next?" Myrna's maid giggled.

"He took me against the wall!" Myrna squealed. "He couldn't wait for us to get to his bed. He tossed my skirts out of the way, lifted me up so I could wrap my legs around his waist. Then he was—ugh. It was better than ever before."

Cairren covered her mouth with her hand,

thinking she would be ill. She couldn't believe her misfortune when the women stopped just outside the door behind which Cairren hid.

"When will you meet him next, ma lady?"

"Tonight, of course. It's not like he bothers with his wife. Why would he when he's bedding me?"

Cairren waited several minutes after the passageway grew silent before she rushed back to her chamber. She decided she needed to take a fresh approach. Rather than hiding in her chamber most of the day and trying to sneak out of the keep between meals, she would leave before the morning meal and not return until after the evening meal. She never walked more than a few miles from the keep, but she spent her days reading and gathering flowers she gave to Wynda. She fished, but tossed them back. She never dared swim in case someone stumbled upon her, but she sat with her feet in the loch for hours until her toes were so pruned, she wondered if they would ever return to normal. She took bread and cheese with her and often picked wild berries. Collette had taught her daughters from a young age which were safe, which were dangerous, and which to avoid if she thought she might confuse one for another. The days were long and lonely, but she avoided overhearing things that sent pain through her chest, and she avoided being trapped. She felt safer roaming the open countryside than she did within the bailey walls.

CHAPTER EIGHTEEN

Samhain was the next day, and Padraig was miserable with the constant reminders that he wouldn't be marrying Myra. The month's separation from Cairren left him feeling hollow, but Myrna had been much more herself, and he once again enjoyed her company. He hadn't forgotten how she behaved when Cairren arrived, and doubt niggled in his mind as he tried to reconcile the Myrna he believed he knew with the one he'd seen. Her vitriol was less caustic, but she still made disparaging remarks about Cairren daily. He realized he'd tuned them out and didn't notice that she said hateful and hurtful things until he heard her speaking with his mother as he passed the open door of a storage building in the bailey.

"Wouldn't it be such a shame if someone were to accidentally bump our village whore into one of the fires?" Myrna laughed.

"Such a shame to be done with the woman who's single-handedly ruined our family," Mary replied.

Padraig waited around the corner to hear if there was more, but the two women moved away from the door. He sighed as he rubbed his forehead. He wasn't sure how seriously to take what he overheard. He didn't believe either woman would murder anyone, but he feared Cairren might still get hurt. As though conjured from his thoughts, he spotted Cairren coming in through the postern gate. As he turned toward her, a guardsman called out, "Kennedys approaching!"

Padraig watched Cairren's head whip up as she spotted mounted riders and a wagon passing beneath the portcullis. She lifted her skirts above her ankles and darted across the bailey.

"Daniel!" Cairren called as she waved. She couldn't believe her clansmen were at Foulis. She'd almost forgotten that the rest of her dowry had yet to arrive. She clapped her hands as the men reined in and the wagon rolled to a stop.

"Aye, lassie," an older guardsman leaped from his horse as she ran headlong toward him.

He opened his arms to her and lifted her off her feet. Padraig watched as she gave Daniel a smacking kiss on one cheek then the other. She tapped his left cheek. "That one is for *Maman*." Then she tapped his right cheek. "That one is for Papa." She kissed the tip of his nose. "And that is for Caitlyn."

"Da, stop keeping my cousin all to yourself. You're not the only one who's been waiting to see her."

"Jamie! You came too!" Daniel lowered Cairren to the ground, but a man closer to her age lifted off her feet once again and swept her into a bear hug.

"Of course, I did. Would you like to see what we brought?" Jamie waggled his eyebrows.

"Oh, Jamie, did you bring it?" Cairren pressed on his shoulders, straining to see into the wagon.

"Maybe. Wouldn't you like to know?"

"You know I do. Stop teasing me."

"Then you shall have to look and see." Jamie tossed her into the air, and Cairren hooted.

"You did! You were able to get it here in one piece!"

Jamie tossed her again, and she clapped. "You brought the wool too."

Jamie tossed her third time before placing her back on the ground. "Aye, Lady Collette threatened to skelp us alive if aught happened to your loom or the wool. But Cairren, that isn't the only surprise."

"What else is there? I know everything else *Maman* and Papa were sending."

"Not everything, Cairren." A deep voice came from the opposite side of the wagon where she hadn't been looking.

"Alex," Cairren breathed. She stepped away from her cousin as Alexander Armstrong reached out his hands. She placed hers in his, and he squeezed them before pulling her in for an embrace that was too intimate for a married woman, but after a month of isolation and hurt, it was the contact she needed to not feel so desperately alone.

Padraig watched as the Kennedys entered the bailey and how Cairren ran to greet them. The first man to greet her was old enough to be her father, and her playful kisses didn't bother Padraig. But he growled low in his throat as he watched the younger man tossing his wife in the air. He'd never heard her laugh, let alone giggle as she did with her family. It didn't matter that the man said he was her cousin; he was too close to her age to be touching her as he did. But the third man who greeted Cairren changed everything. Padraig couldn't hear what they said, and when the stranger cradled Cairren in his arms, Padraig saw red. He charged across the bailey as they pulled apart, but he watched as they held hands again, their fingers intertwined.

"Who're you?" Padraig demanded as he stopped just short of wrenching Cairren away from the man.

Cairren gasped as her eyes flared open, but the man still holding his wife's hands had the audacity to laugh.

"So much for Highland hospitality," the stranger jeered, and the Kennedy men chuckled. "Who're you?"

"I'm the man whose wife's hands you're holding," Padraig snapped. He watched a transformation come over all the Kennedys, and the man who'd been holding Cairren pressed her behind him, as if he were the one who would defend her. Cairren tried to step around the newcomer, but he kept her away from Padraig. Black dots danced at the corner of his eyes as his pulse thrummed at his temples.

"Padraig Munro, this is Alexander Armstrong. Alex, this is Padraig." Cairren tried to make the introductions and once again step around Alex, but he turned to her, lifted her off her feet and set her on the seat of the wagon.

"You keep touching my wife," Padraig snarled.

Alex's hands rested loosely on his belt, but there was no mistaking his meaning. They were there to grab his dirks if he needed them. "You're awfully possessive for a mon who's made it known across the Highlands that he doesn't want to be married. Or at least not to his wife." Alex kept his voice low, and it sounded like the deep rumble of a volcano about to explode. At Cairren's whimper, Alex canted his head to keep his eyes on Padraig while speaking to Cairren. "I'm sorry to be the one who tells you, Cairren. But you should ken that word has spread. It seems you've had a few market days since you married, and people are talking aboot how the recent Munro bride's husband is cuckolding her. I hadn't even known a man could do that, but I heard it too many times to doubt it."

"Ye piece of shite," Padraig hissed as he lunged at Alex. He would never be able to explain how Cairren made it from the wagon bench to standing in front of him before he swung, but she did.

"Stop, Padraig. Alex is one of my oldest and dearest friends. He fostered with us, and we thought maybe one day... Don't fight, please." Cairren stepped closer to Padraig than she had been in weeks. His scent filled her nostrils, and it tempted her to cling to him, but she wouldn't allow herself to become distracted. She looked into Padraig's deep brown eyes and whispered, "You've refused to choose. Don't make me have to."

Padraig's eyes flashed down to Cairren, then to Alex, who wrapped an arm around Cairren's middle and pulled her back against him and then behind him. It was the third time he'd made a move to protect Cairren when Padraig had made none.

"So he's the one you wanted to marry," Padraig accused as his eyes darted between the two.

"I did when I was younger. We thought we were in love for a while." Cairren shrugged as she looked up at Alex. "Then we grew up and realized that we were more like siblings. I told you, Alex fostered with us. I've known him since I was seven. For a while, it just seemed like Alex would be the logical person to marry. He's a neighbor, and we'd known each other since childhood. We even convinced ourselves we were in love."

"But then we realized that marrying someone because it was convenient or because it was just comfortable after so much time around each other wasn't what either of us wanted," Alex explained. "Rather than seeing Cairren as a wife, I went back to seeing her as a sister. It's a much better arrangement."

"Padraig?" Cairren's voice grew hesitant, and both Alex's and Padraig's eyes swung to her. "Where's your mother? I need to ask permission for chambers to be provided for Alex, as the heir to Clan Armstrong, and for Daniel and Jamie. Daniel is my father's cousin, and Jamie is his son."

"Ask permission?" Jamie pushed forward. "This is your home, and we're your family."

Cairren shook her head, praying Jamie wouldn't be as persistent as he usually was. She prayed he would understand the look she gave him, but when he opened his mouth again, she knew he hadn't.

"Why do you sound afraid to speak to your mother-by-marriage, Cairren?" Jamie demanded.

Cairren opened and closed her mouth thrice like a hooked fish. Padraig watched her struggle to decide what to tell the men without lying. He eased her into his embrace and guided her head against his chest before he whispered in her ear.

"Take your family inside for refreshment, and I'll make the arrangements with my mother." Cairren nodded and started to pull away, but Padraig's breath tickled against her once again. "Ren, their chambers will be on your floor. Do you want them to know you don't sleep on the same floor as the rest of the laird's family?"

"No more than I want them to know that the woman you're cuckolding me with sleeps on the same floor as you." Cairren felt Padraig go rigid, but she didn't care. He wasn't the one who was the laughing-stock of the Highlands.

"Then stay with me in my chamber while they're here."

Cairren's lips pinched together, and Padraig noticed the corner of her left eye twitched, but she nodded. She released him and turned to her family and friend. "Let's make our way into the Great Hall. The evening meal won't be long, but I can get you something to drink while we wait."

Padraig watched Cairren disappear into the circle of men who accompanied her into the keep, then turned to look for his mother. He didn't need to go anywhere because Mary and Myrna stood watching.

"How quaint," Mary snipped.

"Mother, I need three guest chambers prepared for the night."

"We don't have room," Mary's haughty tone grated on her son's nerves. He hadn't forgotten what he'd heard earlier. He counted his blessings that their guests arrived when they did. They would keep Cairren safe while he dealt with the inevitable emotional roller coaster Myrna would drag him on the next day.

"We do. Cairren will share my chamber while our guests are here."

"What?" Myrna screeched. "Tomorrow was to be our wedding night, and now you'll have that whore back in our bed."

Padraig's patience snapped. "That's it. I've warned ye aboot the things ye say. What if one of our guests overhears? Do ye want me called out? Do ye want the Munros *and* the Rosses to be shamed across the Highlands? Ye may nae value Cairren, but her clan certainly does. Who do you think people will believe? A man and a woman whining aboot nae getting their way, or a group of warriors defending their lady's honor. Ye return to Belnagown in the morning."

"But what aboot the feast and the festival?"

"Ye should have thought aboot that before ye opened yer gob. Go and pack. We ride out at dawn, Myrna. And dinna think to change ma mind. Tomorrow meant as much to me as it did ye. I'm as heartbroken aboot how our lives have turned out as ye are. But I married Cairren to help this clan. I willna have ye jeopardize that, or this will all have been for naught."

"But Padraig—" Myrna's voice faded as Padraig stormed into the Great Hall only to find Cairren seated at a table below the salt with the Kennedys surrounding her, and Alexander Armstrong sitting so close that she was practically on his lap.

CHAPTER NINETEEN

Padraig ground his teeth as he watched Cairren throughout the meal. She'd politely suggested to his mother that it would be easier if she sat with her clansmen, so Mary wouldn't have to rearrange the seating to accommodate anyone else. Myrna tried to take her usual seat beside him, but he hissed and jutted his chin toward the Kennedys. Myrna sulked, but for the first time, he didn't care. He moved down the table and chose the seat to the right of Wynda.

So much for nae rearranging our seats. Ma wife refuses to sit with me in public. The woman who should have some clue aboot discretion would like to flaunt our relationship under ma wife's kinsmen's nose. And I havenae the cods to do aught aboot any of this.

"You're a dog in a manger," Wynda whispered, and Padraig's head jerked up. She nodded as she glanced out at Cairren, who was laughing for the first time ever in the Munros' Great Hall. "You don't want her, but you don't want anyone else to have her too. Except here's the thing: she's not the one looking for other opportunities. She's accepted where her life has taken her."

"I'm taking Myrna home in the morning," Padraig grumbled. He was unprepared for Wynda to grow anxious and tremble. "What's wrong?"

"Naught. That just won't last for long," Wynda whispered.

"What do you mean? I'm taking her home for good."

"For one reason or another, she'll be back within a sennight. Mark my words."

Padraig kept quiet when Duncan looked at him over Wynda's head, then whispered in his wife's ear. Whatever Duncan said had Wynda nodding. When Duncan turned away, Wynda trembled more, but she kept her eyes down.

When the music began, Padraig rose to ask Cairren to dance, but as he walked past Myrna, she stood.

"It's our last night together, and there will be no tomorrow for us. Can we not dance?" Myrna looked up at Padraig under her lashes, but her coy look no longer affected him as it had for years. He was too annoyed with Myrna and everyone else to want to play flirtatious games.

"Maybe later," Padraig's noncommittal answer brought sparks to Myrna's eyes, but he walked past her before he had to listen to any more of her comments about Cairren. He approached Cairren as Alex stuck out his hand, and she nodded.

"Appears you're too late," Jamie grinned as he lifted his mug of ale. "Maybe you shouldn't have dallied so long."

Padraig glared at Jamie, but it only made his grin broader. Padraig watched as Cairren and Alex danced together. They moved gracefully, and it was clear they'd partnered countless times. A burning sensation took root in his chest above his heart. It tempted him to rub his fist over it to see if he could loosen the pain, but he refused to draw attention to himself. As he watched Cairren smiling at Alex and how he held Cairren in his arms, Padraig realized he was seeing things through Cairren's eyes every time she had to watch him with Myrna. The pain intensified and nearly stole his breath. He snagged a mug of ale as a serving woman walked by.

"Feeling wretched yet?" Daniel appeared at his elbow. "They make a striking couple. What they said earlier was true. They are more like brother and sister, but they would have been good together. Perhaps it would have grown into the love they thought they had, maybe not. But he would have taken wonderful care of her. Do you see how he's listening to her, but his eyes are constantly searching the crowd? It doesn't take longer than two heartbeats to understand your wife isn't safe in here. Why might that be?"

Padraig looked at Daniel and realized the man was waiting for an answer. The question hadn't been rhetorical. "Because they see her as being so different. They assume her difference makes her not good enough. Some even fear it, I suppose."

Daniel nodded. "And what have you done to ensure she's safe?"

"She doesn't like to leave her chamber, so it hasn't been an issue." Padraig shrugged.

"You may be the stupidest mon I have ever met. You cannot be that great an eejit. 'She doesn't like to leave her chamber.' She's scared to leave it, and you're too busy being some lovelorn suitor with a woman who will *never* be your wife." Daniel made a sound of disgust before turning away. Padraig noticed Jamie setting his mug down as he prepared to stand. The song was ending, and Padraig wasn't willing to let another man claim Cairren's attention.

Padraig elbowed his way through his clan members until he reached the corner where Alex and Cairren stood together. Alex's arm was wrapped around Cairren's waist as he whispered in her ear, and Padraig watched the cords in her elegant neck tauten as she lifted her chin to respond. She turned toward Alex, and Padraig could see how Alex's hand rested possessively on Cairren's hip. The man's hand was where Padraig believed only his should be. He wanted to find a cleaver and hack it off.

"You've had enough of my wife's time," Padraig announced, and Alex and Cairren both turned startled expressions at him.

"Alex was apologizing for an incident at court that involved some of his men," Cairren explained.

"What happened?" Padraig demanded. He stepped in front of Alex, his hand resting on the handle of his dirk. "Did one of his men proposition you?"

"Aye, they did," Alex responded before Cairren could. "And they've both received the lash for it. No man should speak to a woman the way they did Cairren, and especially not an Armstrong who kens what Cairren means to me."

"To you?" Padraig snapped. "And just what does she mean?"

Alex unwrapped his arm from Cairren's waist and once more moved to push her behind him, but Padraig snarled.

"You're acting as though I would hurt my own wife. She doesn't need protecting from me," Padraig hissed.

"Doesn't she? Because in the three hours I've been here and the one dance I've had with *your wife*, I've heard five threats to her life, three people call her a whore, and at least five call her a slut. I'd say she bluidy well needs protecting."

Padraig glanced down at Cairren, whose face had gone so pale he feared she would collapse. It was the same ghostly white as their wedding night when her knees gave out. Padraig pulled Cairren into his embrace, and she buried her face in his chest. Padraig whispered, "Did you hear this too, Ren?"

Cairren nodded her head. It had been horrible to hear what people said, and it reconfirmed why she never should have left her chamber. Padraig looked at Alex and then swept his eyes across the clan members gathered. They laughed and danced and drank as though nothing was out of the norm, yet Padraig wanted to rail against them, demand that they cease persecuting Cairren and just let her live her life. Yet what life was there? Even if she weren't in danger, she was still just as unwanted, if not more, than when she arrived.

"We're going abovestairs, Ren. I don't want you down here anymore." Padraig whispered.

"What are you going to do? Lock her in the chamber you're demanding you share with her after keeping her in a guest chamber since you married? Then mayhap you'll come down here and dance away another night with the woman you really treat as your wife?" Alex demanded. "Och aye, thought we wouldn't hear aboot that either, did you? Aboot how she doesn't even have a chamber on the family floor, but the other one does. That's no great secret. We kenned that before we even arrived."

"Enough," Padraig snapped. "If you want to discuss this with me, then do so as a mon tomorrow, away from Cairren. You're doing naught to make her feel better. While you're so busy rubbing it in my face, you seem to have overlooked that you're doing it to Cairren, too." Padraig guided Cairren away from the crowd and up the stairs. He didn't look at anyone but Cairren as they passed the dais. He kept his arms wrapped around her, but when she stumbled on the landing, he lifted her and carried her to his chamber.

Cairren kept her eyes shut as she entered Padraig's chamber. She didn't want to look at the bed that was both the location of her greatest humiliation and greatest pleasure. When Padraig set her on her feet, she turned toward the fire and pulled her Kennedy plaid snugger around her shoulders. Padraig watched, and it struck him that they'd been married nearly two moons, and Cairren still wore her clan's plaid when she should have begun wearing a Munro one on the day they married. He pulled a spare plaid from the foot of the bed before walking to Cairren.

"Ren, this will be far too large, but I can help you fold it into an arisaid." Padraig offered her his plaid, but she stared at it as though it were riddled with vermin. She shook her head. "You should've been wearing my plaid since the day we wed."

"There are always a lot of shoulds," Cairren whispered. "They'll just think I'm mocking them."

"Or they'll know you're a member of this clan."

"Go to bed, Padraig. Go back downstairs. Just go." Cairren turned her back and walked to the hearth.

"I'm not leaving here, Ren. And I want you to have this."

"Why? Why does it suddenly matter?"

Padraig ran his hand through his hair and decided honesty might work for once. "Because I want to see you in my plaid. Because I'm furious that I had to watch another mon hold you in his arms and watch you offer him smiles I've never seen before. I'm angry at my family and Myrna for how they've treated you. I'll kill whoever's been making threats against you, and I will find out who. I'm disgusted with myself for being such a cowardly bastard for not treating you properly. Because I just want one night for you where you aren't scared or abused. You deserve far more, but that's what I can guarantee you right now."

Cairren was about to take pity on Padraig when she recalled what she'd heard that morning as she slipped out of the keep. She'd spotted Myrna entering her chamber as her maid opened the door. In the silent keep, her voice carried. "I barely made it out in time. He wouldn't let go!" Cairren's eyes swept over Padraig's bed. The one where she'd spent one night, and Myrna seemed to have spent all the others. She walked to the door, but before she could pull it open, Padraig's hand covered hers on the handle. She ripped hers away and shoved his chest.

"Leave me alone," Cairren hissed. "Don't crowd me and don't trap me here."

"Trap you here? I'm trying to keep you safe, and we agreed you would stay here while your clansmen are visiting."

"I agreed because I didn't know what else to say at the moment, but now that I'm here, I can't stay. Besides, what will Myrna say if she shows up, and I'm here? Or does she know to expect you at her chamber?"

"What're you talking aboot? Do you mean so she kens when we'll leave in the morn?"

"No, I mean so you can bed her like you do every night."

"Bed her? Now you're just making shite up."

"I am not," Cairren seethed. "I'm not the liar of the two of us."

"Neither am I. I've been honest aboot the situation from the start."

"Selectively, at best. But you are lying now. I've heard her talking aboot it."

"You've been spying on Myrna?"

"That's rich. You assume I'm in the wrong. You're not denying that you're bedding her. You're accusing me of spying. Go to hell." Cairren reached for the door again, but Padraig stepped in front of her.

"How else would you know what she's been saying? Mayhap not spying, but eavesdropping."

Cairren held up her forefinger. "The first time I heard her, I was going downstairs while she and her maid were aboot to enter her chamber. They were discussing the miraculous things you do with your tongue. Apparently, it's so good, she'd steal the crown jewels for it. I wouldn't ken." She held up a second finger. "The next time, I was trying to hide from Duncan when I heard them in the passageway outside the storeroom. I learned she likes it when you take her against the wall." She held up a third finger. "And this very morn I heard aboot how she barely made it out of your chamber in time. You couldn't keep your bluidy hands off her. She's expecting you tonight, so you should go and avoid being late." Cairren stepped back and crossed her arms, her toes tapping, and her eyebrow cocked. She appeared bored as she waited for Padraig to move.

"You're lying, and it's ugly," Padraig accused.

"Oh, because it's not possible that you'd forsake your vows so you can rut with your pretty and perfect lady."

"It's not possible because I haven't. Other than that kiss you saw in the garden, I haven't touched her. Or at least, there have been no other intimacies."

"Then how do you explain what I heard?"

"You must be mistaken."

"It's always so much easier to believe I'm wrong than to accept that she's not perfect. I hate you." Cairren snapped her mouth shut, not having intended to hurl such a venomous phrase, but in that moment, she meant it with her whole heart.

Padraig straightened and looked down at Cairren. Her words stung, and he wanted to lash out, but he forced himself to stop and think for once before he acted. Cairren wasn't a liar, and it was easier to believe she was wrong than try to wrap his mind around what she told him. It was easier to paint her as the villain and keep his pristine image of Myrna intact. "Perhaps she knew you were there each time and was trying to hurt you."

"And that makes it all right? That you're not actually bedding her. She just wants to cause me pain." Cairren shook her head.

"Mayhap. It's not right, and I'm not excusing it, but I know I have slept alone every night that I haven't been with you since you arrived. I have never coupled with Myrna. I've never done more than kiss her."

Cairren's lips drew in tight as she nodded her head. "No wonder you want to couple with me. You don't dare defile her, but you're frustrated that you can only kiss her. Why not use your wife to slake your lust? I'm telling you now, like I told you the night you visited my chamber before my parents left. Leave me alone, or I will scream this keep down. Move."

"And where will you go?" Padraig demanded. "To Alex?"

"Yes!" Cairren hurled at him. She didn't know where she intended to go, but she wanted to hurt Padraig.

"Like hell you are, Ren. You're my wife." Padraig pulled her against him and fisted her hair in his hand, but he would never force her. He waited for her to pull away, to push him away, but her gray eyes with the tinge of green eyes filled with tears as she nodded. He lowered his mouth to hers, careful to go slowly and not frighten her. He would only do what she wanted. Their lips brushed together, and a tingle shot through Cairren's body. She needed to be closer to Padraig, not just skin to skin. She needed to feel safe with him again, like she had for the brief time he sneaked to her chamber each night. The kiss was tender as Padraig eased his tongue into her mouth. He refused to rush, wanting to draw out each moment, making up for the hurtful things said that night. "Ren, will you share my bed with me tonight?"

Cairren looked at the massive bed and remembered how Padraig had been so caring and encouraging their first night together. He'd tended to her wants and her needs, and she'd trusted him. Only to have it all come crashing down. She closed her eyes as tears leaked from below her lids. Her body and her mind were at war. She hungered for the feel of him inside her, but her memory warned her she had no one to blame but herself for the inevitable misery that would come in the morning. She looked at the bed again as she struggled not to cry.

"Cairren, you're the only woman who has ever shared that bed with me." Cairren look up at him, confused and disbelieving. "I've never had a mistress, only women I've visited in the village. I swear to you that I've never coupled with her. You're the only one who's been in my bed besides me."

"I—I—I want to believe you. I choose to believe you; otherwise, I'm the greatest fool for agreeing to staying here tonight."

"You'll stay?" Padraig beamed when Cairren nodded. "I can sleep by the hearth, if you'd rather." Padraig didn't want to, but he would do anything to bring Cairren's smile back. He wanted the one he'd seen directed at Alex and the Kennedys to be the one directed at him.

"I don't want to sleep on the floor." At Padraig's puzzled look, her gazed softened. "That's where I'd end up because I want to spend the night beside you."

They undressed in silence before the fire. Padraig watched the light flicker off of Cairren's bronze skin, and he traced the shadows as they danced across her breasts. He kissed along her neck until he reached the spot behind her ear where he nuzzled and licked. His hand slid between them, and he groaned when he discovered the moisture pooling between her thighs. He flicked his fingers into her entrance, and Cairren moaned as she pressed her hips forward. Padraig sank to his knees, kissing the inside of her thigh as he nudged them apart. A brief thought tapped at his brain as he recalled Cairren saying Myrna had enjoyed being pleasured by his tongue. He knew that wasn't true, but he intended on being sure Cairren learned what he wanted his tongue to do to her. He lapped at her seam and chuckled when she gasped and grabbed a fistful of his hair. He glanced up, and his wolfish grin made Cairren's lips part as she panted. She released his hair and watched as he pressed his mouth to her mons. It surprised him that she'd kept her mound smooth despite their unpredictable relationship. For a moment he wondered if she was doing it for someone else's benefit.

"I just like it better. It's more comfortable," Cairren whispered, reading his mind. "You're the only mon who knows."

Padraig teased her body until she begged for him to bring her to release. She clutched his shoulders to keep her balance as she grew lightheaded from the sensations coursing through her. While tasting her release tempted him, he wanted to be buried inside Cairren for each of the climaxes he intended to bring her. He eased her down, so she straddled his kneeling legs. Guiding her hips, the tip of his cock slid along her seam, and by silent mutual agreement, he pulled her onto his cock as she dropped her weight onto his lap. They kissed as their bodies moved together, and just as every time in the past, Padraig marveled at how being joined with Cairren surpassed any other experience in his life.

The world fell away until it was just the two of them, locked in the throes of passion until Cairren's strangled cry signaled a release that left her breathless. Padraig thrust over and over as she encouraged him to stop holding back. Their movements became frenzied as they each sought to bring the other to climax. When Padraig couldn't withstand the need any longer, he ground Cairren against his rod.

"You are mine, Cairren. I won't let you go. I know what I'm saying, and I mean it." Padraig promised as his seed filled her core. Cairren refused to read more into it, and she didn't want to hear anything that would later crush her. She pressed her mouth to his until their tremors subsided, and Padraig carried Cairren to his bed. They slept little that night as their need was insatiable, and neither was inclined to deny the other.

CHAPTER TWENTY

Cairren came awake to the feeling of Padraig feathering his fingers over her chest. She grumbled and shook her head as she burrowed closer to him. His laughter rumbled deep in his chest.

"I know, little one. I'm tired too. I didn't want you to wake alone and think I'd abandoned you," Padraig whispered. Cairren's eyes fluttered open. "Ren, I don't want to leave this bed or leave you, but there's only one thing I want more than that. I want Myrna to go home. I have to ride out and take her to Balnagown. I plan to return before the evening meal, but it's likely I'll be forced to spend the night while I settle things with her family. They're already angry that the wedding was canceled. That I'm returning her home on the day we were to wed will only make matters worse, but she cannot remain here."

Cairren nodded but remained silent. The return to reality was jarring and disappointing. She looked around the chamber until she found her clothes from the night before. She moved to roll away, but Padraig captured her hand and brought it to his lips.

"Ren, do you have any idea what the thought of returning here and finding you in this bed does to me?" Padraig guided her hand down to his thick rod. "I'm not leaving until I'm certain you understand I'm returning here to you. You have family visiting, so I know you won't stay locked away all day, but I confess the thought of you being in my bed all day, naked as you are now, will keep me hard as a pike. Do you know how uncomfortable that will be on a bluidy horse?"

Cairren giggled as she pulled Padraig over her. "Then let me ease some of that discomfort."

Padraig slid into Cairren and sighed. He rocked his hips over and over until Cairren begged for more. He happily obliged and thrust with as much force as he dared. Cairren never ceased to amaze him with how her body welcomed him despite their difference in size. Each time he feared being too rough, Cairren demanded more. He happily gave it to her until they were both panting and sweating.

"You shall keep everyone waiting," Cairren reminded Padraig. He grumbled, but rose to pull on a fresh leine. Cairren rested on her elbows as she watched the muscles ripple across Padraig's back and chest as he moved. When he moved to pin his brooch to his shoulder, she kneeled at the end of the bed and held out her hand. As Cairren fastened the extra length of plaid, they froze and gazed at one another. It was the most wifely thing Cairren had ever done, a different type of intimacy than any they'd shared. Padraig wrapped his arm around her trim body and pulled her close for a kiss. She cupped his jaw in her hands as his free hand cupped hers. Neither was prepared for the door to burst open or for the scream that followed.

Padraig spun around, shielding Cairren's naked body from the intruder as she scrambled to pull the sheet around her. She pulled the bedcovers to her chin and around body, holding them closed against her back. She peered around Padraig's shoulder and found a snarling Myrna in the doorway. She vibrated from rage as she took in the scene of Padraig and Cairren together.

"Why is she in my bed again?" Myrna demanded.

"It's never been your bed, Myrna. And Cairren is my wife. She's where she belongs."

"What?" Myrna screeched as she stormed into the chamber. "It's supposed to be our wedding day, and yet I come to share horrible news, needing your comfort, only to find you here with this—this mongrel."

"Get out, Myrna, before I throttle you," Padraig warned. "You will not speak to or aboot Cairren like this anymore. Wait for me in the bailey and be ready to ride out in five minutes."

"We can't," Myrna crowed. She sounded a little too self-satisfied for Cairren's comfort.

"And why not? Myrna, I have no patience for you already."

"That's because you don't love me anymore," she wailed. Padraig was stuck once again. Most inconveniently backed into a corner. He wasn't about to confess his love for Myrna while his naked wife kneeled in the bed they'd just shared. But neither did he want to ignore Myrna and not reassure her.

"It's fine," Cairren muttered. "Tell her."

Padraig turned to look at Cairren, and her lack of surprise or hurt made his stomach churn. She was not only prepared for him to choose Myrna in front of her, she expected it. *Of course, she is. When havenae I?*

"Myrna, wait for me, belowstairs. This is neither

the time nor the place for this discussion."

"You're kicking me out?" Myrna pointed at Cairren. "Aren't you done with her yet? I've ignored the fact that you spent the night fornicating in here with her, but now you expect me to wait even longer. No."

Cairren sighed. She was fed up of being in the middle, once again blamed for Padraig's inability to decide. She climbed off the bed and walked across the chamber naked until she reached her clothes. She listened to Myrna hiss and spit, lobbing insults about her skin color. She acted as though she heard nothing. She pulled her chemise on, then her kirtle, but she didn't bother lacing it. She collected her shoes and stockings then looked at Padraig, who she'd felt watching her since she left the bed. When she made to walk past him, his hand shot out and took hers. He gave it a squeeze before turning his attention to Myrna.

"What is this news you claim is so horrible that you burst into my chamber unannounced?"

"It's supposed to be our—" Myrna's mouth drew into a tight pucker when Padraig cursed. "There's a sickness going through my clan. My parents say it's not safe for me to return."

Padraig felt the anger seething out of Cairren, but she didn't move. He looked down, and her face was the image of sympathy and concern, but he could feel the barely contained rage. He darted his eyes to Myrna without moving his head, and he caught the moment of gloating before Myrna turned baleful eyes at him. She rushed forward and pressed herself against Padraig.

"It's so awful, Padraig. I'm so worried for my family, but my parents insist I must stay away."

Padraig didn't move. He did nothing to comfort

Myrna, even though his arms ached to wrap around her and sooth her worry. He'd seen the scorn in her eyes only a moment ago, but she sounded and felt like the Myrna he'd loved for so long. He looked at Cairren when she released his hand, but she wouldn't look at him. He called out, "Ren," as she walked through the door. But rather than look back, she slammed it shut.

"Finally. Now you can stop pretending and hold me the way you want to," Myrna murmured as she stroked her hand over his chest. He looked down at her, but it was like looking at a stranger. He realized he expected to see Cairren there, not another woman. Not even Myrna. It didn't feel right, and something about the timing of a sickness was so calculatingly suspicious that he wanted to ask if she believed he was stupid or just gullible. He settled for another question.

"When did my mother suggest this as a solution to you leaving?"

"I don't understand." Myrna's tone and expression were so confused and innocent that Padraig wondered if he'd jumped to conclusions too soon. But before either could say more, a blood-curdling scream rent the air. Padraig knew it was Cairren before he was through the door. He charged down the passageway as he watched Duncan pulling Cairren toward his chamber. She was struggling, and despite Duncan being smaller in stature than Padraig, he was still far too large for Cairren to fight against.

"Let go," Padraig bellowed.

"Come now, little brother. You were always better at sharing than I was," Duncan jeered.

"Let go of my wife, Duncan, or I will rip you apart."

"The slut offered herself to me, walking around with her gown half hanging off her."

Padraig knew Cairren hadn't laced the kirtle, but it had more than covered her. When he looked at her, there was a jagged tear at the shoulder seam and the sleeve dangled. The gown was pulled down low over Cairren's breasts, but her chemise covered her skin.

"I will kill you." Padraig charged at his brother, knowing the man would defend himself first before worrying about Cairren. Duncan released her as he ran into his chamber and slammed the door shut. Padraig thrust his foot into the door, and the wood splintered from his kick. It swung open, and Padraig cornered Duncan. His fist lashed out, creating a loud crack as Duncan's jaw broke. Padraig grabbed Duncan around the throat and drove him backwards until his head made a sickening thud as it struck the wall. He drove his fist into his brother's eye and then under his chin.

Padraig was beyond the point of any rational thought. He would never forget the sound of Cairren's scream or the sight of her looking for him as Duncan dragged her toward his chamber. He'd never liked his brother, but he discovered in that moment that he held no brotherly love for the man either. Possibly committing fratricide didn't deter him from beating Duncan. He reached for his dirk and pulled the blade free, but before the blade entered Duncan's belly, two small hands tugged on his arm.

"Stop, Padraig. You can't kill him," Cairren begged. "He's your brother."

"And you're my wife."

"What is going on here?" Micheil demanded as he and Mary entered the chamber, a sobbing Myrna leaning against Mary.

"It's her fault," Myrna pointed at Cairren. "She isn't content with just stealing Padraig from me. Now she'd take Duncan from Wynda. She's turning brother against brother." Myrna sobbed as her hand trembled.

"A woman interested in a dalliance doesn't scream like she'd aboot to be murdered," Alex Armstrong said from the doorway. "I've known Cairren nearly my entire life, and I've heard her scream like that only twice before. Once when a wolf attacked us as children, and once when her sister fell into a ravine. That was fear and naught else you heard."

"Take her back to my chamber, Alex, and stay with her," Padraig spoke as he looked at Cairren. She was still gripping his arm, her eyes round with terror. He understood she no longer feared for herself so much as what he would do to Duncan. "I know what I saw with my own eyes, and I will not let my brother abuse my wife."

"Padraig," Cairren whispered. "Look at him. You've broken his jaw on both sides, and you're having to hold him up. He's already passed out. Let him go. Please."

Padraig's eyes lingered on Cairren before he looked at his brother. He sheathed his dirk and let Duncan go, who slid down the wall, still unconscious.

"Go to our chamber and wait for me there, Ren," Padraig whispered. Neither noticed he'd called it their chamber, but others did.

"'Our chamber,'" Micheil hooted. "Finally tired of creeping around at night?"

Myrna looked back and forth as she understood Micheil's meaning. "You've been with her other nights?"

Padraig ignored Micheil and Myrna and nodded

to Alex. Cairren shook her head and crossed her arms.

"Angry at him or not, disgusted with him or not, Duncan needs his jaw set. Padraig and Alex, get him on the bed. You have no healer nor midwife, so unless you ken someone other than me who can set bones, I'm the best chance he has of ever chewing again."

"Don't touch my son!" Mary flew at Cairren, but Padraig stepped between them.

"Touch my wife, and she and I leave," Padraig glared at his mother. "She's right. She can set his jaw, and there are few others who would do as fine a job. Duncan brought this upon himself, but even though he attacked her, she's still willing to help him. Duncan's alive because Cairren stopped me from gutting him. She's a better person than any of us. Alex, give me a hand."

Cairren drew in a deep breath before turning to Mary. She expected the woman to insult her before doing as she asked, but she hoped her mother-by-marriage would see some reason. "Lady Mary, I need whisky and bandages before I can start. Duncan will be in dreadful pain when he wakes, and I don't want that to be in the middle of setting his jaw. Then I need to immobilize it to keep the bones aligned. Please." Cairren stood with her hands clasped before her, her tone as deferential as she could muster.

"Why should I do aught for you?" Mary snapped.

"Because you're really doing this for Duncan," Cairren reminded her.

Mary glared for a moment, then turned away in a swish of skirts. Wynda eased into the chamber and came to stand beside Cairren.

"Are you well? I heard the commotion, but I didn't think squeezing another body in here would do any good." Wynda asked as she took in Cairren's torn gown and the bruise developing on Cairren's cheek that Cairren was trying to hide from Padraig. "I'm so sorry, Cairren."

"I'm well, and don't you dare apologize for him. You might feel bad for me, but don't you for a moment feel guilty on his behalf." Cairren and Wynda embraced as they silently consoled one another, both Duncan's victims.

When Mary returned with the supplies, Cairren had Padraig and Alex prop Duncan up while she poured just enough whisky down his throat to deepen his breathing without drowning him. Mary and Myrna squawked when Cairren climbed onto the bed and straddled Duncan's chest, but Cairren snapped at them, saying they were welcome to the task if they could do it better. Both women backed down and let Cairren work on Duncan's jaw. Once she aligned it on both sides, Cairren wound bandages to keep Duncan from moving his jaw or bumping it in his sleep. Wynda offered to tend to Duncan once Cairren finished, but it was Myrna's lingering look at Duncan that raised Cairren's suspicions. Cairren opted to keep her observations to herself even when Padraig took her back to his chamber and helped her with a bath. He became irate all over again when he noticed the bruise on her cheek and fingerprints on her breast, but she pleaded that all she wanted was for him to stay with her until she fell asleep. Padraig remained with Cairren all day despite Myrna appearing twice to beg him to walk with her. He was unprepared for how little he wanted to see Myrna that day. His only priority was remaining with Cairren until she woke. He could tell she wasn't excited about attending the Samhain bonfires, but Padraig cajoled her and promised never to leave her side.

CHAPTER TWENTY-ONE

Cairren watched the crowd gathered around the bonfires as revelers sang and danced to welcome the harvest season. She remained sheltered by Padraig, Alex, and the Kennedys, and she felt some semblance of normalcy. Padraig fetched a mug of whisky for her and even went so far as to silently sip from it before handing it to her. Her expression softened as she thanked him, appreciative for how the drink warmed her insides. She'd always loved the festivities of Samhain, and the music helped her relax. She hadn't seen hide nor hair of Myrna or Mary, but Micheil wandered through his clansmen; however, he kept his distance from her circle. She wished to dance, but after her two disastrous attempts in the Great Hall, one resulting in a near-elbow to the face and the other listening to threats and insults, she opted to keep her interest to herself.

"Jamie, that lass keeps staring in your direction," Daniel elbowed his son as he pointed to a youthful woman who kept shooting Jamie coy smiles. With auburn hair, blue eyes, and deep dimples, Jamie was a favorite among women for his easy good nature and humor, but he had a sweetheart at home.

"Da, even if Keyla never learned of it, I have no interest in anyone else."

"But the lass looks positively lonely," Daniel continued to tease.

"Then you go dance with her," Jamie challenged.

"And have your mother skelp me alive? Nay thank you." Daniel shook his head with a grin.

Padraig listened to the easy banter between father and son and wished he had such a relationship with his own, but it had been contentious for as long as he could remember, Micheil often pitting brother against brother. While Padraig was the more responsible of the two and the better fighter, Duncan was the favored firstborn and shared a similar personality with Micheil.

"Alex, she's looking at you just as much as Jamie. Why don't you talk to her?" Cairren suggested.

"I think I shall accept that suggestion." Alex grinned and sauntered away. His ebony hair and green eyes were a stark contrast to Jamie's, but the men had become easy friends when Alex arrived to foster. Before Jamie began courting Keyla Kennedy, one of Cairren and Jamie's clanswomen, the two men had been known for the carousing. Cairren imagined Alex continued their legacy even though he'd returned to Clan Armstrong land. She'd once thought him the most handsome man she'd ever seen. Her gaze shifted to Padraig and found him watching her. Without a doubt, Padraig was the most handsome and seductive man Cairren knew. His heated gaze warmed her even more than the whisky.

"How are you, little one?" Padraig murmured near her ear. His breath made her shiver, and while it surprised her to find she was enjoying herself, her body ached to return to the privacy of Padraig's chamber.

"I'm having more fun than I thought I would," Cairren stretched to whisper in his ear.

"As am I, but I can think of something that I would enjoy more than a noisy crowd."

"Oh?" Cairren offered the most alluring expression she could manage, and from the way Padraig's body instinctually moved toward hers, she believed she'd succeeded.

"We've been and we've seen. I think it's time we call it a night, Ren." Padraig's hand that rested on her waist drifted to her bottom and squeezed. His attention had been fixated on Cairren since they left the keep. At first, it had been for her safety, but now it was purely desire. He watched as she swayed to the music and laughed with her friends. They'd exchanged several heated glances, and Padraig wanted nothing more than to strip her bare and feast on the parts of her that were his to admire alone.

"I—" Something darted past Cairren's periphery, and she glanced toward it. Her heart catapulted into her stomach. She pushed past Padraig as she called back. "Jamie, my salve and linens. My chest. Now!"

Cairren watched in horror as a small child toddled too close to the fire. Not an experienced walker, the little girl looked more like a drunkard as she staggered too close to the flames. Cairren's eyes darted about, looking for someone chasing after the child, but no one but she seemed to notice.

"No!" she screamed. "Stop!" When the toddler kept moving toward the flames, she tried Gaelic instead. "*Stad!*"

She ran to the toddler, but she couldn't reach her before she pitched forward. She scooped the lass into her arms and twisted away from the flames, but not before the inferno scalded the child's hands. The scream that the little girl let loose traveled through the crowd, and people turned to look.

A woman pushed through the crowd until she stumbled to a stop before Cairren. "Give me ma bairn, ye witch. Ye tried to kill her. Ye'd burn her to death." The woman yanked the child from Cairren, only making the screams worse.

"Mind her hands," Cairren warned. "They need tending immediately."

"Bitch," the woman hissed.

"Enough, Meg. Lady Cairren just saved Katie's life. Say another word, and I will put you before the lash," Padraig warned.

"Padraig, nay. She's frightened for her child," Cairren argued.

"Then she should have been minding her."

Cairren shook her head. "Accidents happen. But that's neither here nor there. She needs tending. Look. Jamie's coming with my salve." Cairren turned toward the sobbing mother. "Please, will you let me tend to your daughter's hands? I fear that without the salve her hands won't heal properly. The scaring might make them useless."

"Ye're nae touching ma daughter, ye heathen. We dinna want yer kind here."

Padraig opened his mouth, but Cairren's hand on his arm stayed him.

"That's fine. I know that already. But you'd really maim your daughter to prove your hatred?"

The woman looked at her inconsolable child in her arms as she tried to rock her, then at Cairren. She shook her head just as Jamie arrived with a jar and strips of linen. Cairren held out her hands for the child, and the woman slowly relented. Cairren wanted to scream for her to hurry, that she was wasting time that was keeping her child in pain, but she kept silent, unwilling to risk the woman refusing her. As she took the little girl in her arms, she crooned soft sounds until the teary eyes looked at her.

Switching to Gaelic, she said, "I'm Ren. I have a little sister I call Caity. That's my very most favorite name. Just like yours. I'm going to help you, lass, but it will hurt. I'm so sorry, but I must make it a wee worse before I can make it better." She looked at the mother and continued. "I have to move closer to the fire, so I can see. The heat will make it hurt more, but I have no choice."

Padraig and the Kennedys moved with Cairren, keeping a circle around her. She sat on an upended stump and pried the first tiny fist open. She wanted to cry as she examined the damage. The palm was already raw blisters with open skin. The burn was worse than she expected. She held a hand out without turning away, and Jamie handed her the open jar. She settled it between her knees and scooped a gob with her forefinger and put it to her tongue. She couldn't keep from shivering at the bitter taste, but she looked once more at Meg. "Tastes disgusting, but it's not poisonous. If she should ever get some in her mouth, she won't get sick." Cairren knew all toddlers put their hands in their mouth, so her explanation was reasonable, but she wanted people to see she would taste her own medicine.

As she scooped out more salve, she hummed to Katie, using her lap to rock her as she continued to sob but no longer scream. Her clear alto quietened the last of the murmurs in the crowd as she slathered the ointment on the little girl's hands.

> *Ho-ro-ro, hi-ri-ri*
> *Cadal gu madainn*
> *O, hush dhuit, mo phàisde,*
> *Bha do dhùdach na ridire,*
> *Do mhàthair a bhean,*
> *An dà chuid brèagha agus soilleir;*
> *A 'choille agus na glinn,*
> *Bho na tùir a chì sinn,*
> *Buinidh iad uile,*
> *Leanabh a ghràidh, dhuit.*
> *O, hush dhuit, mo phàisde,*
> *Bha do dhùdach na ridire,*
> *O, hush dhuit, mo phàisde,*
> *Mar sin bonnie agus soilleir.*

Cairren was certain the Munros recognized the lullaby that Blair Sutherland taught her in the hopes that one day Cairren would sing it to her own children.

> Ho-ro-ro, hi-ri-ri
> Sleep until dawn
> Oh, hush thee, my baby,
> Thy sire was a knight,
> Thy mother a lady,
> Both lovely and bright;
> The woods and the glens,
> From the towers which we see,
> They all are belonging,
> Dear baby, to thee.
> Oh, hush thee, my baby,
> Thy sire was a knight,
> Oh, hush thee, my baby,

So bonnie and bright.

She gingerly wound the linen strips, covering the tiny hands and wrists. By the time she'd finished, Katie had fallen asleep, soothed by Cairren's voice and exhausted from her ordeal. She brushed hair back from her forehead and gave her one long last look before handing her to Meg. She'd fought the temptation to kiss the lass on the forehead, fearing it would be too much for the Munros. She stood and handed the jar to the woman, then wiped the last of the salve onto a line square.

"You need to apply this every few hours. They will look much worse before they look better. Would you permit me to visit and examine them? They will need the dead skin cleaning away. It's painful to experience and painful to watch. I'd spare you that."

"Why?"

"Why is it painful?" Cairren guessed that wasn't the woman's question, but she would be sure before she volunteered any answers.

"Why would ye help her?"

"She's not even two summers, is she?" Cairren asked. Meg shook her head. "Because I would see her grow up to be a healthy and happy lass, then a bonny young woman. If I have the knowledge and the tools to help, why would I not? She's a wean. She doesn't ken yet why people are different, what makes them good or bad. She only kens kindness, and that's what she needs right now."

Meg stood looking at her daughter who slept in her arms, then nodded. "Will ye come in the morn? Can I ask for ye if I need ye?"

"Of course. Day or night." Cairren smiled as she brushed out her skirts. She turned toward Padraig, who took her hand. The festivities had lost its merriment, and people drifted home. Halfway back to the keep, Padraig stopped and encircled Cairren's waist before kissing her. It was languid and soft as Padraig poured in feelings he didn't understand and was unable to articulate. He needed Cairren to know that he was proud of her, impressed by her knowledge and her character, and that he appreciated what she'd done. But there was more. Something inside of him had shifted while he watched her tend to the little girl. The gentle strength she'd shown, her dignified command of the situation, her empathy to both mother and child was more than he'd ever seen before. He'd imagined Cairren holding their own bairn one day, and he realized as he kissed her, the child had looked like Cairren, not him. The idea made him want to hurry them to their bed rather than run for the hills. And as the kiss drew on, he knew that his chamber and his bed were now their chamber and their bed. He didn't want her to return to the guest bedchamber.

"Stay with me," Padraig murmured against her lips. When she opened her mouth, he dropped a quick kiss to silence her. "I mean in our chamber every night."

Cairren pulled away, and a hard set entered her eyes. Padraig realized that she hadn't understood what he'd tried to convey. She believed he spoke solely from lust. He was sure he'd felt something different from her kiss too, but she was guarded against him disappointing her again. She was prepared to defend herself rather than accept any more failed attempts.

"Ren, I'm not asking just so it's convenient for me to bed you. I'm asking because I want my wife by my side. I want to fall asleep with you in my arms and wake to you there, too."

Tears welled in her eyes as she shook her head. "You're a fickle mon, Padraig. You say that now, the night of what should have been your wedding to another woman. I won't be able to bear the pain when you change your mind again and tell me to leave." Cairren swiped away the tears that fell, glancing around to ensure no one saw her. "Let's get through the next few nights while my clansmen are here."

They walked back to the keep in silence, not saying a word as they undressed. Cairren climbed into bed, still wearing her chemise, but she felt Padraig's arm wrap around her waist as his body slid close to her just as she fell asleep.

CHAPTER TWENTY-TWO

For the next sennight, Padraig lived in a land of limbo. He made progress with his guests each day, training with them each morning and into the early afternoon. They gained a mutual respect between Highlander and Lowlanders. He was sore but satisfied each day as he entered the Great Hall for the evening meal. He avoided Myrna despite her repeated attempts to catch him alone. His heart ached to see the hurt and confusion in her eyes, but he'd spent a great deal of time thinking about the woman he'd seen since Cairren arrived. He didn't want to believe that who he'd witnessed over the past two moons had lurked within Myrna all along. He tried to convince himself that the situation proved too much for her and made her react poorly. But as he watched her silent loathing toward Cairren and continued to hear her agree with his mother's nasty comments, he suspected the hatefulness had always been there. She'd just never had a reason to show it before. He kept his distance, and it allowed him to preserve the image he clung to.

Cairren shared his chamber, and they coupled throughout the night, neither able to deny themselves or the other. But he didn't know where she disappeared to during the day while he and her clansmen were in the lists. Wynda spent her days tending to Duncan, so he knew Cairren wasn't with her. She would smile and say she found things to do, but she never elaborated. The only thing he was certain of was that she worked on a tapestry at her loom, which had been set up in near the window in his chamber. She continued to refer to the room as his, so he didn't press the matter. But he couldn't account for the other hours of the day until she went for walks or rides with Daniel, Alex, and Jamie. As Padraig got to know the men better, his jealousy abated. He understood that Alex and Jamie saw Cairren as their sister, and she was more of a daughter to Daniel.

Despite his offers, Cairren continued to take her meals at the lower table, sitting between Alex and Jamie and across from Daniel. It was clear they guarded her, and guilt ate at him that there was a need and that they were fulfilling what should have been his role. But it was the most lighthearted Padraig had seen Cairren since they met, and so he wouldn't change anything for that.

Padraig made his way through the village, having checked on a croft that suffered roof damage during the last storm. He'd spent the morning away from the lists, making rounds that Duncan couldn't while he convalesced from the injuries Padraig gave him. He was near the outskirts of the village when he spotted Cairren leaving Meg's croft. The women stood chatting in the doorway, and it shocked Padraig to see Meg offer Cairren a hug. He hung back and watched as Cairren kissed Katie's forehead and turned toward the keep. He'd seen she was tempted to offer that affection the night Katie was hurt, but he knew she hadn't dared. She looked back once, and Meg and Katie waved, her little hand still bandaged. When Cairren was out of sight, he went to Meg's croft and knocked.

"Padraig, ye just missed yer wife," Meg smiled as she shifted Katie to the other hip. He could hear her other children playing behind her.

"I ken. I saw her leaving. How're things?"

Meg grinned. "Ye want to ken if I've tried to gut her. Nay, I havenae. She's been an angel to Katie and the other weans. I couldnae do what she does. I have to take maself out when she tends to Katie's hands. I canna manage her cries. I can tell it hurts her heart, but she's braver than me. She's taught the older ones how to keep Katie from putting her hands in her mouth and how to change her bandages. Do ye ken, she's even taught them to sing and count in French? Ma weans speaking French!"

Padraig considered how to phrase his question. "Do you feel comfortable with her in your home?"

Meg grew serious and raised her chin. "Do ye mean, do I fear she'll dirty ma home and ma children? Do I still fear she's a witch? Nay, I dinna fear aught when Lady Cairren visits. She's teaching me to sweeten drinks to hide the taste of the medicinals I give Katie, and she's offered me medicinals for the other weans who canna seem to stop their dribbly noses. They taste horrid without the disguise. Now the weans drink it, and I can see them improving. She's an angel, I tell ye."

"Do the others treat you poorly for allowing Lady Cairren into your home?"

"The first few days, but I think they rather like

listening her to sing to the weans. Other children have asked to come and listen. She never turns them down but always asks permission from me or their mams."

"She asks permission?"

"She says they arenae her weans to do as she pleases." Meg bit her lip. When Padraig nodded, she invited him inside and shut the door before she continued. "I've apologized several times for the unkind things I said to her and aboot her behind her back. She offers a smile and tells me to think naught of it. The kinder and more forgiving she is, the worse I feel. I tried to confess to Father Mitchell, but he said her kind isnae the type of neighbor God intends us to love. That doesnae sit well with me. Padraig, I fear he says that to many people. He's spreading poison and too many people are still believing him. While her clansmen are here, people are on their best behavior, but I'm scared of what will happen when they leave."

"What have you heard people saying?" Padraig forced his tone to remain relaxed and to keep from fisting his hands when what he wanted was to find Father Mitchell and shake him.

"They're believing him that she's bewitched ye with her bed sport. He says that's the only way ye could have turned away from a woman as pure as Lady Myrna. He says she has the devil in her, and that she canna be a real Christian since her mam grew up with a heretic father. That the heresy is in her blood. I dinna ken how that can be, but people believe him because he reminds them that he's God's messenger on Earth."

"Those are dangerous ideas he's spreading, and I won't stand for them. Thank you for telling me, Meg."

"But Padraig, that's nae all. Lady Mary and Lady

Myrna are agreeing with him as though his was the Gospel."

"My mother and Lady Myrna? They're spreading rumors?"

"I'm sorry to be telling ye this, and I ken I'm speaking out of turn against ma clan's lady, but Lady Cairren doesnae deserve this. I ken that now. I just wish I had sennights ago. I've tried to break people's belief of the rumors by sharing what she's done, but a few people have suggested she's bewitched me too. I canna risk ma weans with people saying that."

"I understand, Meg. You've done the right thing telling me. Thank you." Padraig left and made his way back to the keep, mulling over what Meg told him. Nothing contradicted what he knew about each of the people he heard about. He believed Father Mitchell, his mother, and Myrna were continuing their smear campaign, and he believed Cairren was everything Meg described. He just didn't know what to do to stop them when the hatred outnumbered the good.

Cairren enjoyed the only pleasant week she'd had since she arrived. She wove and visited Meg in the mornings, then she spent the afternoon with her kinsmen and Alex. Their presence eased her fears when she was in the Great Hall, and it took her mind off the loneliness she'd experienced and that inevitably awaited her when they departed. Padraig was attentive in and out of their bedchamber, and she even allowed herself to consider the chamber theirs despite only referring to it as his. It surprised her that Padraig kept away from Myrna. The woman's glares intensified, as did her pouts when Padraig was near, so Cairren was confident that Padraig was avoiding Myrna. She just was unconvinced it would last. She was uninterested in playing Myrna's game of manipulation. If Padraig cared for her, it would be because he came to that conclusion on his own. Cairren wouldn't pretend to be someone she wasn't. She left that to Myrna. With guardsmen, albeit Kennedys, finally willing to escort her, she could explore further afield. She paid close attention to where they walked and rode, noting where she believed she could venture alone.

There was only one thing casting a shadow on Cairren's temporary happiness. She was worried about Wynda. She wasn't taking her meals in the Great Hall anymore, claiming that she was busy tending Duncan or too tired and wanted to retire. Cairren suspected the abuse had increased, and Wynda was hiding, so no one saw the aftermath. She'd caught a head cold that passed through the keep, but she struggled to get better, the lack of food and rest wearing her body down. Cairren offered Wynda medicinals, and it was on the morning that Wynda finally agreed that Cairren heard a loud crash as she made her way to Duncan's chamber. She feared he'd fallen from the bed, but when she rushed into the chamber, she found Wynda sprawled across the floor and Duncan standing over her.

"Get out, whore," Duncan demanded.

"I will not," Cairren entered the chamber, leaving the door open. "You struck your wife."

"The lazy bitch is clumsy. Tripped over her own feet."

"Then why are you standing there?"

"To help her, you simpleton. Now get out," Duncan demanded once again.

"I came to give Wynda the medicinals I offered her. That," Cairren pointed to the gash on Wynda's temple. "Needs tending. It's deep."

"She's fine. Leave before I throw you out."

Cairren brandished her dirk that she'd started carrying when she arrived at court. She knew she was unlikely to overpower Duncan, but she intended to do as much damage as she could. "I'll leave, but Wynda comes with me."

"Fine. You can both get the bluidy hell out."

Cairren reached out her hand, and Wynda skirted around Duncan before the women left. In Wynda's chamber, Cairren drew a deep breath before looking at Wynda's face. "This needs stitching."

"Nay, just clean it, and I'll be right as rain."

"Nay. You won't. It'll get infected. I'm stitching this closed, Wynda." Cairren went to where she knew Wynda kept her sewing kit. She lit a candle and passed the needle and thread through it several times before cleaning Wynda's temple. The women sat in silence by the arrow slit while Cairren worked. Wynda barely flinched as Cairren passed the needle through her skin until she had ten clean sutures. Cairren knew Wynda's lack of reaction came from enduring many injuries at her husband's hand. "What was he angry aboot?"

"He didn't like what they served this morn when he broke his fast."

"Didn't like it? It was the same thing it always is."

"Aye. But I suppose that's not what he wanted." Wynda glanced at the closed door before looking at Cairren. "You've delivered bairns before, haven't you?"

"Aye. Plenty while I was still on Kennedy land."

"I think I'm carrying again. I've missed my courses twice now. Could you examine me?"

"That's wonderful news!"

"Shh! Nay, it's not. No one can know, in case I lose the bairn again."

"But if Duncan keeps beating you, you are likely to lose it. Wouldn't he stop if he knew?"

"You'd think, but it's never made a difference in the past."

"But wouldn't Micheil help you with this? It's his grand bairn who might be Duncan's heir."

"Duncan has sworn he'll kill me if I ever tell anyone what happens between us."

Cairren swept an assessing look over Wynda. "Did he force you? Is that how he got you with child?"

Wynda shook her head before lowering it. "I don't fight him anymore. It's not worth it."

"Och, Wynnie." Cairren hugged her friend. "Please, let me help you get back to your people. At least to give you a chance to carry this bairn. If Myrna can claim a sickness is keeping her away from her clan, we can come up with a reason for you to return to yours."

"I'll think aboot it," Wynda conceded. Five minutes later, Cairren confirmed Wynda was carrying and issued her plea again. "Aye. I want to go home now that I know for sure."

"We'll come up with something." Cairren offered her another hug before she returned to Padraig's chamber.

CHAPTER TWENTY-THREE

That night, Cairren broached the issue of Wynda with Padraig, careful not to say anything specific until she knew whether he might be an ally.

"Padraig, I'm worried aboot Wynda. She's not been getting better, and she's lost significant weight while she's been tending Duncan."

"She's always been sickly and thin, Ren. I know you want to help her, but I don't know that there is much to be done. Our previous healer tried," Padraig said as he unlaced Cairren's gown.

"I had to give her stitches today, Padraig. To her face." Cairren turned around.

"Aye, she has a habit of being clumsy," Padraig mused as he tried to work Cairren's gown over her shoulders, but she crossed her arms.

"It's not clumsiness when someone pushes you."

"What're you saying, Cairren? Are you accusing Duncan of hurting her?"

"It's not an accusation when it's true. I heard a crash when I was on my way to give her some medicinals. I thought maybe Duncan had fallen. I entered the chamber and found Wynda on the ground, bleeding, while Duncan stood over her. His hand was raised as if to hit her. She's struck her face on the corner of the chest. I saw the blood on the wood."

"Duncan has a foul temper, which I'm sure is short after a sennight of being stuck in bed. He—"

"Are you excusing what he did?" Cairren stepped away from Padraig, incredulous at what she was hearing. "You condone men, your own brother, beating their wives? Your brother has a broken jaw because he touched me, but you don't care that he regularly abuses Wynda?"

"I didn't say that. But she is his wife. There is naught anyone can do if he chooses to mistreat her."

Cairren stood there aghast. She couldn't believe what she was hearing. Her opinion of Padraig had improved tremendously over the past sennight, and now it crumbled all over again. She pulled her gown back into place. "You should be ashamed. That's cowardice and dishonorable, Padraig. I've forgiven a lot, but I will not turn a blind eye to refusing to protect the weak. That's inexcusable." Cairren walked to the door.

"Where're you going?"

"To sleep in Wynda's chamber."

"Your place is here with me, Cairren." Padraig stood with his hands on his hips. "I'm your husband."

"Isn't that convenient? I don't want to look at you, so I definitely don't want to lie in the same bed as you. I'm telling you, something awful is going to happen to Wynda. And it will be everyone's fault if it does. Because it means we did naught to protect her. I don't want that on my conscience, and neither should you." Cairren yanked the door open and left Padraig staring at the space she had just occupied.

Cairren hurried along the silent passageway until she reached Wynda's door. She knocked softly, but when Wynda didn't answer, she knocked louder. After the third time, she tried the door handle, finding the door unlocked. She entered and screamed, "Padraig! Padraig!"

Before Cairren, Wynda lay on the bed, her eyes open and unseeing, her mouth open as if she'd been trying to cry out. Cairren ran across the chamber and shook Wynda, but her head lolled to the side. "Padraig!"

Padraig heard Cairren's scream as he undressed. He left his plaid behind and ran down the passageway, following Cairren's voice. His family's doors opened as he ran past, and his parents and Duncan stepped out of their chambers. He stormed into Wynda's room to find Cairren sitting on the edge of the bed, holding Wynda's hand. He'd seen death often enough to know that Wynda was no longer breathing.

"Cairren?"

Cairren pointed at Wynda's neck, and Padraig came closer. Even in the firelight, he could see a livid bruise that went around Wynda's neck. Someone had choked her.

"You killed my wife!" Duncan bellowed.

Padraig spun around and shielded Cairren. "She did not. She just left our chamber, and she told me she was coming here. She didn't have the time to do that, and she wouldn't."

"Then who did?" Micheil demanded.

"Her bastard husband," Daniel announced. Everyone turned to see Daniel, Jamie, and Alex standing in the passageway. Daniel pointed to his son and neighbor before continuing. "We heard a crash this morning as we were making our way to gather our weapons before heading to the lists. We saw Cairren run into Duncan's chamber and heard the argument. We hurried out of sight when Cairren and Lady Wynda walked out. We wanted to spare the lady the embarrassment of knowing we heard what happened. But all three of us saw blood on Lady Wynda's face."

"He did it out of vengeance," Jamie spoke up. "We went to speak to him when the women entered Lady Wynda's chamber. Apparently, he enjoys roughing up women. He warned her that she would pay if we interfered. Now we can see he meant it. We never would have left her unguarded if we thought he were a murderer."

"Nonsense," Micheil decreed. "My son isn't a murderer. Everyone knows she was clumsy."

"Clumsy?" Cairren screeched. "You don't accidently choke yourself in your own bed. She was carrying a bairn."

The chamber went silent as all eyes turned to Cairren. She clung to Padraig, and she hadn't even noticed he'd wrapped his arm around her. She buried her face in his chest and sobbed, uncaring that the Munros saw her weakness. Her only friend was dead, and she'd done nothing to save her. She was too late.

"She was with child?" Mary demanded.

"Aye. I confirmed it today when I examined her. After I stitched her forehead." Cairren lifted the sleeves of Wynda's chemise, showing arms mottled with bruises, all clearly fingerprints. "This wasn't clumsiness."

Alex pushed into the room and stood before Cairren and Padraig, but his eyes were only on Cairren's. "Do all the men in this clan beat their women?"

"No, Alex. Padraig has never raised a hand to me, and I don't believe he would," Cairren murmured before turning back into Padraig's embrace. "I—I need to prepare her body for—" Cairren couldn't finish as a sob overcame her.

"Tell me how I can help, Ren," Padraig whispered.

"I can do it myself."

"But you don't have to. Let me help you."

"Lady Mary and I will do it. She will not defile this body and keep it from a proper Christian burial," Lady Myrna's voice seemed unnaturally loud after Cairren's soft one. Padraig realized he hadn't seen her leave her chamber when Duncan and his parents left theirs. He hadn't seen her until now.

"Myrna," Padraig warned.

"Wynda would have wanted us to do it," Myrna argued.

"That's not true. You and Wynda didn't get along. I noticed that lately. Wynda and Cairren were friends; besides, Cairren has proven she's a healer. She says she's done this before. Cairren will do it, and I will stay." Padraig's tone brooked no argument. He could tell his mother didn't want the task, and neither Duncan nor Micheil seemed to care.

Cairren waited until everyone filtered out of the chamber before she turned to Padraig and shook her head. "It's not appropriate for you to be here, but I will accept your help. I should summon maids to assist me, but I want to preserve some of Wynda's dignity. She would never want people to see what I suspect we will uncover. Please have hot water brought here."

While Padraig went to summon a servant to bring buckets of hot water, Cairren set about gathering a fresh chemise and gown along with the soap she'd given Wynda soon after she arrived. Padraig worked silently next to Cairren, doing as she asked while they bathed and dressed Wynda's body. Cairren styled her hair before they wrapped her in a sheet until a funeral shroud could be found. Padraig couldn't believe what he saw when Cairren removed Wynda's chemise. Bruises of varying colors marred his dead sister's-by-marriage body, and scars crisscrossed her abdomen and back. He watched Cairren work with businesslike efficiency, but tears poured forth the entire time. When they finished, Padraig carried Cairren back to their chamber and held her while they waited for the bath he ordered.

Padraig washed Cairren's hair and body as she stared at the flames. He knew she was replaying what she'd seen from the lines etched in her forehead. When he'd rinsed her hair clean, he helped her from the bath, wrapping her robe around her before drawing her back onto his lap as they sat before the fire. Her eyes drifted closed, but her mind remained active.

"I knew the situation was dire, but I had no idea the abuse was as extensive as it was. What we found shocked me, even though I expected bruises and scars. I don't know how she survived what she did. Padraig, I was going to help her run away. I wanted her to leave at least long enough to have the bairn. She admitted she lost the others because Duncan beat her. I should have insisted sooner. I didn't protect her, and yet I stood in judgment of you. I was the coward. I was too involved in my own problems to help my friend. Now she's dead."

"Cairren, you've been protecting her since you arrived. I know you didn't knock that jug over by accident that morning. You did it to distract Duncan and give you an excuse to get Wynda away from him. I know you've been doing that by keeping her company in the mornings."

"And I'm probably the reason for several of her recent beatings. He probably punished her for being my friend. I was so desperate for company that I didn't think aboot that. He probably killed her because of me intervening this morning. I didn't help her. I cost Wynda her life."

"You cannot believe that. Wynda was lonely before you arrived, and I've known that all along. She tolerated Myrna because I asked her to befriend Myrna years ago. But I've noticed they didn't like each other. I thought it was Wynda's fault, but I doubt that now. You're the only genuine friend she's had since she entered this clan, and she was happier for it. I saw it. She cared for you, Cairren, and she wouldn't agree with you blaming yourself. You've done more to help her than anyone. You would have risked your life to get her away, while I disregarded your concerns. I never imagined it was so bad. I swear I would have intervened if I'd had any idea."

"I believe you would have, but she would never have admitted it. Duncan petrified her. He warned her he would kill her if she ever told anyone." Cairren sighed as she clung to Padraig. "Please don't let me go. At least, not until I fall asleep."

"I wouldn't dream of it, Ren." Padraig eased them onto the bed, and Cairren was soon asleep, but it was restless at first. Padraig stroked her hair until she settled, and he watched her sleep. His heart broke for his sweet wife and his gentle sister-by-marriage. They'd both suffered for entering this clan. A clan he'd once been proud of, but now often wished he could leave behind.

CHAPTER TWENTY-FOUR

Cairren stood in the bailey and waved as her clansmen and Alex rode away. Unlike the last time she said her goodbyes to her family, Padraig stood at her side. She smiled up to him and patted his chest before walking into the keep. She wasn't sure where to go. She wasn't in the mood to weave, and there was nothing else for her to do in the chamber she shared with Padraig. She still wasn't comfortable thinking of it as their chamber; there was still too much uncertainty to think of anything in permanent terms. Without Wynda to keep her company, there was no reason to go to her old bedchamber. She wasn't welcome in the kitchens after three unsuccessful attempts to offer her help. She didn't know, nor did she want to discover, where Mary and Myrna were. Duncan was back on his feet, so she preferred to stay away from any dark passageways. She changed into her boots and went for a walk. She'd discovered a valley during one of her rides with the Kennedys and Alex, and she was certain she could make it there on foot.

The day was pleasant, but she appreciated how her plaid kept away the crispness of the autumn morning. She'd agreed to wear Padraig's plaid, but she disagreed that it would help people see that he accepted her. It seemed to do the opposite, as if she committed sacrilege by wearing it. But that morning she was glad to have the wool wrapped around her shoulders. She walked for what she assumed was an hour and discovered the meadow she was searching for. The heather and thistles painted the ground her favorite shades of purple. She'd brought a basket with her, so she gathered heather to use in a fresh batch of soap. When she had all that she needed, she decided she should return to the keep, or at least closer. It was growing warm, and she feared her skin darkening too much if she remained in the direct sunlight.

She passed through a stand of trees and breathed easier in the shade, but when voices carried to her, she halted. She didn't want to be discovered wandering alone, so she ducked behind a tree trunk, straining to hear the voices, hoping to know what danger they might present.

"I couldn't wait any longer for the chit to be out of the way," a man's voice carried to Cairren. She struggled to hear, recognizing the voice was Duncan's. She dared slip closer, knowing he spoke of Wynda, but she couldn't see to whom he spoke.

"She caught us one too many times," Myrna's voice filled Cairren's ears as she drew near to the couple. She could see them lying naked together on the ground. She swallowed her gasp as she watched Duncan playing with Myrna's breast as she stroked him. She ducked back behind the tree. "The stupid bitch wouldn't have kept the secret much longer. You had no choice."

"I just wish I'd done it sooner." Cairren was close enough to hear Duncan suckling Myrna's breast.

"I wish you had, too. There was no way I would have let her bear your heir. If you hadn't beaten it out of her, I would have poisoned it like the last time. At least now we don't have to worry aboot doing either of those." A rustling of leaves beneath them and then Myrna's moan signaled that they were done talking. Cairren peeked back around the tree and spotted Duncan's lily-white backside as he thrust into Myrna. Cairren looked around for a way to escape the trees and make it back to the keep without being seen. Even before what she heard, she didn't doubt they'd kill her if they discovered her alone. Her heart pounded as she tried to figure out what to do.

"By God's bones, Myr. Your cunny is ringing my cock dry. You're so damn tight."

"Or you're so big," Myrna panted.

"Do you tell Padraig that too?" Duncan laughed.

"I wondered if his cock was broken until he started humping his little whore. I even wondered if he was a real mon, or if he preferred being buggered. He never tried to tup me. He claimed it was honor. I think his cock is tiny." Myrna and Duncan chuckled as he rolled off her. "Duncan, you know I haven't been with anyone else since I arrived here. At least not this time."

"You better not be. I'm the only cock you're fucking, understood?" Cairren peeked back around the tree when Myrna yelped. She could see Duncan had a fistful of Myrna's flaxen locks, and his hand was wrapped around her throat. "You like that, don't you?"

Cairren watched Myrna struggle to nod. She turned her back to them yet again when Duncan thrust his fingers into Myrna's sheath. Cairren squeezed her eyes shut, blocking out the sound of them rutting and trying to recall what they'd said. She'd heard them admit to not only killing Wynda, but Myrna admitted to bedding men other than just Duncan. She swallowed bile as she tried to decide what to do with what she heard.

"He's going to send me back, you know." Myrna's voice carried as she and Duncan dressed. "I'm certain of it. He's turned away from me, and I can't lure him back. I don't know that Mary will continue to help even if she wants Cairren gone. Unless I can convince Padraig to keep me, we'll be forced to meet here."

"As long as your messenger is better than the last one. He gave the bluidy missive to Wynda instead of me. That's how she found out aboot us," Duncan grumbled.

"Then we must turn Padraig against Cairren."

"Aye, and the sooner the better."

Cairren held her breath as she listened to the couple mount their horses and ride away. She remained there as her stomach churned, and her heart pounded. *Do I tell Padraig? I doubt he'll believe me. He'll believe I'm being a jealous shrew before he believes his darling has done aught wrong. But that doesn't make keeping the secret right.* Cairren replayed what she heard in her head. *They've sent each other missives. Perhaps one of them has saved theirs. Dare I rummage through either of their chambers? Will what I find even convince Padraig? I'm more likely to be caught than I am to be believed. I wish Maman and Papa were here. They would know what I should do.*

Padraig watched Cairren leave the bailey alone because she'd asked him for space after her family and friends left. He made his way to the lists, but he couldn't concentrate. Cairren had endured Wynda's funeral the day before, and now her friends had departed. He worried about her as he watched her retreat since Wynda's death. She'd become introspective and distant, and he suspected part of it was she expected him to send her back to her own chamber now that it was no longer in use. He had no intention of having Cairren spend another night anywhere but in his bed. By midmorning, he abandoned his training and went in search of Cairren. He looked in their chamber, her old chamber, and Wynda's. He went to the garden and even checked the stables. He asked two villagers as they entered the bailey if they'd seen Cairren among the crofts, but they shook their heads. He figured she must have gone for a walk outside the walls, so he went to the guardhouse.

"Where did Lady Cairren and her guards go?" Padraig asked, his questions directed to any of the men. But he received blank stares in return. "She's not in the keep or the bailey. Her horse is here, so she must have gone for a walk. Where did they go?" He repeated his question.

"We dinna ken, Padraig," one guard offered. "She doesnae tell us when she leaves."

"You mean she just walks out without her guards?" Padraig was incredulous. He didn't think Cairren was that irresponsible.

"She doesnae have guards." Another man, Timothy, spoke up and looked at Padraig as if he were a simpleton.

"Of course, she does. She's my wife and a lady," Padraig countered.

"Ye never assigned her any, so nay one has agreed to go with her," a young guardsman named Matthew stepped forward. He shot an angry look at Timothy. "Or rather, none have been allowed to go with her."

Padraig didn't know if he had ever been as angry as he was now. "She's outside the walls right now without a guard because she was refused an escort." Padraig's ears were ringing.

"She came happy as you please, demanding that men give up their time to play nursemaid to her," Timothy explained. "I told her nay each time. If she'd mattered enough to be protected, ye would have seen to it. We ken ye dinna want her, so we figured this might help things along."

"I didna need to order that she be guarded. *She's ma wife!*" When upset or angry, Padraig's burr overtook his speech. He spun around but stopped. He turned back to the guards. His left eye twitched. "What do ye mean 'we figured this might help things along'?"

Timothy shrugged. "We all ken ye want to marry Lady Myrna. That canna happen if ye're still married to that brown bitch."

Padraig snapped. He lunged at Timothy, his knife in his hand. It entered the man's belly as Padraig's weight pushed the guard back against the wall. "I would cut out yer tongue for saying that, but I never want to see ye again." Padraig drove the dirk deeper into Timothy.

Padraig stepped back and let Timothy's body drop to the floor. "He willfully endangered ma wife's life and insulted her. Let that be a lesson to ye all. Lady Cairren is ma wife, and I expect her to live a long and healthy life at ma side. What I did or didna want *in the past* is irrelevant to yer duty to guard members of this clan, particularly women. From this day forth, if anyone refuses ma wife's request for a guard, ye will meet the same fate as this sod."

Padraig wiped his blade on the man's leine and sheathed it. He ran up to the battlements, looking for Cairren. He couldn't see her near the loch or toward the tree line. She wasn't within sight in the village. He was starting to panic.

"Padraig!" Matthew ran up to him. "She's in the shade by the loch. She likes to sit on the rocks and splash her feet in the water. I dinna ken where she went earlier. She went much further than usual and I couldnae follow her, but she usually doesnae go beyond where she can still see the keep's outline."

"How do ye ken?"

"I keep an eye on her. Timothy wouldnae let any of us accompany her, even though there are a few of us who disagreed with him. Ye ken Meg's ma cousin, and I ken what Lady Cairren's done for wee Katie and the other weans. I dinna think it's right that she nae have someone guarding her."

"And why didna ye come and inform me of this?" Padraig demanded, but he knew the answer before Matthew answered.

"I didna ken how ye would react if I did. I figured it was better to keep an eye on ma lady than to have ye say nay one should." Matthew shrugged, embarrassed.

"Are ye the only one who watches out for her? Would ye agree to be her guard?"

"I would be honored to. And nay, I'm nae the only one. Henry, Peter, and Dougal take turns with me keeping watch." Matthew looked sheepish for a moment before he lifted his chin. "We've followed her before, Padraig. Nae because we suspect her of aught, but like I said, it didna sit right with us that she was outside the wall alone. And well, we feel sorry for her."

Now that Padraig knew where Cairren was, and his heart slowed, he wanted to know more about what Cairren did when she left the keep. He took a deep breath, and his burr slipped away as easily at it had appeared. "Does she leave for very long?"

"Before the Kennedys visited, she would leave before the morning meal and come back as the sun set."

"That long?" Padraig looked out at the loch. "What did she do for that long?"

"Walk mostly. A large circle around the keep, village, and loch. Like I said, never so far that she canna see the keep. But Padraig, we didna realize what she was doing for several sennights. Someone could've nabbed her or killed her with nay chance of making it back to the keep. I dinna ken that anyone would go to her aid if she cried out. Henry, Peter, Dougal, and I make sure we're never on patrol together anymore. As least two of us accompany her whenever we can, even if she doesnae ken it. At the least, we watch her from the battlements."

"Besides going for walks, how else does she spend all those hours?"

"Sometimes she rides. That makes it harder for us to follow without her noticing, but when she sees us, I think she assumes we're on patrol. She sits in the meadow a lot, daydreaming sometimes, reading others. She paddles in the loch and picks flowers. I've seen nay one skip a stone as many times as she does."

Padraig continued to look out at the loch. The youthful man standing next to him knew more about how his wife spent her days than he did. Matthew and three other men had cared more for his wife's safety than he had. He'd assumed that she asked for a guard and was escorted everywhere she went beyond the village. It never dawned on him that any of the guardsmen would dare turn her down. But Innes's words came back to him: *where you lead, they will follow*. Timothy said very much the same thing. They assumed he didn't care enough about her. But to know that members of his clan thought he would welcome her demise so he could marry Myrna was more than he could bear. He still wished he was married to Myrna, though the sentiment seemed to grow weaker each day, more a familiarity than an emotion, but he never wished Cairren would come to harm. The consuming protectiveness that he only seemed to experience with Cairren surged through his veins.

"You, Peter, Dougal, and Henry are now my wife's personal guards. I don't want her to go beyond the village without the four of you with her. She's not to pass through the gates without at least one of you when she goes to the village."

"Yes, Padraig." Matthew pulled his lips in as he considered sharing one more piece of information. "Padraig, she cries every day. Sometimes it's just tears, but many times it's sobs."

Padraig patted Matthew on the shoulder and smiled. "Thank you."

"If it were ma wife out there, I wouldnae want Catriona wandering alone."

<hr>

Cairren leaned against the rock to her side as she twirled circles in the water with her big toe. She'd walked even further than she realized, and her feet were determined to punish her. The cool water eased the blisters she'd worn on the balls of her feet and her heels. She wished she could slide all the way into the water, but she hadn't been for a swim since before her parents left, and the air was far too chilly for it now.

She'd needed the walk to clear her mind and work through her grief from losing Wynda and watching her friends ride away. She had no way to know if she would ever see friends or family again. She'd only wound up with more to cloud her mind and heart when she stumbled upon Duncan and Myrna. The walk back to Foulis had done little to resolve her conundrum. Without Wynda, and solely reliant on Padraig, crushing loneliness threatened to consume her. She swiped away the freshest batch of tears that trickled off her chin.

If only I could slip away under the water, mayhap find a world with selkies rather than people. Or mayhap walk to the end of the world, never to lay eyes on Foulis again. Would that I could walk to Dunure. Perhaps it will come to that in the spring, but I'm likely to freeze into a standing stone if I set off now.

Cairren sighed as she watched the sun shine through the leaves of the tree branches that hung low over the water. She heard someone approach and scrambled to her feet, pulling her dirk free from her belt. She crouched, prepared to defend herself. She knew she'd been followed more than once, but no one ever came this close. When someone pushed aside the branches to her hidden spot, she raised her arm, ready to thrust.

"Put that down!" Padraig lurched backward. "It's me, Ren."

It took Cairren a moment to register what Padraig said and that it was her husband. She stepped back and lowered her knife. She reached for a leaf stuck in

Padraig's hair before retaking her seat on the rock. "You found me."

"Were you hiding?"

Cairren shrugged. "Not from you."

"Your guardian angel told where to find you." Padraig smiled.

"My who?" Cairren's brow furrowed.

"Four of the guards have appointed themselves your protectors." Padraig scooted closer and lifted Cairren into his lap. He needed the contact after learning that she had gone unprotected for so long. "Why didn't you tell me they refused you guards?"

"Because what the mon told me made sense."

"Oh, Ren. I never intended for you to be unprotected. I assumed that as my wife it would go without saying that you were to have an escort any time you left the bailey. I had no idea that you were away from the keep for so long each day. Why didn't you tell me this is how you spend your days?"

"What would I have to do if you refused me the guards or permission to leave the walls?"

"So you figured it was better to wander in an unfamiliar land alone? This isn't Kennedy land, where everyone kens you're the laird's daughter."

"I never left Dunure's bailey without at least two guards. Never."

"Then why would you do something so risky? You could have been taken or killed."

Cairren looked him straight in the eye, lifting her chin. "Would that really be so horrible?"

"What?" Padraig's eyes widened. "How can you say that?" But he knew how asinine the question was as it came out of his mouth.

"It was go on my own or remain a prisoner. I liked

my odds better on my own. At least I'm likely to see my attacker coming out here."

"You make it sound as though something happened in the keep. Has someone tried to hurt you?" When Cairren tried to look away, he pulled her chin toward him despite her resistance. His voice held a warning. "Cairren."

"Duncan has tried to approach me a few times. I ducked away most of the time, but he pinned me against a wall once and has made lewd comments a few times."

"I'll do more than break his fucking jaw."

"No, you won't. Let it go, Padraig. I keep my distance from him. You'll just turn your parents, Myrna, and the clan away from you. It's not worth it."

"You mean you're not worth it. Cairren, you're my wife. I'm tired of having to remind you and everyone else of that. No one has a right to threaten you."

Cairren blew out a puff of air from her nose as she turned her head to look out at the water. "Until a sennight ago, you were still courting Myrna. The Church may say I'm your wife, but everyone kens I'm more your leman than aught else." She sighed. "My kinsmen are gone now. You need not play host to them. We can return to how things were, and I'll stay out of the way. I don't need the escort."

"Absolutely not. Not to any of that shite, Cairren. We are not returning to how things were before. You and I share a chamber now, and I will not agree to any other arrangement. I am not courting Myrna, and I intend to send her home without me as an escort. And you absolutely will not risk your life by leaving the bailey without guards. For all we know, someone may be watching you as we speak, planning to kidnap and ransom you. Or worse, rape you."

"That's rubbish. Anyone who's watched me knows I don't have a guard, and they will have figured out it's because I'm not worth a ransom. As for molesting me, they'd have to touch me."

"I know what you mean by that, but, dear God, Cairren, you couldn't be more wrong. Every mon who sees you fantasizes aboot you. I've seen the looks, I've heard the comments. I hate admitting to how many men would take the opportunity to force you. You're alluring, and while they might spew vulgarities aboot you, they'd also seize the chance to have you." Padraig cupped her chin and rested his forehead against hers. His voice caught as he continued. "I can't bear you coming to harm. I'll escort you myself anywhere you want to go if you won't accept a detail. Please, Cairren. I don't want to lose you."

Padraig meant every word. Cairren had become a fixture in his life, and he didn't want to think about life without her. He'd grown fond of the pint-sized woman in his lap, and he realized that while she wasn't the woman he loved, she was a better person than he imagined. He pressed a kiss to her mouth, and she opened to him as her arms looped around his neck. The kiss grew heated, and Cairren moaned with need. Padraig eased her onto the ground before bunching her skirts around her knees. She pulled his plaid up and wrapped her hands around his length. He'd taught her how he liked her to stroke him, and now she moved her hand along his length, twisting her wrist the way she knew made him impatient to sink inside her. She opened her legs to him as his fingers slid along her seam.

"You're wet for me," Padraig murmured.

"Always. Don't make me wait. Not this time. I need you, Padraig."

"I need you, Ren."

Cairren guided his length to her entrance, and he pushed inside, settling hilt-deep into her heated core. They lay together for a long moment as they reveled in the sensation of being joined. Each time they coupled, it was as though the world around them slipped away. They'd learned to move together, seeking and finding pleasure not only for themselves but for each other. The kisses were hungry, and Padraig thrust with abandonment, encouraged by Cairren's moans and with each tilt of her hips as she met his urgency with her own.

"I don't want to hurt you. These rocks are too rough."

"Nay. More, Padraig. Please don't hold back."

Padraig growled as he surged into her, grinding his pelvis into hers as she dug her fingers into his buttocks. They fell silent except for their pants and the sounds of their bodies slapping together. Cairren squeezed her eyes shut, the cords in her throat straining as she threw back her head and stifled her scream of ecstasy. Padraig didn't hide his release, a deep groan signaling his climax. He held Cairren against him as he struggled to catch his breath. As always happened when he joined with Cairren, possessiveness and protectiveness made him cling to her when they were through, but a softer emotion joined the ragged and harsh ones. He didn't understand what was happening, but he had a sudden desire to profess his feelings.

"Ren, I—I—" Padraig froze as he realized what he was about to say. Her soulful gray eyes opened to him, but he couldn't say it. He didn't know if he would mean it if he said he loved her, he didn't want to do it in the midst of coupling and make her think that was the reason for his feelings, and he wasn't sure if the euphoria was to blame. He had to think of something to say though before she realized what he was avoiding. "I think we should head back before it grows too cold for you."

Cairren's gaze shuttered, but she nodded. Padraig wanted to kick himself for ruining the moment. When Cairren lifted her head, her detached expression made him feel even worse. It was as though she was telling him that she accepted that she only served one purpose in his life, and now that they were through, he could move on. He held out his hand, a peace offering, and she took it as she scrambled down from the rocks, but once her feet were on the ground, she let go. Padraig wasn't ready for this distance between them, physically and emotionally. He wrapped her arm around his as they returned to the Great Hall.

CHAPTER TWENTY-FIVE

Cairren smiled at Henry as he waited beside her at Meg's door. She'd grown accustomed to having an escort again after a week of the four warriors trading off, accompanying her on walks around the loch and into the village. She hadn't dared go farther afield after what she'd heard Duncan and Myrna say. She feared what they would come up with to convince Padraig she'd done something egregious. She knocked twice, surprised when no one answered. Katie's hands were healing well, so she didn't need to make the house call, but she enjoyed Meg's company. A young widow, Meg had her hands full with five children. Cairren was happy to help with cooking and housekeeping, though Meg still tsked when Cairren picked up the broom.

Cairren shrugged to Henry and prepared to return to the keep when she heard a scream that meant only one thing. A woman was in labor. Meg's head popped out of a door a few crofts down as she seemed to search the village. When she spotted Cairren, she dashed to her and Henry.

"It's Catriona. Something's wrong with the bairn.

She's been having birthing pains since yesterday, but naught is happening. Can ye help?"

"Aye," Cairren answered as she hurried to follow Meg. Cairren had met Catriona once when the woman's husband introduced them. Matthew was the guard Cairren trusted most, and she suspected he'd been the one to tell Padraig about her situation. The women entered the small croft while Henry stood guard outside.

"What's she doing here?" An older woman who resembled Catriona demanded.

"I've asked her to help, Elspeth," Meg explained.

"She isnae touching ma daughter. She canna be trusted."

"Hush, Mama," Catriona gasped before screaming again.

"Nay. She's nae one of us. She'll steal yer bairn and make it a changeling."

"Elspeth, Lady Cairren has delivered plenty of bairns, and I trust her with ma own weans. Ye ken that. Let her help. We dinna have any other midwife, and Catriona is suffering."

"Please, just let me examine her," Cairren clasped her hands before her and dipped her chin, deferring to the older woman.

"Aye!" Catriona called out. "Mama, Lady Cairren is helping me. I trust her. I canna do this much longer."

Cairren didn't hesitate. She dropped the basket of medicinals she'd been carrying and pulled off her plaid. "I need hot water and soap, please." She moved to Catriona's bedside and lifted the woman's chemise. She could see the sheet was wet and knew the woman's water had broken some time ago because the rest of the sheet looked fresh. "I'm just going to touch your belly and see what position your bairn is in."

Cairren palpated Catriona's swollen belly and wanted to groan. The baby was breach, and Catriona wasn't much bigger than Cairren. There was little chance she could deliver the baby the way it was positioned now. Once she washed her hands, she examined Catriona further and knew they likely had several hours before she would be ready to push.

"I will be right back." Cairren stepped outside and looked at Henry, who studiously avoided looking at the croft. "Where's Matthew?"

"He's on patrol, ma lady."

"You need to fetch him."

"I canna leave ye, ma lady. Ma orders are to remain with ye at all times."

"Then send someone else, but someone needs to fetch him."

"Ma lady, they willna send anyone to fetch him for a bairn. Women have them every day. He has a duty to his clan."

Cairren leaned forward and lowered her voice. "There is a good chance his wife and bairn will die. So unless you'd like a grave beside them, I suggest you get your arse on a horse and find him."

"But—"

"Henry, I swear to you, I will make your life more miserable than you ever imagined possible if you don't bring Matthew home. He deserves to be with his wife. She needs him, and he deserves to say goodbye if she doesn't make it. What would you do if it were Sarah?"

"Aye, ma lady." Henry took off for the stables, and Cairren went back inside.

"Catriona, your bairn is sideways," Cairren held the woman's hand as she explained the situation.

"Your hips are too narrow to deliver like that. I will be very honest with you and tell you the dangers you and your bairn face. There's a chance your pelvis could crack. You might not walk properly again, or you might not have any more bairns. There's a chance that your bairn could have the cord wrapped around his neck, and the delivery could strangle him, or he could be born a cripple if he becomes stuck. There's also the very real chance you both might die."

Catriona sobbed as her free hand rubbed her belly. Her panic-stricken eyes tore at Cairren's heart. She wasn't prepared to accept any of those possibilities. She glanced at Elspeth and Meg before continuing.

"I can try to turn your bairn, so it's head down. It will hurt just as much as pushing the wee one out, but it's your best chance. Will you let me?" Cairren prayed that not only would Catriona allow her to try, but that Elspeth didn't prevent it if Catriona agreed.

"Aye. Aught to save ma bairn," Catriona sobbed.

"Elspeth, I need you to hold your daughter's hands. Talk to her, tell her a story, sing a song. Meg, I need your help. I will need you to press against Catriona's belly as hard as you can while I try to move the bairn into position. Even when she screams, keep pushing. Can you do that?" Meg nodded. Cairren climbed onto the bed and straddled Catriona's legs. "Get on the other side of the bed."

Elspeth sang as Cairren whispered instructions to Meg. The women worked together until Cairren was confident the bairn was in position. Once Cairren and Meg finished, they helped Catriona off the bed, each holding an arm as they walked around the tiny croft. They paced for hours until Cairren ordered Catriona back into bed, her birthing pains coming too close together for the woman to remain on her feet. She pushed for another two hours, and Cairren was becoming worried that even if Catriona survived, the bairn wouldn't. Catriona was past the point of exhaustion and began swearing she couldn't continue, that she didn't have the strength to push anymore.

The door slammed open, and a windblown Matthew charged inside. "Cat!"

"Out," Elspeth ordered. "Men dinna belong in here."

"Nay," Cairren contradicted. "I sent for him, and he stays. Matthew, Cat needs you. She's exhausted and scared. Climb onto the bed behind her and hold her hands." Matthew scrambled to follow Cairren's orders, encouraging Catriona to keep going. Her husband's presence revived her enough to keep trying. Cairren pressed hard on Catriona's belly, praying that she could ease the bairn further into the birth canal. It was another hour of pushing, but then a large baby boy howled after Cairren slapped his bottom. She cleaned him and presented him to the proud mother and father.

■■■

Cairren was sweaty and exhausted when she walked into the keep. She'd apologized to Henry for threatening him, and he'd been gracious, explaining his wife would have done far worse and might still yet when she learned that he'd refused at first. Cairren swiped her sleeve over her brow as she made her way through the Great Hall and toward the stairs. She wanted a bath and a bed. The noise in the Great Hall made her head hurt, so she attempted to hurry through before anyone noticed her.

"There she is!" Myrna's voice pierced the air. "Look at her! She didn't even have the decency to make herself presentable after meeting her lover."

"Myrna," Padraig's voice warned. Cairren looked to the dais where Padraig, Duncan, and Myrna stood together. Myrna held Padraig's hands as she gazed up at him. Cairren approached as she noticed Duncan's gloating expression, Myrna's look of triumph, and Padraig's anger and hurt.

"She's been out with her lover all day, and you're warning me?" Myrna questioned.

Padraig pulled loose from Myrna and went to stand before Cairren. "How could you?" he whispered.

"How could I what?" Cairren was incredulous. "You don't believe her, do you?"

"She said you and Henry disappeared after going to the village. Neither of you have been seen all day."

"And that means I've been unfaithful." Cairren stepped back and glared at Padraig.

"It makes you look very guilty. I assign men to guard you, you disappear, and Myrna said she saw you both leaving through the postern gate."

"Did she? And you believe her." Cairren looked past Padraig, then back to him. "Why wouldn't you? She's all that's good and pure, and I'm naught but evil and dirty. You'll always side with her first. I've never lied to you, Padraig. Never. But the same can't be said for her. But you still favor her."

"This isn't aboot taking sides. This is aboot ma wife being unfaithful."

"It's only aboot taking sides because I have never strayed. You've gone too far this time, Padraig. I won't forgive you for this. Not ever." Cairren spun around and tried to leave the dais, but Padraig's hand snagged her arm in a punishing grip. He jerked her back to stand in front of him and didn't release her arm. "You and your family deserve each other. Now you're man-handling me. You're no better than your brother."

It was Padraig's turn to jerk back, and Cairren broke free. She sprinted to the stairs and took them two at a time until she reached her former chamber. She slammed the door before locking it and dropping the bar in place. She trembled as she looked around the chamber she hadn't entered in days. She went to the chest that stood at the foot of the bed and lifted the lid. She pulled out a piece of parchment, a quill, and a pot of ink. She sat to the table and considered the letter she was about to compose.

CHAPTER TWENTY-SIX

Padraig was furious. He looked at Duncan and Myrna's gloating faces, then at the stairs Cairren had just disappeared up. He hadn't believed Myrna's story until she cried and kept apologizing for having to tell him what she'd seen. It was the worst feeling of betrayal and loss he'd ever experienced. Myrna said she'd seen Cairren and Henry slinking out of the postern gate. He'd tried to argue that he was her guard and that he was aware she went for walks. But Myrna argued she'd seen Cairren carrying a picnic basket, and the couple kept looking around to see if anyone watched them. When Cairren entered the Great Hall with a basket over her arm, he thought his world would crumble around his ears. Now that Cairren was home and accused him of the wrongdoing, he was seething. He swore to himself that he would wait until he was calmer before he approached his wife, but he would not tolerate her infidelity. He'd remained faithful despite living under the same roof as the woman he loved. That notion gave him pause. He looked over at Myrna, and he found the intense feeling of longer and companionship that used to fill him whenever he laid eyes on her was no longer there. He looked back at the stairs and felt that same feeling but to a far greater degree when he pictured Cairren in their chamber.

"Padraig! Padraig!"

Padraig turned toward Matthew, who ran into the Great Hall, his eyes wild. He'd never seen the man so distraught. He called out, "Aye."

"We need Lady Cairren to come back right away. It's the bairn."

"Come back? What bairn?"

"She delivered ma son today, but now he isnae breathing right. We need Lady Cairren to help him."

Padraig's heart stalled. *A bairn? Cairren spent the day with Catriona? But Myrna said...* Padraig turned toward Myrna, who refused to meet his gaze. He took off toward the stairs, taking them three at a time. When he reached the first landing, he knew not to try his chamber. Cairren wouldn't have gone there. *What have I done? I dinna think I even love Myrna anymore, and yet I believed her without question. I did exactly what Cairren always expects. I abandoned her.* Padraig reached Cairren's door and pounded.

"Cairren, open the door. It's Matthew's bairn. Something's wrong. They need you," he panted at the end.

Cairren listened to Padraig and dropped the quill. She hadn't begun writing her letter, still unsure what to say. She was numb from what Padraig accused her of, and her brain felt like it was in a bog until he pounded on her door. She rose and looked at the two plaids on her old bed. She grabbed the Kennedy plaid before opening the door. She pushed past Padraig without a word and dashed down the stairs. She spotted Matthew but didn't slow to ask him what happened. She raced through the Great Hall and out through the bailey.

"Open the gate," she called as she ran toward the postern hatch. She passed through, hearing Matthew and Padraig only footsteps behind her. She didn't stop running until she reached Matthew and Catriona's croft. She burst inside and stumbled to a stop. The sound of the newborn gasping was weak, but the only noise in the home. "I need boiling water and a sheet now."

Cairren dropped her plaid from her shoulders and ran to Catriona and the bairn. She took the baby boy from Catriona, who cried silent sobs. Cairren cradled the infant in her arms and raised him near her ear, so she could listen to his wheezing breath. She crooned to him as she kept checking on the bucket hanging over the fire.

"What happened?" She asked the room, not taking her eyes off the baby as his face grew a deeper shade of purple, and his breaths drew further apart.

"We dinna ken. One minute he was sleeping in ma arms," Elspeth explained. "The next he was gagging and coughing. It was only another moment before he was gasping. Matthew went for ye straight away."

"You did the right thing." Cairren forced a smile for the terrified parents, but she wasn't feeling at all confident. When the water hissed, she asked for the bucket to be placed on the floor. She sat down with a leg on each side and told Elspeth to cover her, the baby, and the bucket with the sheet. It was only seconds before she was dripping with sweat, but she knew the baby needed the steam to loosen whatever was in his lungs. She remained under the sheet, singing a French lullaby to the babe until his breathing deepened and the wheezing ceased. She ripped the sheet from over them and struggled to her feet. Padraig helped her, but had she not had the baby in her arms, she would have pulled away. "Open the shutters."

Cairren stood before the open window as the cool night breeze streamed in. She held the infant away from her, so he could inhale a few lungfuls of crisp late autumn air. Then she turned him over on his belly, supporting his body and head with her forearm and hand before she thumped his back. The newborn coughed and spluttered, but this time clear fluid spewed forth with flecks of something dark. Cairren recognized it and knew the newborn would likely survive. She repeated the process of holding him before the window, then striking his back until she was confident there was nothing left in the tiny lungs. She swaddled the infant and carried him back to Catriona. "Let him suckle, but be careful that he doesn't guzzle too much. Stop to burp him frequently."

Catriona nodded, her tear-stained face showing her appreciation when she was too emotional to speak. Cairren gave her a gentle hug before nodding to Elspeth and Matthew. She picked up her Kennedy plaid from where someone hung it on the back of the chair and walked to the door where she looked back but mother, father, and grandmother were cooing over the infant. She walked out of the croft without sparing Padraig a glance. She'd been aware of his presence the entire time, but she'd been too focused on the baby to care what he did or where he went. Now he walked in silence by her side. Before they reached the keep, Cairren stopped and turned to him.

"You promised days ago that she would leave. She's still here. You've made and broken that promise more than once already. You believed her and accused me. You were so certain I would betray you, but I have done naught to ever make you doubt my honor. I am so hurt by you right now that I don't know if I'll ever get past this. I can't keep doing this, Padraig. I can't share your bed every night only to have you turn on me when a woman who can't even be faithful to you claims I'm the harlot." Cairren snapped her mouth shut. She hadn't intended to say anything about Myrna, but it slid out. She was too overwrought to think straight.

"What did you say?" Padraig glowered at her. "Now who's lobbing accusations to be spiteful?"

"They're not accusations when they're true. But honestly, Padraig, believe me or don't, I simply don't care to try anymore."

"You're exhausted and don't know what you're saying. A bath and a good night's sleep, and you will feel much improved."

"I don't doubt that I will, but I am still through with you. I'm your wife, so I have no choice but to accept your choices, but I want you to stay away from me." Cairren didn't wait for Padraig to respond before she made her way up the stairs to the keep then to her chamber, where she fell on the bed without undressing or even taking off her boots. She slept through the night and most of the next day.

———

Padraig entered the Great Hall, but neither Duncan nor Myrna were in sight. His parents sat at the dais, the evening meal finished. He was in no mood to talk to either of his parents and tried to make his way stealthily to the stairs, but he wasn't to be so fortunate.

"We hear your little bride has disgraced you yet again. Which guard was it? Henry?"

"My wife made me exceptionally proud today. She saved a mother and bairn's life. Saved the bairn twice, actually." Padraig stood tall and made sure his voice carried.

"That's not what we heard," Mary sniffed.

"And who did you hear it from? Myrna? I was just with Cairren at Catriona and Matthew's croft. I watched with my own eyes as Cairren saved that bairn when it was barely breathing. Matthew told me what she did earlier today to save Catriona. She wasn't with Henry. She ordered him to ride out and get Matthew because she feared he wouldn't see his wife before she died. I can easily imagine why Myrna said what she did, and I ken why you believed her. I'm tired of it. I will take my wife and leave Foulis if this continues. I will not continue to subject her to this hatred."

"You wouldn't dare," Micheil bellowed as he slammed his hand on the table.

"Wouldn't I, Father? Cairren is the oldest child with no brothers. I would be within my rights to seek the lairdship after Innes passes. I could take her home and serve as his tánaiste until the time comes."

"You would choose that—that—ugh—over us?" Mary spluttered.

"Yes." Padraig realized he was telling the truth. He ignored his parents and went upstairs. He looked down the passageway to his door but couldn't bring himself to enter it alone. He made his way to Cairren's chamber and knocked softly. When she didn't answer, he opened the door a crack. He could see she was already fast asleep, so he slipped into the chamber. He eased her boots off and covered her with her

Kennedy plaid. It hadn't escaped his attention that she'd arrived back to the Great Hall in her Munro plaid before they argued, then chosen her Kennedy plaid before running to tend the infant. He stepped away from the bed but wasn't ready to leave, so he moved to the chair beside the table. In the dim light from the banked fire, he noticed writing utensils and parchment laid out. He could see the parchment was blank, and he wondered who Cairren intended to write to. He wondered if it was her parents. He wondered if he would have the Kennedys returning to lob off his head. He turned back to watch Cairren sleep before he dozed off, too.

CHAPTER TWENTY-SEVEN

Cairren woke to the sound of soft snores. As she blinked her eyes open, she realized that it was past dusk, and she must have slept the entire day away. She recognized the snores before she looked to find Padraig seated in a chair with his head slumped against his chest. She rubbed her eyes and sat up; the bed creaking. Padraig jerked awake as his eyes flew open and looked for her.

"Have you been here all day?" Cairren asked.

"Aye. I suppose I was tired too, though I wasn't asleep the entire time."

"What were you doing?" Cairren remembered she'd left the parchment, quill, and ink on the table beside Padraig. She was relieved she hadn't even addressed the missive yet, but it made her wonder if Padraig was even more suspicious of something she hadn't done. Yet.

"I was watching you sleep. You were so fatigued, and you worried me when you didn't rise by mid-morning. I feared you might fall ill."

Cairren heard sincerity in Padraig's voice, but while she appreciated it, she didn't want to hear it.

She wanted him out of her chamber. "As you can see, I was just tired. Thank you for your concern, but I'll be fine on my own."

Padraig didn't miss the hard edge to her voice, and he knew he deserved it, but he wasn't ready to abandon hope. "Myrna left this morning."

"That's nice," Cairren nodded and laid back down. She didn't trust herself to keep her cool facade.

"Isn't that what you wanted?" Padraig rose and stepped to the foot of the bed. Cairren sighed and sat up again.

"You know it is. But I told you last night, I'm through trying. Do as you please, Padraig. Have her go, have her stay. I just don't care anymore."

"I don't believe that, Cairren. Not for a moment. We both know something special has developed between us."

"Yes. We're good in bed together. But that doesn't change the fact that you love Myrna, and you will always choose her before you do me. And I could even live with that if you both didn't have to humiliate me in the process. I will live here and be this clan's healer and midwife to those who will accept my help. The rest of the time, I will continue to keep to myself."

"But that's not what either of us really wants," Padraig argued.

Cairren's temper was frayed to the point where it snapped. "How dare you presume to know what I want? You don't give a bluidy damn aboot what I want. If you did, we wouldn't be in this mess. You see only what suits you, and more often than not, it's me as a disappointment and failure. I don't deserve it, but I suppose it's my lot in life. But it doesn't mean I have to subject myself to it unnecessarily. Get out."

"No."

"Very well, I will leave." Cairren made to stand up, but her legs gave out and the room spun. Padraig lunged forward and caught her.

"You haven't had aught to eat or drink in over a day. Let me have a tray sent up. Cairren?" Padraig felt Cairren's body tremble as the tears sounded as though they were wrenched from her soul. He swept her into his arms before sitting on the bed as she sobbed. She curled tight into his arms as she continued to cry. She'd fought for as long as she could, but despair pushed away the last of her control and strength. She cried for all the hurtful things Padraig had said and done since they met. She'd cried almost every day when she went for her walks or for a ride, but it had been homesickness that drove those tears and hurt from what the clan members said and did. This time it was pure grief for the constant upheaval that went along with Padraig being part of her life. She both loved and hated him, and she couldn't reconcile the two emotions, each fighting for dominance.

Padraig held Cairren until she cried herself back to sleep, his misery bringing him to tears once he laid her on the bed. He had clung to a love for the woman he believed he deserved and who he'd intended to marry even though he barely recognized the woman now. He fought against the love he felt for the woman who had been honest, kind, and self-sacrificing since the moment he met her, and yet he hurt her at every turn. As he observed Cairren sleeping again, he realized he hadn't thought of her skin color in so long he couldn't remember the last time he had. He'd automatically deemed her unfit to be his wife, and yet she stood faithfully beside him no matter how many times he erred. He considered Myrna's departure that morning. He'd given her half an hour's notice to pack and be on her horse. She'd blubbered and begged, but he'd been unmoved by her for the first time. Not even a hint of sympathy existed for her. She'd lied unrepentantly, claiming she thought she was certain of what she saw, and that she loved Padraig too much not to protect him from what she believed was the truth. He'd known she was lying. Her desperation was clear on her face, but he felt no remorse. In her attempt to hold him close, she'd only pushed him further away.

But now, as he continued to watch the silent rise and fall of Cairren's chest, he realized he felt betrayed by Myrna just as Cairren felt betrayed by him. It was a vicious awakening to what Cairren had been trying to point out all along. It was just as well that Myrna left. He preferred to keep the memories he had of them together during happier times. She would always have a place in his heart.

When Cairren awoke the second time, it was morning, and her chamber was empty save her. She climbed out of bed as a knock sounded at her door. She padded across the chilly floor and opened the door to a line of servants with a tub and hot water, brought at Padraig's command. When she finished, she made her way to Wynda's chamber. She'd avoided the room since her friend's death, but she knew no one else intended to sort through her belongings, and she suspected there were items Wynda would want returned to her clan. As she opened the lid of Wynda's chest, Myrna and Duncan's conversation in the woods came back to her. She recalled how they said Wynda learned of their affair because she intercepted a missive meant for Duncan from Myrna. She'd also heard that Wynda caught them together more than once. More memories floated to Cairren as she recalled what she'd heard Myrna telling her maid the three times she overheard them. Now she knew Myrna hadn't been speaking about Padraig, but rather Duncan. That realization eased the pain in her chest a smidge now that she was certain Padraig hadn't been unfaithful to her. He'd denied it, but she'd been just as ready to believe the worst about him as he had been about her two nights earlier. It made her question her right to be so offended and irascible about Padraig's accusation.

Cairren turned her attention back to Wynda's belongings. She lifted out a stack of pristine baby clothes, and she closed her eyes as she thought about the babes Wynda lost, about the babe who died with her. She put them aside before reaching for the Urquhart plaid that lay neatly folded. As Cairren lifted it, her brow furrowed as something shifted within the wool. A stack of missives fell into her lap as she opened the plaid. At first, she assumed they were from her family, but she recalled Wynda was illiterate, and Duncan's name caught her eye. As she turned each over, either the word "Duncan" or a single "D" was inked on the smooth side. It made no sense to Cairren why Wynda would have Duncan's personal correspondence until a sick feeling settled in her belly. She knew what these were, even if she didn't know how Wynda came by them. She turned one over and opened it.

My Dearest Love,

I received your missive and insisted the messenger

wait until I write this to you. It feels like an age since we've seen each other, even if it was only a sennight ago. One moment I can still feel your touch and the next, I feel empty and needy. Needy for what only you can give me. I will meet you in our spot tomorrow, just as you requested. I cannot wait for you to be inside me once more.

Your Loving M

Cairren couldn't believe how brazen Myrna was to send such a letter to Duncan. It took little imagination to know that that the only educated woman whose name began with M and who was familiar with Clan Munro was Myrna. As Cairren looked at the stack of folded vellum, she wondered why Wynda kept them since she couldn't read. Cairren was certain Wynda would never use them to blackmail either Duncan or Myrna, so she could only believe she intended to share them with someone else one day. *Would she have shown these to Padraig? Is that why she kept them? Would she want me to share them, or should I burn them? Would it even do me any good to show him? She's gone now. Does it matter anymore?*

Cairren felt no remorse reading more of the letters. If Duncan hadn't wanted to risk them being found, he should have burned them. They were among Wynda's possessions, and no one else in the laird's family had taken an interest in taking care of Wynda's personal effects. One in particular caught her attention.

My Dearest Love,

Padraig continues to refuse to do more than kiss me. I fear I won't be able to fool him into thinking the bairn is his if he won't relent. I won't be able to stop him marrying that woman the king is sending, and I won't have an explanation for why I'm carrying. If he doesn't bed me before she arrives, I fear I shall have to drink the primrose like last time. He steadfastly insists that we must wait until our wedding night, but I shall continue to chip away at his honor. He and I must marry before it's too late, and as you ken, this is the only way for us to be together. No one will ever know whether it's his bairn or yours that I carry.

Your Loving M

Cairren sat in shock as she absorbed what she read. Duncan had gotten Myrna with child more than once, and she'd ended the pregnancy each time when she couldn't convince Padraig to couple with her. Cairren couldn't help but wonder just how many times that had been over the course of the two years they courted. She tucked the missives in the loose folds of her arisaid until she made it to her chamber and hid them in the false bottom of her own chest. She felt compelled to inform Padraig of what she discovered between the missives and what she'd seen. He deserved to know what had been happening beneath his nose, but Cairren hesitated.

She's gone now. Does it really matter? It won't make Padraig feel any better to ken they played him for a fool. It might make me feel vindicated, but it will only hurt him. But with Wynda gone, Duncan will need to remarry. What if it's Myrna? Argh! But does that matter either? If Micheil agrees, and that's what Duncan wants, then it'll irrelevant whether Padraig kens. Do I tell him to prepare him for that because I suspect that's exactly what will happen?

Cairren didn't know what to do as she sat on her bed and looked at the door. She wondered why it even mattered to her. If she didn't want Padraig, what was the point in fighting for him to move on from Myrna?

Because I don't want to spend the rest of my life living in the shadow of that woman's ghost. Or worse, living one floor above her for the rest of my life. What will I do if she becomes Lady Munro? She'll be worse than Mary. At least Mary leaves me mostly alone now. Bluidy hell. What do I do now?

CHAPTER TWENTY-EIGHT

Cairren picked up her basket of medicinals and left her chamber, leaving her troubling thoughts in her chamber. She found Peter, her guard for that day, and went into the village. She checked on Catriona and Liam along with Meg and her children. Peter informed her that word had spread that she saved Catriona and her baby's life. He looked over his shoulder before telling her that Father Mitchell attempted to say it was witchcraft that she'd used, but Matthew had threatened to beat the priest if he lied again. Matthew swore it was a miracle and hard work. Cairren noticed warmer smiles from people who had always scowled at her. She heard fewer insults than normal, but she wasn't willing to get her hopes up. As they returned to the bailey, a roar reverberated against the walls. Cairren turned toward the lists where she saw men running toward something happening in the middle of the field.

"Lady Cairren, come quick. It's Dougal. He's hurt his arm something horrible. It's nae hanging right." Cairren didn't recognize the man who called out to her, but she picked up her skirts and hurried onto the field. Peter led the way, and Henry soon followed, ensuring she had a clear path to the injured man. She found Dougal, one of the largest men she'd ever met but with a gentle soul, lying on the ground unconscious. His arm hung at an odd angle with the bone protruding from the skin. She pushed her way to the front of the crowd and kneeled beside him.

"There's naught to do for that," a deep voice rumbled behind Cairren.

"Aye. The blacksmith'll have to take it," another man spoke with certainty.

"He was a fine warrior." The final comment made Cairren growl.

"If you think he will die or be maimed for life, you can bluidy well leave this field right now. I don't need you lot breathing down my neck while I fix his arm. Now either shut your gobs or move along. I don't want to hear another word." Cairren turned to find Padraig standing beside her. She nodded to him before removing her arisaid and folding it to place beneath Dougal's arm. "I need whisky. Plenty of it."

While she waited for someone to retrieve what she needed, she looked through her medicinal basket and pulled out what she would use to pack the wound once she'd set the bone. She had bandages in the basket's bottom, so she pulled those out. She sent a warrior to chop two flat pieces of wood to use as splints. When the whisky arrived, she took a healthy swig to the hoots of several men; however, they went silent at her scathing glare. She poured some onto her hands and rubbed them together before using one of the bandages to dry them. She felt along Dougal's arm, and as she suspected, he came alert as soon as she moved it. She helped him hold the jug of whisky to his mouth and encouraged him to drink deeply until his eyes rolled back. She eased his head to the ground and looked up at Padraig.

"I need three men to hold him down while I work." Padraig nodded and pointed to two other men close to Padraig's size. They pinned down each of his legs while Padraig held down Dougal's other arm. Cairren poured whisky on the open wound. Dougal jerked awake and failed his arm. He knocked Cairren over, but she scrambled back to grab his arm before he could do more damage.

"Hold him down," she ordered the other men. "Dougal, this will hurt. I'm sorry. I will set this on three. One—" Cairren simultaneously pushed and pulled, and the bone slid back into place.

"Ye didna say thwee," Dougal drawled.

"I ken, but I needed you to not tense. You would have if you thought it would happen when I said three."

"She kicked me in the shin before she set my nose," Padraig offered. Cairren pursed her lips but smiled.

"I'm certain you deserved it, along with it distracting you." Cairren offered Dougal more whisky before she packed the wound with yarrow and prepared to sew it closed. "Dougal, I ken you live in the barracks, but I really think you should stay with your parents for a wee while. I fear you might develop a fever, and you'll need someone to brew willow bark tea and keep an eye on you."

"Aye, Dougal. Ye'll want yer mam to look after ye," teased a man Cairren believed was named Jonathon.

"*Tha thu nad asal,*" Cairren muttered that he was an arse, and the men who heard howled with laughter.

"We agree wi ye, ma wady," Dougal slurred. This only made the crowd laugh more.

"Can you help me get him up?" Cairren looked at Padraig, and he nodded. Once Dougal was on his feet and mostly upright, Padraig dismissed Henry and Peter to help Dougal to his parents' croft, insisting that he would accompany Cairren.

"Have you been up to the battlements yet, Ren?"

Cairren shook her head as she blinked away tears. She didn't want to weaken to Padraig, but the sound of his special pet name for her tore at her. "This didn't seem like a wise place to come," she answered as Padraig led her up the stairs.

"On a cloudless day, it feels as if you can see for forever." Padraig pointed to the clear sky overhead. They walked in silence until they reached the portion of the wall walk that overlooked the loch. "Cairren, now that one of the major obstacles for us is no longer here, can we start fresh?"

Cairren pushed her hair out of her eyes as the wind lifted it. Padraig was gazing at her with the same softness as when they used to lie in her bed and talk, learning about one another's interests and tastes. It felt as if that were a lifetime ago. She looked out over the fields and considered what she would say.

"What happens if she returns?" she asked at last.

"I don't think she will. She has no reason to."

Cairren turned her head to look at Padraig again, struggling to decide whether to tell him what she knew. "Your family wants an alliance with hers, and your brother is now a widower. Your parents might arrange their marriage."

"Nay. Myrna would never agree. She loves me. She would never agree to marry Duncan."

"You still believe she loves you?"

"Why else would she have fought so much for me?"

"Mayhap because she hates me and hates losing to me? Or at least that's how she looks at it."

"She was fighting for us. Cairren, it matters not anymore what she or I want."

Cairren shook her head. "Want? Not wanted, but want? As in now, not the past. You're unbelievable." Cairren turned away and took a step, but Padraig moved around her, blocking her way.

"That isn't what I meant."

"Then what did you mean?" Cairren demanded.

"She was fighting for us because we loved each other. She wasn't willing to give up on us, even if I want to move on."

"Unwilling to give up on you?" Cairren opened her mouth to say more but snapped it shut and shook her head. "You say you want to move on. How do I know that the first time she comes back here, and mark my words she will, that you won't go running to her like you always do?"

"Because I'm the one who sent her home, and I've been avoiding her for sennights."

"It didn't look like you were avoiding her when I walked into the Great Hall to find my husband holding her hands in front of the entire clan. Again." Cairren narrowed her eyes. "And you seemed awfully eager to hear what she had to say when she was speaking out against me. Somehow I doubt you'd believe me so easily if I told you the truth aboot her."

"What truth?"

"She and Duncan have been lovers for years," Cairren blurted out. She stunned herself and took a step back.

"Why would you make up such a horrid lie, Cairren? You always claim that you're honest. You want me to believe the woman I love and my brother are sneaking around behind my back."

"The woman you love? A moment ago, it was loved. Now you're back to being in love. You fickle fool. I hope she comes back. I hope she marries Duncan. And I hope you have to watch them fuck right in front of you like I did." Cairren spun around and ran along the battlements, uncaring of who watched her, and uncaring that Padraig didn't follow her.

CHAPTER TWENTY-NINE

Padraig watched Cairren run away from him, his heart in his throat as she raced down the slick steps to the bailey and then into the keep. He couldn't believe what she'd said. He replayed what they each said, and he'd gotten stuck in his own loop of thoughts, sometimes saying he was in love with Myrna and sometimes saying that was in the past. He didn't even know at this point, but Cairren's accusations about Myrna and Duncan left him reeling. He couldn't imagine Myrna and Duncan together, but Myrna's suggestion that she lose her maidenhead to another man made him wonder who she had in mind.

Could it have been Duncan? Did she already lose it to him? That canna be possible. I know he wasnae faithful to Wynda, but Myrna isnae his type. Padraig drew up short as he thought about that again. *The Myrna I thought I knew, the one I insist on believing is the authentic version of her wasnae his type. But the Myrna I've seen since Cairren arrived is exactly Duncan's type. Maybe I'm the fool Cairren keeps claiming. But if it's true, I've wasted years being duped and loving a woman who doesnae really exist. And now— and now it's pride that doesnae want to give up on*

Myrna. I dinna want to admit that I've been wrong. It hurts too bluidy much.

Padraig looked back at the keep and where Cairren had been several minutes ago. He needed to know for sure. He needed to know if she could prove it or if she was just making up things to hurt him.

She's nae the spiteful one, though. Her words often hurt, but it's always because I dinna want to accept the truth. I left Myrna alone in favor of Cairren, but ma words never show that. God, could I have been that wrong all along? I think I've known I have been but ma bluidy pride... He pushed away from the wall and made his way into the keep. He needed to finish his conversation with Cairren.

▭

Cairren used the candle flame to ease the wax open from the missive she'd snagged from a Ross messenger. With the single letter "D" on the smooth surface, she'd recognized Myrna's writing. She knew what she was doing was wrong, but she didn't care. She would know one way or another, and she would prove it to Padraig if he wanted the truth. If he didn't, then she would let sleeping dogs lie.

D,

Tomorrow in the woods. I'll be there midmorning. Come to me, my love.

M

Cairren read the missive and quickly closed it, heating the wax to reseal it. She left her chamber and crept along the passageway until she made her way down one flight of steps. She put her ear to Duncan's door, and when she heard nothing, she eased it open. She crept inside and placed the missive on the table before fleeing. She dashed back up to her chamber and considered whether it mattered if Padraig knew. She hadn't intended to tell him, at least not how she did, but the words had flown out of her mouth borne of frustration and endless hurt. She closed her eyes and focused on what her intuition tried to tell her. What did her mind want her to do? The different parts fought one another.

Even if Padraig believes me, and even if he doesn't love Myrna anymore, that doesn't mean he loves me. That doesn't mean things are resolved with the clan. Things may be better, but I'm not deaf to the rumors nor blind to how people look at me. Padraig has kept anyone from being outright aggressive to me, but I still don't belong here.

A soft knock on her door drew her away from her thoughts. She shook out her skirts and opened the door, surprised to find Padraig on the other side. She stepped back to let him in. As Padraig stepped inside, he looked around and memories of the first weeks they spent together sharing Cairren's bed each night flooded back to him. He wanted her back in bed beside him, be it the one in front of him or the one in his chamber.

"I don't want to believe you, Ren, but I know you don't lie." Padraig ran his hand though his black hair and looked at his petite wife, who watched him like a hawk. "Do you have proof of what you said?"

"Aye. I wish I didn't, but I do. Padraig, it doesn't give me any pleasure to hurt you like this. That's not why I told you. Yes, I was hurting and blurted it out, but it wasn't to cause you pain. I'm angry that you never listen to me, never believe me, and yet I've done naught to deceive you. I've been honest from the beginning." Cairren walked to her chest and lifted the lid before pushing various items to the side, so she could discreetly open the false bottom and pull out the letters. When she had the missives in her hand, she stood. Padraig watched her debate whether to give them to him, and he feared they were even worse than he could imagine. She sat on the bed and patted the spot beside her. When Padraig took the space she offered, she handed the stack to him. He immediately recognized Myrna's handwriting, having received plenty of missives from her over the years. He opened and read one after another, the knot in his chest threatening to suffocate him.

"Did you read all of these?" Padraig whispered.

"Aye. I'm sorry, Padraig. I didn't imagine this. I didn't even pick up on the hints Wynda left until after I discovered these in her chest. She couldn't have been able to read them all, but she knew they were important."

"What's this spot she keeps mentioning?"

Cairren sighed, and her shoulders drooped. "It's a thicket near the heather and thistle field. I accidently discovered it the day you assigned me an escort. I was walking back from picking heather," she pointed to the bunches hanging upside down to dry. "And I heard voices. I feared who might be there, so I hid. I recognized Duncan's voice first, then Myrna's. They were—it doesn't matter what they were doing. I heard Duncan confess that he killed Wynda and that she knew aboot their affair."

"None of it was real. Nae even in the beginning." Padraig looked at the missives in his hands and on his lap. Page after page of the truth. That Myrna had never loved him and that she'd been using him to be close to Duncan. She'd loved him all along, but hadn't been old enough to marry him when Micheil sought a bride for Duncan. "I loved a figment of ma imagination."

Cairren laid her hand over his and squeezed but remained quiet. He appreciated her silent strength, but he couldn't sit any longer. He needed to pace. He dropped the missives onto the bed and stalked back and forth across the chamber. Cairren watched him, and he could see the worry etched in the creases across her brow.

"They're still meeting, arenae they?" Padraig demanded as he whirled on Cairren. She leaned away even though she sat on the bed, and he was on the other side of the chamber. She nodded but wouldn't meet his eyes. "When?"

"Tomorrow, mid-morn."

"In the same place?"

"Yes. It's a grove of trees just over an hour's walk from here."

"I know where you're talking aboot. It's halfway to Balnagown. I used to meet Myrna there too. What an eejit I've been."

"Padraig, there's naught wrong in wanting to believe in the best in people. This is a plan they cooked up together."

"And I've been their willing dupe for years. I've been in love with someone who doesnae exist."

Cairren didn't know how to respond. She didn't know if he referred to the past or the present, and it hurt too much to ask, so she opted for another question. "What will you do?"

"I'll ride out early in the morn and wait for them."

"Are you going to confront them?" Cairren stood from the bed. "Padraig, please say no. I don't trust them not to hurt you. If not in the trees, then later. Padraig, Duncan frightens me." Cairren finished in a whisper. Padraig stalked across the room and pulled Cairren into his arms. He tucked her head against his chest and wrapped her in his embrace.

"How can you still care what happens to me? Has he done aught else since that day I broke his jaw or the time he caught ye in the passageway?"

"Vulgar comments from time to time and ambiguous threats, but naught like those two times. But if he killed Wynda to get her out of the way, then I don't doubt he'd hurt you too. I know this is hard, but please, if you ride out there, will you take two guards with you?"

"Nay. I have to do this alone."

"And if you don't come back? Will your pride keep you company in your grave?" Cairren trembled as she imagined Duncan strangling Padraig as he did Wynda. Despite Padraig being bigger and stronger, even a more skilled warrior, Cairren wouldn't underestimate Duncan's willingness to do anything to get what he wanted.

"Vera well. I will take two. Only because it's ma pride that's caused all of yer misery since ye arrived."

"It's not the only cause. I mean, there have been other contributors to my difficult arrival." Cairren shut her eyes as she stumbled over her choice of words yet again.

"Ye are honest, ma little Ren. Ye ken ye once warned me that ye might sound like a magpie. I've never mentioned how beautiful yer voice is. Ye are like the wee songbird. At least I've been right aboot that from the beginning."

Cairren leaned back and smiled. Their gaze grew heated, and Padraig ran his thumb over her cheekbone before lowering his mouth until the heat from his lips soaked into her without so much as touching.

He waited for her to pull away, but she lifted her chin and opened to him. The initial taste of Cairren's minty breath went to Padraig's head. He felt drunk as he pressed his tongue into her mouth. It had only been days since they'd last kissed, but it felt like a lifetime to them both. Anger and frustration gave way to a need to reconnect. They were like magnets, always finding their way back to one another.

They struggled out of their clothes until Padraig could lift Cairren, and she wrapped her legs around his waist. He walked forward until her back bumped against the wall, his cock already buried with in her. She moaned as she rocked against him. He nipped at her shoulder and neck as her arm wrapped around his head, pressing him closer. When he could bear it no longer, his mouth sought hers once again. Their kisses matched the hunger their bodies felt as they moved together.

"Ren, naught can ever feel better, feel more right than being inside ye. It's like coming home every time."

"I wish we could remain hidden from the rest of the world, making our own haven."

Their movements became more urgent as Padraig thrust harder and faster, listening to Cairren's moans of encouragement. He wanted to feel her core tighten around him, knowing that he was the reason for her release. As her body went taut, and she screamed, he felt his seed entering her, and he knew he'd made the right choice, even if he'd nearly lost her more than once. He was the only man who had touched Cairren, and he was certain of it. He never should have let the doubt cross his mind. She was his, and he was hers. He would die proving it if he had to.

CHAPTER THIRTY

Padraig woke to the feel of Cairren stretching beside him. They agreed to have the servants move Cairren's belongings into his chamber, and that she would consider it theirs. They'd lain in bed talking late into the night about what Padraig would do that morning, as well as what they wanted their future to look like together. Neither spoke of love or even any emotions, but they finally created the truce they'd been fighting for.

Padraig kissed Cairren's forehead before lowering his mouth to hers. It was only a moment later that their need consumed them both. Cairren's hand wrapped around his length, stroking him as his fingers dipped into her sheath. She brushed her thumb over the tip of his cock and felt the viscous liquid leaking. She'd offered more than once to reciprocate the pleasure he offered her with his mouth, but he argued he would never expect a lady to perform such an act. As she gazed up at him, she decided her curiosity outweighed his objections. She pushed back the covers and slipped down the bed, her tongue darting out to lap at his tip before Padraig realized her intentions. He groaned as her tongue swirled around the flat head of his cock before sliding along its length. She laved him, wrapping her tongue around him before sliding her mouth over his rod. She eased her mouth down his length, growing accustomed to the feel. When she hummed her appreciation, his cock twitched. Padraig reached for her and snagged her hips. He pulled them toward him until he had a view of his favorite destination.

"If that is how we are breaking our fast, then I shall feast too, little one."

Cairren squealed when she felt his tongue pressed against her entrance, but it soon turned to a moan as his motions matched hers. She cupped his bollocks as her other hand stroked what she couldn't manage. Padraig's hips rocked as his fingers bit into her backside. When his teeth grazed her nub, she drew him in deeper, her cheeks hollowing. She came undone when he added two fingers to his attack on her senses. Padraig pulled her free, setting her on her hands and knees before pouncing. He grasped her hips once again and thrust into her.

"Is this what you want, Ren? Do you want me inside you?"

"Always, Padraig," she panted. She sat up, her back arching as she reached an arm over her shoulder to guide his mouth to hers. They rocked together as Padraig's hands circled her nipple and her nub. Pleasure exploded through Cairren as Padraig continued to piston his hips, thrusting into her over and over until his teeth grazed her shoulder, and he felt his climax tighten his bollocks.

They curled together, Cairren's back pressed against Padraig's chest, panting while Padraig stroked her shoulder. He kissed the satiny skin as his hand slid along her ribs until his hand rested on her belly.

"Mmm, I could fall back to sleep like this," Cairren mused.

"It's still early, little one. Why not go back to sleep? I must leave soon, but I hope to be back before midday. I wouldn't mind finding you just as you are now and making a meal of you again."

"Only if you allow me to enjoy the same courses as you."

"Cheeky," Padraig chuckled as he playfully spanked her backside. "Now that I ken you find me such a delicacy, perhaps I should indulge you whenever you wish."

"You indulge me? I think you found that quite satisfying too."

Padraig rolled her over and kissed her neck as he tickled her. "More than quite. I'd go so far as to say highly."

Their eyes met, and Padraig growled, "Ren."

"Pad—" Cairren was cut off as Padraig's mouth crashed back down to hers, but a knock on the door forced them apart. "Naught good ever comes from people knocking on the bluidy door," Cairren grumbled. Padraig laughed as he handed Cairren her robe, and he wrapped his plaid around his waist. He opened the door and listened to the man on the other side.

"Ren, you're needed in the village. It seems a lad has a fever, and his mother can't get it down. She's asking for your help."

"I'll be there as soon as I'm dressed." Cairren slipped from the bed and pulled out fresh clothes for the day. A rueful smile passed between them as they both hurried to get ready. "Do you still agree to take two guards with you?"

"Aye, I will."

"Take Peter and Henry. I trust them to be discreet. Please."

"They're supposed to guard you, not me."

"I know, and maybe you have better choices, but they're kind to me. They know aught that would hurt you would hurt me. They won't speak of aught they see or hear."

"That is true. Very well, since you asked so nicely." Padraig gave Cairren another kiss as they left their chamber together. Padraig carried Cairren's basket until they parted in the bailey. Cairren hurried into the village while Padraig sought the guards Cairren suggested.

Padraig was growing restless. He'd sent Peter and Henry to wait where he knew they could see the spot he'd indicated but wouldn't easily be able to hear. Padraig suspected Myrna would use the same clearing where they'd met countless times over the two years he courted her. It was past mid-morning, and he feared neither of them would show. A moment of doubt entered his mind that Cairren had sent him on a fool's errand, but he pushed the thought away as quickly as it came to him. They'd finally achieved the truce they should have come to within days of their wedding. He couldn't keep from smiling as he remembered how they'd started their morning together. His mind drifted to how they'd spent much of their night until a horse's whinny brought him to the present. It came from in front of him, so he knew it was his brother arriving first. Padraig glanced at his guards, who had disappeared behind a bush. He knew they were there, but he couldn't even see their shadows. He hid behind the trunk of a large elm and watched as his brother dismounted in the exact place he had dozens of times. Duncan scanned the surrounding area as he tied his horse to a nearby tree.

It wasn't long before the sound of galloping hooves pounded toward him. He checked to his left and noticed a swath of blonde hair floating toward him. He remained out of sight as Myrna rode by, so close he would only need to stretch to touch her. She reined in and reached out for Duncan, who lifted her from the saddle. Padraig thought he would be ill as he watched the woman he once loved and believed he would marry fumble to move her clothes out of the way before his brother thrust into her. He couldn't tear his eyes away as Myrna demanded what she wanted, using words Padraig never imagined she knew. He glanced at the bush where Peter and Henry hid and prayed they weren't watching. He doubted Henry would since he loved and feared his wife, but Peter was a bachelor. The image Duncan and Myrna created was erotic, and had it been anyone else, Padraig might have found it arousing. But he watched as his brother thrust into the love of his life.

Wait. Nay. She isnae the one great love of ma life. I feel naught right now. It's like watching ma brother with a stranger who I know I should feel something for, but there's naught there. I'm nay angry, though I am disgusted, but I'm nae as hurt as I thought I would be. He watched Duncan and Myrna as they grunted and groaned. *If that were Cairren, it would devastate me. I would be ready to rain down Hell's fury on him, and I believe I'd be a blubbering mess while begging Cairren to pick me instead. I thought that's how I would feel now, but I'm just empty.*

Padraig moved back behind the tree trunk until he heard their voices again.

"I've asked Mama and Papa to offer my hand to you. We can finally be together, Duncan," Myrna bubbled.

"Aye. Married," Duncan mumbled.

"You don't sound excited. It's what we've wanted for years." Myrna's brow furrowed. "Isn't it?"

"Myr, there are more advantageous matches that I must think aboot for when I'm laird. We can meet here whenever we want, or you can return as a guest. My mother favors you as a companion."

"What? That isn't what we've talked aboot. I was to marry Padraig so we—you and I—could be together. Now you're considering marrying someone else and just, what, rutting me in the woods for the rest of time?"

"Then come back as my leman." Duncan grinned, and Padraig recognized the expression. It was the smug one he wore when he thought he'd outsmarted someone.

"Your leman?" Myrna's chin jerked forward in disbelief.

"You already are, so why not make it official?"

"Because I'm not a widow or a peasant. I've never married. I can't publicly be your mistress." Myrna shook her head as she narrowed her eyes. "You just wanted to have what Padraig had. Now that he no longer wants me, neither do you."

"You've always been smarter than you look," Duncan sneered. "But I've been tossing your skirts longer than Padraig's been sniffing at them."

"But what aboot our plans? We already ken you can get me with child easier than you ever did that brittle bag of bones. She was worthless as a wife. But not only would I give you sons, but I would be a worthy partner to help you lead."

"I don't need a partner. Not one who's proven to be little more than a whore in a pretty dress. You've admitted yourself that you've bedded my men and half the guards at your keep."

Padraig thought he would be ill as he listened to Duncan announce that not only had Myrna lain with him, but with men Padraig trusted and fought alongside. He glanced at the bush and saw Peter looking at him. The warrior's eyes were enormous as he shrugged. At least it wasn't a commonly known secret. *Small bluidy consolation.* Padraig turned his attention back to Myrna and Duncan as they continued to argue.

"My father has already sent a missive to Micheil, and I know Mary will support my cause."

"Do you really want to watch Padraig moon over his brown bitch? They're practically humping morn, noon, and night."

"What do I care? Perhaps I will marry you and fuck him." Myrna screamed as Duncan grasped her chin and drove her back against a tree.

"And maybe I'll marry you for your pittance of a dowry, then kill you too." Duncan spat. They stared at each other a long moment before Duncan squeezed Myrna's breast and crashed his mouth down to hers. Myrna tugged her skirts up as Duncan's hand disappeared beneath the layers of fabric. After Myrna cried out her release, he spun her around and pressed her front against the tree. He spoke softly, but Padraig was certain he heard his brother say, "I've had your cunny, now I'll have your arse," before he tossed his plaid out of the way. Myrna cried out in surprised pain, but Padraig noticed she smiled and pushed her hips back to meet Duncan's cock as he fisted her hair.

Padraig had seen more than enough. He never imagined that he would witness such carnal activity between Duncan and another woman, let alone the one he'd been set to marry only weeks earlier. He wished for a way to leave without being seen, but he was stuck.

"My little bird," Duncan crooned, and Padraig thought he would be ill. "I think I will marry you after all. Your cunny and arsehole are too good to pass up swiving every night. Did you really fear that I wouldn't?"

Padraig peeked around the tree trunk, curious about Myrna's reaction. He watched her cast Duncan her coy smile, the one that had made him hard so many times. Now it did nothing to stir him.

"I had faith you'd remember why we've been so good together for so long. You wouldn't have kept coming back to me for four years if you didn't know a marvelous thing when you have it."

Four years? They began their affair before I even considered her old enough to court. Disgusting bastard. Disgusting bitch. They deserve each other. He'd heard all he could stomach. He signaled to Peter, who he could see nudged Henry. They crept away from their hiding places on silent feet until they could retrieve their horses. They rode back to the keep in silence.

CHAPTER THIRTY-ONE

Cairren tried not to curl her nose in revulsion as the child sneezed on her again. She felt bad for the little boy who coughed until he was hoarse, but she didn't enjoy knowing she was likely to catch whatever he spewed onto her. She'd helped the little boy, Douglas, and his mother, Athne, since early morning. She'd given him three cool baths despite the woman's protest that bathing so often would only make him worse. Cairren explained that the cool water would help bring down his fever, and while Athne grumbled, she finally admitted that the bath was helping to do what the willow bark tea hadn't.

"Athne, I will leave this coltsfoot for you. Add a little honey when you brew the tea. It will make the tea thicker to coat Douglas's throat. That will help with the cough, especially at night. If he has those bouts of coughing again, you must use the sheet and steaming water that I showed you. It's the only way he'll catch his breath. I've already ground the black mustard seeds. Remember, you can add them to a warm bath or the poultice I made. Only mix it with the poultice when you're ready to use it. If you let it sit, it won't be as effective. I'll come back tomorrow to check on him. When he's on the mend, I'll show you how to make a tea from speedwell. If you give it to him regularly, then he shouldn't get sick again so easily."

Cairren looked at the woman who seemed to stare past her. She turned to find Father Mitchell standing outside the open door. She smiled, but the priest's face grew red, as though she'd insulted him.

"Leave this God-fearing woman's house, you slattern." Father Mitchell barked. Cairren stared dumbfounded, but Athne jumped as if it revived her from a trance.

"She's brewing potions to poison ma wean!" Athne shouted, and Cairren heard the murmur of voices outside, but she couldn't see the people.

"I did not. You asked for me to come here, and I helped relieve your son's fever and end his coughing fits. There's naught wrong with what I used. They're commonly known remedies."

"For a witch who practices the dark arts," Father Mitchell accused.

"Nay. These are remedies your previous healer surely used. Athne, I didn't say aught while I made the teas. All I talked aboot was how to make them yourself."

"Ye would have me poison ma wean. Ye must have thought yer curses."

Cairren looked out the window as a crowd gathered. She couldn't believe the woman was claiming things that would likely get Cairren burned at the stake before Padraig rode back into the bailey.

"Bring the witch out here," Father Mitchell ordered before stepping aside. Two hulking guards dragged Cairren from the croft. She recognized them as the men who'd laughed the second and third times she requested guards. She regretted telling Padraig he should take Peter and Henry with him. Dougal was still injured, and Padraig granted Matthew time off to stay with Catriona and Liam. She didn't have a guard with her that day. As the men dragged her past Father Micheil, he flicked what looked like holy water at her, but it burned when it touched her skin.

"Aughhh," Cairren spluttered as more water hit her skin. She knew it was barely diluted lye. She could smell it, and she didn't understand why no one else seemed to notice.

"It burns her! She is a witch!" Father Mitchell crowed. "Have her locked in the dungeon."

She watched as the crowd stood stunned at Father Mitchell's pronouncement. Many looked around, unsure whether to agree with the priest. Cairren could tell that several were tempted to side with him, heads slowly starting to nod.

"She isnae a witch," Meg's voice called out as she pushed through the crowd. "She's a kind woman who saved ma lassie's hands."

"With her heresies," Father Mitchell sneered.

"Nay. With kindness," Meg argued.

"You've told others that you went outside when Lady Cairren treated Katie. You didn't see the evil she cast over your daughter, but you heard her screams. Why did you do naught?" the priest demanded.

"I refuse to believe this. Ma daughter's hands healed because of Lady Cairren. It had naught to do with evil. It had to do with experience and kindness."

"What aboot Catriona's bairn? She practiced dark arts to bring the bairn into the world, then wove a spell to make him a changeling. That's why the sickly bairn now thrives." A woman's voice called from the back.

"I was with ma daughter and grandbairn the entire time," Elspeth called out. She pushed to stand next to Cairren. "I was doubtful too. Nae because of witchery, but because she's foreign. But I watched. She saved ma lass's life and her bairn's. Padraig was with her when she came back to help wee Liam's breathing. He wouldnae allowed evil to enter our home. He would ken."

"She's bewitched him," Father Mitchell retorted. He flung more lye at Cairren, but she was unprepared. It splashed her face, and she cried out. "See. Proof. It still burns. Lock her in the dungeon."

"Nay!" Meg cried out. "If ye're wrong, Padraig will lash ye all. If ye insist on locking her away, put her in her chamber. But mark ma words, ye will have a reckoning, and it willna be with God. It'll be with Padraig. And for yer sake, ye should fear him more."

Cairren didn't struggle as the men shuffled her away. She entered the Great Hall to Mary and Micheil rushing forward. She witnessed equal looks of shock before smugness replaced it.

"I always knew she was naught but filth," Mary hissed.

Cairren did what she could to keep up with the men, but she stumbled over her skirts several times as they dragged her up the stairs. They thrust her into her chamber, but she didn't hear the door lock from the outside. She put her ear to the door and heard a slight rustling, but she suspected the men were walking away. She ran to the ewer, but it was empty. This wasn't supposed to be her chamber anymore. Her face still burned, but far less than it had when the water first splattered it. She'd been fortunate it hadn't splashed in her eye. She prayed Padraig returned soon, but it was barely midmorning.

Cairren lay on the bed and closed her eyes. She replayed the entire day from when she woke beside Padraig to working tirelessly to help Douglas to the confrontation in the village. Her head pounded as she considered her options. Padraig was but one man. Both of his parents, along with his older brother--who was the laird's heir--and the clan's priest all despised her. They would gladly agree to putting her to the fire now because they had her dowry and no longer had a need for her. This was the excuse they needed to do away with her. The look of confusion and shock on Mary and Micheil's faces made her think they hadn't conspired with the priest, but they would support his accusations. Micheil would decree her a witch and light the straw they would pack beneath her feet.

What am I going to do? I can't stay here. The weather will change soon, and I'll be stuck in the Highlands if I survive long enough to see the next season.

The thought of seasons made her consider how long she'd been at Foulis, and unparalleled fear crept into her mind. Cairren laid her hand over her belly as she counted back in her head.

St Columba's bones! I've been here more than two moons, and I haven't had my courses. Could I be with child? If I am, this changes everything. I can't have a bairn here. Not until I ken that my wean would be safe. If I'm carrying a bairn, then I can't stay. It doesn't even matter anymore whether Padraig cares aboot me.

Cairren pressed against her belly as she stretched out on her bed. As she pressed in specific places, she became fairly certain she was pregnant. She considered other signs that she should have noticed. Her breasts were tender, certain smells turned her stomach, but she hadn't been ill at all. She supposed that was the one warning bell that hadn't rung, and so she had missed the others. She swung her legs over the side of the bed and eased to the door, once again placing her ear against it. There was no sound in the passageway. She pressed down on the handle and waited, but no one tried to storm into her chamber, so she eased it open. She looked down the corridor; there was no one in sight. She slipped from the chamber, careful as she closed the door.

Creeping to the stairs, Cairren looked over the side, but once again, no one was in sight. She lifted her skirts out of the way and hurried down them, sprinting down the passageway to the chamber she shared with Padraig. She pushed open the door, half hoping Padraig would be waiting for her. She pushed the door shut, wincing when it clicked. She hurried to her chest and pulled out the parchment, quill, and ink she was yet to use. She marched to the table, forcing a sense of confidence she knew was fake. She looked at the writing utensils she spread out on the table, and she decided what she needed to do.

Laird Sutherland,

I write to you in need of urgent help. I shall not mince words with my request. I was a friend of your daughter, Blair, while I served Her Majesty at Stirling Castle. As you are most likely aware, I recently married Padraig Munro. My father told me before he left that should I ever fear for my safety, I should make my way to Sutherland. I'm in danger, but I do not believe I can make it to your land unnoticed.

My reception among the Munros has been cold at best and hostile at worst. While my husband hasn't mistreated me, I continue to hear threats and insults.

Today they falsely accused me of a crime while Padraig is away from the keep. He is but one man among a sea of those eager to believe the worst of me. I do not look like those around me, and so my oddity has bred hatred.

As I believe it is not only my own life that it is at risk, I beseech you to help me make it to court. My sister recently filled my position, so I have family there now. My parents will surely make their way as soon as they learn of my arrival. I know the weather will change soon, but I fear being on Munro land through winter as I won't be able to hide my growing concern for too much longer.

If you can send an escort within the next sennight, I will ensure I am ready to depart as soon as the sentry spots your party. No one need ride into the bailey, just close enough for them to announce your presence. I can make my way out on my own.

With gratitude,
Lady Cairren Munro

Cairren hurried to seal the missive but put no name on the outside of the parchment. She didn't press her signet ring into the wax either. She needed to get to Matthew. With Dougal still injured and Peter and Henry still away with Padraig, she could only trust Matthew to ride to Sutherland. It was a day's ride each way. She prayed he would accept her request. She slipped down the back stairway, knowing the servants would be preparing for the midday meal, the chambers already cleaned. As she neared the door that led to the gardens, she pulled her arisaid over her head and tucked her arms inside. She counted her blessings that she was wearing her Munro plaid because she hadn't thought about it until she was ready to step outside. She kept her head down and hurried toward the postern gate. She strained to see who had duty there, but she couldn't see the man's face.

Cairren wanted to weep with relief when she recognized Matthew standing before the portal. He was looking in her direction, so she nodded and crept into the shadows of the garden.

"I will spirit ye away, ma lady. Ma horse is already saddled, and I prayed ye would come this way."

"Nay. Matthew. I can't leave yet. I need you to deliver this message to the Sutherlands. You don't have to ride all the way to Dunrobin, just to the border. There's bound to be a patrol. Tell them the missive is from me and urgent."

"Ma lady, ye dinna understand. The laird has already passed judgment. Ye're to burn this eve. Ye canna stay. We must go away now."

"Tonight?"

"Aye. Please, Lady Cairren. I can explain to Padraig where ye've gone when I return."

"No! You can't tell him where you're taking me."

"I can't lie to him."

"Then don't tell him you're the one who took me. I need more time at Sutherland. If Padraig kens where I am, he'll bring me back. He can't overrule his father. He'll only be punished along with me."

Matthew was slow to nod, but he relented. He pulled the postern gate open, and they slipped through. They were mounted and racing away from Foulis Castle within minutes.

CHAPTER THIRTY-TWO

Halfway back to the keep, Padraig recognized Dougal galloping toward them, holding onto the reins with his good arm. Something was very horribly wrong if Dougal was taking a bone-jarring ride, undoubtedly to find him. Peter and Henry spotted him too, spurring their horses to a gallop alongside Padraig. All three men laid low over their horse's withers until the four steeds kicked up dirt as they skidded to a halt.

"Padraig, they've arrested Lady Cairren. Father Mitchell accused her of witchery and practicing the dark arts. Yer father's already passed judgment. She's to burn tonight."

"What?" Padraig demanded, his head whipping up as though he could spy Foulis from where they sat on their mounts.

"All I ken is that Matthew got her out, and nay one kens yet. Catriona and Meg didna ken where he would take her, but they made it out of the postern gate. The women came to me after, and I rode out as soon as I kenned."

Padraig squeezed his horse's sides as he pushed the horse to eat up the miles that lay between him and his home. He charged into the bailey and nearly vomited when he saw the stake and pyre in the center of the bailey. People milled about in differing degrees of uncertainty and horror. Padraig jumped from his horse and ran toward the crowd, but Meg darted out in front of him. He nearly barreled into her but stopped short.

"There was lye in the water," Meg hissed, but at Padraig's confusion she explained. "Father Mitchell went to Athne's while Lady Cairren was treating Douglas. He accused ma lady of being a witch. When he had her dragged out, he splashed what looked like holy water on her, and it burned her skin. I could smell something wasnae right, so I followed the priest back to the kirk. I was right lucky I did. He was aboot to pitch out the water when the laird summoned him. I nabbed the bucket. He used one of his fancy ones, so nay one can say I did aught with it."

"Where is it?"

"In ma croft."

"Cover it and bring it to me. I need to see the laird and Father Mitchell." Padraig rushed across the bailey to where his father and the priest stood before the stake.

"What is the meaning of this? Why did ye accuse Cairren of something that is a blatant lie?"

"It's no lie, my son," Father Mitchell reached out to put his hand on Padraig's arm, but Padraig knocked it away. "She was accused of being a witch, and the holy water proved it."

"Ye mean this water, Father?" Meg called out. She rushed to Padraig's side and handed him the aspersorium, the holy water bucket. Padraig pulled away the linen cover and jerked his nose back as the pungent odor of lye burned the inside of his nose. A mutinous glare came into Padraig's eyes as they narrowed. He gripped the aspergillum, the holy water sprinkler, and stirred it before flicking water at both Father Mitchell and his own father. Both men yelped, and Padraig flicked it again and again.

"It seems ye're both heretics too since the water burns," Padraig announced.

"That—that can't be," Micheil stuttered.

"Smell yer sleeve now, Father," Padraig instructed, defiance radiated from every inch of his taut body. He was prepared to pounce on either man if he should continue to slight his wife. "Recognize that?"

"Aye. It's lye."

"And it burns, doesnae it?" Padraig held up the aspersorium. "This is the same water Father Mitchell flung at ma wife to implicate her. He lied, and I want to ken why. Now!" Padraig roared the last word. He also wanted to buy Matthew and Cairren time to flee further from the keep, lest his father send warriors out to search.

"Because she doesn't belong here," Father Mitchell hissed. "It's unnatural for a person to have such dark skin and be a Christian. Her grandfather was a heretic, a Saracen."

"And her mother was raised a French Catholic. Lady Cairren met none of her grandparents. They were all dead before she was born." Padraig's voice boomed as he made sure everyone in the bailey listening to the argument could hear. "She attends Mass daily, and it's obvious that she not only kens but understands the liturgy. She's been an exemplary model of Christian kindness and forgiveness. She has turned the other cheek at every slight, and yet, this clan continues to see that and accept that as a challenge to wrong her again and again. Rather than thank her for the dowry that has helped provide needed supplies for this clan, ye've hissed and spat at her. Rather than thank her for tending injuries and illnesses, ye rail against her. Rather than being decent people, ye make me ashamed that the Kennedys ever entrusted ma wife to us."

Padraig paused to catch his breath. He was so angry, he shook. He considered his next words, and he prayed they permeated the hate filled hearts and minds of his clan.

"So what that her skin is darker than ours? Jesus hailed from near where her grandfather came from. The Lord probably looked more like ma wife than any of us. Have any of ye stopped to think of that? I doubt it. Have any of ye stopped to remember the king decreed this marriage? How do ye think King Robert will respond if he hears of this treachery? Better yet, did ye ken Lady Cairren is friends with the Sutherland's daughter? How would ye like an angry visit from our neighbors, who will undoubtedly bring the Sinclairs and the Mackays? I'd wager that ye dinna ken that Lady Cairren's father is Laird Tristan Mackay's godfather!"

Padraig glared at his father but lowered his voice. "Ye're the laird here. It was yer duty to welcome yer daughter-by-marriage. Ye agreed to the marriage and even forced it when it could have been a handfast. This is as much yer fault as it is anyone else's. Ye did this." Padraig pointed his finger at Micheil, then at Father Mitchell. "And ye allowed him to do it too. A bluidy man of God spewing hate at an innocent woman. I may have disagreed with the marriage in the beginning, but ye've surely noticed that I've accepted ma wife. If anyone duped me it was Myrna. I watched Duncan hump her this morn, and I suspect ye've kenned aboot that all along, Father."

"Your father didn't, but I did," Mary spoke up as she approached. "Your brother couldn't legally have her, but you could. She was a far more suitable bride for you, so you and your brother would have both gotten what you want."

"Mother! And Cairren is the one standing accused of heresy when you would have Duncan covet his brother's wife." Padraig didn't bother to hide his disgust.

"She never belonged here. She chased Myrna away and addled your mind. I needed to get rid of her for your sake, my son." Mary tried to reach out to Padraig, but he leaned away.

Padraig looked between his mother and the priest. "You concocted this together. Tell me this, if it had been a woman with skin like yours, would you have been as adamant aboot Myrna staying, or is this purely aboot her skin color?"

"Everything aboot her is foreign and wrong. She speaks French," Mary blustered.

"That's what you have against her? You made me learn French too! She'd lived in the Lowlands her entire life before moving to Stirling. And we all ken that city is in the bluidy Lowlands for all it's supposed to unite us. She's never been to France. She's nae foreign! She's a bluidy Scot. She may nae be a Highlander, but at least she's trying to learn our customs. She's nearly fluent in Gaelic already."

"And how did she learn that, by the way? She arrived here knowing Gaelic, but you claim she's never been out of the Lowlands."

"She asked Blair Sutherland to teach her more than a year ago," Padraig snapped. "She was trying even before she arrived."

Padraig turned to look at the crowd that seemed

unable to look away as Padraig argued with his parents and the priest. He cast a speculative glance at several people and noticed that most of them directed their anger at the laird, his wife, and the priest, not at Padraig and he suspected not at Cairren. "Have many of ye have come to ken ma wife?" Heads nodded. "Who here has been treated by ma wife or has family or friends who have?" Hands raised, some slowly while some shot up in the air. "Have ye heard how she welcomed children to listen to her sing while she tended Meg's weans?" Most heads nodded.

"And she didna do it without asking permission," Meg piped in. "And why was that? Because she respected ye when ye couldnae bother to respect her."

"Let me ask ye this, if it werenae for Father Mitchell's lies and those of ma mother and Lady Myrna, would she still seem so different?" He watched as people glanced sheepishly around them, muttering to those who stood close.

"Nay, I dinna suppose she would," an older woman named Bethea spoke up. "But who were we to argue with them? And why would we have known they werenae telling the truth?"

"Is it still ma wife's skin that matters so much? She's learned Gaelic. She wears her Munro plaid. She is kind to everyone."

"I dinna think most of us are bothered by her skin too much, Padraig," a man spoke up, and Padraig recognized him. It was the man he'd been ready to pummel the night of his wedding when he threw an elbow directed at Cairren's face.

"And why's that, Allistair?" Padraig asked.

"I dinna ken, really. She's just been here long enough, and we see her around enough that we like her."

"I need to ken here and now: if Lady Cairren remains in this keep and with our clan, is she safe? If she isnae, then I will take her away."

"To where?" a woman asked.

"I willna say. If she's nae safe here, then I willna tell anyone where we are going. The point of leaving is to protect her."

"Would you return?" the same woman asked.

"Absolutely nae." Padraig realized he meant that with every single fiber of his being. He would find them somewhere else where he could ensure Cairren was safe and happy, and he wouldn't leave her side.

Padraig watched with confusion as a buzz of whispers went through the crowd before Adam, his father's most senior warrior, stepped forward. He was a wizened bear of a man, surly and obdurate. He rarely spoke up, but when he did, the clan listened. He was a respected member of the council of elders.

"We want Lady Cairren to remain, but the priest must go. We dinna want a man who persecutes the innocent to be teaching us the Lord's word. We dinna need a hypocrite when we can have our healer."

"It's not your decision to make," Mary notched up her chin.

"Actually it is, ma lady," another clan elder, Martin, stepped forward. "As the clan council, we can vote out a priest, just as we can vote out a laird. We've met, and we have decided to relieve Father Mitchell of his duties to this clan. He isnae a Munro to begin with. He's a Mackintosh. He can return to them. We never liked them anyway."

"You did not meet," Micheil spoke up, disliking how things had slipped out of his control.

"We did," Arnold, the oldest member of the council pushed forward, using his walking stick to smack the ankles of people who didn't move out of the way. "We dinna have to meet in yer solar to meet. We've been speaking since this clishmaclavering began. The priest goes, the lady stays, and unless ye care to see yer son oust ye, and nae the worthless one, ye'd do well to mend yer ways. I like Lady Cairren. She eases ma gout."

Several chuckles rippled through the crowd. Arnold had become more reclusive by age and wasn't known to be keen on any strangers, so his approval was close to the Gospel for many people in the clan. Padraig looked to the sky and realized the sun had moved further than he expected. He needed to ride out to find Cairren and Matthew before it grew too late. He prayed Matthew took her somewhere not too far. Now that he was more confident that Cairren would be safe at Foulis, he was ready to hunt down his bride.

CHAPTER THIRTY-THREE

Cairren was nearly frozen as she waited outside Dunrobin's gates. She and Matthew rode through most of the night to put distance between them and the Munros. But they'd had to stop for fear of injuring the horse. She'd caught a few of hours of sleep while Matthew was on watch. She felt horrible for this man, who'd left his wife and newborn bairn to spirit her across the Highlands on no sleep. They hadn't dared a fire, so once Cairren became chilled, she struggled to get warm. The temperature had dropped traveling a day's ride north and toward the eastern coast. She stamped her feet as she breathed on her hands. They'd met a patrol near the border, and she'd breathed a sigh of relief when she recognized Blair's brother, Lachlan. He'd sent a warrior to escort them to the keep, but they'd been ordered to wait while someone delivered her missive. She realized it was just as well that she'd written the letter because it might be what gained them entrance after all.

"Allow them to enter now!" roared a deep voice. "Bluidy eejits for leaving a lady and her escort out in the cold." Cairren could only assume she heard the voice of Laird Hamish Sutherland, and when the irritated man appeared, she was certain of it. She'd seen him at court more than once, but they weren't well acquainted. His stride increased when he spotted her. He helped her dismount and nodded to Matthew. He ushered them both into the Great Hall, indicating to a servant to offer Matthew food and beverage before guiding Cairren to his solar.

"Lady Cairren, I welcome ye to Dunrobin and apologize for yer poor greeting."

"Thank you, and think naught of it, my laird."

"Aye, well, Highland hospitality is something we pride ourselves on. I've read yer missive, and I'm deeply disturbed by what has happened. Can ye tell more, please?"

"I don't know what you know aboot my marriage, but my father wants both my sister and me away from the border. He chose a Highlander for my husband, and my younger sister, Caitlyn, replaced me at court. As you can see, I don't resemble many Scots and definitely do not look like a Highlander. Despite my dowry helping the Munros after their issues with the Mackenzies, the clan refuses to accept me. I've lived with taunts and threats since I arrived, and my marriage has been unpredictable at best. Though I do want to be clear that Padraig has never harmed me and has protected me, but he hasn't done aught to make the clan accept me."

Hamish motioned for her to move closer to the fire, where she rubbed her hands together. The chill finally left her, and she relaxed as her eyes met those of the kindly older man.

"I wrote this missive intending to have a trusted guard deliver it to you, or at least to a man on patrol. But when I went to see aboot a messenger, I learned that the laird had already convicted me of heresy and witchery. The priest splashed me with what was supposed to be holy water; it was actually lye. I wasn't prepared and reacted because it burned, and it was their so-called proof that I'm a heretic. The man who accompanied me helped me escape. No one kens I've come here, and I doubt anyone will suspect it right away. I think they'll assume I fled south rather than northeast. Laird Sutherland, my father said I should come to you if ever I was in danger. You're the only person I ken this far north who I can trust."

Hamish listened intently as Cairren told her tale of woe, but when she came to the part about the holy water, she could tell he barely had a leash on his fury. When she finished explaining what brought her to seek shelter with the Sutherlands, he embraced her. It was the first time she'd felt truly safe since her parents left. While she felt protected when she was with Padraig, fear always lurked at the edges of her mind.

"Lass, it'll be dangerous to travel to Stirling at this time of year. There is a possibility that ye could be caught in a blizzard. That said, I dinna want ye trapped here and away from yer family for the entire winter either. How well do ye ride?"

"Well. I may not be the best horsewoman, but for this, I can become one. I need to get to Stirling where I ken my sister is, and I'm certain the king and queen will provide sanctuary until my parents arrive."

"Do ye believe yer husband will follow ye?"

"Most certainly. That's why I want to leave as soon as possible, my laird. I'm fairly sure that I'm carrying, so I cannot return and put my bairn in danger. He doesn't know since I only figured it out today."

"Does anyone else ken? Could that be part of what caused the incident?"

"Nay. I don't have a regular maid, and the only

woman I was close to died recently." Cairren didn't intend to air the dirty laundry of how Wynda died to respect her dignity, but if pressed she would tell everything she knew. She suspected she would tell the king and queen.

"I would extend our hospitality for the night. I'll summon Lachlan to escort ye. Ye can leave at dawn and meet him where ye found him today. I'll also send a half dozen guards with ye. Yer Munro escort should return home before his absence becomes too obvious."

"I appreciate that, my laird. He has a wife and newborn who I feel guilty for pulling him away from. He offered to bring me, and I had little choice but to accept. But I'd feel better knowing he isn't more involved than absolutely necessary."

"Let me introduce ye to Lady Sutherland. She will see aboot a chamber for ye and some food. Ye must be hungry and tired. Ye must have ridden through most of the night to be here so quickly."

"We did. I thank you for your kindness."

"I have two daughters, lass. I would hope that if they were in a similar predicament, they could call upon a neighbor to help," Hamish assured her. They left the laird's solar, and Hamish introduced Cairren to Amelia Sutherland. She immediately took to the motherly woman, and she was grateful for not only the food and roof over her head but the steaming bath Amelia arranged. Amelia suggested Cairren skip the evening meal in the Great Hall to rest and to keep her presence a secret as best they could. She explained her waiting at the gate where anyone could see her was why Hamish was so angry. He wanted her inside as quickly as possible to hide her identity.

Cairren ate, took her bath, and tumbled into bed. She was asleep in minutes. Dawn arrived too soon, but Cairren was eager to be underway on the mare Hamish lent her. The escort he assigned easily rendezvoused with Lachlan, who felt instantly like an older brother. He reminded her of Alexander and how they'd become fast friends as children. Cairren thought to herself that Maude and Blair were fortunate to have a witty and intelligent older brother. Their first day of travel was uneventful, but as nightfall approached, Cairren grew apprehensive, and the guards grew wary. There was no way to avoid riding dangerously close to Foulis Castle the next day unless they wanted to add days to their journey. Cairren asked Lachlan if it would be wiser to travel at night, but he reminded her that bogs where Munros gathered peat were prevalent on the land surrounding Foulis, particularly to the south. It was too dangerous to ride in the dark, so Cairren accepted another night of sleeping in the cold.

CHAPTER THIRTY-FOUR

Padraig was in a frenzy. Cairren had been away from the keep for three nights, and despite sending search parties in all directions for two days, they'd not found more than a brief set of prints leading about five miles from the postern gate. The ground was too dry in some part and too boggy in others. He had no idea where she'd gone, but he at least breathed a little easier knowing she was with Matthew. He hadn't informed Micheil that Matthew was his wife's guard. Most assumed the warrior was still at home with his wife and son, and for their safety Padraig intended to keep it that way.

When they found nothing of use, Padraig decided he would ride to the Sutherlands, praying that Cairren had sought refuge with her friend's family. The third morning after Cairren disappeared, Padraig mounted his horse and rode out with Peter and Henry along with four other guards he trusted with his life and, more importantly, Cairren's. They set a brutal pace toward Dunrobin, but rain forced them to slow by the late afternoon and made it impossible to continue by early evening. Padraig was miserable, and his mood wasn't caused by the weather. He imagined all manner of horrible things that could befall Cairren and Matthew, and it only made him more anxious with each pounding hoofbeat.

When he and his men made camp that night, Padraig prayed more fervently than he ever had. He trusted Matthew, but he was only one man if they were attacked. He wondered how Cairren faired after a day on horseback. He knew she enjoyed riding because it was one of the few things she could do to pass the day while living at Foulis, but he also knew she wasn't an avid horsewoman and wasn't used to long hours in the saddle. He feared she was suffering already, and the protectiveness that emerged whenever he thought of Cairren filled every space of his heart until his chest burned. He thought of nothing but finding his wife and begging forgiveness for failing her so badly. He thought he'd been heartbroken to see Myrna and Duncan, but once again he realized it was his pride that smarted. He even wondered how he could have believed himself in love with a woman like Myrna when he considered all that Cairren offered with an open mind and an open heart. Losing his wife to the wilds of the Highlands far exceeded any battle wound he'd suffered or having to set Myrna aside.

By the time he arrived at Sutherland, Padraig had been riding two full days. He was drenched and miserable as Laird Sutherland admitted him to his solar. Padraig knew immediately that the man was aware of Cairren's situation and had already lent her aid. He prayed they'd tucked away her in a warm chamber on a floor above him. A servant offered him a drying linen as he entered the chamber, and he ran it over his face and hair, but there was little he could do about his sodden clothes.

"She's nae here," Hamish announced before Padraig could explain his presence.

"But that means she was here."

"Aye. She even said ye'd be looking for her. But she isnae here, and I give ye ma word on that."

"Is she hale?" Padraig begged.

"Her body is well, but her soul is wounded."

"I know, ma laird. I'm deeply ashamed at how I've failed her and how my clan has treated her."

"I hadnae realized that yer priest was such a religious hypocrite. He's naught but a bigot, and I'm sorry, lad, but that makes yer father one for allowing it. Lady Cairren told me aboot the lye water."

"I wanted to dump the bucket on them both but settled for anointing them instead."

"Ye splashed yer father and yer priest?" Hamish was incredulous.

"Once I learned what happened and had the evidence, I wanted--no, needed--my clan to see what they had done to Cairren. When it burned both my father and Father Mitchell, it exonerated Cairren. Though it bluidy well never should have come to that. Laird Sutherland, I need to find my wife. I need to know she is safe, and I need to consider whether we will return to Foulis. Much has changed in the course of a day, but we won't return if Cairren doesn't wish it."

"Ye intend to keep yer wife?"

Padraig bristled and narrowed his eyes. "I dinna keep ma wife," Padraig hissed, his burr breaking through. "She isnae a horse or a dog. I have nay intention of ever setting her aside."

"Ye love her, dinna ye?" Hamish asked speculatively. "But ye havenae figured that out yet, I think."

"I—I'm vera fond of ma wife. I think I may be in

love with her, but I thought I was in love once before, and it turns out it wasnae the case."

"Does this feel the same as before?" Hamish demanded.

"Nae in the least," Padraig admitted.

"Then mayhap it is love. In which case, ye have much work ahead of ye. As I said, she's wounded by what's happened. I havenae seen such sadness in someone's eyes in a long time."

"Did she say aught aboot me specifically?"

"Aye. She said ye've never harmed her and even protected her, but it was never enough. Lad, I think the lass feels for ye what ye feel for her. She isnae sure what to do with that. I imagine it's scaring both of ye."

Padraig ran his hand through his damp hair. He was unsure of what more to tell Hamish; still, Hamish was the closest thing to a father figure Padraig had at this point. Hamish suspected Padraig wanted to say more, so he gestured to a chair, and they both sat before the fire.

"I've desired her from the very start," Padraig began, his burr barely noticeable. He noted that Hamish did nothing to hide his brogue, and Padraig wondered if he should abandon his pretentious accent. "The moment I saw her, my body knew what my mind has taken ages to figure out. But I was certain I was in love with—you know who I was intent upon marrying, don't you?"

"Aye, ma niece-by-marriage, Myrna."

"I'd been courting her for two years, and we were set to marry on Samhain despite her small dowry, but then King Robert's order to marry Cairren arrived two months before the betrothal and wedding. The moment she rode through the gates, my mother and Myrna immediately hated her. It was both her skin color, true, but it was also that I wasn't marrying Myrna. I was torn between a woman I believed I loved and desired and a woman who made my body stir in ways I never imagined. It was obvious to everyone that she wasn't welcome. My clan made that known from the start. Laird Kennedy tried to arrange a handfast instead and willingly gave up Cairren's dowry. But my father conspired with Father Mitchell, and when the wedding began, it was marriage vows and not handfasting ones that the priest said. My father wanted to ensure there was no way the Kennedys could take back the dowry."

Padraig gazed into the fire as he thought back to his wedding night. There was no way he would ever share all the intimacies he and Cairren shared; they were too private. But he would confess some of what Cairren endured.

"There was to be a bedding ceremony, but I refused to allow anyone who wasn't our immediate family to enter. My father and Duncan insulted her. Your daughter, Blair, taught Cairren Gaelic at Cairren's request. She wanted to ken what people were saying aboot her. Wise lass. She translated into French for her parents, and I thought the Kennedy was going to skelp both of them alive. I made the men leave, which meant my mother, Myrna—who I later realized never should have been there, her mother, and my sister-by-marriage remained. My mother accused her of being a whore once she was undressed. Uh—the French have—um—different grooming habits than Scottish women."

Hamish pulled in his lips and lowered his eyes, but when he couldn't keep the smile completely at bay, Padraig understood Hamish knew to what Padraig referred.

"I threw the women out too, but not before my mother insisted Cairren would try to fool us aboot her maidenhead. Cairren offered to give the sheet to Wynda as soon as we had—. Anyway, that didn't satisfy my family or Myrna. Cairren caught me comforting Myrna in the passageway only minutes after I left the chamber where I'd just bedded her. It all went downhill from there. I wanted Myrna, but I wanted Cairren too. I bedded Cairren regularly in the beginning, and she rightly named herself my mistress rather than my wife because I kept Myrna by my side during the day. Cairren and I were at odds one day, then reconciled the next over and over. Myrna remained far too long at Foulis, and I didn't make a strong enough effort to respect my wife."

Padraig dared a peek at Hamish but wished he hadn't. The laird glared at him but didn't interrupt. Padraig gather his courage to continue. Hamish was listening to him, and he needed to share the burden in his heart.

"But eventually, I grew tired of Myrna's hateful comments, and the clan's unwillingness to see the good Cairren did as our healer and midwife frustrated me. I learned the day Cairren fled that many within the clan didn't notice Cairren's skin anymore. But many people believed the hatefulness my mother and Father Mitchell perpetuated justified their animosity and vindictiveness. I understand why they wouldn't go against their lady and their priest."

"That is far more than Cairren shared with me, but I sense ye needed to unburden yerself. I believe ye're sincere in yer regret and yer wish to make things right, but I dinna ken that yer clan has really changed. All I will say is that she headed south."

"I suspected as much, but I don't know if that

means to Stirling or all the way back to Dunure. Please tell me she isn't traveling alone." Padraig watched Hamish as he mentioned both locations, but not even a flicker gave away where Cairren was headed. He'd already decided to try Stirling first, but he would travel all the way to the south of France if he had to.

"Of course, she isnae. Lachlan is with her as well as other guards." Padraig scowled, and Hamish chuckled. "Aye, he's easy on the eyes, but he wouldnae do aught to disgrace a lady, especially Blair's friend. His sisters scare him too much."

Padraig nodded, but possessiveness only fueled his sense of urgency and anger at himself. His wife wouldn't be traveling in the company of men, one of whom many considered one of the handsomest bachelors in the Highlands, if it weren't for him. He accepted the Sutherlands' hospitality before riding out at dawn.

CHAPTER THIRTY-FIVE

It was only Cairren's fourth day on the road after fleeing Foulis and second after leaving Dunrobin, but she was doubting her ability to carry on. It would take at least five more days to reach Stirling. What had been a pleasant ride only two months ago was now unbearably cold. She refused to complain, but she'd left so abruptly that she had no chance to pack extra clothes. Rain left her in permanently damp clothes, and she was certain all of her fingers and toes would chip off before they arrived at their destination. Lachlan and the other men took pity on her and offered extra plaids to wrap around her shoulders and drape over her lap. They stayed as far off the path from Foulis as they could, but they'd had to hide from a Munro patrol that Lachlan's scouts spotted. Cairren wasn't certain, but she thought she saw Duncan among them. She felt like she'd held her breath the entire time they rode the border between Munro and Ross territory, and she expected to see Padraig come charging after her at any moment. It surprised her that they hadn't passed each other, since she was certain he would check with the Sutherlands first. She was positive he would eventually recall that she and Blair were friends.

It had terrified her to ride through Ross territory on her way to Dunrobin. She and Matthew passed the trysting spot where she'd discovered Myrna and Duncan. It made her want to weep when she thought about Padraig and Myrna meeting there throughout their courtship. Myrna's home was nearly halfway between Foulis and Dunrobin, but Matthew skirted away from it. She wore her Munro plaid and hoped that if anyone spotted them, they wouldn't be stopped. On her way south from Dunrobin, she had Sutherland plaids covering her, so she was less intimidated by the possibility of meeting Myrna on the road. She didn't know when next she planned to meet Duncan or how soon she would try to win back Padraig once she learned of Cairren's absence. She dreaded an encounter with Myrna while she was trying to flee. She didn't doubt Myrna would be happy to see the back of her head, but she would undoubtedly crow like a rooster about seeing her as soon as she arrived at Foulis.

She and the Sutherlands had no choice but to ride through Munro land since it stretched east to the coast. Going west through Mackenzie territory would add extra days to their journey. She could practically see Urquhart land on her third day south, and it made her think of Wynda. Tears stung her eyes as she thought about her only friend at Foulis and her untimely death. It made her think of the bairn she believed she carried and all that Wynda lost along with the one that died with her. She was so lost in thought, knowing they were nearly off Munro land, that she was unprepared for the ambush. One moment she was cantering, and the next Lachlan was spurring them into a mad gallop toward the invisible border. While she spotted an ebony head of hair in the center in the pack that chased them, she knew immediately it wasn't Padraig. The man's build was wrong; too short and not broad enough across the shoulders.

Duncan. Why would he chase after me? I thought he'd be the first to escort me off Munro land. He must know we're almost to the border, and it's clear that's where we're headed. Is he just in a hurry to chase us off?

"Lady Cairren, those are Munros, and they aren't a search party. They all carry bows," Lachlan yelled over the sound of the horses. "We need to get over the border now. They outnumber us."

Cairren urged her horse on, but the mare couldn't keep up with the stallions and geldings it rode alongside. While it didn't flag, its stride wasn't as long, and its gait wasn't as quick. The men could tell and remained in a tight circle around her.

"How does he know it's us? Why else would he chase us?"

"He must know you fled to us and figured the only reason we have to cross their land is to escort you."

"Couldn't you be on the way to court for Blair?" Cairren struggled to talk as she gripped the reins and squeezed her thighs tightly around the horse's flanks.

"Not at this time of year."

Cairren fell silent as she focused on encouraging her horse to keep up. She glanced to her left and realized Lachlan was right. There had to be a score of men to the half-dozen Sutherlands. The Munros fanned out, trapping them on all sides but their left. If they went further east, they would be bound in by the Cromarty Firth. They had no choice but to outpace the Munros who were racing to move in front of them.

When arrows began flying from the men ahead of them, Cairren couldn't allow the Sutherland men to die for her. They might have been Lachlan's men and even his guard, but they weren't hers. When the second volley flew toward them. She reined in, the horse behind her nearly ramming hers.

"Lady Cairren, we must go."

"Nay. Let Duncan take me. I won't have your men dead on my account."

"Cairren's that's the point of an escort. Now move!" Lachlan bellowed, but it was too late. The Munros closed in, and Cairren looked at Duncan.

"Let them live, and I go without a fuss. Let them return to Sutherland."

"It's not that simple, bitch," Duncan spat.

The Sutherlands reached for their swords, but Cairren called out, "Wait!" She looked at Duncan, then the other Munros, some sneering at her, others bewildered by the unexpected attack. Cairren mumbled, "that's the politest greeting he's ever given me."

"There's no doubt *it's* coming with us," Duncan chuckled at his own degrading comment. "I just haven't decided how to kill the rest of you."

"Duncan," Cairren tried to reason. "You can't be serious. The Munros would never survive an attack from the Sutherlands, Sinclairs, and Mackays. After Wynda's death, the Urquharts are likely to join in. And it wouldn't surprise me if the Mackenzies' and Sinclairs' alliance isn't finally put to use. The Mackenzies need few excuses to harry you. Let Lachlan and his men go."

Duncan considered what Cairren said, and after a

long moment that seemed to draw on forever in Cairren's mind, Duncan nodded.

"Hand the whore over, and we will let you go," Duncan spat.

"No." Lachlan's answer was succinct, but Cairren shook her head.

"I don't want this," she murmured to Lachlan. "Go home. I don't want Sunderland men's deaths on my conscience for the rest of time."

"And I'm not abandoning a lady to this miscreant."

"You don't have a choice, Lach," Duncan's patronizing tone filled the air. "We outnumber you and will just take her. We have no problem leaving your carcasses to the animals. Mind your business and give her over."

Cairren decided for Lachlan when she swung down from her horse and tossed the reins to a stunned Sutherland warrior, leaving the borrowed plaids on the saddle. She slipped between the horses and walked toward Duncan. She stopped halfway and raised her chin, defiance radiating from her. "Padraig's been looking for me, hasn't he?"

"My stupid little brother is chasing his tail trying to find his bitch. You'd think you were in heat the way he's sniffing for you."

"Then you ken he'll kill you if you harm me."

"So he might. Or he might not, since more of the guards are loyal to me than to him," Duncan's chuckle made a shiver slide down Cairren's back. She knew it wasn't true. While the clan hated her, most Munro warriors didn't respect Duncan. She suspected his only allies were the men who rode with him that day. "I shall take you to face judgment."

Duncan nodded, and a man dismounted and

stalked toward Cairren. She saw the rope in his hands, and she knew they would bind both her hands and her feet. The man produced a strip of Munro plaid and gagged her. She didn't resist, but when she was flung belly-down over Duncan's saddle, she thought she would cast up the bannocks and dried beef she ate to break her fast. He gave her backside a resounding slap. Duncan muttered, "I shall have fun with you before we do aught else."

Cairren tried to rear up and look at Lachlan. She hadn't imagined when she surrendered that Duncan would assault her. She'd assumed that he wouldn't actually want to touch her, that his actions in the past had just been to intimidate her. Now she knew just how deeply she had underestimated him. She tried to catch Lachlan's eye, but it was impossible with the horse's head in the way. The Munros spun around and headed southwest, the opposite direction from Foulis.

Lachlan held up a staying hand until the men disappeared. "To Foulis, and don't spare the horses."

CHAPTER THIRTY-SIX

Padraig decided after leaving Dunrobin to return to Foulis for more supplies and men before he would begin the chase to Stirling and possibly beyond. He was nearly home when he noticed the Sutherland party racing toward him. He reined in and waited, but his heart hammered when he heard Lachlan call out, "Your brother has her!"

Padraig's horse ate up the scant distance and reared when he pulled his mount to a stop. "How?" he demanded.

"He had a score of men who outflanked us and shot at us. Lady Cairren refused to consider evading them, arguing she didn't want to see any of us dead. Honorable, but it put her in your brother's hands. She walked to him willingly, but he bound and gagged her, riding southwest. Fool that he is, he left us alive. I think Cairren's argument aboot what awaited the Munros should we die was convincing. But he had to know we'd go straight to you."

Padraig looked in the direction Lachlan mentioned and wondered if Duncan would ride around the western side of Foulis and then head to Ross territory, where he would receive a warm welcome from

Myrna. But Padraig knew he wouldn't. It would be too easy for Padraig to cut him off, and it would put him in Mackenzie territory. Padraig wondered if Duncan would circle back and hide on Urquhart land or even try to get as far south as the Frasers. He just didn't know.

"He wouldn't dare cross over into Mackenzie territory, would he?" Lachlan asked and brought Padraig out of his ruminations.

"I doubt it. He might continue south to the Frasers, but that's too far to return to Foulis without too many questions asked. He might head to Urquhart la—" Padraig suddenly knew where his brother would head. He couldn't believe he hadn't thought of it immediately.

"Are you planning to share what you've realized?" Lachlan asked as he looked sideways at Padraig.

"He's headed to the caves along the coast of Cromarty Firth where it meets Moray Firth. He'll put Cairren in one of the caves and leave her there for high tide to drown her. It's the easiest place to be rid of her without having to do it himself or worry aboot disposing of her body."

"If that's the case, he probably rode far enough to see us turnaround and then turned east. He has an hour's lead on us," Lachlan noted.

Padraig glanced in the sun's direction and knew they couldn't waste time if they were to be there before the afternoon high tide. He knew Cairren was a strong swimmer, but it wouldn't matter if her skirts weighed her down and the waves bashed her against the rocks. Padraig, Lachlan, and their men spurred their horses to the east as Padraig began his litany of prayers over again.

Cairren swallowed as the jostling and hanging upside down made her gorge rise. She would choke if she were ill with the gag in her mouth. She kept her eyes closed. Watching the ground race by beneath her had only made the sensation worse. She listened to the men, but they didn't speak. She'd been able to tell when they turned east, but she didn't know the geography around Foulis to know where they were going. She knew Cromarty Firth lay to the east, and she suspected that was where they were headed, but she wasn't certain. She remembered Padraig telling her about the caves he'd explored as a child. He and Duncan rode out one day, and his older brother pushed him in just as the tide was changing. The tide nearly sucked Padraig into a cave. He told Cairren he'd never forgotten his fear, but one of his father's guards had ridden after the boys when he learned they'd snuck out. Adam dove in and used his larger body to shield Padraig from the crashing waves until he could drag Padraig ashore. Cairren recalled Padraig telling her that Duncan received a beating for his actions, but he'd grinned at Padraig when his punishment was done, unrepentant for nearly killing his younger brother. Padraig told Cairren that it was that event that made him never trust his brother again. Cairren supposed Myrna's duplicitous behavior surprised him at first, but Duncan's hadn't. He'd told Cairren he wouldn't put anything past his brother's depraved mind. Not after he saw Wynda's body.

Cairren caught a whiff of sea air, and her stomach finally sank, to her body's relief but her mind's horror. She knew her death was imminent. She wondered if Lachlan and the Sutherlands would find Padraig. She had a moment of doubt that he would come for her, if he even guessed where Duncan took her. She almost slid from the horse when Duncan brought them to a stop. He'd fondled her bottom and breasts throughout the ride, even hitching up her skirts to reach his hand beneath to her bare skin. He'd tried to slide his hand between her legs, but she'd pushed her knees against his horse's flank, threatening to push herself off the horse. The horse stumbled a step then tried to rear, and a hard spank rained down on her over her clothes. Duncan continued to touch her, but he didn't risk his horse rearing and throwing them both.

Duncan was none-too-gentle when he yanked Cairren from the horse. Her knees gave out, but when she sank to the ground, Duncan pulled her up by a handful of hair. She yelped behind the gag, and many of the men laughed. She scanned her surroundings, hearing the crashing waves and seeing the expanse of water. They were incongruous, the water flat but the waves loud. She knew it meant the tide was rising, and she knew it meant Duncan would hurry to place her inside a cave. They'd tied her hands in front of her, which made the horseback ride more comfortable, she supposed, but it also meant that she could reach the dirk she carried. It surprised her that Duncan hadn't remembered she carried one and taken it from her. She tucked her belt under her arisaid since no one gave her a smaller plaid and still wore Padraig's. This made it easier for her to move about Foulis with no one realizing she was armed; now that would come in handy. She was certain she could reach it, but she didn't know whether she could saw through the ropes binding her hands and feet before the surf was higher than her head. Not for the first time did she wish she was taller.

Still holding her hair and a rope coiled over his shoulder, Duncan maneuvered her along the uneven path that led to the caves. She caught her first glance at the caves, and her heart sank. The tide was rising, but people could still come and go. It meant Duncan had time to secure her in the cavern rather than just toss her in. She pretended to stumble when they reached the sand, giving her an opportunity to pull the *sgian dubh* free before Duncan pinned her arms down. The short, sharp knife would make fraying the rope easier, even if the blade wasn't very long. She would also use it to stab Duncan, if she had the chance. Cairren trudged along as Duncan led her to the back of a cave. A stalagmite was conveniently located near the back wall. She kept the knife hidden within her sleeve; the blade nicked her with each step, but she figured having the blade poking her was the lesser of two evils.

"I shall remove your gag, so you can scream to your heart's content and ken no one is coming for you. Padraig will never guess to come here, and even if he did, the tide will have drowned you before he figures it out. Perhaps he'll wade down and drag your corpse out. Likely, you'll become food for the fish. There are some rather large ones with pointy teeth just waiting to tear you apart," Duncan chuckled, but it faded when Cairren didn't cringe. She knew the basking sharks were seasonal on the east coast, just as they were on the west. They would already be gone this close to winter. She also knew the water would be frigid.

They splashed through the swishing water that entered the cave along with them. Cairren's boots and skirts absorbed water, already making it hard to walk. She stumbled again and forced herself not to cry out when her dirk poked her. She was certain it broke the skin, and she wasn't excited about blood attracting larger fish. She didn't resist when Duncan tied her to the enormous standing stone, grateful that he bound the rope around her arms above the elbow. It meant she could work the thick coil free.

"If there was only more time," Duncan sighed. "I would have given you a good swiving." His laugh echoed off the walls and sounded more like a cackle. He pulled the gag free before squeezing her chin between his fingers and thumb. "Go ahead and scream. I want to hear your fear as I walk away."

Cairren was tempted to spew the obscenities she'd learned at court and the ones she'd heard from the Munros, but she took care not to antagonize Duncan. She also didn't want him to grow suspicious, so she let loose an ear-piercing scream as he moved toward the entrance. As soon as she could no longer see Duncan, she began working on the ropes. She would take her chances if he were to return, but she wouldn't lose a minute while the tide surged toward her, splashing over her knees. The saltwater spray stung her eyes, and the frigid water splashing her face felt like shards of ice, but she worked quickly to cut the ropes. She grew impatient as the minutes passed, but it was awkward trying to drag the knife along the rope, especially without cutting herself. The water had reached her mid-thighs when the length gave way. She inched her way to the side of the cave where she saw a ledge that was wet but not submerged. She squatted, trying to keep her skirts out of the way as she worked to free her feet. She knew she had a better chance with her stronger legs propelling her through the water than her arms.

Once her feet were loose and she'd kicked off her

boots, she ripped at her skirts just above her knees. Her muscular legs would do her little good if they were tangled in fabric. She ripped a hole in the material, but it was hard to cut it. She stood on the hem, pulling the fabric taut, making it a little easier to tear. When she had a hole large enough for her fingers, she kept her feet on the hem of the skirt but took a large step forward while pulling up on the part her fingers held. The skirt tore, and she continued taking steps toward the mouth of the cave until the ledge ran out. She'd ripped a large enough hole that when she bent over and leaned against the wall, she could step through it. She gathered the material between her teeth and split the rest of it off. She was breathless by the time she finished. She pulled her arisaid loose. Her only regret to leaving it behind was that it was Padraig's; she couldn't care less that it was a Munro plaid. She watched the tide push it into the cavern before sucking it back toward her. The rushing water now submerged the ledge, and the water was rapidly rising to her waist. She tried to use the last few minutes she had to loosen her wrists. Between the knife and her teeth, the rope grew slack, but not enough to break through or to slip her hands out. She knew the bone chilling water would only make the fibers more rigid, but she had no choice. She had to abandon the cave, or it would become her coffin.

Dunure Castle had a secret passageway that led below the cliffs to Browney's Cave. Her parents insisted that their daughters know how to make their way through the tunnel and out to the postern gate. They'd shown the girls how to scale the rock face to find the key that unlocked the gate, allowing them freedom to the Firth of Clyde. She'd learned to swim in the firth and was grateful she knew what to expect as the icy water continued to rise. It didn't make it feel any less cold, but it also didn't steal her breath. Her father taught her to count how long each inward and outward surge lasted, so she would know when to surface and cling to the rocks. She tried not to dwell on the inward surge, which appeared more powerful, lasting longer than the outward.

I can't wait any longer. I chose to go with Duncun not only to save Lachlan and his men but because I thought it was my best chance to save my bairn. Waiting in this cave will surely kill us both.

She put the handle of her *sgian dubh* in her mouth and eased into the water, gingerly feeling around with her legs for any outcroppings of rocks she hadn't spied as she entered. She waited through two sets of surges to get a feel for the waves' strength. When the third outward surge began, she dove under the surface and kicked as hard as she could as she counted. Just before the movement shifted, she surfaced. She used her fingers to grip the rocks as best she could, but the strength of the rushing water pushed her back a couple of feet. She dove again as the tide sucked the water from the cave. She kicked even as the muscles in her legs rebelled against working in the freezing water.

You can't give up. It's not aboot you anymore. You have someone else to think aboot. Cairren reminded herself once again of the babe she suspected she carried. She would do anything she could to protect the life that might be growing within her womb.

It took Cairren four rounds of swimming with the current until she emerged from the mouth. She had to contend with the crashing waves and spray pushing her toward the jagged rocks. She found a rock she could wrap her legs around and clung to it, as she heaved and spat saltwater. She glanced around, trying to get her bearing. She could see where Duncan brought her down to the cave, but the high tide covered the pebbly beach. She wasn't sure that even if she made it there that she could reach up to climb the rocks to the part of the path free of water. She considered turning her back to the waves and trying again to free her hands, but she knew the rope wouldn't give now that it was wet. She would do better to save her energy.

Cairren looked across the cave's mouth and tried to see if there was another path up the cliffside, but she couldn't see anything. It would be hours before the tide went out, and she would freeze to death before then. She had no choice but to try to at least cling to the rocks along the shore where the beach had been, rather than remaining in the middle of the opening to the cave. She gripped her dirk between her teeth again and drew in a deep breath. She prayed she was strong enough not to be dragged back into the cave. She pushed away from the rocks, kicking and using her arms to pull her through the water. When her lungs couldn't last any longer, she kicked to the surface. She'd traveled further than she expected, but the cliff still appeared elusive. She didn't give herself time to think beyond drawing in another deep breath before diving under.

CHAPTER THIRTY-SEVEN

Padraig peered over the edge of the cliff at something dark floating in the water. He strained to see before it sank beneath the water. A few seconds later, it surfaced once again, closer to the shore. "By God, it's Cairren!"

Padraig eased his way along the shale path as Cairren's face came into focus. He knew when she spotted him because she kept her head above the surface despite the waves crashing into her. As she drew closer, he saw her mouth move, but the wind and waves drowned out the sound. He continued down the path with Lachlan, Henry, and Peter on his heels. When he reached the end of the trail before it disappeared under the water, he lay on his belly, waiting for Cairren to be close enough to lift her out of the water. She bobbed nearer until he heard her voice. Muffled, it was still the sweetest sound he'd ever heard.

"Padraig!" Cairren called. She kicked and used her arms under water to pull her along as she strained to keep her head above water. She'd considered rolling onto her back, but she wanted to see where she was going, not where she'd been. She wasn't interested in cracking her head into the rocks. When she was where she thought the beach began, she tried to lower her legs and brush her feet against the ground. It was deeper than she expected, and her head dipped below the surface. She came up to the sound of Padraig's panicked voice.

"Cairren!" Padraig screamed frantically. "Cairren!"

"I'm here! I thought it might be shallow enough to stand," Cairren called back, but Padraig shook his head. "It won't be. The tide makes it too deep. You'll have to reach up to me. You might need to climb up the rocks until we can grab each other's hand."

"I can't." Cairren choked on a mouthful of water as she raised her hands in the air. "I can barely grip aught, let alone climb."

Padraig couldn't believe his eyes. His tiny wife had swum out of the cave and around the protruding cliff and rocks with her hands bound. He'd never been prouder than he was as he watched her continue to swim closer. He stood and pulled off his boots. He handed his sword to Lachlan before stripping off his plaid. "She'll need it more than me." Turning, he yelled out, "I'm coming down to get you, Cairren. I'll get you out."

"Nay! The surf is too rough, and I think there are rocks down here. You can't jump."

"Then I'll ease my way in, but I'm coming to get you, Ren."

Cairren smiled despite being half-frozen when she heard his pet name for her. Somehow it made things just a wee bit better. She drew as close to the rocks as she could and treaded water as Padraig eased his way into the surf before dropping the last couple of feet. He swam to her and pulled her into his arms.

"I'm going to kiss you breathless as soon as I get you on shore, Ren," Padraig pledged.

"Aught if it will get me warm," Cairren replied as her teeth chattered. With Padraig near her and rescue close by, she noticed the full force of the bitter cold.

"We'll build a fire and get you warm. I promise. Climb onto my back and loop your arms over my head."

Cairren followed his directions but giggled as his hands touched her bare calves then slid up her leg. "That tickles. But Padraig, I'm indecent. I cut my skirts short, so they wouldn't suck me under. My legs are bare from knee down, and I have no shoes."

"I wouldn't care if you were naked if it means you're safe. I'll get you covered in my plaid sharpish."

"Bah! I'd care if I was naked!"

Padraig marveled at Cairren, her sense of humor still plucky despite her condition. He looked up to the rocks as he reached them. "Get a fire going!"

"Padraig, you won't be able to scale that with me on your back." The cliff looked far higher above the water than it had at a distance. Even where Lachlan and the others stood waiting seemed too far.

"You're my Ren. Just like the wee songbird. You're naught more than a feather on my back. Hold on, little one." Padraig found his first finger holds, his feet feeling for notches beneath the surface. When he was certain he could make his first move, he pushed with his legs, reaching for the next finger hold. He repeated the motion as Cairren clung to him. He knew she squeezed her eyes shut and tucked her head to not have to look. "We're almost there, little one."

They emerged from the water, and Cairren wanted to cry with relief. But when Padraig didn't move, she opened her eyes. She looked around and then over Padraig's head. She realized the problem immediately. There was nowhere within reach that Padraig's fingers could grip.

"Hold my feet," Lachlan instructed Peter and Henry as he laid on his belly. He hung Padraig's plaid down the rock face. "Grab on, we'll pull you up."

Padraig grasped as high on the plaid as he could, twisting it around his wrist before grasping with the other hand. When Lachlan began pulling hand over hand, Padraig assisted the efforts by walking up the rocks. Cairren's legs were locked around Padraig's trim waist, her feet clasped together at the ankle. She did all that she could not to pull Padraig backwards. When they were within reach, Henry and Peter helped pull Cairren onto the path before tugging Padraig up.

"You'd do well to eat fewer meat pies," Peter teased, but Padraig wasn't listening. He'd already yanked his plaid from Lachlan and wrapped it around Cairren. Their mouths crashed together as relief and need swirled together, culminating in a searing kiss that left them breathless and clinging to one another. Padraig lifted Cairren into his arms and carried her to the fire the other men had already started. Padraig was relieved to see that the men had already hunted rabbits and were preparing them for the spit.

"Get the spare plaids from my pack," Padraig instructed Henry. Padraig looked down at Cairren's blue lips and the blue veins that showed in her eyelids. He needed to get her warm. When Henry handed him the two extra plaids, he carried Cairren among the horses and set her down. He spotted a knife in a nearby saddlebag and used it to cut the ties from Cairren's wrists, upset by the rope burns on her skin. He whispered, trying to save her some embarrassment. "You need to take what's left of your gown off, or you'll freeze to death. I need to get you warm."

"I need help. My fingers don't want to do aught." She turned her back to him, and he was tempted to slice through the laces, but he wasn't sure if she would have to don the remnants of her gown again. He tugged them free and helped her ease the gown and her chemise off before he whipped off his leine. He swung two plaids around them and pulled her against his body.

"How're you warm? How's that even possible?" Cairren's teeth chattered.

"I'm touching you. You heat my blood, little one." Padraig kissed her again, his cock insistently pressing against their bellies. "What I wouldn't give to be alone with you, Ren. I would worship every inch of you."

"Just hold me for right now. I was so scared."

"I'm sure you were, little one, but I have never been so proud of anyone. You're the bravest person I've ever met."

"Hardly. I'm not the one who's ridden into battle."

"But you have," Padraig insisted. "Each time you stepped out of your chamber, our chamber, you were prepared to go into battle. I can't imagine how you got out of the cave, but you did. You never cease to amaze me," Padraig murmured the last sentence against her lips before they once more fused their mouths together. Holding the plaid fisted in one hand, Padraig used the other to explore Cairren's body. Her hands roamed over his, leaving trails of fire wherever they touched. "They know I'm trying to get you warm, but can you stay quiet?"

Cairren nodded as she strained on her toes to reach

Padraig's mouth. He lifted her, and she wrapped her legs around him once more. He slid into her sheath, and he struggled not to groan at how right it felt to bury himself inside his wife. His arm wrapped around her waist kept her pinned against his body as they moved together. When their pace didn't satisfy either of them, he pulled the plaids so Cairren could grasp where the ends met. With both hands free, he grabbed her bottom and rocked into her. She laid her head on his shoulder, kissing his neck as he thrust over and over. When her release swept through her, she clenched her eyes and her jaw to keep from crying out. Padraig surged into her twice more before he stilled. They held one another, Cairren wrapped around him like a bear on a tree trunk. She never wanted to let him go, yet she knew she couldn't stay with him. Coupling only reminded her that it wasn't just her life she risked. She'd chosen what she thought was the safer option when she agreed to go with Duncan. She thought she was less likely to die from an arrow wound if she capitulated. She never imagined Duncan would try to drown her. She was more convinced than ever that her home could never be Foulis.

"Do you feel warmer?" Padraig grinned, and Cairren shot him a rueful smile. He continued to hold her as his hands rubbed more warmth into her. She was still chilled, but he was no longer fearful that she would succumb to hypothermia. When her lips no longer showed any hints of blue, they shuffled to his horse where he pulled out two spare leines. He helped her into one and couldn't avoid laughing when the garment that hung to his knees trailed on the ground. "You look adorable," Padraig chuckled.

"I look like a child playing dress up," Cairren huffed, but she grinned.

"Come. Let's get you by the fire and something to eat."

"Do you have any whisky?" Cairren grinned even wider.

"Aye, you ken we do." Padraig led Cairren out to the fire, the two plaids wrapped around her on top of the leine. Once she was settled with her fingers and toes pointed toward the blaze, Padraig pleated his plaid and put it back on. He came to sit beside her and passed her the whisky she asked for. The men hooted as she took a long draw and didn't hiss or choke. She felt the warmth all the way to her feet and knew she'd had enough.

"Will we spend the night here?" Cairren whispered.

"Nay. Once you've eaten and are warm, we'll return to Foulis." Padraig watched Cairren's reaction, but her eyes were guarded as she watched the rabbits roasting.

"Once I've eaten? You didn't say we."

"Aye. Both rabbits are for you. And before you protest and say you don't need that much, yes, you did. You used much of your endurance in that icy water. You need your strength even if the ride isn't that long." Padraig saw she was still prepared to argue. "For me. Will you please do this for me?"

Cairren gazed into Padraig's eyes and saw remorse and fear still shone in his deep brown eyes and the creases in his brow. He seemed to have aged in the few days they'd been apart. She felt guilty for the worry she'd caused, but she didn't regret fleeing. She wasn't eager to return to Foulis either.

"Must be we go back?" Cairren whispered. "I'm scared, Padraig. You can't gainsay your father, and

Duncan is obviously a danger to me. Did your father send Duncan after me?"

"I don't know the answer to your second question, but we can go back. The clan council removed Father Mitchell and intends to send him back to the Mackintoshes. It disgusted them to discover what he'd done. The elders want you to return, and you have their vote of confidence. Many admitted, even Alistair who tried to elbow you on our wedding night, that they still see you as foreign, but it no longer scares them. They are willing to change. Those who you've tended appreciate your dedication. It was my mother and Father Mitchell, along with Myrna, who perpetuated the hatred. The clan didn't dare speak against their lady and their priest. They followed where they were led. And I know I contributed to that, Ren. I've failed you time and again. Bluidy hell, I've said that time and again, but I want you to come home. The clan has pledged that it's safe for you."

Cairren wanted to believe Padraig. She wanted to make their marriage work because she believed she'd fallen in love with him, but she didn't trust the Munros in the slightest, especially not after the future laird nearly drowned her. She looked at the ground and considered what she would say. She'd just coupled with Padraig, and the memory of their intimacy tempted her to give in, but as her stomach grumbled, she remembered that it was no longer just about her. She would buy herself some time.

"Very well. But I'm still scared, Padraig. Your father and Father Mitchell wanted to burn me alive. Your mother would have thrown the first spark. Your brother left me for dead. There's no one left in your family who doesn't want me gone."

"I'm not leaving your side," Padraig assured her.

"You can't be tied to me day and night," Cairren said as she shook her head.

"Let's get through tonight, Ren, then we can make decisions."

Cairren nodded, but she already knew what she would do. She felt like God smiled upon her when Padraig insisted that Lachlan and the Sutherland guards should accept Munro hospitality for the night. When Padraig slipped away for a moment of privacy, Lachlan approached Cairren.

"You still want to go to Stirling, don't you? Probably even more than before."

"I do. I don't want to hurt Padraig. That was never my goal, but I can't remain at Foulis. I know Padraig wants to hold out faith in his clan, but I have none."

"My men and I will take you, but do you think Padraig will let you leave?"

"Aye, I do. Not without trying to convince me to stay, but I believe he wants what's best for me. He has to know that remaining will never work." Cairren watched the spot where she'd last seen Padraig. "I'll pack a satchel and be ready before dawn. I dislike it, but I may be sneaking out."

"I figured as much. Do you want me to get him in his cups?"

At first Cairren shook her head; then she nodded, only to shake it once again as Lachlan chuckled. "Let me talk to him and see if I can reason with him. If he refuses, then helping him drown his sorrows might not be that bad." Lachlan stepped away when Padraig appeared, smiling at Cairren as he went to check his horse.

"What was that aboot?" Cairren couldn't miss the suspicion in Padraig's voice.

"He just wanted to check on me. He was being kind."

Padraig watched Lachlan over Cairren's head. Something didn't sit well with him, but he tried to convince himself that he was just being possessive of his beautiful wife. He reminded himself that he'd just reunited with her, and she'd given no indication that she wanted to be anywhere but with him. Once the fire was out, Padraig helped Cairren mount in front of him, and they rode for Foulis.

CHAPTER THIRTY-EIGHT

When Cairren passed under the portcullis, she felt the same fear as she did the first time she entered the bailey. She looked around as people milled about and watched the riders dismount. She stayed close to Padraig's side, and his arm wrapped protectively around her shoulder made her feel a little less anxious. She breathed easier when she noticed the stake and pyre no longer stood in the center of the bailey, and no one ran at her with a flaming torch. Cairren looked at the steps leading to the keep's main doors. She recognized members of the clan council standing at some distance from Micheil and Mary. She didn't see Duncan or Father Mitchell, and she had to admit relief when she didn't see Myrna, who she half-expected to find waiting for Padraig. Padraig shared on the ride back that neither Duncan nor Myrna knew what Padraig discovered. Duncan hadn't been in the bailey when Padraig argued with his parents and the priest. He'd still been with Myrna.

"Lady Cairren," Arnold called out as he hobbled forward on his walking stick. "On behalf of the clan council, we are relieved to see ye returned to us hale and hearty."

Cairren didn't know what to say. There was no possibility they knew what Duncan had attempted. Before she could respond, Mary's shrewish tones filled her ears.

"You want us to believe she's a proper Christian when she walks around in naught but a mon's leine. Disgraceful."

Padraig stepped forward, but Cairren put a staying hand on his arm. If there was even a remote possibility that she would stay, she needed to discover what would happen if she asserted herself.

"I'm wearing my husband's leine because I destroyed my gown. Do you ken where your other son is? Has he returned from his errand to drown me?" At the stunned gasps from the surrounding people, she suspected her questions were unexpected, but Mary's face didn't change. "Were you the one to suggest he take me to the Cromarty caves and drown me in the Moray Firth? Because that's where he took me after trying to kill Lachlan Sutherland and his guards. My husband's leine was the only thing appropriate I had after having to cut my body free from a standing stone, before I sliced away the bindings at my feet. I had little choice but to cut the bottom of my skirts so they wouldn't pull me to the bottom of the firth. Since neither you nor Duncan bothered to get to know me, you never learned that my father taught me to swim in the Firth of Clyde. Not so different from Moray, just not quite as bluidy cold."

"Explain this," Arnold demanded, but his eyes were on Micheil and Mary rather than Cairren.

"I left here when you sentenced me to death for a crime I didn't commit. I went to the Sutherlands, and the laird offered me escort south. We were just a little past here when Duncan and a score of men attacked, shooting arrows at us. I turned myself over to Duncan, praying he would keep his word and allow Lachlan and his men safe passage home. Duncan had me bound and gagged before throwing me over his saddle. He forced me to ride from here to the firth on my belly." Cairren wasn't about to speak of the other things Duncan did while they shared a horse. "He took me to the caves, where he tied me to a standing stone. He removed my gag and ordered me to scream, so he could enjoy hearing my cries, knowing no one would come for me. Daft man didn't check to see if I had any knives. I cut myself free and swam out."

"Impossible," Micheil argued. "If he intended to drown you, then it was when the tide came in. You couldn't have swum out. You're lying."

"And you're deaf," Cairren countered. "Did you not hear me say that my father taught me to swim in the Firth of Clyde? It's not some placid loch. Do you not ken that Dunure sits on a cliff with caves beneath it? Where do you think I learned? He taught me how to escape should I ever need to. I never dreamed it would come in handy, but I'm glad my father thought of it. I swam out and around the outcropping. I was making my way to the cliffs when Padraig and the other men arrived. Padraig jumped in and pulled me out."

"The lass hadn't time to cut her hands free," Padraig added. "She did all of that just by kicking and determination. I don't know any mon who'd be that quick-witted and brave." Padraig pulled her closer to his side and dropped a kiss on her forehead as she looked up at him.

Cairren looked around at the stunned faces, and

she witnessed more anger directed at the laird and lady than she did toward her. She saw sympathy and pity when people looked at her. She smiled when Catriona stepped forward, holding her son in her arms. She smiled warmly at Cairren before looking around.

"I ken I'm nae a member of the laird's family or part of the clan council, but I would like to ken what's to be done aboot the two attempts to murder Lady Cairren." There was a chorus of agreement as more people stepped forward to demand answers to similar questions.

Adam raised his hands, and the clan fell quiet. "Before that is decided, we need to ken if the laird will accept the council's judgment as binding."

Micheil raised his chin, arrogance making him ugly. "I'm still laird here. This is my clan to run as I see fit. I may have been fooled once by the priest, but that doesn't change who Lady Cairren is, and she is not one of us."

Padraig lunged at his father, even though he felt Cairren try to pull him back. He noted his father's personal guards moved to separate them, but they weren't as quick as they should have been. "Then return her dowry if she's no use to the clan," Padraig demanded.

"When the Kennedy returns the bride price," Micheil countered.

"How soon can you send a messenger?" Cairren infused innocence into her voice, but the steely challenge was written across her face.

Adam once more intervened. "Does this mean we are to understand that ye willna accept the council's judgment, Micheil?"

"It means that this is my clan to do as I see fit." Micheil pounded his fist into his hand. "Be glad I changed my mind not to have her burned at the stake."

"Changed yer mind?" Arnold guffawed. "We threatened to put ye up next since that so-called holy water burned ye too. Ye're naught but a blathering fool, just like yer father was, and just like yer worthless heir. We'd do well to be done with this one and his wasted spawn and have Padraig in charge."

Padraig and Cairren froze as the murmurs spread through the crowd, and far too many heads nodded for Cairren's comfort. She stepped to Padraig's side, her eyes wide with worry. He glanced down at her; her uncertainty was as clear to him as his own. The situation was not going in a direction that either expected.

"And I'll have my guards imprison anyone fool enough to cross me, you treasonous bastards," Micheil roared.

"Then what will ye do with Duncan?" Meg asked. "It isnae just Lady Cairren's word or Padraig's. Duncan involved the Sutherlands. This willna go over well with Lachlan's da. Laird Sutherland isnae kenned to forgive those who harm his kin."

A calculating gleam entered Micheil's eyes, but it fizzled when Lachlan stepped forward. "We expect my Uncle Liam to visit in a sennight. I'm sure he'd be happy to ride with my father to recover my body should you go through with whatever your scheming mind is conjuring."

Lachlan's subtle reminder that the Sutherlands and Sinclairs stood as one force created further dissention among the crowd. "Nay!" "By God!" "Bluidy hell, that's all we need." And those people who had turned loyal gazes toward the laird and lady began to look away.

"Let me pose another question," Adam's booming voice hushed the clan members. "Does Lady Cairren have a place among our clan? A place where she is safe and welcome?"

The bailey grew deathly quiet as people looked around, but no one spoke. Cairren glanced over her shoulder at Lachlan, and he nodded his head. The clan was still frightened to support her against the laird and lady. As long as that was the case, there was still too much danger for Cairren to remain.

"Natter amongst yourselves," Padraig grumbled. "I'm taking my wife to our chamber. She's had enough of an ordeal this past sennight to last her a month of Sundays." Padraig guided Cairren up the stairs, ignoring his parents. He cocked an eyebrow at a servant who stood staring too long. "Food and a bath."

Cairren felt chilled, and it had nothing to do with the air temperature. Being inside Foulis only brought her unhappiness and trepidation. Other than coupling with Padraig, nothing good had happened since she stepped foot in the castle. She'd held out hope that the clan might surprise her, and they had. She'd expected swords drawn and pitchforks pointing at her, but the clan was more welcoming than she imagined. But their fear of the laird and lady outweighed even their fear of her being different. She couldn't blame them when she reminded herself that their entire livelihood depended upon remaining in the laird's good graces. Clan members worked in the keep and industries within the bailey wall, but they also farmed the land that belonged to the laird. The servants, craftsmen, and tenant farmers would have nowhere to go if the laird evicted them from the land they worked or, worse, banished them from the clan. Micheil held control, not with respect but with fear. Cairren understood that and pitied the clan, but she wouldn't jeopardize her babe for them.

CHAPTER THIRTY-NINE

Padraig wanted nothing more than to soak in a hot bath with his wife leaning back against him, or better still, draped over him. He was hungry, tired, and irritated. He'd expected his parents to put up an argument, but he'd also seen his mother's reaction when Cairren asked her about Duncan. He knew she was involved in Duncan's plan, and it wouldn't surprise him if she were the mastermind. His father was stubborn and too prideful.

And I wonder where I get it from. What has it gained either of us? The clan doesnae respect him. He only has control because he intimidates everyone into going along with him. I should have had faith in the clan council, but they've dragged their feet to intervene. Pride goeth before the fall, and I've tumbled head over heels. Perhaps I should have listened a little better to ma Bible lessons. Pride has lost me ma wife. I ken she still wants to leave. Do I take her to Stirling? Do I insist she stay? That'll only make her run away with Lachlan. Do I trust him to take her? That I ken is a nay. I dinna trust anyone with Ren's life.

"Padraig, did you hear me?" Cairren's voice broke through his thoughts.

"Sorry, Ren. I was lost in thought," Padraig smiled sheepishly.

"I need to talk to you," Cairren said as they entered their chamber. Her eyes swept around the room, a chamber filled with her best and worst memories.

"I ken. You're still going to Stirling, aren't you?" Padraig saw no reason not to go straight to the point.

"Aye. I can't stay here. Not as long as your parents and Duncan live here, and that will be for many years."

"Then let's go to Dunure." Padraig hesitated as he wondered if she wasn't only leaving Foulis, but leaving him.

"I will think aboot that. If I can spare anyone traveling in winter, I will. The weather is changing, and I don't ken that I'll make it to Stirling before the first snowfall. Dunure might be too far."

"Before you make it to Stirling. So you're going without me?" Padraig's voice grew quieter with each word. The realization that Cairren might ride away without him and never return made him want to heave or cry, perhaps both.

"You can't. You're still Duncan's second. You have duties here, and you will be Duncan's heir until he has a son. We have no way of knowing when that will be."

"The way he and Myrna are, it should take aboot a sennight. They'll likely wed soon."

"I will not live under the same roof as her again. She'll only be worse once she and Duncan are openly allied."

"Then allow me to stay in Stirling until we can go to Dunure," Padraig tried to reason.

"And do what? Become a courtier? The queen might accept me among her matrons, but what will you do? Spend all day, every day in the lists? You'd be miserable."

"I'd be with you," Padraig insisted.

Cairren's shoulders slumped. They'd come to an impasse, their differences too irreconcilable to move forward. She wouldn't remain at Foulis with his family governing her life, and he couldn't leave because he was duty-bound to remain. "Let Lachlan take me to Stirling. Time apart might not be horrible."

"Yes, it would. Ren, I want you by my side, not halfway across the country. We have much to overcome, much for me to prove. How can we do that with you in Stirling and me in the Highlands? Unless you don't want to work things out." The idea crushed Padraig when he said it out loud. It was one thing when it was a thought silently swirling around in his mind. He could push it to the side, pretend like it was never there. But he'd said it aloud, and it was very real, hanging in the air between him.

Cairren wanted to avoid answering. She wanted to skirt the issue, but she knew Padraig would realize what she was doing and persist until he got an answer. She opted for honesty. "I don't know."

Padraig nodded. He supposed it was better than her saying no. Her admission was the last thing said before the servants arrived with food and the bath. Padraig looked keenly at the tub, but Cairren's eyelids were already beginning to droop. He needed to get her fed, warm, and clean before she climbed into their bed.

Our bed. That's the last time I might ever think of it that way. But who am I kidding? I have nay one to blame but maself. I could have done the honorable thing and sent Myrna away before Cairren even arrived, but I didna. I wanted to have everything, a wife to bed and another woman to love. I did this. I destroyed our chance. I'm more to blame than ma parents, Duncan, and Myrna combined. I pledged maself to her, and didna mean any of it except for the part aboot nae sharing ma bed with another woman. Why would I have needed to? All I did back then was lust for her. Things couldnae be more different, yet they're still the same. She canna stay.

Padraig pushed his self-recrimination aside as he helped Cairren bathe, then encouraged her to eat. It wasn't until after she climbed into bed and fell asleep that he ate and bathed himself. He slid into the bed next to her, and she rolled closer, curling against him. He knew she didn't realize what she was doing, but even in sleep, part of her knew that she belonged at his side. He would take her to Stirling, but he wouldn't relinquish his wife.

CHAPTER FORTY

Cairren awoke from the deepest sleep she could remember and found Padraig wrapped around her tightly. It was as though he shielded her from the world. She lay without moving as she absorbed the warmth of his body and the security it offered. When she arrived at Foulis and met him, she never imagined she would sleep next to him. She assumed they would remain distant, constant enemies. His presence now was familiar and comforting. But it also wasn't enough.

Cairren tried to slip from her cocoon, but Padraig pulled her back against his chest and nuzzled her neck. "Fifteen more minutes, Ren. Then we'll get ready to leave."

Cairren rolled toward him, their eyes locking on one another. Without words, their mouths came together. Padraig's tongue flicked Cairren's lips as she parted them for him. Their tongues tangled and dueled as the kiss combusted into a need that could only be satisfied one way. There was silent acceptance that this might be the last time they ever coupled, and both needed it to say goodbye. Padraig's hand caressed her breasts as she arched her back to him, her mewls fueling his desire as he tweaked her nipples. When his fingers grazed over her belly, Cairren shivered then moaned when those questing digits dipped into her entrance. She pressed her hips to meet his hand.

As she rocked to each thrust, his thumb circled her nub until she writhed with a burning need to feel him inside her. She reached for his length, stroking him as he worked her core. She moved slowly as she marveled as she always did that something so hard and forceful could be so smooth. She swept her thumb of the head of Padraig's cock, swirling what leaked from the tip. When neither could bear the foreplay any longer, Padraig rolled between Cairren's legs, and she guided him to her entrance. Padraig paused as once more their eyes met. They both saw a depth of emotion in their partner's eyes that conveyed as much as their joining and far more than words could. Padraig surged into her, and Cairren's head tilted back as she moaned. Her exposed neck was an invitation Padraig wouldn't resist. He kissed the satiny skin and along the taut cords until he reached the erotic spot behind her ear. Cairren's body burst, as if into flames, as her release spread from deep within her core.

Padraig wished they could freeze in time just as they were, the emotions and sensations suspended, but reveled in until eternity. He would forsake his duties, his birthright, everything if he could remain with Cairren. Her tight sheath pulled him deeper with every thrust until there was nowhere further to go. They couldn't be more joined than they were with him buried within her core, their mouths pressed together, and their arms wrapped around one another. There was nothing between them, nothing that could separate them as they moved as one, a practiced synchronicity. They hurtled toward their climax, crying out together. As Padraig's release filled her, he knew that there was no claim to Cairren greater than their lovemaking. It tempted him to proclaim his love, but it felt pathetic and manipulative to make that declaration as Cairren was set to leave. He would use their journey and their time in Stirling to prove it.

Cairren had never felt more cherished or deeply in love than while she and Padraig made love. She knew that their coupling was no longer just two bodies coming together. She could see the deep emotion in Padraig's eyes, and she knew what she felt. But he made no professions, and she'd sworn to leave. She considered telling him how she felt, but it would only make the journey and his time in Stirling more uncomfortable. She knew he would argue against it, but she would send him back to the Highlands while she waited out the winter at Stirling Castle. It might not have been what she wanted, but it was what she knew was right. She wouldn't swear never to return--she carried his child after all. She prayed that their time apart would be what they needed for Padraig to convince the clan she belonged. But both her head and her heart told her she was fooling herself, trying to ease the impending pain. She was certain Padraig would never take their child from her, but she wouldn't deny him time with their babe. She assured herself that they would cross that bridge when they came to it.

As Padraig withdrew from her, Cairren wanted to cling to him, not ready for them to part. She knew she couldn't. It was her desire to leave that would separate them. She swallowed the lump in her throat as she willed herself not to cry. She rolled to her side of the bed and inhaled deeply as she geared herself to dress and leave their chamber for the last time. She never imagined she would feel so conflicted, or that she would question her decision so much. Her eyes landed on her chest, and she knew that was the most she would take with her. She would leave her loom behind since there was no way to carry it with them. All her other worldly goods had been part of her dowry and now belonged to the Munros. She didn't hear Padraig approach, and jumped when he placed his hands on the outside of her shoulders. He nuzzled her neck and placed a kiss on her pulse point.

"I will ensure you get your loom. It's special to you, and I wouldn't deny you something you love." *I wouldnae deny ye aught.*

"Thank you. That means a great deal to me," Cairren choked out. She didn't resist leaning back against his chest, and he wrapped his arms around hers. Padraig kissed the crown of her head, then pulled his arms away. He watched as she hurriedly packed her satchel with items she would need during the six-day ride. When she finished, Padraig carried it out to the bailey where a stable hand already saddled her horse. Lachlan and his men were checking their mounts. Padraig scanned the waiting steeds and didn't see his among them. He scowled at Lachlan, who only shrugged. Padraig ordered his horse prepared as he approached Lachlan.

"I will accompany my wife. You and your men may return to Dunrobin," Padraig announced, but Lachlan shook his head.

"I trust you--sort of--but I don't trust any of your guards. My father tasked me with seeing Lady Cairren to Stirling, and that's what I shall do."

"Your company is not needed," Padraig growled.

"That's where you are wrong. You have a choice,

Padraig: let us ride with you or we ride behind you. But either way, Lady Cairren remains within my sight."

"Why does this matter to you?" Padraig's eyes narrowed.

"Don't be like that. I have no designs on your wife. She is my sister's friend, and my father is concerned aboot her. I'm concerned, too. What kind of mon would I be if I weren't after yesterday?"

Padraig nodded begrudgingly. He didn't want to admit it, but he felt better travelling with more men, ones who had proven they were willing to defend Cairren. "Very well. Let me arrange for my men." Padraig turned away to find Matthew, Peter, Henry, and Dougal approaching with their satchels and bedrolls. All four men looked forlorn, and it made Padraig wonder if they weren't all a little in love with his wife. He watched with amusement as Cairren stepped in front of Dougal and shook her head emphatically. He couldn't see her finger, but could see her arm move and knew she was wagging her finger at him.

"Absolutely not, Dougal. You'll do more harm than good."

"Ma lady, I've travelled with three cracked ribs."

"And how was that? Not so enjoyable, I bet."

"Hurt a damn sight less than this," Dougal grumbled.

"And I'll feel wretchedly guilty the entire time," Cairren cocked an eyebrow and lifted her chin defiantly. But she softened her tone when she added, "Dougal, I trust you with my life, but I don't want you to come to harm for my sake."

Padraig stepped forward and looked around. "What I need most from you, Dougal, is to remain here and keep an eye on my family and the guards. I need to ken whether it'll ever be safe to bring Lady Cairren back. I trust you."

Dougal looked between Padraig and Cairren then nodded, some of his sense of purpose restored. Cairren looked at Matthew, and her brow furrowed. "Are you sure you want to leave Catriona and Liam for so long?"

"Ma wife practically pushed me out the door and told me there'd be nay more bairns—nay more practicing making bairns—if I didna accompany ye, ma lady." Matthew blushed as he listened to Peter, Henry, and Dougal guffaw. Matthew elbowed Henry, who stood closest to him.

"He's telling the truth, and ye should keep yer gob closed, Henry, or I'll tell Sarah," Catriona said as she walked up. Henry fell silent, but Peter and Dougal only laughed harder. Catriona stopped next to Cairren and smiled widely. "I wanted to thank ye one last time, ma lady, for saving me and ma bairn."

"And thank ye for saving ma lass, ma lady," Elspeth said as she joined the two women. "I regret what I said when ye first arrived. I'm truly sorry, Lady Cairren. Ye've proven to be better than any pale-skinned lady."

An awkward pause followed. "I'm glad you changed your mind, Elspeth." Cairren wasn't sure what else to say after Elspeth's last comment. It didn't seem appropriate to agree.

"Lady Cairren, I would say the same," Meg approached from behind Cairren. "I said wretched things to ye at the bonfire. I wasnae taking enough care of ma wean, and it was easier to blame ye than to admit I made the mistake. Ye have been a true blessing. I dinna ken how ye can always be so gracious. I couldnae."

Cairren could only nod as she looked at the three women before her. She realized that while it wasn't many, she'd made three friends without realizing it.

"Lady Cairren?" A timid voice called out, and Cairren looked beyond Meg's shoulder to see Athne creeping toward them. Tears streamed down her face, and she looked terrified to come closer. Cairren passed an assessing gaze over Athne, taking in her body language and realizing the woman was afraid of rejection. Cairren nodded and forced a smile. She didn't trust the woman after Athne had denounced her and corroborated Father Mitchell's claims. "Lady Cairren, I need to tell ye and Padraig the truth aboot what I did. Now that Father Mitchell is gone, I amnae so scared."

"You feared Father Mitchell?" Padraig asked.

"We all did," Meg blurted. Cairren suspected as much, but she smiled at her outspoken friend. She liked that Meg wasn't shy about speaking up, especially once she was on Cairren's side.

"Ma lady," Athne knotted her fingers so tightly that they were white. "I accepted yer help because I kenned ma wean needed it, but it was Father Mitchell and Lady Mary who told me to ask. Father Mitchell said he would come to ma door, and I was to accuse ye of witchery. He warned that ma soul and that of ma wean would be eternally damned and that the laird would banish ma family if I refused to rid our clan of —of—vermin," Athne choked out the last word.

"My mother was there?" Padraig asked, appalled.

"Aye. She said she would see ma husband removed from the guards if I didna say exactly what she told me." Athne sobbed, sniffing her nose. "Ye were so kind to me and ma wean, Lady Cairren. I'd seen how ye'd helped others, and I was sure ye could help ma wee one. But I couldnae risk ma family, ma lady."

"Athne, I understand. I believe I would have done just as you did, if they put me in that position. I believe there's naught I wouldn't do to protect my children. They wronged us both, but I respect that you're making amends," Cairren responded.

"I want to, ma lady. I wish ye werenae leaving. Ye're good for our clan. Did ye ken that the weans ye taught to sing in French have taught the others? They asked while ye were gone why ye werenae here to teach them more." Athne looked back and waved over a girl of seven or eight. "This is ma lass, Sorcha."

Sorcha bobbed a wobbly curtsey and held out a doll to Cairren. "I made this for ye, Lady Cairren. Do ye see how I used brown wool for her hair and skin, just like ye have? Isnae she pretty? I tried to make her look like ye."

Cairren's eyes watered as she squatted down to eye level with the girl. "This is the most thoughtful gift I have ever received. You're a kind lass, and I will cherish this always." Cairren fell backwards with an oomph as the little girl knocked her over with her embrace. Cairren giggled as the girl squeezed her thin arms around her neck. She wrapped her arms around the girl in return. Padraig helped her to her feet, and she brushed off her skirts. She never imagined such a warm send-off, but she reminded herself that these people in front of her were but a tiny part of the clan.

"Lady Cairren," a gravelly voice called out. "A moment, please." Cairren recognized Adam and remembered that he was the one who saved Padraig from the cave when Duncan pushed him in years ago. Adam glanced at the others but returned his focus to

Cairren, who wasn't sure what the gruff warrior wanted.

"Good morn, Adam," Cairren greeted him.

"Good morn, ma lady." Adam cleared his throat, but his voice was still deep. "I dinna ken if Padraig told ye what happened at that cave when he was a lad. But I ken how hard it is to swim out from there. He and I nearly died that day. It was by the grace of God that it happened just before the tide truly changed. If I'd nae gotten there when I did, I dinna believe Padraig would be alive. I dinna believe either of us would be alive if I'd jumped in any later. I canna believe ye did it with yer hands bound."

Adam cleared his throat again. He appeared uncomfortable when he glanced at Cairren, but his face broke into a wide grin when he looked at Padraig. The sun-weathered skin crinkling beside his eyes. "I jumped in without a stitch on, kenning even a leine would weigh me down. I dinna ken how ye did it with any part of yer heavy gown on." Adam grew serious and bowed to Cairren. "But it isnae just that feat that makes me admire ye more than anyone I ken. I could have, should have, spoken out against the laird and lady. It was ma duty as a member of the clan council to balance Laird Micheil's power, and I didna. Ye've taught many of us a valuable lesson, ma lady. Honor, integrity, and strength have naught to do with anyone's skin. I'm sorry I didna defend ye. I swore as a young mon to protect all members of the clan and the laird's family. I never specified what color their skin had to be. I meant it to be everyone, and it should have been everyone. I humbly apologize, Lady Cairren."

Padraig had never heard Adam speak so much at one time. He witnessed the tears that gathered in the aged warrior's eyes, and it shocked him to see anything but the sternness he'd always known. Not for the first time in his life, he wished Adam had been his father. Adam was the man who taught him to hold a sword and to ride a horse. He'd been strict and relentless, but Padraig owed Adam a debt of gratitude for what he did to raise Padraig to be the warrior he was now.

Cairren came to stand before Adam and shyly wrapped her arms around him. "You remind me of my papa. Thank you," she whispered. Adam froze for a moment before he returned the embrace, his massive arms and chest dwarfing Cairren. When Cairren pulled away, she noticed they'd gathered a crowd. The expressions many wore confused her, but none were hostile. Some looked bewildered, others curious. Many looked regretful, and a few appeared disinterested. But she didn't fear anyone, and no one was glaring at her. She noted that the laird and lady were visibly absent, and she didn't know if Duncan had returned.

"Who's going to treat ma gout?" A reedy voice demanded. Cairren chuckled as Arnold cracked his walking stick against the offending ankles of anyone standing his way. "Ye were set to leave without even a fare-thee-well."

"You shall have your proper goodbye, Arnold. It comes with these instructions: no rich foods, keep your feet up at night, and soak them in lukewarm water if they swell too much." Cairren offered her advice with a smile. She imagined the man was eighty if he was a day, but he wasn't in his dotage. His mind was sharp, and he was in fine health other than his gout. She didn't doubt he had several more years of abusing ankles ahead of him.

"If Adam and his ugly mug got an embrace, I shall demand one too." Cairren's face relaxed into a soft smile as she reached out to him. He murmured against his ear. "I'll work on them all. Ye're too good for us to never come back."

Cairren nodded, but she wouldn't make false promises. She doubted she would ever return to Foulis. It had been a temporary stop on a much longer life journey. She turned toward Lachlan and his men, who stood idly watching. She'd forgotten about them and felt bad for keeping them waiting. She glanced up at Padraig, who smiled at her. The regret in his eyes felt like too little, too late to Cairren. He helped her mount before she, Padraig, and the extra men he'd gathered, along with the Sutherland men rode out. She didn't look back.

CHAPTER FORTY-ONE

Cairren swallowed her tears as she moved behind a tree, one of her spare chemises and her knife in hand. Her courses began on the third day of their trek to Stirling. Disappointment unlike anything she ever imagined overwhelmed her when she realized she wasn't pregnant. The babe would have been her only reason to remain tied to Padraig. There was no reason for them to remain married, and no reason for Cairren to even consider returning to Foulis.

Cairren tore the chemise into strips and prayed Padraig didn't inquire about what was taking so long. He'd taken her to the stream to bathe, even offering to help her with a grin, but she complained that the water reminded her of how cold she was the last time she was submerged. She turned her back and hurried to wash while keeping her chemise from falling into the water. Now that she'd torn through her second spare chemise, she didn't see how much longer she could avoid discussing her courses with him, as she had laundry to do. She hadn't shared her suspicions about being with child, and now she was relieved she hadn't.

Cairren dried her tears and stepped around the

tree to where Padraig stood with his back to her. She tapped his back as she walked by. They'd slept next to one another the previous three nights, but hadn't made their bedrolls into one. Neither hinted at slipping away for a tryst, and neither attempted any affection. It was as though any connection they'd had evaporated. As she approached her bedroll, she noticed Lachlan watching her. When he cocked an eyebrow, she shook her head. He'd deduced that she thought she was expecting, and apparently he'd figured out that she wasn't. He'd asked her discreetly during their first stop the day they left Foulis. Cairren supposed it was because he had two sisters that he was aware of such things. She'd caught Padraig looking at her midriff more than once since they left, but he said nothing. She suspected he'd noticed her courses hadn't started since she arrived at his home. Like many women her age, they were irregular; they usually came three months apart. It was only because that length of time drew out that made her wonder. She realized she'd been hoping to find firmness in her belly, and so she had. Recognizing her error didn't make it any less painful to accept that she wouldn't have Padraig's child.

She slid into her bedroll and pulled both her Kennedy and Munro plaids around her. Flurries fell throughout their fourth day on the road, and the temperature was still falling. She shivered as she tried to get comfortable. She went rigid when she felt Padraig move his bedding closer, but she couldn't contain the sigh of relief when his heat encircled her.

"What's wrong, Ren? Are you not feeling well?" Padraig feared the journey in the foul weather was proving too much for Cairren.

"I'm feeling fine, Padraig," Cairren reassured.

"That doesn't tell me what's wrong."

"There's naught wrong, naught that needs fixing."

"Then you're hiding something from me," Padraig accused.

Cairren looked over her shoulder, glaring at me. "You dare accuse me of hiding things? You're a master of that craft."

"You're still not answering. Why are you evading my concern?"

Cairren rolled onto her back and looked at Padraig, who rested on his elbow. "Very well. I got my courses yesterday. I'm disappointed." Cairren tried to roll back, but Padraig snagged her shoulder.

"You're disappointed that you're not with child. Did you think you were?" Padraig felt the heat rising in his neck as his anger blossomed. He understood Cairren intended to keep that news from him. She would have gone to Stirling, even Dunure, and not told him that they were having a child.

"I suspected I was. I wanted to be, but at the same time, I thought I'd found a sound reason for leaving Munro land: I convinced myself I was having a bairn."

"That's why Lachlan insisted on coming. He knew, and I didn't." Padraig made to roll away, but Cairren grasped the front of his leine.

"Oh, no, you don't. You wanted to know, so now I'll tell you. It terrified me I would end up like Wynda," Cairren blurted.

"Wynda? Bluidy hell." Padraig stared aghast at her. "I hadn't thought of that. You wanted to leave because you feared our bairn was in danger."

Cairren nodded as tears created rivulets down her cheeks. She wanted to curl into a ball and forget about the cramps she felt, and the emptiness in her heart. "I wouldn't have kept our child from you, Padraig. I wasn't even certain. I suspected it more than aught, but without waiting longer or seeing a midwife who could better examine me, I went by missing my courses. It was enough to make me certain I couldn't stay. And I didn't tell Lachlan. He guessed."

"What aboot now?" Padraig's voice rasped. He shut his eyes when he saw the resignation in her face. "You still want to go to Stirling."

"It's for the best, Padraig."

"I want to snap at you and ask for who, but I know the answer to that."

"My intention isn't to hurt you, but neither do I want to die young."

There seemed little to say after that. It was reasonable, and Padraig knew it. He didn't want Cairren to die young either, and her comparison to Wynda shook him to the core. He thought about Cairren nearly drowning, and he knew it would have been history repeating itself. He reached out to wrap his arm around Cairren, but left it suspended as he whispered, "Let me hold you tonight, Ren."

Cairren said nothing, but inched closer until her head rested on Padraig's shoulder and her arm draped across his chest. He held her close, kissed her forehead, and closed his eyes, but he didn't fall asleep until well after he was sure she had. He would never walk away from Cairren again, but he suspected he was in for a fight.

CHAPTER FORTY-TWO

Cairren swept her eyes over every surface in the chamber she'd shared with Laurel Ross for three years. The familiarity was comforting after the heated conversation she had with Padraig. He'd argued against her returning to a ladies-in-waiting chamber; he'd wanted her to share a suite with him. She choked out that it would be harder than ever for her to part with him if they shared a chamber. Then she played her trump card: she needed time with her sister. They'd assigned Caitlyn to Laurel's chamber when Cairren left. She looked at the bed and smiled. It would be barely large enough for the two of them, but it reminded her of when they were children.

Padraig had thrown his hands in the air and given in. He swore he wouldn't do anything to keep the sisters apart, even if he grew lonely in his chamber by himself. Cairren had embraced him out of habit. It was their first affection since she shared a bedroll with him two nights earlier. They'd both been unsure what to do once they were in each other's arms. They pulled apart and looked in different directions. She'd tried to convince him to leave as soon as he knew she was settled, but a vein pulsed in his temple so hard that she feared it would rupture. She kept her thoughts to herself after that.

Cairren sat on the end of the bed and waited for Caitlyn and Laurel to return. She knew they would venture back to their chamber soon to dress for the evening meal. She didn't have long to wait before the women entered and stopped short. Caitlyn recovered first.

"Cairren!" The sisters flew into one another's arms and nearly knocked each other off their feet. "What're you doing here? I never expected to—" Caitlyn broke off, neither wanting to state the truth: that they had expected they would never see one another again.

"It was Myrna, wasn't it?" Laurel whispered.

"She contributed to it, but she wasn't the only reason I've returned," Cairren admitted.

"Were they hateful and dreadful to you?" Caitlyn demanded with righteous indignation.

Cairren drew in a breath and nodded. "How are they to you here, Caity?"

"Better than they were when you arrived. I suppose I'm light enough that I pass inspection. What happened, Cairren?"

Cairren looked at Laurel, who looked miserable and embarrassed. "Laurel, I must thank you for warning me aboot Padraig and Myrna. It still hurt to see them together when I arrived, but at least it didn't shock me. Nay, that came soon after." Cairren walked over to Laurel, who'd moved out of the sisters' way. She took the other lady's hands in hers. "You are not your sister. I don't hold her actions against you."

"Thank you," Laurel whispered. "But I am sorry for what she did. I already know much of it. She sent me missives boasting."

Cairren took a seat on the bed again and patted the space beside her. Caitlyn joined her, and Laurel took a seat on her bed.

"What did she do?" Caitlyn asked.

"She wasn't willing to give up Padraig. And he wasn't willing to give her up either. We married the day after I arrived, and naught good happened after that." Cairren shrugged. "Padraig is a handsome mon, and he finds me appealing. We got along in private, but every morning, he went in search of Myrna. He refused to send her home, and when he suggested it, she found ways to stay. I made friends with my sister-by-marriage, Wynda, but Duncan, my brother-by-marriage, caused her death. It only grew more miserable after that. Even when Myrna eventually left, the clan was still hostile to me. My mother-by-marriage and the clan's priest fueled rumors aboot me." Cairren avoided giving more details, in part because it hurt to rehash the past when she would have to do it before the king and queen, and also in part because she didn't want to frighten her sister.

"What did they say?" Caitlyn asked, her eyes wide.

"Naught that I want to repeat, but they accused me of heresy. I sought shelter with the Sutherlands. I must see Blair soon and thank her. I suspect Lachlan is already with her. He and several Sutherland men travelled with us when my plan was to come here." Cairren didn't want to share what happened with Duncan and the caves, but she couldn't keep something so dire from her sister. She suspected King Robert would force her to give a full recitation, so she saw little point in holding back from Caitlyn and Laurel. "There was an incident before I left Foulis for the last time. Duncan took me to some caves where the

Cromarty and Moray firths meet. He intended to leave me there as the tide rose. I was able to get free, and Padraig and Lachlan, with their men, pulled me from the water. We returned to Foulis, and my reception was far warmer than ever before. But I still believe it's for best that I returned to court."

Laurel and Caitlyn sat in stunned silence as Cairren shared the abridged story of the past months. Caitlyn's mouth was agape while Laurel's eyes were as round as saucers. Laurel recovered first. With much hesitation, she asked, "Do you ken aboot Duncan and Myrna?"

"Yes. You obviously do. Have you always known?" Cairren asked.

Laurel nodded sheepishly. "I caught them once several years ago. It was what made Myrna push my father into sending me here. It had naught to do with finding a husband who'd accept my small dowry. She wanted me away so I couldn't tell anyone." Tears welled in her eyes. "I knew Myrna would make your life difficult, but I never imagined the things she boasted in her letters. And I never imagined Duncan would kill Wynda or try to kill you. I swear I would have warned you away. I would have told your parents everything and saved you the suffering. I knew Wynda. She was kind, and she never deserved what Duncan did to her."

"How did she die?" Caitlyn whispered.

"He strangled her." Cairren bit her lip to keep from crying. "I found her on her bed. I'd convinced her that morn to return to her clan. I don't ken if Duncan learned of it or something else made him do it. But she was with child. Naught happened to him. Lady Mary was aware of the affair the entire time. While Duncan was married to Wynda, he could only have Myrna as his mistress. They concocted the plan to have Padraig fall in love with Myrna and marry her, so she would be closer to Duncan. She would have passed off Duncan's bairns as Padraig's. She was carrying when I arrived, but her attempts to seduce Padraig failed. I can only imagine what she did, but I ken it wasn't the first time."

"My sister has a black soul. I don't know why. She's naught like the rest of us. She's always found pleasure in hurting other people, and she found a kindred spirit with Duncan. They make one another worse. Cairren, I'm sure there's more you don't want to speak of, but I really am so very sorry. I swear I would have spoken up."

"I know, Laurel. They will see the difference between you and your sister all the way in Heaven. St. Peter won't blame you for the sins of your sister. I don't blame you. It sounds like you've suffered enough from her," Cairren sympathized.

"What will you do?" Caitlyn asked.

"I suppose I shall have to seek an audience with the queen or more likely the king. It was King Robert's order that Padraig and I marry. He won't be happy to learn of all that happened. I won't lie, but neither will I tell more than I must. I realized as I was leaving, that just as there is naught inherently evil aboot my skin, there's naught inherently evil within most of the Munros. They haven't met people from foreign lands like we do at court. They aren't educated like many of us. And they are at the mercy of their laird. If their laird denounces someone, accuses them of being unworthy, then they take their guidance from him. When their priest threatens damnation, and they've been raised to believe he's God's voice on Earth, they believe what they hear. What choice do they have? I'm not excusing those who were cruel to me, those who wanted harm to befall me. But I understand how they were sheep who blindly followed their shepherd. Many accepted me, even seemed to want me to stay. But Laird and Lady Munro and Duncan pose too great a threat to me. And if Duncan marries Myrna, I will never return while they are at Foulis. My life would be forfeit the moment I arrived. Their hate is too complex, borne of too many things, to ever overcome. And I don't want to try. The effort will never be worth the risk."

"What will happen with you and Padraig?" Caitlyn wondered.

"I don't ken. He's offered to go to Dunure with me, but he has duties at Foulis. And until Duncan has a son, Padraig is his heir, second in line to the lairdship. He can't abandon his clan."

"But he wants to leave? He's willing to?" Laurel was incredulous. "He must love you far more than he ever imagined he loved Myrna."

"Imagined?" Cairren's brow furrowed.

"That wasn't love." Laurel shook her head. "She did and said everything she thought would make him trail after her. She became the person he wanted to fall in love with, but that was never, ever her. It can't be love when it's based entirely on a falsehood. Infatuation, certainly. Love, never. I suspect Padraig clung to what he knew, what he believed in and didn't want to accept was false. It would be hard to admit he'd been so greatly fooled."

"It was his pride, and he admitted as much," Cairren sighed.

"Does that mean you've forgiven him for what you must have suffered?" Caitlyn's temper flared as she listened to Laurel describe the woman who was the bane of her sister's existence. She grew frustrated listening to what sounded like Cairren accepting less than she deserved.

"It means that I can look back now, and some of it doesn't hurt as much. Some of it, I may never get past. But I have gotten to ken Padraig, and I have seen how he's changed. He's matured significantly in a brief time. He's become a mon I care for."

"Yet you're here, and you haven't agreed to him joining you at Dunure," Caitlyn pointed out.

"I don't know what I will do. My priority was to get away from Foulis and Padraig's family. They're what's keeping me from considering a return. I have decided naught beyond that. I suppose it'll depend upon what King Robert and Queen Elizabeth decide. And it may be several days before I'm summoned before them."

A knock at the door had all three heads turning at once, and they laughed. Cairren went to the door and opened it a crack. Padraig stood on the other side. She opened it wide enough to slip out. When he looked over her head and nodded, she suspected he'd caught sight of Laurel.

"I wanted to be sure you were settled and that you'd seen your sister," Padraig confessed. He appeared shy and unsure for the first time. It lent him a boyish charm when he didn't know where to look. She half expected him to scuff his boot on the floor.

"I'm well, Padraig. I didn't tell Caitlyn and Laurel everything, but they have the gist of it. They deserve to know, and I would rather they hear my version than whatever gossip will spread." Cairren bit her lip and debated whether to tell Padraig what she learned from Laurel.

"What is it? You're debating whether to tell me

something. Is it aboot Myrna, something Laurel told you?"

Cairren nodded but remained quiet. The silence drew out between them until Padraig finally nodded. "Laurel knew aboot you and Myrna before I left. You ken she's the one who warned me. She also kenned aboot Duncan. She discovered them together years ago—even before you began courting Myrna, so Myrna convinced Laird Ross to send Laurel here. He thought he was sending his daughter to find a husband, but Myrna was banishing her. All so that Laurel couldn't share Myrna's secret. Laurel's upset and feels guilty for what her sister did."

"Laurel may be older and can have a wickedly sharp tongue to those she doesn't like, but I know now that she has none of the cruelty and manipulativeness that Myrna does. Laurel's shallow, but she wouldn't devise such an elaborate plan kenning it would hurt so many people."

"You're right. I wasn't sure that I should bring up Myrna. I—I don't know how you feel aboot her right now."

"You want to ken if any part of me still loves her. Nay. I don't. My anger has settled, though I admit the hurt hasn't. I've had long hours on horseback to consider what was beneath my nose, but I never paid enough attention to see the truth." Padraig's lip curled in disgust. "I saw what I wanted. Now I realize Myrna became the person I wanted to see. She said and did what she knew I wanted from a wife. I should have kenned she was too perfect."

"That's just what Laurel said," Cairren whispered.

"There's so much I wish I could take back, Ren. But I can't." Padraig ran his hand through his hair.

"I know. And I'm not angry with you like I used to be. Though it's sad to say this, you haven't hurt me in a while."

Padraig turned to the wall and rested his forearm against it before leaning his forehead on his arm. "No wife should ever be in a position to say that."

"The past can't be undone, Padraig. What is done is done. She's not a part of our lives anymore, and you're not the same mon I met."

"I hope I'm a better one," Padraig whispered.

"I believe you are."

Padraig straightened and looked at Cairren's earnest face. He wanted to believe that she loved him as much as he did her. He was tempted to tell her right there in the passageway how he felt, but Cairren deserved better than an admission when anyone could overhear. "Will you allow me to escort you to the evening meal?"

Cairren was prepared for the request, and she'd already decided she would accept. She didn't want the entire court buzzing about them sitting separately. There would already be talk about her staying in a ladies'-in-waiting chamber rather than the suite assigned to Padraig or a matron's chamber. "I would like that. I'll be ready in a quarter hour."

"I'll wait for you here. I would like to meet your sister. Would she be able to sit with us?" Padraig feared Caitlyn might want to gut him, but he understood the sisters had a unique relationship that differed from Duncan's and his. He knew the sisters were close, and he didn't want to keep Cairren from spending time with Caitlyn. He realized he didn't even feel the need to talk to Cairren or garner her attention. He simply wanted to be close to her. Cairren slipped into the chamber with a smile.

CHAPTER FORTY-THREE

Padraig was unprepared for the attention Cairren's return generated. The ladies-in-waiting tittered and peeked at him, which was annoying, but harmless. It was the men he wanted to run his sword through. He noticed immediately that the men's gazes were lascivious and predatory. His neck hurt from being on a swivel as he glanced around and found one man after another ogling Cairren. He showed his support by keeping his arm around Cairren as they walked through the Great Hall. He steered the ladies toward a table occupied by members of Clan Fraser of Lovat. He avoided the Rosses and gave the Mackenzies a wide berth. Once the meal began, Padraig relaxed. But when the music started, his hackles went back up.

"I don't want to dance with any of them, Padraig," Cairren whispered. He saw her nervousness, and he felt the tension radiating from her.

"We are still newly married. I will explain that I refuse to share. If you will dance with me, then I shall merrily twirl you aboot. If you'd rather remain here, then we shall. If you want to retire, I will escort you to your chamber. I—"

Cairren giggled and placed her hand on Padraig's

arm to stop his babbling. "I know, Padraig. Let's sit for a while and watch. I can point people out." She looked around, then discreetly pointed to their left. "Look. There's Lachlan speaking to his sister, Blair. They're standing with Arabella Johnstone. She was their sister Maude's close friend. Arabella and I grew closer when Maude and Allyson Elliot both married. I'd like to speak with her at some point, but there isn't a rush to do it tonight. There will be time."

Nay, there willna. Padraig wanted to blurt out his thoughts, but he kept them to himself. *We willna linger here. I already ken Cairren was right. It'll make me miserable stuck here. I need to convince her we should set off for Dunure within the next couple days, or the weather will make that choice for us.*

"Alex," Cairren rose to greet Alexander Armstrong. He bent over to kiss her hand, and Padraig watched the smile that brightened Cairren's face. It was the same one she'd worn while Alex and her clan members visited. She had not flashed it since.

"What brings you to court, Cairren?" Alex posed the question to Cairren, but his gaze was on Padraig.

"We have some clan business to attend to, and I wanted to see Caitlyn. I feared I might never see her again, so when the opportunity arose, I made my way here."

"And you're sharing a chamber again, just as you did when you were young," Alex arched an eyebrow. Cairren refused to take the bait.

"For now. I've missed her, and Padraig understands."

"You're an understanding husband," Alex taunted, but before Padraig could respond, Cairren rushed to speak.

"He is. I'm grateful for the time with my sister. I

don't ken when I will see her again, and Padraig knows this is important to me."

"As you say. Would you dance with me?" Alex looked directly into Cairren's eyes as though he searched for the truth to her sudden reappearance at court. She wouldn't lie to her childhood friend, but she wouldn't volunteer more. She felt that was all she did since she arrived. Pick selective bits of her story and evaded the rest.

"Not tonight, Alex. I'm fatigued, and prefer to sit this out. Another night."

"I shall hold you to that." Alex nodded before slipping back into the crowd.

"I'm surprised you didn't make an exception for Alex," Padraig mused.

"I didn't want to answer questions that I didn't want asked. And I am tired. I think I would prefer to retire."

Padraig didn't ask questions, rather offering him her arm. He noticed the attention that continued to follow them, but he preferred looking at Cairren, who walked with the dignity she had whenever put in the spotlight before his clan. He marveled at her silent strength, but he knew it exhausted her. When they arrived at Cairren's door, Padraig felt like he had when he began courting Myrna, uncertain of what to say or do.

"Goodnight, Padraig," Cairren murmured. She hesitated as though she weren't certain what came next, but then she turned to her door.

"Goodnight, Ren."

Cairren looked back over her shoulder before passing through the doorway.

Morning came, and Cairren woke before Caitlyn and Laurel. She was unaccustomed to court hours after living in the Highlands for months. She hadn't danced most of the night away like the women she shared the chamber with. Her friend and sister would likely sleep until close to midday since it was clear the queen didn't expect them to join her on her morning constitutional. Cairren dressed and slipped from the chamber. She made her way through the winding passageways until she stepped into the brilliant sunlight. She didn't hear voices, but she heard the crunch of footsteps. She waited for Queen Elizabeth and her matrons to round the corner before dropping into a deep curtsy.

"Lady Cairren, I hadn't expected to see you, yet there you were at the evening meal." Queen Elizabeth flicked her hand, and Cairren rose. A speaking glance sent the other women away. The queen's assessing gaze missed nothing as Cairren stood still. She wouldn't speak unless asked a question. "Why have you returned?"

Cairren knew the queen was often direct, but she hadn't expected her to be so blunt so soon. "I would seek an audience with the king, Your Grace."

"Walk with me." When Cairren took her place one step back from the queen on the woman's left, Queen Elizabeth continued her questioning. "What reason could you have to see the king? Is your husband not handling clan matters?"

"Padraig will surely speak to the king and keep him abreast of the politics and happenings on Munro territory, but I would speak to the king aboot something else."

"You are being evasive, not reserved, Lady Cairren. My patience is thin already this morning. Come to the point."

"Yes, Your Grace. My marriage hasn't been what my parents intended, nor what I imagine the king intended. While most of the Munros have been merely inhospitable, there was an attempt on my life." The queen came to such an abrupt halt that Cairren nearly stepped in front of her. Only months after her joint coronation with Robert the Bruce, the English King Edward Longshanks captured Queen Elizabeth, and she spent eight years under house arrest while her sister-by-marriage and Isabella MacDuff were kept in cages suspended outside separate castles. After the harrowing experience, the queen took threats and mistreatment of her ladies as a grave offense. "Explain," she commanded.

"The clan's priest accused me of heresy and witchery after I became the clan's healer and midwife. He hates me to his very core. He sprayed me with barely diluted lye, and when I flinched, he claimed that it burned, and this was proof that I was a witch. My father-by-marriage was prepared to put me on the stake."

"That is outrageous," Queen Elizabeth declared.

"Your Grace, that wasn't the event to which I'd referred," Cairren grimaced.

"There's more?" the queen demanded incredulously.

"Aye, Your Grace. I made my way to the Sutherland and sought refuge from him. Laird Sutherland directed Lachlan to accompany me here, but my husband's brother, Duncan, absconded with me. He tried to drown me in a cave on the shore of the Moray Firth."

"And where, precisely, was your husband during

all of this?" The queen's tone made Cairren fear for Padraig's life.

Cairren shifted uncomfortably, and Queen Elizabeth's eyes shot up. "During the incident with the priest and the doctored holy water, he was away from the keep. He became aware that the woman he intended to marry before me was having an affair with Duncan. By the time he returned, I'd already escaped the stake and was on my way to Dunrobin. He followed me there, but I'd departed by the time he arrived. He intended to gather more supplies and men before following me to Stirling. But just before he reached Foulis, he encountered Lachlan, who explained what happened with Duncan. Padraig figured out where Duncan took me and came for me."

"He rescued you from the cave. How heroic."

"Aye, Your Grace." Cairren reasoned that Padraig had saved her, so she didn't feel compelled to share her part in her own rescue.

"I suspect there is far more, but I think it is best saved for the king. Come along, Lady Cairren. You have a meeting to attend."

"Yes, Your Grace." She hurried to keep up with the queen's brisk pace. Before she realized where she was, she followed Queen Elizabeth into King Robert's Privy Council chamber.

"Lady Cairren," the russet-haired monarch greeted her. She'd known Robert the Bruce since the day she arrived at court, but he didn't intimidate her any less after three years of living at his court. "I noticed you arrived with your husband. You were not expected."

"It was a rather unexpected journey."

"Do tell," King Robert said as he gestured to a chair. He ordered everyone from the room, leaving only Queen Elizabeth, Cairren, the king, and his guard. "I suspect this shall take a while."

Cairren inhaled deeply before she told the king and queen everything but the most intimate details. She relayed the duplicity of the wedding, the humiliating bedding ceremony, Padraig's ongoing relationship with Myrna, Duncan's attack on her and Padraig's reaction to it, and Wynda's death. She paused until the king nodded for her to proceed. She explained how she became the clan's healer and midwife and how that improved relations with some of the clan members, but not enough to avoid the accusations of witchcraft made against her. She was clear on the details as she explained Myrna, Duncan, and Lady Mary's roles in the deceit and danger she faced. By the time she came to the end of her tale, she was emotionally depleted and wanted nothing more than to curl into a ball beneath the table.

"This is beyond the pale, Lady Cairren. I promise you that I never would have decreed that you marry Padraig Munro if I'd known what a weak and fickle mon he is, or how shameful the Munros are."

"Your Majesty," Cairren bowed her head toward the king. "Padraig is not a bad mon, but everyone he trusted played him false. I no longer fault him for all the choices he made."

"Why have you come here?" the Bruce asked.

"I could no longer remain at Foulis, among the Munros, without fearing my imminent death. I returned here knowing my sister was in residence. I would request your permission to remain, either until my parents can escort me home or until the weather clears and I can travel with guards."

"So you are leaving your husband," King Robert was not asking a question.

Cairren nodded. "We cannot reconcile what stands between us. Please let me be clear that I don't hold Padraig at fault for why we cannot remain together. He has duties to his clan he cannot abandon, and I cannot stay while his family intends me harm." Cairren steeled herself for what she was about to request. "Your Majesty, I would petition for an annulment."

"You know that isn't possible, Lady Cairren," Queen Elizabeth spoke up.

"Your Grace, during the wedding Father Mitchell asked if there was any impediment we knew of that could keep us from marrying. He stated that if we withheld secrets within our hearts, if we were not forthcoming in why we shouldn't marry, then the union would be void in both God's eyes and the law's." Cairren blinked several times as she thought about how to make her argument. "We both made our pledges knowing they weren't true. Neither of us spoke up to admit we didn't intend to keep all of our vows. We promised to love one another, but we both knew we entered the marriage under false pretenses while Padraig loved another woman. That lie makes our marriage unlawful and is grounds for an annulment."

"That is very shaky logic, Lady Cairren," the king warned.

"Your Majesty, Padraig deserves a wife who can live with him and share the responsibilities of his position. He deserves to have children people won't ostracize if their skin is too dark. I deserve not to live in fear that my next breath shall be my last. This annulment is best for everyone. My father agreed to give up my dowry to allow Padraig and me to handfast. This relationship would have ended in a year and a day. I do not doubt he will forgo its return if I am granted permission to return to Dunure."

"And who would you marry instead?" Queen Elizabeth inquired.

"I don't have an answer to that, Your Grace. I don't intend to remarry soon."

"Is your husband aware of your appeal?" King Robert raised his chin and looked down his thin patrician nose.

"No, he is not, Your Majesty. He knows I'm of the opinion that we are at an impasse."

"But he doesn't share that opinion, I take it." King Robert continued to look down his nose.

Cairren knew the king was testing her, but she was resolute. "As I said, Your Majesty, Padraig would accompany me to Dunure, but he has duties to his clan that he cannot dismiss."

"Your husband would give up his place among his clan to live with yours," Queen Elizabeth surmised. "And you won't accept that."

"Your Grace, it's not aboot what I want. It's what is best for our clans. That was the reason for our marriage in the first place." Cairren paused as she considered her wording. "Your Majesty, I cannot in good conscience draw Padraig away from his clan. They need his guidance and leadership now, and it will only become more necessary in the years to come."

"You're saying his father is failing to lead his clan, and his brother will do no better. I gathered as much from your tale. You are an honest woman, Lady Cairren. No one has ever spoken a word against you, and you endured much while at court. I can't fathom how you endured what you did with the Munros. Ladies are not meant to ride into battle as you did every day. I will petition the Pope, but as we are not reconciled, I am not confident that you shall receive the outcome you wish. That said, my excommunication means I am no longer bound by the doctrine of the Church. As king, I assert I have the power to grant your petition. However, before I answer one way or another, there is much I need to consider."

Cairren swallowed. She understood that was the king's indirect way of informing her that he would speak to Padraig. She could only imagine how well that would go over. She'd prayed King Robert would grant her request and that he would make the decree official.

"Thank you, Your Majesty, Your Grace." Cairren waited for the king to nod before she rose and curtsied. She glided to the door, but once in the passageway, she ran to her chamber.

CHAPTER FORTY-FOUR

Padraig expected the king would summon him, but he hadn't anticipated it would be the morning after he arrived. He was accustomed to the Bruce making visitors wait days before granting them entry into the Privy Council chamber. From there, it could be several more days before the audience occurred. It shocked him to stand before King Robert before the midday meal.

"Munro, I've learned that Clan Munro failed spectacularly in offering Highland hospitality to your wife. How would you explain your wife's reception, and more to the point, how would you describe your marriage to Lady Cairren?"

"It has been a source of great dishonor and shame," Padraig admitted. "I suspect you have spoken to Lady Cairren, so I shall keep this succinct. I failed my wife when she arrived as my bride. While I intended to keep my vow of fidelity, and I did, I entered my marriage believing I was in love with another woman. I intended to marry Lady Myrna Ross at Samhain. Then your order came for me to wed Lady Cairren. I couldn't imagine forsaking Lady Myrna, and when Lady Cairren arrived..."

Padraig swallowed before clearing his throat. The chamber suddenly felt sweltering. "Lady Cairren was not what any of us expected. She wasn't what I expected. I could see how my clan reacted, and it made me resent being forced to put aside Lady Myrna. I thought I could balance having my wife and the woman I loved. While not intentional, I didn't prevent myself or others from humiliating Lady Cairren. It took longer than I care to admit for me to realize that the woman I married was far better than the woman I thought I loved. I have worked to make amends with Lady Cairren, and I believe my clan will accept her. But I cannot deny that my family does not."

"So you didn't love Lady Cairren when you pledged to do just that. You didn't intend to allow your love for her to develop because you believed you loved another. Did I understand you?" King Robert's focus on a singular point made Padraig wary. He wasn't certain the direction in which the conversation headed, but he suspected he would be miserable once he got there.

"Yes, Your Majesty."

"What made you realize that you weren't in love with Lady Myrna?"

"At first, I was sympathetic to what I believed she felt. I was heartbroken to see her suffer from her disappointment and grief that our lives would not be bound through matrimony. I excused her vicious and vindictive tongue as that of a prostrate woman who saw little future. But as time went by, I realized Lady Cairren conducted herself with dignity and kindness at all times, even in the face of Lady Myrna's scorn and abuse."

Padraig paused as memories of Cairren's determination and strength flashed before his eyes. He wondered how he could have ever failed to see what Cairren offered beyond their bedchamber.

"It was impossible not to draw a comparison and see that it was Lady Myrna who came out lacking. I could no longer make excuses or justify her behavior, and so I saw through the façade." Padraig looked away from the Bruce as he told the last part of his story. "Lady Myrna never intended to be faithful to me. She never was. She and Duncan have been involved for years, long before I began courting her. They conspired to convince me to marry Lady Myrna, so she could live at Foulis and continue her affair with Duncan."

King Robert looked at the Highlander for a tense moment. "While you appear contrite, Padraig, I cannot overlook how the marriage began. You didn't enter the marriage truthfully, and you made a false promise to love Lady Cairren. She has already admitted to the same falsehood. It is because of this that I lean heavily toward granting your wife's petition for an annulment."

"Her what?" Padraig rose from his chair so abruptly that it tumbled over. Guards rushed forward, but the king waved them away. "Cairren asked for an annulment?"

"Aye, just before I summoned you. The queen and I spoke to your wife, and she recounted her experiences with your clan. I'm of a mind to agree that it is not safe for her to return. I also acknowledge that you both made false statements during your wedding. You've corroborated her claim that you both entered the marriage under false pretenses and didn't intend to uphold your vows."

"But I lo—" Padraig snapped his mouth shut. He

would not profess his love for the first time to someone other than Cairren.

"That may be all good and well, but your marriage was a mistake."

"No, it wasn't," Padraig argued. When King Robert's face grew red, Padraig apologized. "Please forgive my rudeness, Your Majesty. I wasn't prepared for this. Needless to say, it comes as a devastating shock. I hoped you would assist me in convincing Lady Cairren that we should retire to Dunure. Together. I didn't expect to learn my marriage would be deemed void."

"It might have been prudent to tell your wife your feelings before you arrived here," Queen Elizabeth spoke up for the first time.

"I see that now, Your Grace." Padraig glanced down before looking the king in the eye. "Is my marriage over?"

"Not yet." King Robert drew out his pause, and Padraig knew he was doing it to torture him. "I shall grant you a day to convince your wife to remain married."

Padraig's shoulders slumped. "Your Majesty, I do not see that as possible. As long as my father leads the Munros and my brother is his heir, Lady Cairren won't return. Duncan is likely to marry Lady Myrna, and she and my mother under the same roof will only endanger Cairren. I cannot take her back with me. She will not agree to me joining her at Dunure. Her sense of honor and duty is too strong. While they are two of the traits I admire most aboot her, they are most inconvenient right now."

King Robert chuckled and nodded. "Then I shall grant you up to a fortnight. There is much to this story I still wish to investigate. Laird Kennedy also needs to be made aware that his daughter has sought safety here. I will be sure the mon kens you accompanied Lady Cairren and what your intentions are, but he will be angrier than a bear woken before spring. I forewarn you: you may not live long enough to enjoy your marriage."

"I understand, Your Majesty."

"I suggest you find your wife." King Robert offered him a rueful smile as Padraig bowed and left the Privy Council chamber.

CHAPTER FORTY-FIVE

Padraig pounded on Cairren's chamber door so hard that the wood shook. "Cairren, open the door." He pounded again. The sound echoed through the passageway, but Padraig couldn't care less if he drew attention. He intended to speak to his wife. He'd passed Caitlyn, who confirmed Cairren was in their chamber. He was in the middle of his third round of knocking when the door flew open.

"Padra—" Cairren wasn't given the opportunity to speak. Padraig pulled her into his arms as he kicked the door shut. His mouth slammed down onto hers. They battled for control of the kiss as it became a conflagration of pent-up need and unresolved pain. He lifted her, and her legs came around his waist as he backed her against the door. The kiss carried on until they were breathless, and Padraig's stubble abraded Cairren's lips and chin. Padraig lowered her to the ground, and they stared at one another.

"I love you, Ren. I won't accept an annulment." Padraig heaved a deep breath as he tried to slow his racing heart, the accelerated pace the result of their breathless kisses and his anxiousness over their impending confrontation.

"Padraig, you have to go home, and once there you need a wife who can be at your side."

"Or maybe you already have another husband in mind," Padraig flung at her. "Are you planning your wedding to Alexander?"

"Alex?" Cairren asked incredulously. "First, if I wanted to marry Alex, I would have done so years ago. Second, I don't want to marry anyone who isn't you. And third, you're a jealous arse to accuse me of that."

"I am jealous. And possessive and protective. I'm not giving you up, Ren. I will give up my family, but I won't give you up."

"You shouldn't have to choose."

"Maybe, but I have. You are my wife, and I love you."

Cairren stared into Padraig's eyes that were such a deep brown they appeared nearly black. She remembered once wondering if their color reflected his soul; now she knew they didn't. When meeting his gaze became too hard, she closed her eyes, but that only brought forth their most intimate memories. "You've said that twice."

"Said what?" Padraig tried to follow her thoughts.

"You've said 'I love you' twice. I need to catch up. I love you, Padraig. It's why I'll let you go. I don't want to because I love you, but I will because it's what's best."

"No, it bluidy well isn't what's best. You believe you can decide for me. Do you want me deciding for you?" His eyes narrowed. "I think I shall. You are taking me with you to Dunure because that's what's best for you."

Cairren was too overwhelmed after her conversations in the garden and Privy Council chamber. This was more than she had the strength for. She fell against Padraig's chest as his arms came around her. "This is where I want to be for the rest of our lives. I don't mean court," she clarified. "I mean in your arms."

"And this is where you belong. It's where I belong. Cairren, I don't want to anywhere without you. Foulis is a keep. A stack of bricks I've lived in since I was born. Home is in your arms."

"When did you become so sentimental?" Cairren smiled.

"Around the time I pulled my head out of the pile of shite I was rolling around in."

"Lovely," Cairren chuckled. She slid her hand up Padraig's chest until she could cup his jaw. "And I love you. There's been so much hurt between us already. I don't want to cause more. I don't want you to resent me."

"There will never be aught more painful than living without you," Padraig lifted her hand from his cheek and kissed each of her fingertips.

"Where do we go from here?"

"Our chamber." Padraig chuckled when she playfully scowled. "Right now, you're coming to our chamber where I intend to make love to you, wife. After that, we can decide if we'll go to Dunure or if we'll remain here."

Cairren squealed as Padraig swept her into his arms and walked to the door. She leaned sideways and pressed down on the door handle. She squealed again when Padraig pretended to drop her, but she realized he'd done it to make her cling to him. As he carried her through Stirling Castle to their chamber, she cared not that people watched, pointed, and whispered. As they undressed amid kisses, she was thankful her courses had ended, and she wondered if this might be the time that they actually conceived.

Padraig carried her to the bed and eased her onto the mattress with a tenderness that made Cairren's heart feel too large for her chest. He climbed onto the bed and straddled her legs. As his eyes swept over Cairren's petite frame, she marveled at how different their bodies were yet how well they fit together. When her eyes landed on his cock, it twitched, and Padraig growled before pouncing.

Their kisses grew more urgent with each swipe of their tongues. Padraig's large palm covered Cairren's breast as he kneaded the aching mound of flesh. He shifted to bring her breast to his mouth. He used the tip of his tongue to circle her nipple before flicking it, then drawing it into his mouth. Before Padraig touched her on their wedding night, she'd never imagined that a man suckling her nipples could be so erotic. Now her breasts ached for his attention. Cairren cupped them in offering, one that Padraig gladly accepted. She arched her back to bring them closer to Padraig's mouth as he shifted back and forth between left and right. His fingers left a trail of fire as they brushed along her belly until they reached her slit.

"This isn't just coupling or me just bedding you, Ren. I want you to ken that I'll never look at we do as just aught. Making love to you means more to me than I have words to express," Padraig confessed.

Cairren grasped his upper arms as she smiled at the love that shone in his eyes. She let her knees fall wide, and she lifted her hips. "Then show me, *mo ghaol.*" My love. Padraig had never heard words that made him feel more invincible than the endearment Cairren offered in Gaelic.

"*Tha gaol agam ort nas motha na tha tonnan aig a 'mhuir, mo chridhe,*" Padraig whispered. From the brilliant smile he received, he knew Cairren understood that he'd said "I love you more than the sea has waves, my heart." But then her smile turned nervous, and his heart melted. He guessed she was piecing together a reply.

"*Agus bidh gaol agam ort nas fhaide na a 'ghrian, a' ghealach, agus na reultan a 'deàrrsadh.*" Padraig's heat overflowed with pride that his bonny Lowland bride made such an effort to speak his native tongue. His heart was brimming with the depth of emotion he felt as she told him, "and I shall love you longer than the sun, the moon, and the stars shine."

Padraig pressed his hips forward, easing his sword into Cairren's tight sheath. He pulled her leg over his hip as he thrust, over and over, into her. Her mewls of need and desire encouraged him to drive into her harder with each surge until she screamed his name. But Padraig refused to end their lovemaking. He returned his mouth to her breast, tugging her nipple with his teeth as he ground his pelvis into hers. He felt the spasm begin again within Cairren's core. She clung to him, certain she would float away on a cloud of pleasure. It was only as she climaxed a third time that Padraig granted himself the release he had struggled to control. He rolled them so that Cairren lay draped across his chest. Her long chestnut hair had come unbound and spread across her back and his ribs. One of Padraig's hands stroked the silky strands as the other cupped her bottom. As they basked in the afterglow of their passion, the world beyond their bed had ceased to exist.

CHAPTER FORTY-SIX

The fortnight the king offered Padraig passed faster than either Padraig or Cairren expected. She'd sent a missive to her parents giving them a sense of the most pressing matters without sharing the details. It snowed twice in the first three days they were at court, so Cairren pleaded that her parents not to make the journey to Stirling in the inclement weather. Padraig considered traveling to Dunure in the foul weather a risky enterprise, but he scowled and huffed when Cairren pointed out the alternative was to remain in Stirling. When the couple stood, holding hands, before King Robert at the end of the second week, the Bruce simply sighed and shook his head. He waved them away, chuckling as they rushed back to their own chamber. He knew the young couple's destination and desire.

How many of these young women have Elizabeth and I married off? My brother Edward and Elizabeth, Isabella and Dedric, then Maude and Kieran. Allyson —God bless that woman—and Ewan, Cairstine—and who would have ever guessed she would marry, I thought she wanted to be a nun—and Eoin. Thank the saints the Gordon twins are no longer bachelors. And now Cairren and Padraig. I wonder who shall be next. I'll sort through that pile of missives another day.

⸺

Padraig dismissed his guards to return home the morning after they arrived in Stirling, once he saw flurries dancing in the wind. There had been silent opposition, but Padraig refused to keep his men from their families for an entire winter. The mountain passes would become untraversable if too much snow accumulated, so it shocked him when he opened the bedchamber door and found Dougal and Matthew on the other side.

"What's happened?" Padraig demanded.

"Who's there, Padraig?" Cairren asked as she came to stand beside her husband. "Matthew? Dougal, what are you doing riding all the way here? Why isn't your arm still in a sling?" Dougal offered her a guilty smile.

Padraig bade the men enter, and Cairren built up the fire. The couple waited impatiently as the two warriors warmed themselves.

"Padraig, ye tasked me with keeping ma ears and eyes open, and I did," Dougal began. "Laird Urquhart sent men to claim Lady Wynda's belongings. Duncan got into an argument with the men; nae surprising to anyone. He refused to allow them to enter the keep, and in the process of insulting them and Lady Wynda, he let it slip that he killed her."

"I knew I should have returned her belongings sooner." Cairren lowered her eyes and shook her head. She felt guilty that she'd put the task off.

"Aye and nay, ma lady," Matthew picked up the story. "The men rode out without a word once they realized what he confessed. Many thought that was the end of it, but I kenned no mon—no laird—would allow another mon to murder his daughter and turn a blind eye. The Urquharts rallied the Mackenzies and let raids on villages along the borders with both clans. We didna ken which way to turn. Duncan rode out to where the three territories met, assuming his men would follow him to their deaths, and some did. Many fought with honor to protect our villagers, but nae Duncan."

"Padraig, yer brother's dead," Dougal said in a low tone. Both guards waited for a reaction from the couple, but Padraig and Cairren stood in stunned silence, looking at one another. "That's nae all. Padraig, the laird is demanding ye come home now that ye're his heir."

Padraig's jaw hardened. "That won't happen. Not as long as my father is laird. I won't return without Lady Cairren, and I won't take her back."

Matthew rubbed the back of his neck. "Aboot that. Yer father wants ye to return, so ye will convince the council to allow him to remain the laird. They're trying to oust him in favor of ye."

"And he thinks I'll return to defend him? The mon is barmy," Padraig spat.

"Aye, and we all ken it now too. When ye left, he raged for days," Dougal explained. "The vile things he spewed shocked us all. The clan wasnae having his threats against ye and Lady Cairren. Tension grew as the clan saw the mon yer father really is. Then yer brother died. The mon isnae right in the head anymore. He walks around the keep talking as though Duncan is standing beside him. He keeps swearing vengeance against the Mackenzies and Urquharts, but when he isnae spewing rubbish, he's in his cups.

He willna be leading any raids, and Adam willna take men in the laird's stead."

"The council is running the clan, but they arenae comfortable doing that for long when there's an heir who's more than capable to lead," Matthew finished.

"Matthew, I never wanted the lairdship. I dinna want it now," Padraig's brogue slipped out. The news of his family's implosion troubled him, but he wouldn't shift his priorities. The most important thing was keeping Cairren safe.

"They figured ye'd say as much," Dougal nodded. "The council sent us to make ye an offer."

"I amnae interested. I dinna want to hear it. Ye've made a lengthy trip in foul weather, and I appreciate it, but I amnae returning to Foulis," Padraig insisted.

"They'll send yer mother back to Clan Rose," Matthew blurted.

"You get that from your cousin," Cairren mused. When three blank male faces turned to her, she smiled. "The way you say things in a rush before someone can disagree. You get it from Meg."

"More like the lass got it from him," Padraig quipped. "He's quieter now that he has a wife."

"Humph," Matthew scowled. "Either way, they'll send yer mother back to her brother if ye and Lady Cairren return."

Padraig glanced at Cairren, then shook his head. "Nay. This is all too neat and tidy. One moment the clan canna be rid of Lady Cairren fast enough, and now they beg for her return. I dinna believe that. Mayhap they need me to return and ken I willna without Cairren. How do I ken they arenae lying to fool us?"

"We wouldnae have come, Padraig," Matthew persisted. "We watched over Lady Cairren even before ye assigned us the duty. We wouldnae risk her life if we didna believe it was right for her to come back."

"I trust ye both, but this doesnae sit right with me. I need to speak with Lady Cairren," Padraig replied as he wrapped his arm around Cairren's shoulders. "Go to the barracks, and I will find ye tomorrow. I willna decide aught now."

Cairren and Padraig stood together as the guardsmen trudged out of the room.

"I like the way you speak," Cairren smiled.

"The way I speak?"

"Aye. When you sound like a Highlander."

"Ye like ma burr, do ye?" Padraig nipped at Cairren's neck.

"Vera much," Cairren giggled. Padraig pretended to nibble along her neck and ear, eliciting more giggles. It was a carefree sound that he was unaccustomed to hearing from Cairren. He liked it, but he feared returning to Foulis would mean the end of such laughter, and would signal the end of her carefree days. He didn't doubt that she was up to the task of being the lady of the clan. He doubted his clan was up to the task of having her as their lady. He didn't want to make a choice that would end her giggles.

"Vera well, wee one. I shall sound the way God intended. If ye ask nicely," Padraig teased. Cairren sucked in her lips as she glanced below Padraig's waist. Her mischievous expression nearly made Padraig forget what they needed to discuss. "I'll be the one asking for that later, cheeky."

Cairren grinned as Padraig led her to a chair where he sat, then pulled her into his lap. She tucked hair behind his ear and sighed. "I don't know what to tell you. I never imagined any of this would happen.

One moment, I'm running away to avoid being burned at the stake or drowned. The next, two of your most trusted warriors are practically begging for us to come back. I trust Matthew and Dougal, and I believe what they said. I just don't ken if I trust what life will be like if I return."

"That's ma fear. Adam and Martin still have many years ahead of them, but Arnold is auld. He seems spry, but he was auld before I was born. The rest of the council follow their lead for now, but I dinna ken what'll happen once they're gone."

"Wouldn't you have been there long enough to have a voice in who takes their places?"

"Aye. But I wonder how people will act without those three to be the voice of reason. I dinna ken if people would listen to me and younger council members as well as they do Adam, Martin, and Arnold."

"What if we return, and your father refuses to step down?" Cairren asked.

"That's what I'm wondering too. But regardless of what we choose, we must inform the king." Padraig ran his hand over Cairren's arm as she leaned against his chest. He wished they could stay as they were, and he wished the outside world would stop intruding.

"Perhaps it would be better to do that first," Cairren suggested. "If he decides for us, it won't matter what we think." Her anxiousness eased as she listened to the steady beat of Padraig's heart.

"If we returned, what would ye do?

"I suppose I'd take over your mother's duties. I would oversee the running of the keep."

"Nay. I meant what would ye do if ye were me?" Padraig clarified.

Cairren was unprepared for him to ask her opinion

on clan leadership matters. She knew her father often sought her mother's opinion and advice; she just hadn't anticipated Padraig doing the same. "I would make peace with the Urquharts by returning not only Wynda's belongings, but anything remaining of her dowry that can be spared. Then I would offer to foster Laird Ross's grandson, with the stipulation that if Myrna comes within sight of Foulis, you won't hold me responsible for what I do. I would do these two first because they take the least amount of time and effort."

"That's fair. What would ye do after that?" Cairren's suggestions and how quickly she rattled them off intrigued Padraig.

"I—me, not you—I would reassure Laird Sutherland that I'm well and happy that you and I have resolved what stood between us. Then I would—this time I mean you—I would trade our wool for their grain. The raids before I arrived destroyed much of the harvest. I'd offer the trade as a step toward forming an alliance with them. An alliance with the Sutherlands will keep the Mackenzies from being a menace."

Cairren watched Padraig as he listened to her suggestions. She was unsure whether he would appreciate her ideas, but he nodded his head while she spoke, encouraging her to continue.

"You'll have to survey the damage from the raids," Cairren continued. "For now, I would relocate villages that lie too close to the boundary. Bring them further onto Munro territory, but double the patrols. The boundaries are obviously too easy for the Mackenzies to reach, but too far for us to protect easily. It doesn't matter how much farmland is available near the boundary—or how rich the soil is—if there's no one alive to work it or if the crops and homesteads are constantly destroyed."

"I'd like to nominate ye for laird," Padraig teased.

"Those are just ideas," Cairren shrugged.

"Dinna do that, Ren." Padraig eased Cairren away from his chest. "Dinna make yer ideas sound less important because they came from ye. It's the opposite. The suggestions are more valuable to me because they're yers. I trust ye."

Cairren smiled and nodded before easing back against Padraig's chest. "When should we seek another audience?"

"Regrettably, sooner rather than later. If we're to travel into the Highlands, we must leave within the next day, two days at the most. I fear we're going to struggle to get through the mountains."

"Aye then, let's make our way back to the Privy Council chamber and find our place in line," Cairren grumbled, and Padraig laughed. He wasn't eager to leave the privacy of their chamber to mill about with frustrated and bored courtiers and petitioners.

CHAPTER FORTY-SEVEN

Padraig and Cairren left their audience with the king in stunned silence. They'd been unprepared for King Robert to order the clan council to remove Micheil as laird. Cairren nearly fell over in shock when the king refused their suggestion that Mary retire to her clan. He said he only trusted nuns to keep her from causing more havoc. He suggested a couple of abbeys in the Hebrides and one further north, in Sinclair territory. Places so remote that both her clan of origin and clan-by-marriage would soon forget her. The Bruce asked what Padraig intended to do if he accepted the laird-ship—a responsibility the king made clear he expected Padraig to take. Padraig shared Cairren's suggestions and was emphatic that they were recommendations from Cairren. The king was pleased and agreed with her ideas. There had been nothing more to say, so they were dismissed. Still reeling from his orders, they returned to their chamber and began packing. It was only after their satchels were closed and waiting at the foot of their bed that they were ready to discuss the decision made for them.

"I can't believe, just like that, we're returning to

Foulis, and you're to be the laird. Is it divine intervention?" Cairren mused.

"I dinna ken. I suppose we'll see soon enough if it's that or the Devil's curse." Padraig encircled Cairren's waist and dropped a kiss on her nose. "I wouldnae say this in front of the king, but I need ye to ken that we will leave the moment ye dinna feel safe or ye're unhappy."

"We can't do that. Not once we're the laird and lady. Duty doesn't work that way."

"It does when yer first duty is to yer wife. I ken sometimes duty will come before what we want. But I willna let it come before yer safety. I willna tolerate any disrespect to ye. I willna waiver on that either." Padraig's expression was so serious that Cairren knew arguing further would be pointless.

"I'd like to see Caity again before we leave," Cairren shifted the subject.

"Shall we go now?"

"Nay. We have a couple of hours before she'll be excused from the queen's solar."

"How shall we ever pass the time, *mo chridhe?*" Padraig was already unlacing Cairren's gown as she reached to unfasten his brooch.

"I don't know, but I'm sure you'll show me." Cairren waggled her eyebrows before her gaze dropped below Padraig's waist.

"Cheeky lass. I love ye, Ren." Padraig tipped Cairren's chin up and brushed a soft kiss across her lips.

"And I love you, even if you're a wee bossy at times."

"Bossy, am I? Then I order ye onto this bed to enjoy yer husband's loving ministrations."

"Aye, ma laird," Cairren giggled as she raced to

the bed, and howled with laughter as Padraig snagged her around the waist, then tossed her onto the bed. They were not bored while waiting for Cairren's sister.

Cairren laughed with her sister throughout the evening meal after convincing Padraig to sit with the Armstrongs. She watched Caitlyn and Alexander, and she wondered if she'd missed something over the years after she and Alex agreed they didn't suit. She elbowed Padraig, cocked an eyebrow, and tilted her head. But he was clueless, furrowing his brow and shaking his head. Cairren leaned in and whispered her suspicions and watched understanding bring a smile to his face. Cairren danced with Alex and Lachlan in between dances with Padraig. She visited with Blair, and they once more promised to visit one another the next time Blair traveled home to Dunrobin.

Padraig arranged for their horses to be saddled and waiting for them as the first rays of sunlight peaked over the horizon. The Sutherlands joined them in the bailey to see them off. It was a tearful goodbye as Caitlyn and Blair wished their siblings godspeed. Cairren and Lachlan both turned back to wave goodbye before they passed under the castle's portcullis.

The roads were clear of snow for the first three days of their journey, but as they entered the mountains, snow covered much of the trail along the steep ridges. Padraig's heart was in his throat as he watched Cairren in front of him. He'd debated whether he should lead as they walked beside their horses, or if he should remain behind Cairren so that he never lost sight of her. She smiled back at him as she walked on the inside of the path, her body brushing against the rock face as her horse plodded along. Padraig was certain the icy wind that whipped through the ridges chilled Cairren to the bone; he promised himself that he would feed her until she could eat no more once they arrived at Foulis. He would see that she gained some meat on her bones, lest she freeze in the Highlands. Everyone breathed easier once they left the Cairngorm Mountains in their shadows.

The last two days of travel proved that Scotland could experience all four seasons in a matter of days. They left the last traces of snow behind them only to have buckets of rain dumped on them until the last two hours of the ride to Foulis. The clouds cleared, the sun shone, and it was warm enough for Cairren to push her arisaid off her head. She drew in a breath of the fresh Highland air, easing some of the anxiety that intensified as they drew nearer to their destination. She glanced at the men who surrounded her and found Padraig watching her. His smile warmed her more than the sun.

"Perhaps the Lord is letting us know there is a bright future ahead of us," Cairren mused.

"Or mayhap He is shining a light on the truth. That ye're an angel sent down to us."

"I don't know aboot all that, but I'm holding onto hope," Cairren returned his smile.

"I'm clinging to it," Padraig frowned.

"Don't do that. You'll give yourself wrinkles, and I like your face as it is," Cairren teased.

"Aye, we all ken how much you like your husband's face," Lachlan interrupted. "You two can't stop making cow eyes at one another. Makes the bannocks hard to keep down." Lachlan's teasing tone took the bite out of his comments, but Cairren's cheeks went red. It had been too cold to think about slipping away to tryst, but she and Padraig found snuggling close together and sharing their plaids allowed for certain intimacies.

Cairren returned her eyes to road ahead of them as the tops of Foulis's tower came into view. Padraig drew his mount closer to hers and reached out to cover her hand. She spread her fingers so his could entwine with hers. She shot him a thankful smile, and he nodded. They'd discovered during the journey they were starting to read one another's thoughts. Their gazes and body language expressed what they couldn't say out loud. It was a level of intimacy Cairren never thought to share with her husband. She'd seen her parents communicate in such ways throughout her life, but it seemed impossible to fathom when she arrived at Foulis the first time. Now, as the keep became more visible, she relied on Padraig's silent support. He'd pledged over and over throughout the journey that if she didn't receive a respectful welcome, they wouldn't even dismount. He swore the first time anyone said or did anything to offend or threaten her, they would leave and never look back.

She'd never imagined Padraig would become a doting husband to her. She'd feared she would spend much of her life watching Padraig treat Myrna the way he treated Cairren now. But reflecting on Padraig and Myrna's relationship, she'd seen an indulgent man giving in into the whims of a self-centered, entitled bitch. Cairren had a moment's remorse for her choice of words, but she knew of no other that seemed adequate without being vulgar, even in her own mind.

She doubted that Padraig and Myrna would have ever developed a relationship with depth, even if Duncan hadn't been in the middle. Perhaps Myrna would have matured, or perhaps she would have remained selfish and hateful. Either way, Cairren was glad Myrna was no longer a part of their lives, for Padraig's sake and for her own.

Their party rode through the gates with Matthew and Dougal leading the way. Padraig refused to ride anywhere but beside Cairren, just as he had throughout the entire journey. He cared not that people expected him to ride at the front of the group; he wouldn't entertain Cairren being out of reach in case of an attack.

The Highland air felt fresh, lighter than it had during Cairren's first time in Foulis. An invisible cloud had lifted over the Munros' keep, and Cairren felt it. She noticed smiles where before there had been doubt and suspicion. Children whose parents had held them back at Cairren's first arrival ran out to greet their party. Suddenly Cairren felt wary. The change was too significant to feel authentic.

Catriona, Meg, and Elspeth stood by the keep's steps, waving their greeting, though Lady and Laird Munro were noticeably absent. At first Cairren breathed a sigh of relief; then she realized that their absence could not be solely due to their hatred of her. She was uncertain how the clan would receive news of Lady Munro's banishment, and the impending reaction made her stomach churn. She turned her gaze away from the women and the keep, and saw Peter and Henry standing among the guards assembled behind the clan council. She darted a glance at Padraig, who was also looking in that direction. He hadn't dismounted, and she took her cues from him.

"Padraig, Lady Cairren, we are most grateful for yer return," Martin welcomed them. He'd been the quietest of the council members who defended her. Cairren surmised that he was not a talkative man by nature, so it surprised her when he spoke first. She dipped her head in greeting.

"Ye say ye're grateful, but I dinna ken that everyone shares yer sentiments," Padraig called out. Many heads jerked back in surprise to hear his brogue. "Ma wife likes it," was all the explanation he offered before continuing. "The council may lead the clan now, and I may become laird, but the clan will decide tonight whether ye accept Lady Cairren. Each member of the clan over the age of three-and-ten will swear their fealty to Lady Cairren. I will decide whether we stay by how many make that oath and whether I believe yer sincerity. We will leave in the morn if I am nae satisfied."

Cairren kept her chin up and her back straight, giving no sign that Padraig's order came as a surprise. Her eyes swept the crowd to see how they received Padraig's mandate. The number of nodding heads disconcerted her after her time with the clan. She noticed one warrior sneering at her, and Padraig must have, too. He nudged his chin in the man's direction, and Henry and Peter dragged him away. From her perch upon her horse, she watched as Peter held the man, and Henry plowed his fist into the man's face and abdomen.

"I warned ye once before, I will treat any slight or disrespect to Lady Cairren as harm done to me." Padraig voice was loud and firm. "Whether I become yer laird or nae, I will see ye punished. If I am laird, ye will go before the lash. If the harm is too great, ma wife and I leave."

Cairren didn't agree with the use of corporal punishment for this, but she understood Padraig's need to assert himself, especially if he would soon lead the clan. And she didn't doubt his retribution would be swift if how he'd beaten his brother indicated his protectiveness. She hoped she could convince him of a lesser punishment as she suspected, inevitably, someone would run afoul of her.

"Padraig?" A man Cairren didn't recognize stepped forward. He appeared to be a farmer or villager. "Padraig, might ye banish the offender rather than ye leave? I dinna want to believe Lady Cairren will come to harm now that we arenae believing Lady Mary and Father Mitchell, and we dinna fear yer father or brother. I dinna like saying that it might. But if it were, that doesnae mean we all want Lady Cairren mistreated. We dinna all want to be punished."

Padraig considered the man's comments and nodded. "That would be something which ma wife and I would decide together. If I become laird, then Lady Cairren becomes the lady of our clan. She will receive the honor and courtesy that goes with that position." Padraig turned to Cairren and held out his hand. When she placed it in his, he ran his thumb over the back of hers. "Before we step foot on Munro soil and before I escort ma wife into our home, I owe her an apology. It wasnae just ma family and our guest who are to blame for leading the clan to believe mistreating ma wife was acceptable. I shoulder that guilt, too. I didna treat Lady Cairren with the honor and care she deserved both as ma wife and as a person. Laird Kennedy told me 'where ye lead, they follow.' I didna appreciate his guidance, but I understand now. Lady Cairren, I am truly sorry for the pain I caused ye, for the blind eye I turned to others hurting ye, and for nae being the husband ye deserved. I love ye, Ren."

Cairren swore to herself when she arrived the first time that she would never let the Munros see her cry; she would never show weakness. But now happy tears streamed down her cheeks, even as she turned a brilliant smile toward Padraig. She cupped his face with her hands, grateful their horses stood still, and spoke for all to hear. "I love you too, Padraig." Then she offered him a kiss that left no one in doubt of the love and tenderness they shared.

Their homecoming had been a tumultuous day. They entered the keep to find Micheil intoxicated and mumbling to an invisible Duncan. As soon as he saw Cairren, he'd pointed his finger and screamed, "the Devil's bitch," before clutching his chest. He collapsed before them, but he still breathed. Cairren, much to her distaste but, was driven by conscience to examine him. The best she could diagnose was an apoplexy. She warned that he might recover, but it was just as likely that he wouldn't. He hadn't opened his eyes in hours, and the clan took it as a message from God that He wanted Padraig to serve as their new laird. The clan council disappeared into the laird's solar, and both Padraig and Cairren expected to wait hours before hearing their decision. The men were in and out in less than five minutes. They'd elected Padraig as their laird and held a special election to officially declare Cairren as Lady Munro.

As their laird, Padraig delivered the news that King Robert wasn't satisfied with his mother returning to Clan Rose. Instead, she was banished to

Murkle Priory, far north in Sinclair territory. Padraig delivered the directive to his mother while Cairren went to their chamber abovestairs to bathe. Even a floor above the fray and with the door closed, Cairren could hear Mary's vitriol as she raged against Cairren, using curses in Gaelic that Cairren didn't understand. From the way Padraig's hair stood on end once she finally saw him, Cairren knew either Mary's tirade infuriated him, or he'd had to restrain his mother as they moved to the woman's chamber. Cairren feared it was both when several clan members apologized on Mary's behalf for what they all heard.

Before the meal began, Cairren slipped away from Padraig and spoke to her friends. It was odd, but comforting, to realize she had friends among the Munros. She asked the question she knew Padraig wanted answered as much as she did.

"What's become of Myrna?" Cairren feared her rival would appear on their doorstep by morning.

"That's quite a tale. She rode into the bailey easy as ye please," Meg began. "She said she'd come to see Padraig. To resolve their disagreement. We kenned she wasnae telling the truth, but we thought she'd come to torment ye, ma lady. When she learned of Duncan's death, she fell into the screaming ab-dabs. It was like naught ye've ever seen before, ma lady. Nay one could understand what she was going on aboot. Ranting like a banshee."

"Aye, Lady Mary tried to get her under control. Do ye ken what Lady Mary did?" Catriona's eyes widened, but she grinned. "Slapped her."

"Aye. It stunned her enough to stop her squawk-ing," Meg laughed. "But then she started bellowing that it was Lady Mary's fault that she'd never married Duncan and how it was Lady Mary's fault that

Duncan didna kill Lady Wynda sooner. Then, ma lady! She said what none of us can get over. She blurted out that she'd flushed bairns from her belly with the primrose tea just as Lady Mary told her, but now she has naught to remember Duncan by."

"Aye, nae *a* bairn but bairns," Elspeth hissed.

Cairren was already aware of what the women told her, but it stunned her to learn they knew too. She looked in Padraig's direction as he laughed with the loyal men who were to remain her personal guard. "Did aught else happen?" Cairren wasn't sure she should ask, but she couldn't deny she was curious.

"Aye," Meg continued the story. "Ma sister's husband's brother's friend told us what he heard when he was on patrol near their border. He likes to blather aboot with anyone who will listen. He ran into a Ross patrol, and they told him everything. Come to find out, ma lady, her father nearly had his own apoplexy. Lady Myrna hid in her chamber for nigh on a sennight before she dared show her face again. Laird Ross was still livid! He signed a betrothal contract with some lesser MacGillivray chieftain. I dinna ken how, but he persuaded the Church to shake a leg and nae post the banns. Laird Ross said there wasnae any point since Duncan was dead, and she wasnae a maiden. She's already married, ma lady."

Cairren struggled to keep up with Meg's recitation of what happened while she and Padraig were away. She didn't think they'd been away long enough for so much to happen, but she realized it had been nearly a month. She thanked the women for sharing the latest news. What she learned tempted her to dash across the Great Hall to Padraig to crow about Myrna's fall from grace. But she still wasn't wholly convinced that Padraig was over his love for Myrna.

She feared it would hurt him to learn what became of her.

Padraig watched Cairren speaking with the women who'd become his wife's champions. He noticed her smile grew the longer they spoke, and he wondered if they were telling her what the men had shared about Myrna. When they began the story, he thought he would feel some tug at his heart, something like nostalgia or maybe even sympathy. Instead, he was relieved and vindicated. He tried not to become smug as he listened to her future, to be married to a man old enough to be her grandfather but still in need of an heir. She would get to put her experience to use, since the man was known to be randy and demanding.

He watched Cairren wind her way through the crowd, receiving smiles and greetings. He realized he trusted his clan enough to not fear Cairren walking alone. He sensed Matthew, Peter, Dougal, and Henry were watching her, ready to defend her should they think someone threatened her. He encircled her in his arms and dropped a kiss on her puckered lips.

"Did the women tell ye aboot Myrna?" Padraig watched as Cairren considered her answer. She nodded her head but offered no comment. "Ye dinna have to worry that I'm hurt by the outcome. She got what she deserved. Or she will get what she deserves. Cairren, she has nay hold over me anymore, and there isnae room in ma heart and ma mind for any woman but ye."

"You are sentimental," Cairren giggled, but her brow furrowed at Padraig's intense gaze.

"Nay. Dinna stop. I just never thought to hear ye laugh so merrily here."

"Neither did I, *mo ghaol*. I suspect I haven't won

over nearly as many as would have us believe I'm welcome. But I think between your edict and the others' judgement, those who still disapprove of me will remain quiet. I can live with that. I'm so happy that what began as naught but hurt and anger has grown into love and forgiveness. I don't imagine everything will always be cheery, but I no longer live in fear." Cairren stood on her toes and strained to reach Padraig's mouth until he dipped his head. Their kiss was just as passionate as the one they shared before the kirk on the day they wed, but it held promise and tenderness neither expected they would share. "I'm glad we are no longer enemies, Padraig."

"Aye. I much prefer ye as ma equal and nae just a lover." Padraig returned her kiss before they took their seats as the clan gathered before them.

Cairren watched as the last members of Clan Munro approached and kneeled before Padraig and her. She never expected that she would become Lady Munro, or that the clan she believed would always shun her, even try to kill her, now jostled each other to pledge their loyalty to her. She glanced at Padraig, who watched her as they sat in chairs side-by-side and held hands.

Cairren pushed the hair back from her face. She struggled to catch her breath after walking up the flight of stairs to the family chambers. She paused to stretch her back, her hands pressing against the back of her hips. A sharp kick made her think her bairn understood they hadn't reached their destination. As she walked into the nursery, she heard Padraig's deep rumbling laugh before she spotted their three sons rolling and tumbling over their mountainous father. When Padraig learned Cairren was pregnant the first time, he swore he would never be the father he had. He begged Cairren to tell him everything Innes did to learn what made the man into a father her daughter doted upon. They'd laid in bed together night after night as Cairren told him more stories from her childhood and described her relationship with Innes.

There hadn't been a day since their oldest son was born that Padraig's relationship with their children didn't remind her of how much her father loved her. He was a devoted husband and father who made time for his family and considered their needs as much as he did the clan's. Their love grew stronger with each passing year, even in times of struggle and challenges. The Munros' feud with the Mackenzies grew less volatile once Padraig become laird, but there were still raids and skirmishes along the border from time to time. They'd faced a year with flooding in autumn and blizzards throughout winter. They'd worried that food stores would run short, and it had challenged them to provide for the poorer and older members of their clan.

And, as they expected, in the early days after their return there were incidents where clan members revealed their true colors by disparaging Cairren, but the clan's judgement was swift. Padraig had the ultimate word on the guilty party's punishment, but the clan rendered theirs before Padraig could declare his. They shunned and publicly shamed those who spoke against Cairren. There were only a handful of times when Padraig felt his only recourse was the lash, and he banished a couple who refused to show remorse.

It took more than a year for Cairren to trust the clan without reservation. She'd doubted how long the members' reformation would last. But without Padraig's family, Father Mitchell, and Myrna to poison people's minds, Cairren discovered that the Munros lived by the Highland code of honor. She came to respect them as they respected her, and she found friends among the clan. She never felt isolated anymore. In fact, she wished for more time when people didn't surround her. She and Padraig slipped away when they could for lengthy walks and rides. He even took her back to the coast many times, but they never ventured near the caves.

During their first spring visit to the loch after they became laird and lady, Padraig confessed to watching Cairren swim with her parents and what he'd seen when she slipped behind the bushes to dress. He admitted how his body reacted to seeing Cairren for the first time. It didn't take long for them to strip bare and enter the water so Padraig could show how he'd felt. The clan soon learned not to venture near the loch when Matthew, Peter, Dougal, and Henry blocked the path. It became a special place for the couple, and Cairren was fairly certain they'd conceived at least two, if not all, of their children there.

"Ren, how're ye feeling?" Padraig said as he lay on his back, their middle son, Alexander, soaring through the air in his hands. All the while their youngest son, Adam, draped himself over Padraig's middle. Their oldest son, Innes, bounced on Padraig's bent, raised legs.

"I'm well, but I'm not sure I can say that for you," Cairren chuckled. She lifted Innes off of Padraig's legs, much to the child's consternation. Padraig tucked a boy under each arm as he stood. Alexander and Adam hooted with laughter as Innes wrapped himself around Padraig's leg. He walked them around the nursery until he was out of breath.

"I think your da needs a nap just like you lads," Cairren once again lifted Innes off of Padraig's leg.

"But we arenae tired, Mama," Adam mumbled around his yawn.

"I ken, wee one. You can have a body rest if you aren't sleepy," Cairren compromised but smiled at Padraig over the children's heads. Both parents knew the boys would be fast asleep before they left the nursery. They crept out the door, then Padraig swept Cairren into his arms before carrying her to their chamber.

"I think ye were right, Ren. I do need a nap. But I canna sleep without ye by ma side," Padraig grinned. He lowered her feet to the ground before resting his hand on her rounded belly. "Do ye think we'll have a lass this time?"

"Not bluidy likely from how this bairn flips and kicks. If we're having a lass, then she will get into more trouble than her brothers," Cairren grumbled, and her belly shifted. Once again, it was as though the babe had a point to make, leaving Cairren shaking her head. "I've had another missive from the Sutherlands. It seems we're all in a race to see who will have the most bairns. Isabella just had hers, making five weans for her and Dedric. Maude and Kieran had their fourth. Blair just discovered she's on with her third. And Allyson and Cairstine are both expecting their fourth."

"What do ye expect when none of their husbands can keep their hands off their wives." Padraig nibbled at Cairren's neck, adding, "It's why we're to have our fourth any day now. I canna stay away, and ye do naught to discourage me."

Cairren chuckled, "So it's my fault?"

"Aye." Padraig nipped at her earlobe as he pulled the laces loose from Cairren's kirtle. "Or mayhap it's yer parents who are to blame, for making such a bonnie lass."

"I don't know aboot bonnie when I'm as wide as the side of a stable." Cairren rubbed her hands over her belly. Despite her expanding middle, she felt nothing less than beautiful and cherished by Padraig.

"I think we need less blathering and more me proving just how bonnie ye are." Padraig led them to their bed, and as they laid facing one another, he grew somber for a moment. "I love ye and our lads and this bairn more than I ever kenned a heart could."

"Mayhap King Robert should set aside his crown and become a matchmaker. He's done better with the couples he's matched than any of us thought. I may not have appreciated it in the beginning, but there isn't a day that goes by that I'm not grateful that the king ordered us to marry. I love you, Padraig."

"And I love you, Ren." He sealed their devotion with a kiss.

THANK YOU FOR READING AN ENEMY AT THE HIGHLAND COURT

Celeste Barclay, a nom de plume, lives near the Southern California coast with her husband and sons. Growing up in the Midwest, Celeste enjoyed spending as much time in and on the water as she could. Now she lives near the beach. She's an avid swimmer, a hopeful future surfer, and a former rower. When she's not writing, she's working or being a mom.

Visit Celeste's website, www.celestebarclay.com, for regular updates on works in progress, new releases, and her blog where she features posts about her experiences as an author and recommendations of her favorite reads.

Are you an author who would like to guest blog or be featured in her recommendations? Visit her website for an opportunity to share your insights and experiences.

Have you read *Their Highland Beginning, The Clan Sinclair Prequel?* Learn how the saga begins! This FREE novella is available to all new subscribers to Celeste's monthly newsletter. Subscribe on her website.

www.celestebarclay.com

Join the fun and get exclusive insider giveaways, sneak peeks, and new release announcements in

Celeste Barclay's Facebook Ladies of Yore Group

THE HIGHLAND LADIES

A Spinster at the Highland Court
BOOK 1 SNEAK PEEK

Elizabeth Fraser looked around the royal chapel within Stirling Castle. The ornate candlestick holders on the altar glistened and reflected the light from the ones in the wall sconces as the priest intoned the holy prayers of the Advent season. Elizabeth kept her head bowed as though in prayer, but her green eyes swept the congregation. She watched the other ladies-in-waiting, many of whom were doing the same thing. She caught the eye of Allyson Elliott. Elizabeth raised one eyebrow as Allyson's lips twitched. Both women had been there enough times to accept they'd be kneeling for at least the next hour as the Latin service carried on. Elizabeth understood the Mass thanks to her cousin Deirdre Fraser, or rather now Deirdre Sinclair. Elizabeth's mind flashed to the recent struggle her cousin faced as she reunited with her husband Magnus after a seven-year separation. Her aunt and uncle's choice to keep Deirdre hidden from her husband simply because they didn't think the Sinclairs were an advantageous enough match, and the resulting scandal, still humiliated the other Fraser clan members at court. She admired Deirdre's husband Magnus's pledge to remain faithful despite not knowing if he'd ever see Deirdre again.

Elizabeth suddenly snapped her attention; while everyone else intoned the twelfth—or was it thirteenth—amen of the Mass, the hairs on the back of her neck stood up. She had the strongest feeling that someone was watching her. Her eyes scanned to her right, where her parents sat further down the pew. Her mother and father had their heads bowed and eyes closed. While she was convinced her mother was in devout prayer, she wondered if her father had fallen asleep during the Mass. Again. With nothing seeming out of the ordinary and no one visibly paying attention to her, her eyes swung to the left. She took in the king and queen as they kneeled together at their prie-dieu. The queen's lips moved as she recited the liturgy in silence. The king was as still as a statue. Years of leading warriors showed, both in his stature and his ability to control his body into absolute stillness. Elizabeth peered past the royal couple and found herself looking into the astute hazel eyes of Edward Bruce, Lord of Badenoch and Lochaber. His gaze gave her the sense that he peered into her thoughts, as though he were assessing her. She tried to keep her face neutral as heat surged up her neck. She prayed her face didn't redden as much as her neck must have, but at a twenty-one, she still hadn't mastered how to control her blushing. Her nape burned like it was on fire. She canted her head slightly before looking up at the crucifix hanging over the altar. She closed her eyes and tried to invoke the image of the Lord that usually centered her when her mind wandered during Mass.

Elizabeth sensed Edward's gaze remained on her. She didn't understand how she was so sure that he was looking at her. She didn't have any special gifts of perception or sight, but her intuition screamed that he was still looking.

A Spy at the Highland Court **BOOK 2**

A Wallflower at the Highland Court **BOOK 3**

A Rogue at the Highland Court **BOOK 4**

A Rake at the Highland Court **BOOK 5**

An Enemy at the Highland Court **BOOK 6**

A Saint at the Highland Court **BOOK 7**

A Beauty at the Highland Court **BOOK 8**

A Sinner at the Highland Court **BOOK 9**

His Highland Lass **BOOK 1 SNEAK PEEK**

She entered the great hall like a strong spring storm in the northern most Highlands. Tristan Mackay felt like he had been blown hither and yon. As the storm settled, she left him with the sweet scents of heather and lavender wafting towards him as she approached. She was not a classic beauty, tall and willowy like the women at court. Her face and form were not what legends were made of. But she held a unique appeal unlike any he had seen before. He could not take his eyes off of her long chestnut hair that had strands of fire and burnt copper running through them. Unlike the waves or curls he was used to, her hair was unusually straight and fine. It looked like a waterfall cascading down her back. While she was not tall, neither was she short. She had a figure that was meant for a man to grasp and hold onto, whether from the front or from behind. She had an aura of confidence and charm, but not arrogance or conceit like many good looking women he had met. She did not seem to know her own appeal. He could tell that she was many things, but one thing she was not was his.

His Bonnie Highland Temptation **BOOK 2**

His Highland Prize **BOOK 3**

His Highland Pledge **BOOK 4**

His Highland Surprise **BOOK 5**

Their Highland Beginning **BOOK 6**

The Blond Devil of the Sea **BOOK 1 SNEAK PEEK**

Caragh lifted her torch into the air as she made her way down the precarious Cornish cliffside. She made out the hulking shape of a ship, but the dead of night made it impossible to see who was there. She and the fishermen of Bedruthan Steps weren't expecting any shipments that night. But her younger brother Eddie, who stood watch at the entrance to their hiding place, had spotted the ship and signaled up to the village watchman, who alerted Caragh.

As her boot slid along the dirt and sand, she cursed having to carry the torch and wished she could have sunlight to guide her. She knew these cliffs well, and it was for that reason it was better that she moved slowly than stop moving once and for all. Caragh feared the light from her torch would carry out to the boat. Despite her efforts to keep the flame small, the solitary light would be a beacon.

When Caragh came to the final twist in the path before the sand, she snuffed out her torch and started to run to the cave where the main source of the village's income lay in hiding. She heard movement along the trail above her head and knew the local fishermen would soon join her on the beach. These men, both young and old, were strong from days spent pulling in the full trawling nets and hoisting the larger catches onto their boats. However, these men weren't well-trained swordsmen, and the fear of pirate raids was ever-present. Caragh feared that was who the villagers would face that night.

The Dark Heart of the Sea **BOOK 2**

The Red Drifter of the Sea **BOOK3**

Leif **BOOK 1 SNEAK PEEK**

Leif looked around his chambers within his father's longhouse and breathed a sigh of relief. He noticed the large fur rugs spread throughout the chamber. His two favorites placed strategically before the fire and the bedside he preferred. He looked at his shield that hung on the wall near the door in a symbolic position but waiting at the ready. The chests that held his clothes and some of his finer acquisitions from voyages near and far sat beside his bed and along the far wall. And in the center was his most favorite possession. His oversized bed was one of the few that could accommodate his long and broad frame. He shook his head at his longing to climb under the pile of furs and on the stuffed mattress that beckoned him. He took in the chair placed before the fire where he longed to sit now with a cup of warm mead. It had been two months since he slept in his own bed, and he looked forward to nothing more than pulling the furs over his head and sleeping until he could no longer ignore his hunger. Alas, he would not be crawling into his bed again for several more hours. A feast awaited him to celebrate his and his crew's return from their latest expedition to explore the isle of Britannia. He bathed and wore fresh clothes, so he had no excuse for lingering other than a bone weariness that set in during the last storm at sea. He was eager to spend time at home no matter how much he loved sailing. Their last expedition had been profitable with several raids of monasteries that yielded jewels and both silver and gold, but he was ready for respite.

Leif left his chambers and knocked on the door next to his. He heard movement on the other side, but it was only moments before his sister, Freya, opened her door. She, too, looked tired but clean. A few pieces of jewelry she confiscated from the holy houses that allegedly swore to a life of poverty and deprivation adorned her trim frame.

"That armband suits you well. It compliments your muscles," Leif smirked and dodged a strike from one of those muscular arms.

Only a year younger than he, his sister was a well-known and feared shield maiden. Her lithe form was strong and agile making her a ferocious and competent opponent to any man. Freya's beauty was stunning, but Leif had taken every opportunity since they were children to tease her about her unusual strength even among the female warriors.

"At least one of us inherited our father's prowess. Such a shame it wasn't you."

Freya **BOOK 2**

Tyra & Bjorn **BOOK 3**

Strian **VIKING GLORY BOOK 4**

Lena & Ivar **VIKING GLORY BOOK 5**